W9-AGI-765

NO GOOD DEEDS

"Laura Lippman is among the select group of novelists who have invigorated the crime fiction arena with smart, innovative, and exciting work. She consistently delivers the goods."

George Pelecanos

"The best authors deepen their detectives, turn caricature sketches into character studies and hone familiar rhythms until a P.I. or an amateur sleuth feels like an old friend . . . [Lippman's characters'] lives have evolved with every volume but [their] core values have remained reassuringly familiar . . .

It's impossible not to like the complex, all-too-real Monaghan, a strong, wry detective prone to 'derailing my own gravy train.' How can you resist a tough cookie who is nonetheless sentimental enough to turn down all work around Valentine's Day, which is to private investigators what April 15 is to accountants?"

Washington Post Book World

Books by Laura Lippman

LAURA LIPPMAN

NO GOOD DEEDS

HARPER

An Imprint of HarperCollins*Publishers*

HARPER

An Imprint of HarperCollins*Publishers*
10 East 53rd Street
New York, New York 10022-5299

Copyright © 2006 by Laura Lippman
Excerpt from *What the Dead Know* copyright © 2007 by Laura Lippman
Author photo by Jan Cobb
ISBN: 978-0-06-057073-6
ISBN-10: 0-06-057073-3

First Harper paperback printing: March 2007
First William Morrow hardcover printing: July 2006
First William Morrow special printing: July 2006

HarperCollins® and Harper® are registered trademarks of HarperCollins Publishers.

Printed in the United States of America

Visit Harper paperbacks on the World Wide Web at
www.harpercollins.com

10 9 8 7 6 5 4 3 2 1

For the Thursday crew

And for Brendan and Willa,
for being there every day

NO GOOD DEEDS

WHEN I WAS A KID, MY FAVORITE BOOK WAS *HORTON Hears a Who*, and, like most kids, I wanted to hear it over and over and over again. My indulgent but increasingly frazzled father tried to substitute *Horton Hatches the Egg* and other Dr. Seuss books, but nothing else would do, although I did permit season-appropriate readings of *How the Grinch Stole Christmas*. See, I had figured out what Seuss only implied: Those Whos down in Who-ville, the ones who taught the Grinch what Christmas was all about? Clearly they were the *same* Whos who lived on Horton's flower. That realization made me giddy, a five-year-old deconstructionist, taking the text down to its bones. The word was the word, the Who was the Who. For if the Whos lived on the flower, then it followed that the Grinch and his dog, Max, did, too, which meant that the Grinch was super tiny, and *that* meant there was no reason to fear him. The Grinch was the size of a dust mite! How much havoc could such a tiny being wreak?

A lot, I know now. A whole lot.

My name is Edgar "Crow" Ransome, and I indirectly caused a young man's murder a few months back. I did some other stuff, too, with far more consciousness, but it's this death that haunts me. I carry a newspaper clipping about the shooting in my wallet so I'll be reminded every day—when I pull out bills for a three-dollar latte or grab my ATM card—that my world and its villains are tiny, too, but no less lethal for it.

Tiny Town is, in fact, one of Baltimore's many nick-names—along with Charm City and Mobtown—and perhaps the most appropriate. Day in, day out, it's one degree of separation here in Smalltimore, an urban Mayberry where everyone knows everyone. Then you read the newspaper and rediscover that there are really two Baltimores. Rich and poor. White and black. Ours. Theirs.

A man was found shot to death in the 2300 block of East Lombard Street late last night. Police arrived at the scene after a neighbor reported hearing a gunshot in the area. Those with information are asked to call . . .

This appeared, as most such items appear, inside the *Beacon Light*'s Local section, part of something called the "City/County Digest." These are the little deaths, as my girl-friend, Tess Monaghan, calls them, the homicides that merit no more than one or two paragraphs. *A man was found shot to death in an alley in the 700 block of Stricker Street. . . . A man was killed by shots from a passing car in the 1400 block of East Madison Street. . . . A Southwest Baltimore man was found dead inside his Cadillac Escalade in the 300 block of North Mount.* If they have the victim's name, they give it. If there are witnesses or arrests, the fact is noted for the sheer wonder of it. "Witness" is the city's most dangerous occupation these days, homicide's thriving secondary market, if you will. We're down on snitchin' here in Baltimore and have the T-shirts and videos to prove it. Want to know how bad things have gotten? There was a hit ordered on a ten-year-old girl who had the misfortune to see her own father killed.

Here's what is *not* written, although everyone knows the score: *Another young black man has died. He probably deserved it. Drug dealer or drug user. Or maybe just in the wrong place at the wrong time, but he should have known better than to hang around a drug corner at that time, right?* If you want the courtesy of being presumed innocent in certain Baltimore neighborhoods, you better be unimpeachable, someone clearly, unambiguously cut down in the cross fire. A three-year-old getting his birthday haircut. A ten-year-old playing football. I wish these examples were hypothetical.

I'm not claiming that I was different from anyone else in Baltimore, that I read those paragraphs and wondered about the lives that preceded the deaths. No, I made the same calculations that everyone else did, plotting the city's grid in my head, checking to make sure I wasn't at risk. Shot in a movie theater for telling someone to be quiet? Sure, absolutely, that could happen to me, although there aren't a lot of tough guys in the local art houses. Killed for flipping someone off in traffic? Not my style, but Tess could have died a thousand times over that way. She has a problem with impulse control.

But we're not to be found along East Lombard or Stricker or Mount or any other dubious street, not at 3:00 A.M. Even when I am in those neighborhoods, people leave my ride and me alone. Usually. And it's not because I'm visibly such a nice guy on a do-gooding mission. They don't bother me because I'm not worth the trouble. I'm a red ball walking; kill me and all the resources of the city's homicide division will be brought to bear on the investigation. I'll get more than a paragraph, too.

In fact, I think I'd get almost as much coverage as Gregory Youssef, a federal prosecutor found stabbed to death last year. Perhaps I should carry a clipping of that case, too, for it was really Youssef's death that changed my life, although I didn't know it at the time. But I'm not likely to forget Youssef's death soon. Nobody is.

The hard part would be fitting me into a headline. *Artist? Musician?* Only for my own amusement these days. *Restaurant-bar manager?* Doesn't really get the flavor of what I do at the Point, which is a bar, but increasingly a very good music venue as well, thanks to the out-of-town bands I've been recruiting. *Scion of a prominent Charlottesville family?* Even if I were confident I could pronounce "scion" correctly, I'm more confident that I would never pronounce myself as such. *Boyfriend of Tess Monaghan, perhaps Baltimore's best-known private investigator?* Um, no thank you. I love her madly, but that's not how I wish to be defined.

I think I'd prefer the simple appellation City Man, the everyday superhero of the headlines. City Man is a fixture in the local paper, too. He wins prizes, he's nominated for national posts, he sues giant corporations, he goes missing on occasion. City Man is eternal.

The everyday homicide cases, those one- or two-paragraph news stories I told you about—those guys never get to be City Man. They are allowed to represent only vague geographic areas—a Southwest Baltimore man, an East Baltimore man, a West Baltimore man. They're even denied their neighborhoods, which in Baltimore is like being denied a piece of your soul. They are not universal enough to be City Men, not emblematic enough to be Collington Square Man or Upper Park Heights Man or even Pigtown Man.

And yet they are. They are more representative of this city than we want to admit. A homicide occurs here, on average, every thirty-six hours. In certain neighborhoods homicide is a way of life, if you'll permit the oxymoron. Yet other neighborhoods assume that it's their right to remain untouched by this plague and are horrified when the covenant is broken. A few years back, when Tess was still a reporter, a Guilford couple were killed in their mansion, and the city freaked. It was one thing for "those people" to murder each other, quite another if they were going to start crossing the invisible boundaries, killing rich white people in their homes. Within two days an arrest was made, and Tess told me a fake headline circulated the newsroom via the computer system—A RELIEVED CITY REJOICES: THE GRANDSON DID IT.

A man was found shot to death in the 2200 block of East Lombard Street late last night. Police arrived at the scene after a neighbor reported hearing a gunshot in the area. Those with information are asked to call . . .

Just another little death—unless you know the big picture. Once you learn the complex story behind even one of those one-paragraph homicides, once a single life is illuminated, you can't stop thinking about all the other victims, wondering what their stories are. Were. To read the newspaper with this kind of attentiveness is to become Horton the Elephant, besieged by all those tiny beings from Whoville. You are the only one who hears, the only one who knows, their only possible salvation.

And, like Horton, all you can do is hold on tight to that dandelion of a world curled in your trunk and pray you don't get locked up for listening to the voices that everyone else swears aren't there.

PART ONE

Smalltimore

Sunday

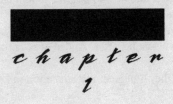

chapter
1

T ess, do you know who the Baltimore Four were?"

It took Tess Monaghan a moment to surface from her own thoughts, but she eventually came up for air, leaving behind the various newspaper articles and computer printouts strewn across her dining room table—and rug and hallway and breakfront—in seemingly random stacks that were actually quite methodical. She had tried to confine this project to her office, but with the presentation now just twenty-four hours away, such compartmentalization had to be sacrificed. The future of Keyes Investigations Inc., the lofty-sounding name that encompassed exactly one employee—three if you included the dogs, who accompanied her to the office every day—was riding on this assignment.

"I should hope so," she told her boyfriend, Crow, who had found a corner of the dining room table large enough to hold a bowl of cereal and the *New York Times* acrostic, which he was working between bites with his usual infuriating nonchalance.

"Any native Baltimorean who doesn't should have his or her birth certificate revoked."

"Well, it's not like they were super famous, not as famous as the guys who came after. And it was before you were born."

"My father didn't neglect my education in key areas, I'm happy to say."

"Your dad didn't know either. I asked him the other day at work, and he said it sounded familiar, but it didn't make much of an impression on him."

"Didn't make much of an impression?" Tess, who had been on her hands and knees, the better to crawl through her paper labyrinth, rocked back on her heels. "It was only one of the transforming events of his life."

"Wasn't he already married when the Vietnam draft started?"

"What are you talking about?"

"What are *you* talking about?"

"The Baltimore Four—Palmer, McNally, Cuellar, and Dobson, the four Oriole pitchers who had at least twenty wins in the regular season in 1971."

Crow laughed in his easy way, a laugh that excused her ignorance—and his. "I'm talking about four antiwar activists who poured blood on records at the U.S. Customs House in 1967, sort of a run-up to the Catonsville Nine. Philip Berrigan—Berrigan, Lewis, Mengel, and Eberhardt. I heard about them when I was making my rounds at the soup kitchens last week."

Tess was staring at a photograph of a dark-eyed, dark-haired man. "You and that do-gooder crowd. Just remember, no good deed—"

"Goes unpunished. Jesus, Tess, you'd probably have mocked Gandhi if you met him."

"Not to his face."

"Anyway, I think they were pretty cool. Berrigan and that group. Can you imagine someone pouring blood on records today?"

"Yes. And I can imagine that person being detained at Guantánamo without legal counsel, so don't get any ideas."

Tess returned to sorting her papers, only to find her shoulder-length hair falling in her face. It was an impossible length—not quite long enough for the single braid she was trying to coax back into being after an untimely haircut, but too long to be allowed to swing free. She fashioned stubby pigtails on either side of her head, securing them with rubber bands, and went back to work.

"Hey, you look like Dave Grohl from the Foo Fighters," Crow said approvingly. "Circa 1999. You going to wear your hair like that tomorrow?"

"It's a thought." An amusing one, actually: Tess as her authentic self, in her favorite sweats, henley shirt, and ad hoc hairstyle, standing in front of the buttoned-down types that had infiltrated the local newspaper. But at the prices the *Beacon-Light* editors were paying, they expected and deserved the bogus Tess—hair slicked behind her ears into some semblance of order, a suit, real shoes with heels, which Tess actually liked, as they made her almost six feet tall. "I can't believe they want a PowerPoint for this thing. I'd rather spend the afternoon at Kinko's, photocopying twenty-five sets of every package, instead of fighting with my scanner to load all these images."

"Why is a newspaper hiring a private detective for consulting work anyway? Shouldn't their own reporters know how to do this stuff?"

"They've had an exodus of senior staff, which they've replaced with a lot of inexperienced kids. Feeney thought it was his lucky day when he got promoted to city editor, but herding these rookies is more likely to put him in an early grave."

"So what are you supposed to do?"

"They've asked me to take three recent cases in the news and use them as sort of intellectual object lessons, walk them through all the possible scenarios in an investigation."

"WWTMD—What Would Tess Monaghan Do?"

Tess laughed. "Sort of. Thing is, I have the leeway to work in some, uh, more legally ambiguous ways. I can lie about who I am, pay people for information. Reporters can't. Or shouldn't. So this is going to be mostly about public information, especially stuff that's *not* online. The Internet is amazing, but you need to leave the office now and then, interact with people. A good courthouse source is better than the world's fastest search engine."

"It's just so strange, you in bed with the *Beacon-Light*. Feeney, sure. He's your friend. But you've always hated all the top editors at that paper, especially after the way they hyped your—" Crow stopped to find a precise term for the events of almost a year ago, the trauma whose aftermath had driven them apart for a time. "Encounter."

Encounter. Tess liked that. Euphemisms had their uses. "Encounter" was so empty, so meaningless, incapable of holding the horror of the attack, the greater horror of what she had been forced to do to save her life. She reached for her knee, for the fading purplish scar that paradoxically soothed her when the most troubling memories surfaced. A souvenir of the "encounter."

"The money is to drool for. And February was so slow this year. I have to make it up somehow, especially now that I have a car payment."

"Things will pick up."

"They better. I have that other gig—the investigation of that charity that you're going to help me with—but that's small potatoes. I need this."

What went unsaid between them was that February was

unusually slow because Tess, reunited with Crow—again—had decided she believed in love. Again. And as a reconstituted convert to love, she had declined all offers to gather evidence of cheating spouses around Valentine's Day, which is to private investigators what April 15 is to accountants—busy, exhausting, extremely lucrative. It was a costly bit of nobility, but she had no regrets. Pangs of anxiety when she had balanced her accounts and paid her bills on February 28, but no regrets. So far.

"How can a newspaper that's cutting staff afford to pay you so well?"

"It's a classic example of how corporate accounting works. On the local level, there's not enough money to hire reporters. But I'm being paid out of the national office in Dallas, and they're awash in money. My fee might seem outrageous to us, but it pales when compared to the two million in consulting fees they bestowed on the departing CEO."

And when Tess had taken the job, she had every intention of phoning it in, just freestyling her way through the symposium, and who cared if it was all bullshit and blather? As it turned out, Tess cared. The work ethic passed down by both parents kicked in as surely as the recessive gene that had made her eyes hazel. In the end she would rather grumble about being underpaid than endure the shame of underperforming. Besides, Feeney had gone to bat for her. She wouldn't want a lackluster presentation to taint her old friend.

Crow, still in pajama bottoms and a T-shirt as Sunday crested noon, pointed a bare toe at the stack nearest him, topped by the photograph of the handsome dark-eyed man that Tess's eyes kept returning to, almost in spite of herself.

"What are you going to tell them about the Youssef case? It's hard to see how you can think of an angle that hasn't already occurred to the newspaper. Much less the Justice Department, the FBI, the Howard County police . . ."

"Oh, that one's about reading between the lines. The investigation—and the story—has stalled for reasons that no one wants to discuss in public. I'm going to connect the dots."

"Can you prove your theory?"

"No, but that's the beauty of the project. I don't have to *prove* anything. I just have to have plausible explanations."

"Homicide as intellectual exercise. Seems like . . ." Crow bent over his puzzle, filled in a line. "Bad karma. Eight letters. Yes, exactly. It fits. Done."

"It fits your puzzle. Gregory Youssef created his own karma."

Assistant U.S. Attorney Gregory Youssef had disappeared on the eve of Thanksgiving and was found dead late on the day the media insisted on calling Black Friday. The first twenty-four hours had promised a sensational story with national implications—a federal prosecutor, one assigned to anti-terrorist cases, kidnapped and killed. Youssef had been sitting down to dinner when he was paged to the office—or so he told his wife. No record of that page was ever found. He returned downtown. Sixteen hours later his body was discovered on the Howard County side of the Patapsco River, not far from I-95. Early speculation centered on the terrorism cases he had just started working and the tough sentences he had won on a handful of drug cases. The U.S. attorney vowed that such a crime against a federal officer of the court would not go unpunished. For the entirety of Thanksgiving, it had seemed there were only two stories in the world, as reporters alternated their live feed from the yellow police lines at the murder site to the lines of the hungry at area soup kitchens. Death and hunger, hunger and death.

But the Youssef story receded from the headlines before most Maryland families had finished their turkey leftovers. The feds, who usually bigfooted such cases, pulled back with amazing and uncharacteristic grace, all but insisting that Howard County detectives take the primary role. The U.S. attorney stopped appearing hourly in front of local television cameras and, coincidentally or no, resigned at the end of the year. Suddenly everyone seemed content to shrug and deem it a genuine mystery, despite some precise evidence about Youssef's final hours—an ATM withdrawal in East Baltimore, the discovery of Youssef's car just off one of the lower exits on the New Jersey Turnpike.

Then there was the very nature of Youssef's death—dozens and dozens of stab wounds, made with a small knife that was never found. It was when Tess learned of this detail that she decided that Youssef's murder had been intensely personal. Possibly a crime of revenge, definitely one of rage. The ATM withdrawal? That was in an area known for prostitution, including male prostitution as practiced by out-of-town boys who considered themselves straight even as they took other men's money for sex. The information that Youssef was a devout Christian with a pregnant wife had only confirmed Tess's suspicion that this was a man with a secret life, one that his former colleagues were intent on masking.

But no one wanted to dwell on such details when the victim was such a well-intentioned striver, the son of Egyptian immigrants, a man who had dedicated his professional life to the justice system because he was horrified to share a surname with the first man who attacked the World Trade Center. What heartless soul would make his widow confront her husband's conflicted nature in the daily newspaper? Gregory Youssef was like a bad smell in a small room: People stared at the ceiling, waiting for the rude fact of his death to dissipate.

Yet the longer it lingered, the worse it looked for law-enforcement officials, who were supposed to be able to solve the homicide of one of their own. Even if the newspaper hadn't told her to prepare a dossier on this case, Tess would have been drawn to it. The Youssef murder was juicy, irresistible.

"Thing is, the newspaper has nothing to gain by pursuing the story," Tess told Crow now. "If my theory is right, it will just piss everyone off. But until an arrest is made, there will be rumors and conspiracy theories that are even worse. The U.S. attorney set the tone for the coverage. The moment the body was discovered, he should have been using codes to slow the reporters down. Instead he revved them up, let the story run wild over the weekend, then tried to back away from it."

"Codes?"

"If he had considered how . . . well, personal the murder looked, he might have managed to indicate that to reporters, off the record. Wink, wink, nudge, nudge. It's done all the time. Or was, back in my day." Tess had worked as a reporter for only a few years and accepted long ago that she was more temperamentally suited to life as a private investigator. But she still had some nostalgia for her newshound phase.

"So why isn't the prosecutor doing that now?"

"You can't put the news genie back in the bottle. Now everyone is left hanging—the poor saps who got stuck with the case, the widow. It was kind of unconscionable, if you ask me. But if an arrest is made, this stuff is going to come out, and the reporters need to anticipate it. Bet you anything it will be some young country guy, one of those 'straight' teenagers who comes down here and turns tricks but doesn't like it much. Or someone like that weirdo from Anne Arundel County, who drove to Baltimore just to pick up gay men and try to kill them."

Crow made a face.

"Yeah, I know. It's a distasteful topic, even in the abstract. That's why this gig pays well."

"Are your other scenarios unsolved homicides as well?"

"Nope. I've taken on that perennial favorite: Can it be proven that State Senator Wiley Staunton doesn't actually live in the district he claims as his home? Hard to prove a negative, but it turns out the *Beacon-Light* reporters neglected to pull a pretty basic record—the guy's voting registration. He may represent the Forty-seventh, but he's been voting in the Forty-first for the last sixteen years. That's a story in itself. You'll probably see that on page one of the paper by week's end. I've also got a nice tidbit on the governor—"

"The extramarital affair?" That particular rumor about Maryland's governor had hung in the air for months, like a shiny helium balloon bobbing over the heads of children, tantalizingly out of reach, suspiciously unchanging in its proportions and altitude.

Tess snorted. "He *wishes*. An extramarital affair is positively benign when compared to what I found in the governor's garbage. Two words: 'adult diapers.' "

"Is it legal to search the governor's garbage?"

"Better question—should the state's chief executive violate federally mandated privacy laws by not shredding confidential documents about his employees? That's the *real* find. The diapers were just a bonus. If anyone wants to threaten me with charges for Dumpster diving on private property, I'll just wave those. Not literally, of course."

"But as you said, the reporters can't break the law."

"True." Tess allowed herself another pause-and-stretch on her crawling path among the documents. "But they can use information of dubious provenance if they don't probe too closely the whys and wherefores of how it was obtained. My hunch is that this whole enterprise is sort of . . . an overture on the newspaper's part. I think Feeney's bosses would like to figure out a way to put me on retainer."

"To what purpose?"

"You know how banks and businesses can launder dirty money? A private investigator could launder dirty information for a media outlet. Take credit reports, for example. I can get those in a heartbeat. Fact is, so could the *Blight,* using its own business offices, but that would be unethical—and illegal."

"Then wouldn't it be equally wrong to get the same information from a third-party source?"

"Probably. But newspapers are so besieged right now. On the one hand, they're all playing Caesar's wife, suspending and even firing reporters for the tiniest slip-ups. But they're also trying to compete with the weekly tabloids on the gossip front."

"Would you be interested?"

"I'd like to avoid it. It's one thing to run a daylong seminar on how PI techniques can be applied to investigative reporting. If they like me, I could parlay that into a national gig. But actually working on stories? I'll probably say no."

"Probably?"

"If money continues tight . . ." She tried for a lighthearted shrug.

"I could kick in more. There's no reason you have to carry the mortgage alone. I'm not asking for equity, just saying I could pay rent."

"I don't see how you could contribute more than you do. I know what you make, and my dad's much too cheap to give you a raise."

"I'll give up my MBA classes, get a part-time gig, find some money . . . somewhere."

"No, no. Don't sweat it. We just need to implement some belt-tightening measures—fewer steaks from Victor's, more wine from the marked-down barrel at Trinacria. And maybe—" Tess turned her gaze on the two dogs that had been keeping mute sentry at Crow's elbow, in hopes that a bite of cereal might fall. Esskay, the greyhound, was the unlikely alpha dog of the pair, while Miata was the world's most docile Doberman. "And maybe stop feeding those two parasites altogether."

Esskay's ears actually seemed to twitch in alarm, while Miata's sorrowful eyes held, as always, untold worlds of misery. Tess and Crow laughed, snug and warm on a rainy Sunday, delighted with the mundaneness of their problems. So money was tight. So Tess had a job she didn't particularly relish. Things would work out. They always did. Until they didn't.

Gregory Youssef's face stared up at her from the floor in mute reproach. He had almost movie-star good looks, but his image had grown meaningless from repetition, another face in the news. They all ran together after a while. *The guy who killed his wife, the guy who got killed, the guy who raped and pillaged his company.* Four months after his murder, all Youssef's face evoked was a vague sense that one had seen him somewhere before. *Oh, yeah, that guy.* Everyone knew of him, yet no one really knew him. As Tess studied the photo, it seemed to dissolve into a series of dots until his face disappeared completely, became an abstraction. Yet he would never become abstract or obscure to his widow. Tess hoped Mrs. Youssef had found a version of the truth that allowed her peace, no matter how wrong it might be. Who could be mean enough to begrudge her the myths that would pull her through, the story she was even now preparing to tell a child who had never known his father? Besides, Youssef's secret life, whatever it was, didn't void his love for his wife. People were more complicated than that.

The problems of three people didn't amount to a hill of beans, Bogart tells Bergman. But a hill of beans can seem mountainous when it's your hill of beans. Tess actually felt a tear welling up in her eye, and she swabbed it with a corner of her T-shirt. What was wrong with her? She had started crying over *The Longest Yard* last night, too, although she had told Crow it was because she was imagining what a desecration the remake would be. Truth was, she had been blubbering for Caretaker, the sly fixer who could anticipate everything but his own death.

She *must* be premenstrual. Or more anxious about her financial status than she was willing to admit. She shouldn't, in hindsight, have turned down all that work around Valentine's Day. A fussy private detective was a paradox, like a gardener who refused to touch soil or mulch or fertilizer. Tess had come to embrace Dumpster diving, because a hot shower banished the experience so readily. Entering a man's secret life, even in theory, made her feel far dirtier.

Now Youssef's staring face seemed castigating, accusing. Tess placed a stack of papers over it and returned to the confidential documents she had found in the governor's trash, including copies of several e-mails that would seem to indicate that the governor's wife had been directly involved in a smear campaign against the Senate president. Really, couldn't the state of Maryland afford to requisition a shredder for the governor's mansion?

Monday

chapter
2

SHIT."

Crow couldn't have been inside the Holy Redeemer parish hall more than ten minutes tops, dropping off produce that the East Side soup kitchen would stretch into salad for three hundred. How had his right rear tire, which had started the journey as plump and round as the others, gone so suddenly flat?

Worse, it wasn't even his tire. It was Tess's, on her precious Lexus SUV, which she had lent him reluctantly because Sunday's rain had turned to Monday's snow and sleet—what the local weather forecasters called a wintry mix—and Crow had deliveries to make all over Baltimore. She had insisted on taking his Volvo for her shorter trip downtown. The Volvo wasn't bad in the snow, but it needed a new muffler and a brake job that Tess thought Crow couldn't afford. And it was easier to let her continue thinking that for now than to get his car repaired.

"You want help changing that, mister?"

The young man seemed to appear from nowhere on the empty street. Fifteen or sixteen, he was ill dressed for the weather, a fleece hoodie thrown over baggy jeans and no gloves on the raw, chafed hands that—oh, so providentially—held a tire tool. At least he had a pair of Timberlands, although the brand had lost its cachet. Maybe that was the reason he was willing to expose the pristine suede to the elements.

"I mean, if you've got a spare, I can take off the lug nuts." He brandished the tool in his hand.

How *convenient,* as Tess would have said. But then, Tess would have been onto this kid the moment he appeared. Crow had allowed him the benefit of the doubt. Only for a second, but it was that split second of optimism that defined the difference between them. He was the original half-full guy, while she saw everything as half empty.

"I can change my own tire," Crow said shortly. "Is it simply flat, or did you puncture it?"

The young man widened his eyes in an excellent show of innocence, undercut only by their amber color and cat shape, which suggested an innate cunning. "Hey, I just happened to be walking by earlier and I saw it was flat, so I went home and got this. I didn't do shit to your tire."

"Sure." Crow popped the trunk, grateful that Holy Redeemer was his last delivery of the day. At least he didn't have to shift boxes of food to get to the spare. He moved quickly and capably. It wouldn't be the first tire he had changed, or even the worst circumstances under which he had changed one. The ever-shifting precipitation was now a light, fluffy snow, and the wind had died. In early winter such a snowfall would have been picturesque. In the penultimate week of March, it was merely depressing.

"You need help?"

"Not really."

Still, the young man lingered, offering commentary as Crow worked. "That's a little tight, ain't it?" he said of one lug nut. Then: "That's a decent whip, but I prefer the Escalade or the Expedition. Like they say: If you gonna go, go big. These Lexuses is kinda small."

And finally, when everything was done: "So can I have ten dollars, man?"

Even Crow found this a bit much. "For what? Giving me a flat tire or irritating the hell out of me while I changed it?"

"I *tol'* you, I didn't do shit to your tire." A pause. "Five dollars?"

"I don't think so."

"C'mon, man. I'm hungry."

It was a shrewd appeal. A white man in a Lexus SUV bringing food to a soup kitchen should be suffused with guilt and money, enough to throw some cash at a hungry adolescent, even one who had punctured his tire.

And it worked.

"You're hungry?"

"Starvin'." He patted his stomach and pushed out his lower lip. He wasn't exactly a handsome kid, but there was something compelling about his face. The eyes might seem sly, but the grin was genuine, almost sweet. "Like those commercials. You know, 'You can feed this child for seventeen cents a day—or you can change the channel.' 'Course it's more than seventeen cents here. We ain't in Africa, ya feel?"

"Okay, get in the car, we'll go buy you a sandwich."

"Naw, that's okay. I just wanted to buy groceries and shit."

"How many groceries can you buy for five dollars?"

"I could get a sandwich, a bag of chips, and a large soda down at the Korean's."

"What about the Yellow Bowl? I'll spring for a full lunch." The Yellow Bowl was a well-known soul food restaurant not too far away.

An Elvis-like curl of the lip. "I don't eat that country shit."

"Look, you name the place and I'll take you there for lunch."

"Anyplace?"

"Anyplace in the Baltimore metro area."

"How about Macaroni's?"

"Marconi's?" The choice couldn't have been more surprising. The restaurant was one of the city's oldest, a fussy, white-tablecloth landmark where H. L. Mencken had dined in his prime. The only thing that had changed since Mencken's time was the wallpaper and a few members of the waitstaff. Tess, of course, loved it. But then, Tess suffered acutely from Baltimorosis in Crow's opinion, a disease characterized by nostalgia for all things local, even when their glory days preceded one's own birth by decades. A nonnative, Crow was less susceptible.

"Are you sure you want to go to Marconi's?"

"Macaroni's."

Crow decided to chalk the choice up to that weird gentry vibe in the bling culture, the same impulse that had made Bentleys and Burberry plaid so popular. The kid was trying to aspire.

"Doesn't matter how you say it, we'll go there. It's on me."

"Man—I got things to do. Can't you just give me a dollar or two?"

"What do you have to do? Go find another mark, slash his tire?"

"Didn't do shit to your tire." Still, he got in the car.

"My name's Edgar Ransome, but people call me Crow."

Lately he was wishing that weren't so. Childhood nick-
names didn't wear well as one approached the age of thirty.
They yoked you to the past, kept you infantile. But he also
didn't feel like an Edgar, Ed, or Eddie, and his last name
sounded like a soap opera character's. "What's your name?"

"Lloyd Jupiter."

"Seriously."

"I am serious."

Lloyd scrunched down in the seat, sullen and unhappy at
the prospect of being forced to eat at one of the city's best-
known restaurants. He did not speak again until Crow pulled
up in front of the old brownstone on Saratoga Street.

"What's this shit? I thought we were going to *Macaroni's*."

"Look at the sign, Lloyd. It's Marconi's."

"I know what it says. I can fuckin' read. But I wanted to
go to the Macaroni Grill out Columbia way. They got a salad
bar. My mom took me there for my birthday once."

Crow considered persuading Lloyd to settle for Marconi's
French-influenced menu, force-feeding him shad roe and
lobster imperial and potatoes au gratin and vanilla ice cream
with fudge sauce. It had to be a thousand times better than
any franchise restaurant. Instead he turned the car around
and headed south to the suburbs, to the place that Lloyd
Jupiter had specified. A deal was a deal.

"Where is it, exactly?" Crow and Tess didn't spend much
time outside the city limits.

"Out Columbia way," Lloyd repeated. "On that highway,
near that place."

"The mall?"

"Naw, on the highway to the mall. Across from Dick's
Sporting Goods."

"You get those Tims at Dick's?"

Lloyd rolled his eyes, perhaps at Crow's use of the shorthand for Timberlands, perhaps for some other unspecified ignorance and whiteness and general uncoolness on Crow's part. "Downtown Locker Room."

"That the place to go, huh?"

Lloyd shifted in his seat, stiff and uncomfortable. Did he think that Crow was cruising him, taking him out to lunch and studying his material desires in order to extract some kind of sexual favor? Street-level life in Baltimore, as Crow thought of it, was viciously homophobic. Tess had that much right: White country kids would turn tricks and still consider themselves straight, but black kids simply didn't try to play it that way. You were queer or you weren't. And if you were, you'd better be ready to get your ass kicked or kick back.

Tess would laugh at him later. Laugh at tenderhearted Crow, insisting on buying lunch for the street kid who had punctured her tire and tried to extort money from him. Roar at the idea of taking said kid to Marconi's, then acquiescing to his desire for the chain-restaurant glories of Macaroni Grill, slipping and sliding along slick highways on a day when people who didn't have to drive were being exhorted to stay at home.

Still, he couldn't help loving her, although loving Tess Monaghan was a challenging proposition, what a union man might call the lobster shift of romance. The summer he was nineteen, Crow had worked for exactly three days at a factory owned by a family friend. His job was to insert a metal fastener in a hole on a piece of cardboard, which would later be assembled into a floor display for a mattress. Because he worked the late shift, the lobster, he had received an extra twelve cents an hour—the lobster-shift differential.

He often thought that there should be a Tess differential as well. Not that life with her was as mind-numbing as those three days in the factory. Quite the opposite. But she required a lot of extra work.

*   *   *

There was a short wait at the Macaroni Grill—it was twelve-thirty now, and the restaurant's vestibule was filled with a backlog of not-quite-homebound families, desperate to amuse their children on a snow day when there wasn't enough actual snow to do anything outside. Crow and Lloyd sat on a bench opposite a row of newspaper boxes, and Crow bought a paper, but Lloyd wanted nothing to do with it, not even the comics or the sports section, although he did ask Crow how the Detroit Pistons had done the night before.

"Tell me about yourself, Lloyd."

All he received was a narrowed-eye look in return.

"That's my girlfriend's SUV you vandalized, by the way. Her new-to-her precious baby." Tess had bought the Lexus from a dealership that insisted on calling it preowned, a semantic shenanigan that had so annoyed Tess that she walked out in the final round of negotiations. The salesman had knocked off another five hundred dollars to get her back to the table.

"It *looked* like a woman's car," Lloyd said. "That's why—" He stopped himself.

"What? That's what you were counting on when you slashed the tire? A woman who would need help changing the tire?"

"Didn't do shit to your tire."

"Well, you're lucky she wasn't driving it today. She's a lot tougher than I am."

Lloyd gave Crow a look as if to say, *That's not so tough.*

"For one thing, she's licensed to carry a gun."

"She a cop?" This prospect was clearly unnerving.

"Private detective."

Lloyd couldn't maintain his studied indifference. "For real? Like Charlie's Angels and shit?"

"A little more down to earth. Skip traces, insurance stuff, missing persons, financial background checks."

"She ever kill anybody?"

"Once. It was self-defense. . . ." He had Lloyd's full attention now. Tess would rather that Crow post nude photos of her on the Internet than speak of the near-death encounter that had thrust her onto the front page last year. The scar on her knee was slowly disappearing, but Crow had noticed how often her fingers went to that spot, fingering the lumpy, purple-white line as if it were a crooked pennywhistle. *Hot cross buns. Hot cross buns. One gunshot, ten gunshots, hot cross buns.*

He had a scar, too, but Tess seemed to forget that. Everybody had scars, one way or another.

"She know kung fu? I do."

Lloyd jumped to his feet, executing a mishmash of moves that appeared to have been gleaned from films such as *The Matrix, Hero,* and *Crouching Tiger, Hidden Dragon.* His impromptu performance alarmed the mostly white, all-suburban audience of waiting families. It wasn't Lloyd's race so much as his loudness, the sudden movements. That just didn't play in Columbia.

"She has her methods."

"Is she like the White She Devil in *Undercover Brother?*" Lloyd struck another pose, shaking his head violently from side to side as if trying to dislodge a bug from his ear. Crow considered himself well versed in all forms of pop culture, but Lloyd had left him behind with that reference.

The pretty brunette hostess hurried forward, ready to seat them even though several other parties had been waiting longer.

"Where do you live, Lloyd?" Crow asked as he watched Lloyd tuck in to his salad-bar creation, more cheese than lettuce. Cheese, lettuce, and nothing else.

" 'Round."

" 'Round where?"

"I don't like to specify too much about myself. But you know, I turned sixteen last fall. They can't make me go to school anymore."

"So what are you doing if you don't go to school?"

"I worked for a man 'round the way."

The past tense didn't escape Crow. "Doing what?"

Lloyd gave him a look. "You sure you're not a cop?"

"I'm a bartender." Not quite the truth, but more expedient than trying to explain his jack-of-all-trades role at Pat Monaghan's bar, the Point.

"Why you so interested in me?"

"Because you're a person, sitting opposite me in a restaurant. Why wouldn't I be interested in another human being?"

Lloyd pointed a fork at him. "A human being that you think slashed your tire."

"Well, didn't you?"

Lloyd grinned. He was so long and bony, thinner than even Crow had been at that age, and he was rampaging through his salad as if he hadn't had a solid meal for a while. Weekends were light on free food in the Baltimore area, with only a few churches open for business. That's part of the reason Crow had started using his day off to take supplies to the smaller soup kitchens, the ones that didn't get as much publicity as the name-brand charities.

"Did *not*. Word. But I saw the guy who did, and I told him that an old lady had seen him and called the police and he better run. I told him I'd hold his tool for him so the police wouldn't pick him up. Then I waited for you to come back. Tire was already flat, right? No harm in helping out."

His last words echoed in Crow's brain. It was true, despite what Tess maintained. There could be no harm in helping anyone.

"Lloyd, tell me straight: You got a place to sleep tonight? The temperature's supposed to go down into the twenties."

"I'll be fine."

"Okay, but when I take you home, I'm taking you to an address and watching you go *inside*. In fact, I'm coming inside with you and meeting your folks."

"Uh-uh."

"Why not?"

"Some white dude bring me home, my mom starts asking questions, and she'll figure out that I wasn't up to any good, and I'll be *beat*."

Lloyd's tone and reasoning were persuasive, but he had hesitated just long enough for Crow to know he was lying.

"But according to you, all you did was take advantage of someone else's crime."

"Yeah, but she won't believe that. My mama ain't got much use for me."

"Lloyd—do you live with your mom? Or any adult? Is anyone looking out for you?"

Their entrées arrived—the speed of the service was setting records, as if the staff could not be free of Lloyd and Crow soon enough—and Lloyd busied himself with spaghetti and meatballs. He ate as a child might, Crow noticed, holding the fork in his fist, cutting the strands instead of winding them around the fork.

"I'm not dropping you off on the street, not in this weather. Either I take you to a place where an adult comes to the door and vouches for you or I'll find you a shelter bed—"

"No fucking shelters!" Lloyd almost yelped in his distress. "You show up there, you young, they call juvenile services or social services and they haul you away for what they say is your own good. That ain't for me."

"Then I'll take you to where I live. Just for the night,

okay? You can sleep in the spare bedroom, and I'll take you back to the neighborhood tomorrow morning. Even drop you off at school, if you like."

"Told you, I'm sixteen. I don't have to go."

"Fine, Lloyd. You don't *have* to go. But do you want to go?"

"Hell no." His look was scornful, contemptuous of the very idea that one could want to go to school if it wasn't required by law. Crow decided to change his tack, to become Lloyd's supplicant, allow him the illusion that he had the upper hand in their dealings.

"Here's the thing, man. I need you to tell my girlfriend what happened with her car. She's going to be pissed about the tire, and she's not going to believe me."

"What—you whipped?"

"A little," Crow said. "A little."

Of course, if he were truly cowed by Tess, he wouldn't dare bring Lloyd Jupiter home with him.

"Women," Lloyd said with a world-weary sigh, as if he had a lifetime of experience.

"They can be demanding. But they're usually worth the effort."

"True dat," Lloyd said, reaching for a fistful of garlic bread. "Can I have dessert?"

chapter
3

"S̲URVEILLANCE ISN'T FOR AMATEURS," TESS MONAGHAN told the bright young faces that stared unnervingly up at her from the seats of the *Beacon-Light*'s small auditorium, a spanking-new addition to a building that seemed to be under constant renovation. "Remember the *Miami Herald* and Gary Hart? They staked out his apartment but didn't realize it had a back door. There's no such thing as partial surveillance. That's a classic amateur mistake."

"But you *were* an amateur, right?" one of the men asked. It was that logy middle section of the afternoon, the Q-and-A portion of her presentation, and Tess had long ago figured out that this particular reporter was far more interested in his own Q's than in anyone else's A's. She wasn't sure of his name, which had been given in a flurry of handshakes and greetings over coffee at 10:00 A.M. and reiterated during the lunch break. The men here all looked alike—Ivy League preppy with floppy hair, khaki trousers, and button-down shirts with sleeves rolled up to the exact point just below the elbow, almost as if they had been measured with a ruler. And all white. The male reporters picked for this tutorial in investigative techniques were extremely white, *white*-white, so white that they made Tess doubt her own credentials as a Caucasian.

As for the women, there were only two, and they were a study in contrasts. One was a demure blonde afraid to make eye contact, while the other was an exotic blend of races who might have wandered in from the Miss Universe pageant. The newspaper probably counted her three or four times over when cooking its diversity stats.

"If you mean I had no formal training as a private investigator, then yes, I started as a self-taught amateur. But I apprenticed to a PI, as required by law, and took over his agency when he retired to the Eastern Shore."

This was true, as far as it went. Tess seldom bothered to explain that she had never met her mentor face-to-face. Edward Keyes was a retired Baltimore cop and old family friend. As a former detective, he was given a PI's license automatically and then "hired" Tess. He had signed the incorporation papers, expedited her license, and sold her the agency for a dollar, all without leaving his home on the Delaware shore.

"Tess was a reporter at the *Star*," Kevin Feeney put in. "But in just three years, she's had a lot of success running her own business."

"Are you expanding?" the same floppy-haired man demanded. "Taking on staff? Landing big corporate accounts?"

"Well, I got this one." This earned her a generous laugh. Apparently her interrogator wasn't popular with his colleagues either. "As for expansion, I don't think I'd be particularly good at managing others. 'Hell is other people,' as

Sartre said. Instead I work with a loose network of female
PIs, nationwide. We trade out our time and brainstorm together, but we remain independent contractors."

"Why all women?"

"Why not?" No laugh this time, just stony looks of con-
fusion, although Tess thought she saw Miss Universe hide a
smile behind her left hand while raising her right and waiting to be recognized. The men raised their hands, too, but
they seldom waited for Tess to call on them.

"Is your work dangerous?" Miss Universe asked.

"Not if I'm doing it right."

Her one insistent questioner was not done. "But you
killed a man, right? Didn't you have to kill someone in self-
defense?"

Her grin faded, and behind the podium her hand reached
instinctively for her knee. "Yes."

"How does it feel—"

"One more question," Feeney cut in. "Preferably from
someone who hasn't asked one yet. Then it's back to work."

"Do you actually *enjoy* what you do?" asked a man at the
back of the room. "Your work seems even more dependent
on human misery than journalism is."

The question caught her short, no glib reply at the ready.
Tess knew she liked working for herself and was proud of
the middle-class living she had managed to achieve, touch-
and-go as it could be at times. Just a few years ago, she had
been living in a below-market rental in her aunt's building,
carrying balances on her credit cards, scrimping and saving
for the tiniest indulgences. Now she had a house that was ap-
preciating so fast the tax bill was threatening to overtake the
mortgage—and that was without the city's assessment division catching up with all the improvements made since she
bought the little bungalow.

But did she enjoy her job? The means to the various ends

were often unpleasant, a constant reminder of humankind's capacity for venality. If no one ever cheated an insurance company, much less a spouse, if no one tried to outthink security systems or steal others' identities . . . well, then, Tess wouldn't have been able to purchase a Lexus SUV, even a used one.

She had reunited a family, she reminded herself. Safe-guarded a secret that the entire city held dear. Eased a woman's tortured conscience, stopped a monster in his tracks, cleared a man's reputation. Saved the lives of three children, whose father remained on friendly terms with her. In fact, Mark Rubin wanted Tess and Crow to attend second-night seder at the family's house next month.

"Yes," she said. "I do. I really do."

After a polite round of applause, the star reporters of the *Beacon-Light* filed out in dutiful, orderly fashion. Ah, Hildy Johnson had long ago left the building, no matter which gender embodied the part. Once they had cleared the room, Tess turned to Feeney and rolled her eyes.

"In my day it was the television reporters who asked how one felt."

"Sorry, Tess. I told them to avoid that subject out of common courtesy. He's not the sharpest crayon in the box. If he were a Crayola, he'd be burnt sienna."

"Burnt sienna? Feeney, only one person in this entire room even approached beige."

"I mean he'd be one of those second-class colors that no self-respecting kid touches until all the good ones are gone."

"Ah, but in that case," Tess said, "he *would* be the sharpest crayon in the box."

Feeney laughed. "There are days when I wish I had one of those little built-in sharpeners at my desk and I could just insert their heads in there. Don't get me wrong. They're good kids, bright and earnest. But they're inexperienced and they don't know the city. Aggressive, yet hamstrung with fear. It ain't the best combo. That's why I was hoping a maverick like you might fire them up, inspire them to 'think different,' as that ungrammatical ad campaign had it."

"The best question I got all day," Tess said, "was if they made female-friendly equipment for bladder relief."

"I must have stepped out during that part. Do they?"

"Yes, but I prefer the old-fashioned way whenever possible. Speaking of which . . . ?"

"Down the hall, on the left."

The newsroom that Tess walked through bore little resemblance to her beloved Baltimore *Star*, dead for almost a decade. In fact, it no longer resembled the *Beacon-Light* newsroom of just two years ago. Reporters often complained that modern newspaper offices could be insurance companies, but Tess thought the *Beacon-Light* looked more like an advertising agency where the employees had been kept in sensory deprivation tanks for too long. There were few flashes of personal identity in the pretty maple-veneer cubicles—no toys or rude posters or dartboards with the boss's face pinned to them, things once common to newsrooms. It took a moment longer to identify what else was missing. Laughter. Chatter. Noise of any kind. No one was joking or shouting or even berating someone over the phone. H. L. Mencken had once complained that copy editors were eunuchs who had never felt the breeze on their faces. But with telephones, the Internet, and e-mail, far too many reporters spent their entire days staring into the sickly glow of computer terminals, removed from human contact. They were at once more connected and less connected.

Still, stupid and impertinent questions aside, Tess's gig was a godsend—a nice chunk of guaranteed cash for very little effort—and Feeney was probably right when he said that she could spin it into a regular venture, flying to newspapers and television stations all over the country. With budgets cut to the bone, the big media companies would rather pay a onetime fee to a PI than hire seasoned editors and reporters.

Her cell phone vibrated, and she glanced down: Crow, although their wireless service announced him as E. RANSOME. A daytime call from him was rare enough to give her pause; he was not much for idle chat, and he understood that her work often prevented her from answering the phone. Besides, Crow's own days were fuller and fuller, almost frighteningly so. "He's growing up right before your eyes," Tess's friend Whitney had observed, meaning to make a joke. After years of a rather feckless, careless existence, Crow seemed to have found his inner workaholic, throwing his energy into creating a reputable music club in the most unlikely corner of far west Baltimore, then trying to eradicate hunger in his spare time. The change encouraged Tess, but it also unnerved her a little, as all change did.

"What's up?" she asked.

"We're going to have a houseguest tonight. Just wanted to give you a heads-up."

"Cool. Some college friend passing through?"

"No, more of a friend in need."

"A friend?"

"Well, a new friend. An acquaintance."

"Crow—"

"Tess, I met this kid, and he doesn't have anywhere to go or anywhere to stay, and—I just can't leave him on the street in this weather, and he doesn't want to go to the shelters or the missions, and who can blame him?"

"Crow, you are out of your fucking mind."

"Why? It's just one night."

"There are a thousand whys, but I can't have this conversation outside the ladies' room at the *Blight*."

The use of the paper's nickname earned her a stern look from a beetle-browed woman stalking by, legal pad in hand. It wasn't very gracious, disparaging the paper on its own premises.

"I'll tell you what: We'll meet for dinner somewhere, and I'll size this kid up before you bring him into—our house." She had almost said "my," a bad habit. "I could be at the Brass Elephant in half an hour."

"Lloyd's underage. We can't take him to a bar."

So it was Lloyd now, underage Lloyd. "What does he want, an expense-account dinner at Charleston?"

"What he really needs is a home-cooked meal, something that will stick to his ribs. I was thinking lamb stew, some chipotle muffins." He was trying to soften her up, naming two of her favorite dishes. It was working.

"Okay. To *dinner*. I'm not guaranteeing him a bed for the night. I get to reserve judgment on that until I meet him."

"Tess, I'm not the naïf you like to make me out to be. I've got some street sense."

"Of course you do," she said, but her assurances rang hollow even to her.

She pushed her way into the ladies' room. This, too, had been upgraded, the once institutional green-and-peach color scheme replaced with gleaming stainless steel and stark white tiles. A young woman, the multinational brunette from the presentation, leaned toward her lovely reflection, inspecting her invisible pores, her nonexistent lines. Asian? Black? Latina? Possibly all three.

"Your talk was *fascinating*," she said when she caught Tess's eye in the mirror. "Completely opened up my mind to new ways of reporting."

Tess wanted to take the compliment, but the gushing was too rote.

"Please don't suck up. It makes me nervous."

"That's refreshing," the girl said, returning her gaze to her own face. "The men around here can't get enough smoke blown up their butts. I tell you, it's exhausting."

Tess laughed with relief. Here was the smart-aleck attitude she remembered, the coarse vocabulary she expected from journalists.

"I'm rotten with names. You're . . ."

"Marcy. Marcy Appleton." Tess tried not to smile. It was such a hilariously all-American, blond-cheerleader name. The girl's accent was midwestern, too, with broad *o*'s and *a*'s. "I cover federal courts."

"You really want to do investigative stuff?"

"It's the most prestigious thing you can do here, now that they're consolidating the national bureaus throughout the chain. And everyone knows that the foreign bureaus will go next. Which sucks, because I came here banking on a post in Asia. I'm fluent in Mandarin, and I traveled throughout the region between college and grad school. Know who they sent to cover the tsunami? Thomas H. T. Melville III, who's barely mastered English."

"He's . . ."

"The idiot who started to ask you what it felt like to kill someone."

Marcy paused, took a pot of gloss from her purse, and rubbed it gently over her lips. Apparently she wanted to know, too, but was too polite to ask outright. Tess opened her own leather satchel and revealed the Beretta that she always kept at hand.

"I didn't always carry this. Now I do."

The girl nodded. She was perhaps six or seven years younger than Tess, but she seemed to be from another generation or perhaps even a different species, one characterized by boundless confidence and self-esteem. "And I guess you don't use it as a figure of speech anymore. It would be impossible to say 'I want to kill so-and-so' once you've done it literally."

"Yeah," Tess said absently. "Yeah." She was thinking, *Actually, I want to kill my boyfriend.*

"There was one thing you said—about the Youssef case—that didn't exactly track for me."

"Yes?" Tess suddenly didn't feel as kindly inclined toward the girl.

"The federal courthouse is my beat, although all the boys keep trying to bigfoot me on the story. Only nothing's coming out. It's not the most leak-happy place under any circumstances, but the discipline on the Youssef murder is remarkable. I can't get the feds to speak, even off the record, about what a piss-poor job the Howard County cops are doing, and I can't get the Howard County cops to say anything about what the feds should or shouldn't be doing."

"The old divide-and-conquer technique, huh?"

"Exactly. You were probably a good reporter in your day."

"Merely adequate. But the closemouthed atmosphere you're describing—that only supports my theory, right?"

"I suppose so." Marcy frowned. She really was lovely. With a face like that, she probably wasn't used to not getting what she wanted from men, and the federal bureaucracy was dominated by men, although the acting U.S. attorney was a woman. "The thing is, Youssef was a flirt. I always thought he was kind of hitting on me. But, you know, it would have been unethical to act on it. He was a source."

"And married."

"Oh, yeah," Marcy said, although this seemed a secondary concern to her. The paper's ethics policy probably didn't cover adultery, just sex with sources. "Still, he definitely had an eye for women."

"Good cover for a closeted man, don't you think? They can be the worst Lotharios of all. Or maybe he was bi. Or his killer could have been a *female* prostitute. His wife was eight months pregnant at the time. The particulars remain the same. It was vicious, it was personal—and no one wants to talk about it."

"Maybe," Marcy said. "I don't know. In the end it's so hard to know what goes on in anyone's head."

"Keep that kind of talk within these walls. Out there never admit that you don't know anything. *They* don't."

Emerging from the sanctuary of the ladies' room, Tess almost tripped over a lurking man, a whey-faced middle-aged version of the young comers she had been instructing all day. Introduced to him that morning, Tess had already forgotten his name, but she retained his bio: a new assistant managing editor, imported from Dallas just a few months ago, according to Feeney. Rumor was that he had been installed by corporate with orders to gut the newsroom budget. When that was accomplished, he would be rewarded with the top job.

"Initial feedback on your presentation was very positive," he said. He had that unfortunate bad breath that nothing can mask, so it ends up being bad breath with a minty, medicinal overlay. "The reporters said you had lots of insight into out-of-the-box thinking."

"I hope no one actually said 'out of the box.' Or if they did, they were promptly fired."

"We're a union paper, we can't fire anyone," the editor said, wringing his hands mournfully. Hector Callahan, that was his name. Hector-the-Nonprotector. Hector-the-Nonprotector-Complete-with-Pocket-Protector-Who-Liked-to-Talk-About-News-Vectors. Tess was training herself to use rhymes as mnemonic devices.

"I was joking."

"Oh." He looked puzzled, as if jokes were an archaic social custom. "You know, I think that there could be a place for you here. On staff. Well, not on staff—we couldn't offer benefits—but on retainer, as a consultant."

Here was the offer that Tess had dreaded, the one she must sidestep adroitly if she was going to turn this into a traveling gig throughout the chain's holdings.

"That would create all sorts of conflicts of interest for me. Few clients are going to feel comfortable working with a private investigator who also works for the local newspaper."

"But if we did it on a case-by-case basis—the Youssef matter, for example. If you, as a private detective, fleshed out your theory—did some actual legwork to verify your . . . um, suppositions—and brought that report to the newspaper, then we could report your findings."

"You mean, I could be the messenger that everyone wants to shoot and the paper could claim it was just reporting what someone else said. It would be an ingenious way of advancing a salacious story—and then the paper could promptly back off, throw me to the dogs if I made even the tiniest mistake. Have your dirt and make me eat it, too."

"Being on retainer for the paper would be a steady source of income that would help you weather the . . . um, droughts endemic to small businesses such as yours."

He said "small businesses" as if the very concept were distasteful, as if it smelled as rotten as his breath.

"You sound almost as if you know something of my finances, Hector." She managed, just, not to add the rest of the rhyme now bouncing in her head. *Hector the Nonprotector / Likes to Talk about News Vectors / Does he have a brain, this Hector? / That is simply mere conjecture.*

He smiled, expelling another puff of minty-bad breath.

"We do know how to do some basic investigative work.

Just think about it, Miss Monaghan. Don't be so hasty. Don't make your decision now. Think about it, sleep on it."

Somewhere in Tess's brain, a cautionary voice reminded her to count to ten, to wait before saying the words springing so automatically to her lips. But the voice was too faint, too weak. Sentences were already forming and heading out into the world, as impossible to marshal as the wind.

"You know, whenever anyone tells me to think about a proposition, he—and it's almost always a he, come to think of it—seems to disregard the fact that I *have* thought about it. Thought about it, considered it from every angle, and rejected it. So no, I'm not going to think about it. You don't need a PI on retainer. You need to devote more resources to hiring experienced reporters who can do the kind of investigative journalism you want, or else come to terms with the fact that you're putting out a piece-of-shit newspaper that's interested only in its bottom line."

Hector backed away from Tess, then turned and, in his haste to escape from this Cassandra-like creature, caromed off the wall with a loud thud, righted himself, and limped into the newsroom, favoring his left hip.

"What was that noise?" Marcy asked, coming out of the bathroom, hands smoothing her silky brown hair.

"Me, derailing my own gravy train."

chapter
4

GABE DALESIO DEBATED WHETHER HE WOULD NEED A COAT to dash over to the courthouse for the 3:00 P.M. initial-appearances hearing, running through the pros and cons with the same swift analysis he brought to everything he did. *Pro:* There was snow on the ground. *Con:* The snow had pretty much stopped. *Pro:* It was still cold. *Con:* If he stopped at the smoking pad afterward, the men who smoked—the DEA agents, Customs, ATF, even IRS—almost never wore top-coats, no matter how bitter the day, and Gabe wouldn't want to look like a pussy. Six months in, he was still enough of a newbie to worry about the impression he made on the guys. If he could only impress them, maybe they would start bringing him cases and he wouldn't have to play second goddamn chair on other AUSA's cases. The smoking pad was usually a reliable place for nicotine freaks to bond, but he had yet to make a single real friend.

If only the boss smoked. *That* would be a golden opportunity. But the interim U.S. attorney was a pinch-faced, uncharmable woman. Lesbo? Gabe didn't automatically assume that a woman was gay just because she was immune to what all his female relatives had long assured him was a completely irresistible charm. Still, one had to consider the possibility. He almost hoped for her sake that she was, because he couldn't imagine what kind of man would want to be with her. *Fug*ly bitch.

He left his coat in his office, a decision he regretted when he felt the air. He regretted it more when he finished the mind-numbing routine of extraditing the lowlife of the day and saw that two middle-aged secretaries were the only people on the slice of patio allotted to the federal courthouse's smokers. They welcomed Gabe nicely enough, and he flashed his boyish smile. Force of habit. Besides, secretaries were always worth sucking up to, although these two didn't seem particularly interested in him. Perfunctory greetings exchanged, they turned back to their conversation, which centered on what they had done over the weekend.

Weekend talk—that was the mark of going-nowhere losers in Gabe's head, people who were always talking about their weekends, either the one just past or the one about to come. It was why he had been such a bad fit in Albuquerque with all those outdoorsy types, whose jobs seemed to exist only to support their skiing and hiking habits. That and the fact that he didn't speak any Spanish beyond *sí* and *huevos rancheros*, and he couldn't give a shit about immigration casework. Gabe didn't even like three-day weekends, feeling they disrupted the rhythm of work. January and February had been a bitch for just that reason. The Christmas holidays finally over, all he had wanted to do was work, get some traction, and here came Martin Luther King Day and then Presidents' Day. The city even took a holiday for Lin-

coln's birthday, which he found totally bush. But then he
found everything about Baltimore bush league.

Gabe wasn't a monk. If he met a woman worth dating,
he'd take her out to a restaurant, try to extract the reasonable
quid pro quo. (And any woman who said she didn't operate
on a sliding scale, who claimed to behave no differently
whether it was the Double-T Diner or Charleston, was lying
through her teeth.) He went to the gym, sometimes took in a
Ravens game, although the brokers' prices were steep and he
couldn't accept anything from anyone. The ethics policy for
federal prosecutors was about as strict as they come: Nothing from nobody. They couldn't even accept freebies to re-
distribute to orphans, for Christ's sake. But Gabe was cool
with that. He wasn't consciously preparing himself for Senate confirmation down the road, but he'd be ready just in
case. His life was going to be so clean it squeaked.

Besides, what was wrong with dreaming big? You had to
be able to envision something in order to achieve it. Once,
he had read this interview with the guy who did the Dilbert
cartoon, and he said he had used visualization techniques,
that self-actualization thing where you write down what you
want every day, over and over again. Gabe had been a little
scared to try the writing-down part—it would be too embarrassing if someone found those hopeful sentences, as damn-
ing as a teenage girl twining her initials with some
boy's—but yes, in his mind he pictured himself in the robes
of the federal judiciary. Look, someone had to be a federal
judge. Why not him?

He took one last greedy drag, staring balefully at the
ridiculous piece of modern art on the tiny patch of courthouse lawn. It was Gabe's understanding that the twisty
piece of orange, blue, and yellow metal had long been the
unchallenged title holder for ugliest piece of public art in
Baltimore, but it had gained some serious competition from

a towering man-woman figure outside the train station. That hermaphrodite monstrosity had been the first thing Gabe had seen when he made the trip down from New Jersey for his job interview, this giant male-female of steel, with a pulsing purple-blue light where the heart should be. It completely dwarfed the train station. Gabe was no philistine, but what message was such a statue trying to send? *Welcome to Baltimore, the capital of androgyny. Welcome to Baltimore, the land of hollow people. Welcome to Baltimore, pre-op tranny capital of the world, where you can't tell the men from the women.* The last was kind of true, actually.

Gabe had been lured to Baltimore by the former U.S. attorney, a gung-ho guy who spoke passionately of nailing corrupt public officials, who dangled the bait of vast conspiracies and career-making casework. An Italian-American, he had bonded with Gabe over their loathing of *The Sopranos, The Godfather*, and every other guido stereotype. Truth was, Gabe sort of liked mob shows, not that he was the kind of guy to park himself in front of the television on a regular basis. Anyway, he was only half Italian. His mother was German-Irish. She had the Irish charm, if not the German mania for cleanliness, and her emotions ran as freely as water. Meanwhile his Italian dad was as starchy and reticent as any WASP, a shirt-and-tie civil servant. So Gabe could, and did, play his identity numerous ways—Horatio Alger boy made good, solid middle-class citizen used to creature comforts, arm-waving Italian, poetic Irishman, orderly German. Some people might call that phoniness, but Gabe considered his ability to fit in with others a social nicety. He didn't lie, not exactly. He just played up whatever part of himself made others feel comfortable.

He put his cigarette out in the ceramic container, one of those overdesigned contraptions intended to be mildly decorative. *Someone made that,* Gabe thought, although probably not in this country. That was someone's job, poor bastard. Most people had jobs like that. Meaningless, disposable, of no import. Whatever his frustrations, his work mattered. He never lost sight of that.

He checked his watch and realized he needed to get to the staff meeting. An oddity, scheduled for day's end on a Monday instead of a Friday, suggesting that it might actually be about something. But whatever the topic, it would circle back to the Youssef case. All the meetings did.

He arrived for the 4:30 P.M. meeting at exactly 4:29. Punctual but busy, that was the message to send. Show up five minutes early and everyone wondered why you were so free. One second after the boss, and you were toast. With the calculation that Gabe brought to everything at work, he chose a seat in the middle of the room, one where he could make eye contact with the boss but also steal looks at Lombard Street if it got too deadly dull.

He listened attentively, looking for opportunities to contribute, but only if he could be original, meaningful. No talking for talking's sake. Still, no matter how on point Gabe was, he never seemed to earn more than an impatient frown. The boss woman just wasn't in his corner. True, she hadn't hired him and she wasn't here for the long term, but her indifference bothered Gabe. Why didn't she like him? He was good and eager and hardworking. In his head he was a rising star, and his inability so far to persuade others of that fact had been the biggest shock of his postcollege life. After a lackluster year with a Wall Street firm, he decided the federal system would be more of a meritocracy, less inclined to be impressed by prestigious law schools and things like law review. Albuquerque had been okay, but Baltimore was supposed to be closer to the center of things, especially terrorism. So he came back east, only to find out that they now thought Al Qaeda was infiltrating Mexico. Gabe never seemed to be in the right place at the right time.

The meeting was just a regular staff meeting, a nuts-and-bolts thing, but the boss lady did bring up Youssef at the end.

"I know you don't want anyone in this office to talk to the press about Greg," said one of the more senior prosecutors, a woman on whom the boss just doted, Terri Hamm. She got the hot cases, the big drug dealers, the gang members who were getting federal death-penalty sentences. Again, it was a matter of having the connections, of knowing the agents who would bring you the good stuff. Youssef had been doing a lot of those cases before he moved to antiterrorism.

"I don't want anyone in the office to talk to the press, period," Gail said, and everyone laughed dutifully. A joke, but not.

"The thing is, that lets the Howard detectives off the hook, because no one's calling them on what a shitty job they've done. And the less that's said, the more people on talk radio feel free to indulge in wild speculation, some of which leads right back to this office. We look awful, through no fault of our own."

"It is a delicate situation," conceded the boss. "But I'm more concerned with Greg's widow than with public perception. And I don't think talk radio represents mainstream opinion."

"Still, it shakes people's faith in our overall ability," Terri Hamm said. "The one thing we're supposed to be able to do is solve the death of one of our own. Why can't the Howard County police at least provide updates, let people know that the case isn't completely stalled? They were pissed when the one fact about the ATM got out, but that wasn't our fault."

"We have no official role in this, although an FBI agent is acting as an unofficial liaison. And what's the use of announcing they've developed leads if they don't want the leads to get out? I think they're right to hold back the information about the toll plaza and the ATM card."

Although Gabe's gaze was focused, his expression appropriately serious, he allowed his mind to wander. He had barely known Youssef, who was killed two months after Gabe started, and what he had known made him resentful: the Egyptian wonder boy, the son of a Detroit deli owner. Youssef had gotten a lot of hot assignments for the wrong reasons, in Gabe's opinion. It was sheer public relations. *Forget Abu Ghraib, forget Guantánamo—look at this handsome A-rab who's working for the U.S attorney.*

Still, Gabe's brain was poking at something almost in spite of itself, prodding and nudging. He risked a question, despite the fact that Gail was clearly ready for the discussion to end.

"The toll plaza—are we talking about the fact that the car went through cash booths, even though it was outfitted with an E-ZPass?"

"Yes. Clearly the driver didn't know that Greg had E-ZPass on his car—or thought that going through the cash tolls would keep the device from being activated. So we still know exactly when he went through the McHenry Tunnel and when he entered and exited the New Jersey Turnpike."

"But there's another time, right? Not just on the trip north, when we think the killer panicked and headed to a place he knew so he could dump the car and get away, but on the trip *out* of the city, right?"

The boss lady sighed, not bothering to conceal her impatience. "Yes. What's your point, Gabe?"

"Nothing."

But something had clicked for him. He just didn't want to feel his way through the idea in front of this throng.

*　　*　　*

The meeting ended, and Gabe's little brainstorm might have moved on, replaced by his own work, uninspiring as it was. But on his next trip to the smoking pad, he saw Mike Collins, a DEA agent, the kind of guy that other guys wanted to impress, even if he wasn't the star he used to be. Collins had a fierce rep. Strong, broad-shouldered, laconic, Collins never wasted a word. He barely wasted a facial expression.

"You and Youssef were buddies, right?" Gabe ventured.

"We worked on some cases together. I wouldn't call him a friend."

"But you knew him, right?"

That earned only a slow, terse nod.

"So did you see him as a secret faggot?"

"I don't talk shit. About anyone." With just that handful of words, Collins made it clear that Youssef didn't deserve to be gossiped about, while Gabe did.

"I'm not talking . . . shit." The phrase sounded thin and mealy in his mouth. "I'm interested in some facts that don't seem to fit."

"Such as?"

"I'm just working off hunches right now. I'm not saying I can shoot down the working scenario. But it's something I want to think about."

Collins stared at him for several seconds before speaking. No more than three, but they were exceptionally long seconds, in which Gabe had time to consider every way he was inferior to this man. He tried to stay quiet, imitate Collins's style, but he broke down, rushing to fill the silence.

"It's the toll plaza. Not on the trip north. The first time, on the way out of the city to where he and his trick are going to do . . . whatever."

Collins still didn't speak.

"He must have been behind the wheel on the trip out,

right? If he picked someone up and was taking him to a safer place to . . . rendezvous. Why doesn't he use the E-ZPass lane? He did coming into the city, earlier that night."

"Maybe he didn't want to leave a record of his movements. People in our line of work tend to be paranoid." Collins managed to make it sound as if Gabe were not in that group, not one of them.

"But if you've got the thing, it still registers. Using a pay lane doesn't keep it from engaging."

Collins shrugged. "Depending on traffic, you can't always control what lane you end up in. Especially coming onto the highway from Boston Street, as Youssef is thought to have done. That would have been the fastest way from Patterson Park. You get hemmed in by the trucks, you go where you can."

"Okay, sure, on any given night. But this was the night before Thanksgiving."

This time Gabe waited Collins out, using his cigarette as a prop. True, he drew on it until it was almost burning ash between his fingers, but he didn't start babbling again.

"So?" Collins finally asked.

"I happened to drive home that night, to my folks' place in Trenton. And every toll lane along I-95 was stacked to hell and back. I would've killed for E-ZPass. If I weren't a law-abiding type"—he allowed himself a nervous laugh here, but Collins didn't join in—"I would have risked running it in some places. And here's Youssef, trying to get his dick sucked or whatever he does, then get home in a reasonable amount of time so his wife will buy his work-emergency excuse, and he just sits there in line, as if he had all the time in the world?"

He barely felt the frigid air, except in his exposed fingers. He was that flush with his insight, that proud of the detail he had caught. Collins was nodding and taking it in, his esteem for Gabe growing larger by the second, silent as those seconds were.

Then Collins stubbed out his cigarette in the sand-filled ashtray and said: "You think a lot about what goes on in the mind of a guy who's about to get his dick sucked by another guy?"

With that he walked away, leaving Gabe feeling very small and very cold. Except for his face, where the blood now rose, flaming the handsome, symmetrical features that his female relatives always swore would grease his way through life.

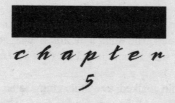

chapter
5

T ESS ARRIVED HOME TO THE USUAL HAVOC OF A CROW-
prepared meal, which she never minded. He was not
only an excellent cook but a considerate one as well, insistent on cleaning up after himself. So it was easy to tolerate
the by-products of his feasts—the bursts of flour, the drib-
bles of olive oil, the littered countertops.

Crow's guest, however, was a tougher sell. The sullen teen
was sitting at their dining room table locked in a staring contest with the dogs, both of whom seemed highly skeptical.
Esskay's instincts weren't worth much; the greyhound dis-
approved of anyone who didn't fawn over her. Miata, shy
and reserved, was a better barometer. Her narrowed gaze
and the slight rumble in the back of her throat did not speak
well for the young man facing her.

"Hello," Tess said.

He looked harmless enough—a skinny, almost scrawny
kid with close-cropped hair and skin the color of a full-

bodied lager. His most striking features were his amber eyes, one with a black dot in the iris, and slightly pointed ears, which gave his face an elfin cast.

"Hmmmmmph," he said, not lifting his gaze from the dogs' glare.

"Lloyd, this is my girlfriend, Tess," Crow called from the kitchen. "Tess, Lloyd Jupiter. He's going to be staying with us for a while."

"A while?" Tess echoed. "No, I'm *not*," Lloyd said.

"Well, you're definitely staying here for the night."

Tess poured a glass of red wine for herself and Pellegrino for Lloyd, who sniffed suspiciously at the bubbles before he sipped it.

"This 7-Up got no taste," he said.

"It's water. I'm afraid we don't keep soda in the house. Where do you go to school?" She was determined to be a good hostess.

"I don't."

"Where did you go before you dropped out?"

"Didn't say I dropped out."

"Sorry—I just assumed. So did you? Go to school and then drop out? Graduate early? Or are you just truant?"

"I was over at Clifton Park. It didn't have much for me."

"What do you do now?"

"I get by."

"Puncturing people's tires and then offering to help change them. I heard." Crow had briefed her on that part while she was driving home, perhaps banking on Tess's inability to work up a truly righteous rage at him while distracted by rush-hour traffic.

"I *didn't*. Another kid did it. Look, you got television? Xbox?"

"There's a television in the den, which doubles as my office and our guest room. No Xbox or PlayStation, I'm afraid. The only computer game we have is the chess software that came loaded on my laptop."

"Can I see it?"

Tess took him to her office and set up the wireless laptop. Lloyd didn't actually know how to play, she noticed. He asked for the computer's recommendations and sometimes tried to move pieces in ways that were promptly disallowed. But it was a game on a screen, which seemed to satisfy him.

"Hey," he said after a moment. "This computer's talking to me."

"Well, it gives you suggestions—"

"No, it's talking to *me*, in this, like, little box. Asking me about"—he squinted at the screen, sounding out the words—"the giant scam."

"What?" Tess leaned over his shoulder and saw the instant-message box that had opened in the corner. She must have logged on to her IM account by force of habit. The Snoop Sisters—the unfortunate Yahoo group name used to identify the women PIs with whom Tess worked—were enjoying a live chat, and Gretchen from Chicago had assumed it was Tess who was online. Gretchen's question was pretty much the way Lloyd had conveyed it, albeit even ruder: **So how was the giant scam you perpetrated on Christy Media Inc.? Any chance of the rest of us getting cut in on this action?**

Not really here, Tess typed back, reaching around Lloyd, who seem to draw himself in as if terrified of contact. **Guest using computer. Will provide details via tomorrow's digest.**

"What is that?" Lloyd's voice was animated for the first time.

"Just IM."

He looked mystified, but he didn't ask for clarification. Lloyd seemed resigned to not understanding things.

"IM, instant messaging. If you have friends logged on to a computer at the same time, they can communicate by typing."

"How?"

He had her there. Tess didn't have a clue how the technology worked.

"It's like a phone, sort of, only it's attached to a computer keyboard. Didn't they have computers at your school?"

"Yeah, but they didn't always work and we just used them to, like, write stuff. I been on the Internet at the public library a couple of times, but that was before you needed a library card to use it." The topic seemed to embarrass him, and his eyes slid away from hers, toward the piles of paper that had migrated back to her office when she finished prepping late yesterday. "Is that your boyfriend?"

He was pointing to the photo of Gregory Youssef, which topped her file on the case, and it took enormous effort on Tess's part not to laugh. Other than dark hair, Crow and Youssef shared absolutely no resemblance. White men must all look alike to Lloyd.

"That's the federal prosecutor who was killed."

Another blank look with no follow-up.

"Right before Thanksgiving. Remember?"

"Oh, yeah, when they jacked everybody up."

It was Tess's turn to look confused.

"They, like, picked up every player in the neighborhood, took 'em downtown on all kinda bullshit. Then, like that"— he snapped his fingers—"they let 'em all go. Most of 'em, at least. Some they put charges on, just for the hell of it, or 'cause they was paper on 'em. But they knew all along it wasn't any of them that messed with him."

Of course, Tess thought. In the first forty-eight hours, when it was assumed Youssef's death was job-related, they had probably looked closely at his drug cases, then released the men they had detained without so much as an apology.

"They decided his death didn't have anything to do with being a prosecutor after all," she said. "The investigation indicated it was personal."

"Girlfriend?"

"Not exactly."

"So they ever find who done it? They usually pretty good at finding out who kills white people."

There was no edge of resentment in Lloyd's voice, no political undertone. He was speaking a simple fact. A private-school teacher had been shot and killed in the parking lot of a suburban mall just this month, and suspects had been in custody within forty-eight hours. Meanwhile the board listing Baltimore City's homicide victims—mostly young black men—was flush with red, the color used to indicate open cases.

"No, they've yet to make an arrest in the death of Gregory Youssef."

"You—*who*?" His voice cracked a little.

"Gregory Youssef, the prosecutor. His murder remains unsolved. That guy." She tapped the photo.

Lloyd turned his attention back to the computer screen, his posture rigid, his fingers poised above the keys like a bird's talons, curved and prehensile. He seemed not offended but suddenly annoyed by Tess's presence, irritable. "How come the horses can't move straight?"

"The knights. And I don't know the whys of chess. Crow's good at it, but it doesn't play to my strengths. I suck at what our chief executive calls strategery. I prefer the Pickett's Charge approach to life."

"What?"

"Gettysburg?" It didn't seem to register. "The Civil War?"

"Oh, yeah. That."

"Gettysburg was one of the pivotal battles in the war, the so-called high tide of the Confederacy. Pickett went straight up the middle—and lost all his men."

"Well, that was ignorant," Lloyd said, and Tess really couldn't disagree. Truth be told, she had no admiration of Pickett, and she had related the story just to make conversation. Her tactics were quite the opposite of Robert E. Lee's. She wanted to lead Lloyd back to the story of Gregory Youssef, and she didn't dare do that too directly. How could one know the name but not his face, or the larger story of his death?

But the name had clearly meant something to Lloyd—something that terrified him.

"So," she said, coming into the kitchen and closing the old-fashioned swinging door behind her. When she had overseen the renovation of the house, her father and Crow had tried to persuade her to create a great-room effect, allowing the living room, dining room, and kitchen to blend into each other. But Tess had decided to respect the bungalow's old divisions. Tess liked walls. "What the hell are you up to?"

"Nothing but lamb stew."

"We can't run a shelter, Crow. Not for even one kid."

"Tomorrow I'll take him by South Baltimore Station or someplace like that, see what they can do for him. But I couldn't leave him out there tonight."

"South Baltimore Station is for adult addicts in recovery, and it has a waiting list. Does he have a substance-abuse problem?"

"I don't get that vibe from him."

"He seems to be familiar with neighborhood dealers. He knew they all got 'jacked up' when investigators thought Youssef's murder was connected to his job. The very mention of Youssef's name made him jumpy and anxious."

"Knowing drug dealers in his part of Baltimore is like knowing Junior Leaguers in Roland Park. You make small talk with plenty of young Muffys and Paiges down at Evergreen Coffee House, but that doesn't mean you put on a big hat and sell lemon sticks at the Flower Mart."

"Fair enough. But he's a dropout who tried to cadge money out of you, changing a tire that he punctured."

"No, another guy did it. He just bird-dogged that guy's scam. It's very enterprising, if you think about it."

"That's a distinction of little difference, Crow. What do you really know about this kid? Just who have you brought under my—our—roof?"

"Taste this." Crow spooned a little lamb in her mouth, but all the rosemary and garlic in the world couldn't distract her.

"One night only," she said. "Then he goes."

Summoned to dinner, Lloyd said a brief prayer over his food, which made Tess squirm a little at how much she took for granted in her life. And someone had dinged manners into him along the way, although the job wasn't entirely finished. He gamely tried the lamb stew, chewing as if he were being forced to consume balsa wood but ultimately cleaning his plate. He then poked at the salad, clearly suspicious of the dark green leaves and toasted nuts.

"This lettuce go bad?" he asked Crow.

"It's spinach. We eat it for the lutein."

Lloyd pointed with his fork. "This a peanut?"

"Pistachio."

"For real?" He shrugged and ate it, without enthusiasm, but also without resistance. When he took a bite out of the chipotle corn muffins that Crow had made from scratch, however, he bellowed as if something had bitten him.

"I thought they was cornbread," he said after gulping down half his glass of water—tap water this time, at his request. "Shit's all hot and spicy."

"They're corn muffins with chilies in the batter," Crow apologized. "They just caught you off guard."

"My mother says right people put sugar in their corn-bread," Lloyd said as if announcing a core belief on a par with monotheism. "I coulda eaten cornbread without sugar, but this shit is just *wrong*."

"Where is your mother?" Tess asked. "What's her name?"

Ignoring her, Lloyd tried another bite, and it did seem to go down easier now that he knew what to expect. And he had no quarrel with dessert—a choice of chocolate, pistachio, or straw-berry ice cream from Moxley's, served with homemade brown-ies. His plate cleared, he stood to return to his chess game.

"Want to give me a hand cleaning up?" Crow asked in his easygoing way.

"You cooked. Why doesn't *she* clean?"

"Sometimes she does. But Mondays are my day off and she worked today, so I don't mind carrying the full load."

Lloyd looked at Tess, sitting at the table with her glass of wine, scratching Esskay behind one ear. "Did you go spying today?"

"Spying? Oh, no. I just gave a presentation down at the newspaper, talked about investigative techniques." Curious to see how he would react, she embroidered a bit. "That's why I had that picture of Youssef."

"You got nunchucks?"

"Excuse me?"

"Nunchucks. For kung fu." Lloyd did a demonstration that owed more to *Karate Kid* than it did to John Woo.

"I have a gun. That's the best form of self-defense."

"'Can I see it?"

"No." But Lloyd's question reminded Tess that she needed to lock the Beretta in the safe next to her bed. She didn't always remember, but with a young guest in the house, she had to be at her most conscientious.

She came back and watched Lloyd clear the table, which had more than its share of suspenseful moments. Her everyday dishes were also her only dishes, a mismatched collection of state commemoratives culled from flea markets and yard sales. They would be impossible to replace, except via eBay, which always struck her as cheating. The quest should be as important as the object when one was a collector. But Tess was trying not to be a person who prized things too highly, so she clenched her jaw and let Lloyd go, reasoning that his agreeable helpfulness was more important than keeping North Dakota in one piece.

After dinner they watched *Minority Report* on DVD, which Lloyd seemed to like once he got used to the idea that it was supposed to be the future. "Parts of Baltimore look worse 'n that," he said dismissively of Philip K. Dick's Washington as imagined by Spielberg and his designers. The movie over, they left him to his own devices, telling him to feel free to use the television or Tess's laptop. "You can also read anything you like," Crow said, gesturing to the shelves in Tess's office.

"You got any comics?" Lloyd asked.

"No, but I've got some books about comics," said Crow, ever game. He brought down Michael Chabon's *The Amazing Adventures of Kavalier and Clay* and Jay Cantor's *Krazy Kat*, then grabbed an omnibus volume of Dick. "And this is the book that inspired the film we saw tonight."

Tess stifled a laugh, but not the surge of affection behind it. Where some might have seen an almost woeful ignorance in Crow's suggestions, she understood that he loved these books. And whatever Crow loved, he wanted to share. Besides, Lloyd might like Philip K. Dick, although she would have been inclined to start him on Richard Stark or Jim Thompson, something hard-boiled and brutal.

Curled up in bed with her own book, *Behind the Scenes at*

the Museum, Tess finally had a chance to tell Crow what had been bothering her all evening.

"He didn't recognize Youssef's face. But the name—the *name* seems to bother him. He changes the subject whenever it comes up."

"So?"

"How do you know the name but not the face? Sure, certain beat cops are known on the street. But I'd be surprised if the average street kid could name the Baltimore state's attorney, much less an assistant U.S. attorney. If you've heard of Gregory Youssef, it's because he was murdered. But Lloyd hadn't made that connection. He knew that a prosecutor had been murdered, he knew the name Gregory Youssef. But in his mind the two had nothing to do with each other."

"Hmmmmmm." Crow was lost in the world of Bernard Cornwell.

"Hey. *Hey.* I'm just as interesting as the Napoleonic era," Tess said.

"Prove it."

In her opinion she proceeded to make her case quite persuasively.

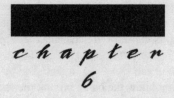

chapter
6

BARRY JENKINS WAS THE TYPE OF GUY WHO ALWAYS
found a way to turn his weaknesses into strengths.
Slow, stocky, and patient, he had learned early to make the
choices that rewarded his build and temperament. In high
school he crouched behind home plate as a catcher, blocked
on the football team, then dated the girls who were impressed by such achievements. *Work with what you've got,*
he told the guys he had mentored over the years, *and you'll
always get ahead.* And for most of his time in the FBI, that
advice had proved golden.

The bar at the Days Inn on Security Boulevard also fell
squarely into the category of working with what you were
given. While the other federal agencies were downtown, the
FBI was tucked away in this butt-ugly bit of suburbia near
the Social Security complex in Woodlawn. This physical
distance from the DEA, ATF, and IRS guys was supposed to
emphasize the Bureau's superiority. At least that had been

the rationale once upon a time, and that attitude still prevailed. So let those other guys sip imported beer and cocktails in those desperate-to-be-chic downtown bars. And never mind that most of his coworkers went to an old-fashioned tavern in the heart of old Woodlawn. Barry *preferred* the bar at the Days Inn, a straight-up, honest place. Back in the day, it had been a family-owned motel with pretensions and a fancy restaurant, Meushaw's. That is, Barry's family, which really didn't have anything to compare it to, had thought it ritzy. His folks had brought him here for supper after his first communion, and Barry had considered himself pretty worldly, ordering the chicken Kiev. In fact, it was at the moment that his fork pierced the breaded crust and butter oozed forth that he had vowed to have a life where he would see Kiev, or whatever it was called now, see the whole wide world. And he had. He could honestly say he had done what he dreamed of doing when he was a kid, and how many people could make that claim?

Sure, the younger agents considered Jenkins washed up, one of those doddering types just marking time until he hit mandatory retirement. But that assessment, like Meushaw's demotion to the Days Inn bar, was all about appearances, wasn't it? Jameson's was Jameson's no matter where you drank it, or in whose company. Barry was still Barry—shrewd beneath his good-boy exterior, analytical, easygoing with people. It just depended on how you looked at things, and Jenkins was an expert at considering situations from every angle. He could always see the whole where others saw parts, hold the whole playing field in his head. "Court vision," they called it in basketball, but that was one game Jenkins had never played. No speed, no jump. Again, it was all about knowing what he could do and what he couldn't, and the latter knowledge mattered just as much, if not more. If Barry were one of the fabled blind men locked up with the elephant, he would feel it from tail to trunk, bottom to top, and when he left the room and removed his blindfold, he would know it was a goddamn elephant.

Mike Collins arrived at 10:00 P.M. sharp, on-the-dot punctual as always, which accounted for his nickname—"Bully," short for Bulova, or so the official story went. It had proved to be an unfortunate nickname for a while there, but Collins had ridden out that mess like the soldier he was. Big and handsome, he could have stepped off a recruiting poster—if the DEA had recruiting posters. But what made Collins remarkable, in Jenkins's opinion, was that he actually had all the qualities that people projected onto this kind of masculine attractiveness. Nerves of steel, balls of brass, heart of gold. All those metals.

"I can't believe you wanted to meet in this shithole," Collins said after ordering a bottle of Heineken and bringing it to Barry's table, one of several along the bank of windows that overlooked this unlovely stretch of Security Boulevard. But the table was isolated, and the reflection made it easy to see if anyone was in earshot.

"I like it out here," Jenkins said, thinking, *I don't drive to you. You drive to me.* "Why'd you want to meet anyway?"

"This kid prosecutor tried to chat me up on the smoking pad today, make conversation about Youssef."

"So? That's bound to happen from time to time. A person's coworker gets killed, it's natural to gossip about it."

"He noticed something about the E-ZPass. Youssef used it on the way into town, when he was coming up 95 from his house. But on the way out, he went through a pay lane."

"We've been over that. The pass works whatever lane you choose."

"Sure, which makes sense when the killer is heading north afterward. But this prosecutor pointed out that traffic was backed up that night, said it wasn't logical to sit there in a long line when a guy's trying to get out, get some satisfaction, get home again."

Jenkins took a drink, which burned a little. Reflux. Even his own body was turning on him. "He's right, but what's it to him?"

"My opinion? He's sniffing around, looking for a way to insert himself."

"So what did you say?" He tried to keep his tone super casual, although Jenkins always worried a little about Collins on the verbal front. Their extremely unofficial task was to gather information, not disseminate it. Jurisdictional proprieties may have placed the case under the Howard County police, but that didn't mean the federal agencies weren't going to keep tabs on it. Headquarters had technical oversight, but the locals wanted their own eyes and ears. Of course, it was a sign of how queasy the case made everyone that they let Jenkins be the liaison. If they really cared what had happened to Youssef, they would have wanted someone in better standing to play monitor.

"I said"—Collins paused, clearly proud of himself—"I said, 'Do you spend a lot of time thinking about what goes on in the mind of a guy about to get his dick smoked by another guy?'"

"Good answer." In his relief Jenkins bellowed a bit, sounding like the guy on the old quiz show with the families. The original emcee, the cocky Brit from *Hogan's Heroes*, not the nondescript guy who had the hosting duties now. "That'll keep him away from it."

"For now," Collins said. "But I think he might keep poking."

"Who is this guy?"

"One of the newer hires, been relegated to second chair so far. Booted a come-up or two, but all the young ones do that."

"Have I—"

"No, he's too new. And too gung ho. What do you want to bet he'll try to take anything to court when his time finally comes?"

"Sounds too stupid to be trouble," Jenkins said, knowing that stupid people could be extraordinary trouble, the very worst kind of trouble. *Fat, drunk, and stupid is no way to go through life, son.* What movie was that? *Animal House.* Jenkins had been just a little too old to get that when it was released—out of college, already at the Bureau, already a father—but his older nieces and nephews repeated lines from that movie as if they were the Baltimore catechism. Fact was, Jenkins had felt a pang of sympathy for the would-be keepers of order—Marmalard, Neidermeyer, and most of all, Dean Wormer. Well, the world had learned its lesson, hadn't it? You sacrifice order at a price. Learned it late, but learned it at last. Jenkins had been one of the voices scream-ing in the wilderness along with John O'Neill, another FBI agent, another guy they screwed over just because they didn't like his personal style. O'Neill had tried to tell them about the impending threat from Osama, but no one wanted to hear. They busted his balls over a briefcase, forced him out. September 11 was O'Neill's first month on the job as head of security for the World Trade Towers, and the one man who had been screaming about bin Laden since the bombing of the USS *Cole* ended up dead. You want to keep planes from crashing into buildings, you need a few more Dean Wormers in the mix.

"He's ambitious," Collins said. "You can almost smell it on him."

"Ambitious *and* stupid? Now, that's something we can work with. If it comes to that. For now, stay still. Can you do that for me, Bully? Stay still, stay quiet."

"Absolutely."

Collins tipped the lip of his bottle against Jenkins's shot glass, and they both drank. Jenkins studied the amber legs running down the inside of his glass. He had watched the bartender pour it straight from the Jameson bottle, but he was suddenly dubious that he had gotten what he paid for. Would the bartender have dared to pull such a trick on him? Yeah, he would have. Because the only thing you got for being a regular in the Days Inn bar on Security Boulevard was loser status, even in the eyes of the losers who took your generous tips and smiled to your face, pretending fealty. No one had a nose for weakness like the bowed and bloodied.

That's why Jenkins liked Collins. Loyal as a dog. Loyal as the lion was to the guy who pulled the thorn from his paw. Collins would die for him, literally. The kid loved him more than his own kids did.

Then again, Jenkins hadn't divorced Collins's mom and taken up with a cocktail waitress who ended up being Miss Ballbuster of the new millennium. Fuckin' Betty. Jenkins had learned the hard way that a guy didn't have to have much money to attract a gold digger. Betty had seen the way he lived in New York—the restaurants, the clubs—and never made the distinction that it was because of his status in the Bureau, not his salary. And when the status was gone, along with those paltry perks—poof, so was Betty. Neatest little magic trick he had ever seen, a 120-pound woman disappearing into thin air. He tried to tell her that they would live better in Baltimore, that most agents preferred it over New York or Washington. Betty didn't buy it.

But then, Betty knew her strengths, too. She claimed she was thirty-five when they met, but she was most certainly on speaking terms with forty. She was one of those natural hard-bodies, a freak gift from the gods, because the most strenuous thing Betty ever did was lift a glass to her mouth.

The face—the face had been hard, too, and not in a good way. She had required a good thirty minutes at the dressing table each morning to get it to live up to the body, to mask the lines she'd gotten from squinching up her features and thinking about how she was going to separate this guy or that guy from whatever he had. The way Betty saw it, she had maybe one more husband left in her, and she couldn't afford for it to be Jenkins, not once he was all but demoted.

He glanced at his own reflection in the window. Eighteen months. Eighteen months to the mandatory retirement age. He could walk now with a decent enough pension, but he wouldn't give them the satisfaction. He'd do his time, get to the end, then set up the sweetest little security gig he could find. In the meantime he would pretend he gave a shit about solving the Youssef case. A loser, even his enemies would concede that. It wouldn't be his fault if an arrest were never made. All anyone really wanted was for it to recede in the public imagination, an easy enough trick. The average joe couldn't hold a thought for twenty minutes, which is why all the world's problems kept being trumped by the missing-white-woman-of-the-week.

He caught a vision of his retirement party, sad and empty. In fact, it would probably look a lot like this—him and Collins, huddled at a table together, two pariahs. In a fair world, a true meritocracy, they would be known for the heroes they were. But Jenkins knew that nothing was more unfair than the bureaucracies allegedly devoted to justice.

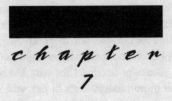

chapter
7

LLOYD HAD TO WAIT UNTIL ALMOST MIDNIGHT BEFORE THE house was quiet and he was sure that everyone was asleep. It had freaked him out a little, the sounds of sex coming from the other bedroom, not that he hadn't heard those noises before. Made them, too, but that was different. These people were *old*. Well, not old-old, but old enough. And weird. It was like the Brady Bunch parents rocking the bed, like his mama and Murray, and who wanted to think about that shit?

The woman did have a nice shape, though. Solid, not that skinny, flat-ass body that so many white women prized. But she had to be his mama's age, or close to.

Lloyd Jupiter's mother, Berneice, had been sixteen when he was born, and she hadn't done so bad by him. Not great, but not particularly bad, all things considered. She had pretty good judgment about the men she brought home, if you didn't include Lloyd's father in the mix. He was locked up or dead. At any rate, he hadn't been around for years. Her latest man, father to Lloyd's youngest brother and sister, was downright reliable, sticking with her two years now. Which was good for his mama, but not so good for Lloyd, 'cause Murray was one of those Jamaican tight-asses who had some definite ideas about what Lloyd should be doing, like school, and not doing, like just about everything else.

Given the tension between Murray and him, Lloyd hadn't been around to see his mama for a while. She was beginning to ride him, too, which wasn't like her. Before Murray, Lloyd had always been able to charm her, get his way, shake a few dollars loose from her billfold. After all, he was her firstborn, and she felt guilty about so much—his useless father, how her attention got stretched with the addition of each new kid. In her way, she loved him best.

But the last time Lloyd had dropped by, she'd been out-and-out pissed at him—furious over the rumor that he'd been working for Bennie Tep, even more furious at the news that he'd been let go. The truth was somewhere in between. Lloyd didn't work for Bennie, but some of his buddies did, and they let him hang. Bennie liked Lloyd. People always liked Lloyd, if he wanted them to. But he wasn't allowed any role in the main business, not after a few disastrous attempts at playing tout. He could do the math, but those fiends were fierce, rushing him so that he lost his place in the count. Which was fine with Lloyd. He hated *all* work, hated anything with a boss—jobs, school, family. He needed to find a way where he could be the man in charge, but he wasn't sure what that was. Dr. Ben Carson had come to his grade school when he was a kid, and that had seemed kind of cool, a black man opening up little children's hearts and fixing them, but it meant so much school, and Lloyd was through with school the moment he turned sixteen last fall.

"I heard about you," his mother had said, her voice shrill,

her finger in his face. "Getting high and shorting the count. You incompetent, a fiend, or just a thief?"

He had shrugged, refusing to align himself with any of those piss-poor choices.

"You know, you can't even work at McDonald's if your cash register is light at the end of ev'ry shift."

"I ain't gonna work at no fuckin' McDonald's."

"Honey, that's what I'm saying. You ain't gonna work anywhere, you don't get your act together."

It was a lot of shit to put up with, just for five or ten dollars. He could panhandle that much in a good afternoon.

He hadn't been getting high anyway, not really. He smoked a blunt now and then, nothing more. What was wrong with that? Look at these two, guzzling all that wine with dinner. Well, okay, they didn't guzzle exactly. It wasn't like they were tipping Thunderbird from a paper bag. But that stuff fucked up all different parts of your insides, while weed just messed with your lungs a little, and you had to smoke a lot to do real damage. He had learned all that back in school, the various dangers of drugs and alcohol and cigarettes, and while they tried to say that weed was bad, Lloyd knew it wasn't. Sick people got to smoke it in some states, so how bad could it be?

He crept out of the half-ass room they had stuck him in and paused in the hallway, listening. The dogs were his main concern, especially the Doberman. The big, rat-looking dog didn't seem so much a threat, not unless it got close enough to breathe on you. Dog's breath was *nasty*. He waited, his lies ready—*just going to the bathroom, needed a drink of water*—but nothing happened. No boards creaking, no long toenails clattering on the wooden floors, no lights coming on.

Time to go.

Part of his brain warned him to do just that, only that. *Go*.

Just get away from these people, put some distance between him and them, and hope he never saw them again. In the most paranoid part of his brain, he had almost persuaded himself that he'd been set up, that the woman had sent her whipped boyfriend to go looking for him and drag him back here, knowing what he'd done. But naw, that couldn't be. It was just his usual shitty-ass luck, the life of Lloyd. Try to make a buck, nothing more, end up with this gung-ho dude and his detective girlfriend, who seemed to know something that nobody was supposed to know. Why wouldn't she stop saying that name? Youssef. Youuuuuuuuuuuuuusseffffffffff. Like she could read his mind. No, the smart thing was to get out.

Thing was, he had come over the threshold with plans, and Lloyd always fell in love with his own plans. If he pictured himself doing something or having something, no matter how small, he had to try to follow through. There had been a poem in school about how bad that was, putting off a dream. Lloyd had allowed this guy to bring him here because he thought there would be something in it for him, and he had been clocking stuff from the moment he got inside the house, calculating what he could carry, what he could sell. In his head he had already made fifty, a hundred dollars easy.

He retreated into the study and surveyed the portable goods available to him. It was some trifling shit. The jewelry would be in the bedroom, obviously off-limits now. He should have sneaked back there earlier. No, never mind, the woman didn't look like someone who went in for good stuff, judging by her watch and the small gold hoops in her ears. But there was the laptop and a digital camera. Also some DVDs, although they didn't look like the kind that would generate much cash. They all had the same title. He sounded it out silently: *Cri-ter-ion Collection*. Wasn't that the guy who wrote the book about the dinosaurs? Lloyd had liked that book, even better than the movie, because the book didn't let anyone off the hook. The mad-scientist dude was pecked to death by his own little monsters, while the movie made out that he was some white-bearded Santa Claus guy. Villains needed to be punished proper, in Lloyd's opinion, although he didn't always agree with the movies on who the villains were. Like, *Spider-Man 2*. That octopus dude had a right to be pissed.

No, wait: "Criterion Collection" must be the company that made these DVDs. The real titles were for sure bizarre. *Yojimbo. Rashomon. Ran.* Ran from what? They were in black and white, too, which meant they weren't worth carrying out of here. Too bad, because they looked kind of interesting, like old-fashioned kung fu movies. *Throne of Blood.* That one he had to take, even if he didn't have a DVD player his own self. Dub did.

There was a big jar of change, but it was too large to carry, and fishing out the quarters would make too much noise. The other electronics were all too big, too, and not at all up-to-date. No flat screen, no plasma, just a shitty-ass Sony no more than nineteen inches, although it would still bring a little something. Then again, he was taking the Lexus, so he could carry more. But he had to travel part of the way on foot, at the end. So this was all he was going to get, one armful's worth.

At the last minute, he opened up a little box he had spied on her desk, a blue oval with a horned horse painted on it, to see if jewelry might be hidden in it. Unicorn, that was what you called it. Not horned horse, unicorn, and this unicorn was hiding a stash of weed. They had *weed.* Fuckin' hypocrites, like all grown-ups. Okay, not exactly, it wasn't as if they had been in his face, wagging fingers, saying no-no-no like his mama, who used to say yes an awful lot, pre-Murray.

She was clean now, which should have been good, but it wasn't somehow. Man, it pissed Lloyd off for reasons he couldn't quite explain even to himself, this stash tucked away in a painted box. He pocketed the box, then headed out into the hall, laptop under his arm.

The big dog, the scary one, had nosed its way out of the couple's bedroom and was now staring at him. Lloyd froze in place, petrified. He hated dogs. He expected this one to start barking and growling, giving him up. He began working on a story. But the dog just regarded him with sad, judging eyes, not unlike his mama's. *Oh, Lloyd,* the dog seemed to say. *Stupid Lloyd. Bad Lloyd.*

The dog didn't try to keep him from going, though. Again, just like his mama.

The alarm system in the house was no problem. He had made it a point to watch that Crow dude disarm it when they came in, so he punched in the code now, taking it off instant, then grabbed a set of keys from the hooks by the door and sailed into the cold night. It was creepy here, almost like country, super silent and darker than any night he had ever seen, even when he was out at Hickey, not that you were given a lot of chances to stare at the night sky when you were locked up.

Shit. Another car, a real piece-of-shit thing, was blocking the Lexus. He hadn't counted on that, another car being in back of the one he wanted, but yeah, she had to drive something home. Worse, it was a stick, which was *weak,* unless it was a Maserati or something like that. Lloyd didn't know how to drive stick. He'd just have to make it out on foot.

Still, again—it was so hard to abandon his beautiful plan, having already spent the money he planned to make five times over. The house was on a little rise. Maybe he could roll the hooptie out into the street by releasing the parking brake, then come back for the Lexus and head out the other

end. What did he care if the Volvo blocked the bottom part?
It was a weird-ass street, narrow as an alley. The houses on
the opposite side, the ones whose backyards came up to the
edge, were big and fancy, but the houses on this side were
nothing great. Where the fuck was he anyway? He hoped he
could find his way home from here. He had tried to pick out
landmarks on the drive here, and he was pretty sure he could
work his way back to Cold Spring Lane, which meant he
could find Greenmount and then home, but he couldn't
swear which direction he needed to go. The dude had all but
kidnapped him, forced him to come here. All he was doing
was freeing himself, like a slave escaping the plantation.

He opened the door of the Lexus to stash the goods, and
it shrieked. Fuck, *that* was alarmed, too, and the piercing
sound filled the night. He had forgotten about the car alarm.
He'd have to take the Volvo now, make a quick getaway.
He'd driven stick on a video game at ESPN Zone. How different could it be? But while he managed to get the engine
to turn over, release the parking brake, and roll back, the car
stalled out as soon as he tried to put it in a forward gear. As
he struggled with the gears, gravity took over, and he found
himself rolling backward, faster and faster. At first he continued trying to start the car, then realized he might be better off applying the brake. But nothing happened, no matter
how hard he pressed—*shit*, that wasn't the brake. The brake
was in the middle. He slammed both feet down on it *hard*
and triumphantly brought the car to a stop in the middle of
the cross street at the foot of the drive.

He sat there no more than a second, breathing hard from
the rush of it all, trying to gather his thoughts, which weren't
at their sharpest. *Go back? No. What, then? Get away. Go.
Run.* But even as he fumbled with the Volvo's door, a huge
old boat of a car appeared out of nowhere, bearing down on
him. It was enormous, the biggest car-car that Lloyd had

ever seen, almost as long as a limo, and strangely noiseless, but maybe his hearing was off—or stunned from the alarm on the Lexus. No, he could hear his own breath, he just couldn't hear the approaching car's engine. It was like a ghost car, drifting toward him, showing no sign of stopping. Slowly, gracefully, it rolled, rolled, rolled—and struck the Volvo smack in the side.

Lloyd hit the steering wheel with a jolt, but the Volvo was an older model, with no airbag to slow him down. Ribs smarting, he jumped from the car, even as an old man—a very real red-faced, flesh-and-blood old man—emerged from the ghost car and began yelling at him.

Lloyd didn't wait to hear what the man was screaming or to offer the opinion that it was the old man's fault for not braking to avoid the stalled Volvo, or at least trying to steer around it. The guy clearly had had time to avoid the collision, but Lloyd had no intention of pursuing that argument. No, Lloyd ran, heading up the hill beyond the ghost car, although he had a vague feeling that Cold Spring Lane and the city he knew was the other way. He ran through the midnight-quiet streets of this strange neighborhood, wondering how long a black man could run here without being noticed and, inevitably, arrested.

He reached what appeared to be a main street, slowing down to a fast walk, his lungs on fire. He would still be regarded with suspicion here, but he wasn't quite as out of place. There were bus stops and shit, so he could always say that's where he was headed if anyone pulled him over.

It was a long and miserable walk in the night air, with slippery patches of ice underfoot. The sounds of sirens in the distance made him jumpy. By luck, and luck alone, he managed to find his way back to Cold Spring, which took him to the Light Rail station. Here, at least, he wouldn't look out of place.

Stomping his feet in the cold, waiting for the train to come, he couldn't help feeling . . . well, *angry*. It pissed him off, having to leave that laptop and digital camera behind. He wanted someone to blame for his troubles, and he decided it was all that woman's fault. She would probably make a big stink, too, even though he had left her stuff behind and it wasn't his fault that old car had rammed him. The dude—the dude, he would want to let it go, but the woman was tougher. She had a mean streak. He'd been stupid. No, he'd been greedy, which was worse. Can't ever leave well enough alone, was the way his mother put it, and maybe she was right. But at the time Lloyd had just thought of it as getting a little bonus, of making up for the bad luck that seemed to dog him everywhere. He had the worst fucking luck.

Gregory Youssef. It had been a name to him, a name and four numbers, nothing more. He hadn't thought about that caper for months. Favor done, opportunity lost, just another day in the life of Lloyd Jupiter, the can't-win-for-losingest loser to ever come out of East Baltimore. Shit. *Shit*.

He hadn't known until tonight that the killed lawyer had been *that* guy, that the name he had buried in his memory was of any concern to anyone other than the guy himself. Did that make him an accessory? No, but it meant he had been played.

He was so fucked.

The train hissed into the station. He didn't have a ticket, but he was counting on getting a few stops down before the conductor caught up to him and threw him off. As it turned out, he made it to Howard Street before anyone approached him, and he was able to run, avoiding the citation.

It was so cold he didn't even try to get back to the East Side, just went to the downtown parking garage where the homeless men slept on the steam grates. He hadn't been there for a while, but he remembered that it was around the corner from that weird-ass orange, blue, and yellow statue.

He was too late for the sandwich run, which some church group did about 10:00 P.M., and the best spots were taken, but he still found himself a manhole cover with some hot air coming up. You got kind of damp sleeping that way, but it was warm and safe. Relatively. He took his coat off and bunched it under his head to make a pillow, and his body's exhaustion overwhelmed his mind's jumpy agitation, pulling him into sleep almost immediately. He dreamed about horses, Corvettes, and pork chops.

When he woke up at dawn, his jacket looked as if he had chewed on it, just a little bit. He went out into the day, blinking, almost expecting to find some cops just outside the garage.

But there was no one waiting for him, absolutely no one at all.

Tuesday

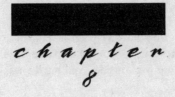

chapter
8

W HAT DO YOU MEAN, CROW WON'T PRESS CHARGES?"
Whitney Talbot's voice, never demure, was like a
ship's horn when she was surprised or outraged. It sliced
through the midday din of Matthew's, which, admittedly,
was not difficult to do. The sixty-year-old restaurant took
up only the front half of an old rowhouse, and there were
few diners at this time of day.

Still, even in a place used to voluble and excitable customers, Whitney attracted attention. She always did. Tess,
who had known her since college, had decided having Whitney as a friend was like traveling around Baltimore with a
white Siberian tiger. Seldom dull, always the center of attention, but also a little unpredictable.

"Lloyd has a jacket—" Tess began, shaking hot pepper
flakes over the traditional tomato pie. Whitney was having
the house specialty, a crab pie, but shellfish-averse Tess
never risked contact with the local delicacy. Unless she was

desperate to leave a social occasion early. Then a little ana-phylactic shock was just the ticket.

"A jacket? Did he steal that, too?"

"A *record*. He's already been in Hickey for auto theft. Crow doesn't want to bring charges because he'll almost certainly end up back inside. And maybe not as a juvenile this time."

"But even if he's not a car thief, he's still guilty of leav-ing the scene of an accident, right? And you have to tell po-lice who he is, or you're liable."

"Crow gave them a fake name," Tess said, still feeling sheepish for letting that bit of deception fly. "Bob Smith. No one batted an eye, even when Crow helpfully added, 'That's Bob with one *o*.'"

"Isn't it illegal to lie to cops?"

"Sort of. But with no real injuries, the cops aren't exactly making this a priority. And Crow told them the truth when he said he didn't know how to find our houseguest again. You know what's really embarrassing? I think the cops thought it was some kind of kinky pickup. Two white sub-urbanites cruising for decadent thrills, bringing home a young hustler and getting metaphorically screwed instead. They've probably opened a pervert file on us."

If Whitney's voice was loud, then her laugh was a bor-derline bray. "It sounds like the damage was pretty minor," she said at last. "Other than that done to your reputations with Northern District, I mean. You said the other guy had nothing more than a crumpled bumper, and the Volvo's such a junker you can't really damage it."

"Yeah, but he's claiming the impossible-to-pin-down soft-tissue injury. Worse yet, the responding cops let him go without administering a Breathalyzer. Believe me, he would have flunked. You could smell the gin on him ten feet away. Everyone in the neighborhood knows about Mr. Parrish. He goes over to the Swallow at the Hollow, then literally coasts home, sliding down Oakdale and then making the turn toward his house on Wilmslow. He rationalizes that it's not *driving* drunk if his foot isn't on the accelerator and the engine is off. Just coasting drunk."

"Well, it's not like Crow has any money. Can't get blood from a stone."

"If Parrish has a cagey lawyer, they might go after *me*—through my homeowner's or the umbrella policy I carry for the business. And my carrier won't be so blasé about accepting Crow's bogus Bob Smith story. They could refuse to cover me, and even a small settlement would wipe me out right now."

Whitney didn't laugh at this. Despite being born rich—or perhaps because of it—Whitney took money very seriously.

"Then Crow's being an idiot. This kid doesn't deserve his nobility. You took him into your home, fed him, gave him shelter, and how did he reward you? By trying to steal from you and wrecking Crow's car. You've got to convince Crow to tell the truth and press charges."

Tess sighed and focused on her pizza, but even a Matthew's tomato pie could not soothe her. With Crow this morning, she had taken Whitney's side of the argument. She had, in fact, been far more shrill and unkind. The past twelve hours had been a series of shocks—the jolt of the Lexus's alarm, the cold air that hit them as they raced outside with only jackets and boots added to their nightclothes, the dogs trotting excitedly behind. The scene at the bottom of the hill, with Mr. Parrish stalking around his car in inebriated indignation, saying some terribly racist things about what and whom he never thought he would see in Roland Park. It was Mr. Parrish's diatribe, as much as anything else, that had hoisted Crow with his sanctimonious petard. By the time the police arrived, he was adamant that Lloyd—well, Bob—was their guest and that he had implicit permission to use Crow's car. And the fact was, Mr. Parrish's mammoth Buick had struck the Volvo so far back along the midsection that Tess was inclined to agree with Crow: Lloyd was stalled in the street at the moment of impact, so Mr. Parrish was to blame for the collision. After all, the one thing that they *hadn't* heard that night was the Volvo's engine, and it was a noisy, raucous car, audible for blocks.

Even so, Crow shouldn't have given the police a false name for Lloyd. That had been rash, a mistake that was sure to come back and haunt them. The boy was still liable for leaving the scene of an accident, although, given the small stakes—no real injuries, the minor damage to Mr. Parrish's car—Tess doubted that the police would spend a lot of time trying to find and arrest him. And the insurance companies wouldn't be much interested in him either. Lloyd had no figurative pockets, shallow or deep, under any name, so Crow's carrier couldn't transfer the fiduciary responsibility to him. Yet Mr. Parrish would collect nothing if the case were treated like the theft that it was. No, as long as Crow claimed that Lloyd had his permission to use the car, Crow would be on the hook for everything. Tess's only hope was that Mr. Parrish's insurance company, once it ferreted out how few assets Crow had, would give up.

Tess worked a lot with insurance companies. The industry's very aversion to paying out large sums had generated several small ones for her over the years, so she would never stoop to gross generalizations where agents and actuaries were concerned. She hated to think what another Tess Monaghan might do if presented with such a case. She would make short work of the assignment, getting Mr. Parrish a nice little check and never caring what happened to the irresponsible driver on the other side of the equation.

"Crow may be a soft touch, but that's a large part of who

he is," she said to Whitney now. "You of all people should get that. You're the one who told me we had to stop trying to change each other."

"He could stand to toughen up a little bit. It's not just the car—it's being naïve enough to bring this kid home in the first place. Whatever story he's feeding the insurance company doesn't change the fact that you nursed a viper in your bosom, as Aesop would say. Took the kid in, gave him a meal and a warm place to sleep, and he rewarded your hospitality by trying to steal from you."

"The moral of Aesop's story was that you *can't* change someone's ingrained nature."

"*Exactly.*"

"No, I mean this kid did seem to have some genuine sweetness to him. And he wasn't very good at lying—not when the name of Gregory Youssef came up."

"Really? Do you think—"

The two old friends, who had once rowed in perfect sync at moments, were still capable of thinking that way. Tess knew that Whitney's mind had jumped to the obvious conclusion— a young man from the East Side, not far from the neighborhood Youssef was last known to be. Police had assumed that Lloyd was a hustler. Wasn't he, in a sense?

"No," Tess said, shaking her head. "He didn't know what Youssef looked like, so he can't be the pickup. Besides, you don't see a lot of black kids hiring themselves out as trade. It's a weird racial division. White boys from farm country do it, sometimes. They rationalize they're not gay, just taking advantage of gay men. But the black kids don't go for that double standard."

"All the more reason to be covert about it."

"Uh-uh." Tess took another bite of pizza. The crust recipe was said to be secret, which compelled her to analyze it every time she visited. It had a pastry feel, flaky and light. And

Matthew Ciccolo had started as a baker. A little sugar, perhaps more lard? "Remember, he knew the name, not the face. He'd clearly never seen the guy in his life. But Lloyd knows *something*. And he's not the kind of kid who's going to speak voluntarily to the cops—not without a charge hanging over him, which would force him to make some deals fast."

"You've got the auto-theft thing."

"I'm not sure that's enough of a threat to get Lloyd to talk to the cops. You know what the antisnitching culture is like in Baltimore." The city had been abuzz for weeks about a homemade DVD, *Stop Snitching*, that showed an NBA player hanging with drug dealers, making ominous threats about what happened to those who cooperated with the police. "But it might be enough leverage to get him to talk to a reporter. Which would sort of make up for the fact that I embarrassed Feeney by telling his boss to go fuck himself. The thing is, we have to find Lloyd."

"I'm in," Whitney said, eyes gleaming. It was what made her such a satisfactory friend. She was always up for whatever Tess was planning, even when she didn't have a clue what it was.

"We'll need your mother's car. And"—Tess looked up, catching the waitress's eye—"an order of curly fries."

"Are the curly fries the bait?"

"No, my dear. *You* are."

"Here?" Crow asked.

"Almost. A little higher. A little to the right—and yes. *Yes.*"

Kitty Monaghan stood in the center of her ever-expanding bookstore, Women and Children First. It was a family enterprise, twice over. Tess's aunt, her father's only sister, had acquired the old pharmacy from Tess's maternal grandfather, who had presided over the spectacular rise and even more spectacular fall of Weinstein's Drugs.

Kitty was having far more luck at the corner of Bond and Shakespeare streets, although it had required endless ingenuity on her part. Over the years the bookstore had enlarged its original mission, adding annexes known as Dead White Men and Live! Males! Live! But instead of the ubiquitous coffee bar, Kitty had put the old soda fountain back into service, providing an array of ice cream drinks and baked goods. She let people drift in with coffee from the Daily Grind and Jimmy's and perch at the counter for hours, buying nothing more than a newspaper and a cookie. Somehow she made a profit.

Now she was creating a gallery space within the store, and Crow was helping her install the first show, a grouping of tin-men sculptures—a firefighter, a policeman, a dog walker, an astronaut—all with the same conical tops, yet somehow distinctive, too. Most of the pieces stood no more than three feet high, but there was one life-size one, and Kitty had decided she wanted it suspended from the ceiling so it appeared to be flying. It was an angel, after all, its face at once goofy and benevolent. An angel with the best of intentions, one that would try to take care of you and probably would succeed in the end, but not without a few bumps along the way.

Kitty agreed with Crow's assessment of the angel's character.

"Like Clarence in *It's a Wonderful Life*," she said, offering Crow a glass of real seltzer. Not the store-bought variety but the stuff that had to be delivered by a New York deliveryman. Kitty's life was full of people who fell over themselves to do her favors. Crow had come under her spell almost five years ago, when he took a job as a part-time clerk here—and then he met Tess. Crow studied the angel again. Now the smile seemed more mocking than kind.

"I used to think I was going to be an artist, remember? An artist, a musician . . . all I've ever really been is a dilettante."

"You'll always be an artist, Crow. No matter how much you throw yourself into business, you're not going to be able to snuff out that part of yourself. Tess fell in love with you when you were a bookstore clerk, remember?"

"And fell out of love with me. Remember?"

"Her faith faltered once or twice along the way. Her faith in herself, not you. Besides, you're the one who bails, leaving when things don't go exactly the way you want. You first bolted when she admitted she was *attracted* to someone else. You did the same thing when she said she wasn't sure she wanted to get married. Not that she didn't love you or didn't want to be with you. Just that she was unsure of marriage—and of your motives for proposing when you did."

"I love her. That's not a motive."

Kitty may have carried the name and looks of an Irish-woman, but she had the soul of a Jewish mother. Throughout the conversation she had been working behind the counter, heating a cheese tart, slicing fruit, then placing it all before Crow on a large Fiestaware platter. He hadn't even realized he was hungry, but he fell on the food happily.

"Of course you love her. But you asked her to marry you because you felt guilty about what she went through when she was almost killed. Which, by the way, was entirely her fault. Not yours."

"She was targeted by a psycho. That's not exactly something she brought on herself."

"Fair enough. But the *way* she chose to handle it—that was her decision, before and after. No one could have protected her. How do you think her parents felt? Or me? Or Tyner? We were all horrified, after the fact."

"Okay, but why doesn't she want to get married? Her parents are happy enough—"

"Now. They were a little feistier when Tess was young, always bickering. They found it fun and even erotic, I think, but try to explain that to a five-year-old. The main thing is, I don't think Tess wants to have children, not yet. And what's the point of getting married if you're not going to have children?"

Crow thought he had her at last. "Kitty, you got married for the first time in your forties. Are *you* planning to have children?"

"I'm not playing by anyone else's rules," she said, smiling.

Crow was too distracted to notice how neatly Kitty had sidestepped his question. The physical activity of setting up the exhibit had provided only a temporary reprieve from the thoughts that had been troubling him all day. He had always known it was risky keeping secrets from Tess, no matter how benign. She despised looking foolish under any circumstances. As much as she fibbed and lied her way through her professional life, she was scrupulously honest in her personal one and expected the same from others.

But really, there had never been any point in full disclosure and, more important, never an appropriate time. He'd been waiting for all the stars to align, for Tess's business to pick back up, so she wouldn't feel pitied or patronized. Perhaps he should volunteer the information now, to soothe her fears over what the insurance companies might do to her. But she would be angry, and he hated to invoke her wrath, especially when things between them were so smooth, almost honeymoon-like.

Or had been, before he brought home a joyriding thief who tried to burglarize them.

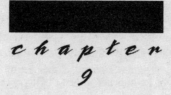

chapter
9

B Y SUNDOWN IT WAS CLEAR THAT LLOYD'S ONLY CHOICES
for the night were the streets or one of the mission
shelters, which he despised, with their enforced God shit,
not to mention all the other rules. Might as well live with
Murray's bullshit, in that case. And some of the hard-core
men smelled so, a nasty funk of wet clothes and body odor
and cheap wine. He had been trying to panhandle enough to
get into the motel over on North Avenue, which wasn't fussy
about ID and age as long as you had cash, but he hadn't
come close to scraping up the almost forty dollars he
needed. As a panhandler Lloyd lacked the natural advantages—no gimp, no limp—and while kindhearted women
sometimes gave him a few dollars for food, he could never
pull off those big scores, the ones that involved a lot of talking, a complicated story about a broke-down car or a bus, the
one where you took the person's name and swore to Jesus
that you would repay them soon. No, all he had was fifteen

dollars and some change, and the only thing that was good for was getting stolen.

Maybe his mother would actually take him in for the night. She'd do it for sure if he offered her the fifteen dollars, or even ten, but a mother should stand her boy to a bed for free. Plus, he *hated* Murray, Jamaican motherfucker always talking about the value of hard work. Home was almost as bad as the missions, especially if Antone, the four-year-old, was still peeing the bed.

Dub's flop, though. That would work. Cold, but free. Lloyd would buy a sub and a Mountain Dew.

He stopped at Lucy's and ended up getting a chicken box, which he wolfed down on the steps of an abandoned house a block away. He had meant to take it to Dub's, share a little, but it smelled so good and *warm*, and it was heat that Lloyd craved as much as anything. He was down to the bones of the chicken, the Styrofoam box balanced on his knees, when he felt a vicious clap across the side of his head that knocked him to the street, the remains of his meal scattering.

"What the fu—"

The two boys who had jumped him worked silently and quickly, turning out his pockets and taking his change. They must have followed him from Lucy's. It was business to them. They had seen him with cash and they wanted it, so they took it. Lloyd had no allegiances, no real backup. He was a free agent, and a free agent was prey. It made him angry, but it was like a mouse getting angry at a cat. Way of the world, outside his control.

Luckily, he had stashed the unicorn box in an inside pocket, deep inside the folds of his jacket where they couldn't feel it. And at least he had finished his meal before they jumped him.

Knees and ego bruised, he collected himself with as much

dignity as possible and limped toward Dub's house of the month. It was boarded up, like most of the houses in the block, but Lloyd knew how to swing open the plywood on the door and crawl over the threshold. Cold, but not as cold as outside, and Dub had collected a good pile of blankets from the Martin Luther King Day giveaway at one of the soup kitchens.

"Hey," Dub greeted him. He was reading a book by flashlight. Boy was a fool for schoolwork. "There's a spot over there."

"You wanna work tomorrow? I'm bust."

"I could do it after school, if you wanna."

"Midday's better. More places. We gonna have to go work some strange territory, we wait until after school."

"Got a test. And you know I can't cut, or they gonna send a note home and find out I got no home to send it to."

"Don't know why you're still fuckin' with that school shit."

Dub shrugged, pretending he didn't know either. But Dub was smart. The teachers were always marveling at his brain, and they didn't know the half of it. No one over at the school knew that his mother was in the wind, or that he hunkered down in vacant rowhouses with his brother and sister, Terrell and Tourmaline. If Dub stopped coming, the whole Lake Clifton faculty would probably take to the streets searching for him. And if he ever got busted for one of their "enterprises," as Lloyd liked to think of the cons they pulled, those teachers would go to court, ask the judge to forgive and forget. Dub, not Lloyd. No one at the lake remembered who Lloyd was.

But Dub never got caught at anything. That's how smart he was.

Lloyd picked his way among the others that Dub took in, preferring a spot by the wall, just one less person next to him. Once situated on his blanket, he took out the unicorn box, but he didn't open it or propose smoking what he had brought. Dub was like a churchwoman when it came to drugs, didn't want them anywhere near his brother and sister. Was it truly less than twenty-four hours ago that Lloyd had first seen this box, slipped it into his pocket, his head full of plans? He was going to sell the laptop and the camera, buy his mother some flowers or a pair of gold earrings, show up all flush, say he had a job.

But there would have been questions, he admitted to himself now, too many questions, and Murray would have broken him down, accused him of lying, which Lloyd would have denied with outraged innocence, because by then he would totally believe his own bullshit. It wouldn't have been at all like he imagined.

Seemed like nothing ever was. The thing he had done last fall—but he hadn't *known*. It was just a favor. He'd bet Le'andro didn't know what it was all about either.

It was almost ten o'clock, and even the cleaning crew had cleared out of the U.S. attorney's offices, but Gabe Dalesio was still at his desk, looking at office reports. Page after page after page of the most mundane stuff. The target discussed women and television shows, the Ravens, the relative merits of local sub shops. But he never alluded to drugs or crime, not unless he was using some elaborate code that they had failed to discern. Perhaps the sandwich orders could be translated into drug transactions. For example, "with hots" might be— But no, it just wouldn't hang together. There was no doubt the guy was a dealer, given that it had gotten to a Title III. But he was cautious and disciplined—although not so disciplined that he eschewed landlines.

It hadn't been Gabe's bright idea to go after this particular dealer. But he had inherited the case, so he had to make it work. Some previous AUSA had been shrewd, shedding this loser. Who had initiated it? Gabe flipped back through the file. Gregory Youssef. Of course. No wonder the guy had lobbied to get into the antiterrorism unit, with these kinds of dog cases dragging him down. No one was going to make a name for himself with this shit.

Gabe's thoughts returned, as they had almost obsessively over the last twenty-four hours, to yesterday's conversation with Collins, out on the smoking pad. *Do you spend a lot of time imagining what it's like to get your dick sucked by another guy?* A day later, Gabe still wasn't sure what the snappy comeback should have been. He almost felt obligated to get one of those fat secretaries to lie down on his desk, timing it so Collins would be passing by his just-ajar door, know that he was verifiably straight.

He walked over to his window, which afforded a slice of a view, if you could call it that—office buildings, an old Holiday Inn with a revolving restaurant on top, that strange Bromo-Seltzer Tower glowing blue. He should have held out for a real city, Boston or Chicago. The guy who hired him had done a total sell job, claiming that Baltimore was the best office for those who were aiming up, up, up. Close to D.C., easy to stand out, blah, blah, blah. Yeah, and that guy was now hiding out in some high-priced law firm, trying to sock away enough money to retire in style.

Traffic was light—nothing happened in Baltimore at night—but there was a steady stream of brake lights in the street below. He thought again about the lines at the toll-booths. No one would wait in those fucking lines who didn't have to, regardless of the circumstances. It would be automatic to head toward the flashing yellow light, to glide through as you had dozens of times before. Youssef had used his E-ZPass coming into the city, up I-95. Why would he have been so patient going out?

Because he wasn't at the wheel of his own car even then. Because the person who was driving didn't know that the car was equipped with E-ZPass, and Youssef didn't tell him. Why? Because he didn't see any reason to expedite his own kidnapping. And if he was kidnapped, then it was a federal crime, and Gabe's office had every reason to stick its beak in.

The idea delighted him so much that he brought up his hands and smacked them against the glass, in essence high-fiving himself. And if Youssef wasn't driving . . . well, then what? How did that jibe with what everyone thought they knew? If Youssef's piece of trade had already freaked out, where was Youssef? Dead already—but no, he'd clearly been killed where he was found. There had been no blood evidence in the car. Still, he could have been in the trunk, or hog-tied in the backseat, although that might have caught the eye of even the most brain-dead toll taker. But if he had been in the car, alive and sentient, he could have jumped out when the car slowed for the toll, run to the little office maintained by the transportation police.

"Steady, now," Gabe addressed his reflection in the window. "Stay cool." He wouldn't make the same mistake twice, running to someone to get affirmation for his latest brainstorm. He would hold this insight close, continue to mull.

He would make his name on the Youssef case, not on Youssef's hand-me-downs and leftovers.

Wednesday

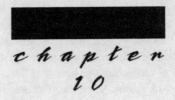

chapter
10

WHITNEY GLIDED TO THE CURB IN HER MOTHER'S MERcedes station wagon, an older model that, in the WASP fashion, had not been particularly well maintained. The once-burgundy exterior had faded to the color of a scab, and the window glass was clouded with age.

Still, the car looked like a rich woman's ride, especially after its deluxe treatment at Wash Works just that morning. A burst of opera escaped when Whitney opened the door, so loud that Whitney must have had the radio set at eardrum-bursting levels. She removed the key from the ignition, took a second to adjust the cashmere scarf draped around the shoulders of her mother's old mink, and cut across Mount Street without looking in either direction, clearly expecting traffic to stop for her. It did. In her hands—encased in leather driving gloves, naturally—she carried an open cardboard box filled with bags of Otterbein Cookies, purchased so recently that one could almost smell them. She could not have been more obnoxiously conspicuous, her presence all but screaming, *Look at me! Rob me! Carjack me!*

Excellent, Tess thought from her hiding place in the alley. Whitney was like a piece of cheese in a cartoon, a yellow triangle so toothsome that the mouse in this game of cat and mouse would never notice the figurative box poised overhead, ready to slam down when the stick was removed.

Granted, it was their fifth stop this afternoon, and the plan had yielded no results, although several local soup kitchens had been happy to receive the red-and-white bags of chocolate chip and lemon sugar cookies from this glamorous and heretofore-unknown benefactor. And most of the providers were familiar with Lloyd, Whitney reported back, although they just smiled and shook their heads ruefully when asked where he might be found. Tess and Whitney were running out of stops and cookies, and while Whitney had drawn plenty of stunned looks, Lloyd had yet to put in an appearance.

Still, Tess was certain that the kid's ruse wasn't a onetime gig. In fact, once she had thought it through, she found his scheme rather brilliant. Stake out a street near one of the local soup kitchens, pick out a car that clearly doesn't belong to the neighborhood. In the case of her Lexus, the parking sticker for the Downtown Athletic Club had marked it as an outsider's vehicle. Whitney's Suburban, while clearly a rich person's car—only the wealthy could afford to fill the bottomless gas tank—wouldn't register as rich in Southwest Baltimore. But her mother's Mercedes station wagon, with its I ♥ CORGIS bumper sticker, all but screamed its Greenspring Valley pedigree.

Crouched behind a ripe, overflowing trash can, Tess kept an eye on the street. A short kid, round of face and body, ambled toward Whitney's car and, with a quick look around, bent over and jabbed something in the tire. *Damn.* But she had warned Whitney that it was likely the tire would be slashed, not just flattened. "Mother has a full spare" was Whitney's airy response.

The more troubling fact was that this squat kid clearly wasn't Lloyd. It would be a hollow victory, nabbing the wrong culprit. Maybe the tire scam was to inner-city neighborhoods what the squeegee market used to be.

The fat kid, who had the wonderful ability to move swiftly without appearing to, sauntered away. Just as Tess was debating whether she should chase after him, she saw Lloyd coming down the block, tire tool in hand, positioning himself. *Another kid did it. I didn't do shit to your tire.* Wasn't that what Crow said Lloyd had insisted, over and over, with winning sincerity? It had been a technical truth, then. One boy slashed it, another offered to fix it.

Whitney left the soup kitchen, once again making herself as ostentatious as possible—tossing her blond hair, shooting her cuffs, revealing her watch and gold bangle bracelet, also borrowed from her mother. Playing her part brilliantly, she headed back to the car as if it never occurred to her that anything could be amiss, opening the driver's door. It was then that Lloyd materialized at her elbow.

Tess couldn't hear their initial exchange, although it did strike her that Whitney was overplaying the damsel in distress a bit, flailing her arms and even chewing on a gloved knuckle at one point. Finally Whitney popped the trunk and then, as she and Tess had rehearsed, began filling Lloyd's arms with the remaining boxes of cookies, ostensibly to get to the spare.

"The tire's just here, under this compartment," she was braying when Tess crept up behind Lloyd.

"Hey, Lloyd," Tess said.

They had anticipated that his instinct would be to hurl his armful of cookies and make a run for it. But Tess had also counted on a split-second delay, a moment in which Lloyd would hesitate—and be lost. Even as he tried to throw the cookies at Tess, Whitney stepped forward and pushed him into the open luggage compartment, then slammed the door shut and locked it with the button on her key ring. The Mercedes may have been more than a decade old, but the era of child-safety locks had already been in full swing then. The old station wagon also had a mesh screen separating the luggage compartment from the rest of the car, an option added for Mrs. Talbot's beloved but lively corgis. Lloyd was trapped. He banged on the windows with his fists, cursing them, but there was nowhere he could go.

Tess kept watch over him, even as Whitney ran around the corner to the Lexus, fetched her spare from Tess's trunk, and proceeded to change her own tire, a task made slightly more difficult by Lloyd's heaving body, which rocked the Mercedes a little.

"What now?" Whitney asked, eyes gleaming.

"I don't know." Tess raised her voice so Lloyd might hear her over his pummeling fists. "What now, Lloyd? Cops? Division of Juvenile Services? Your call."

"Fuck you, bitches!" he yelled back. "You can't make me do shit! You got nothing on me! I didn't *do* anything!"

"I saw it, Lloyd. I know you're working with that other kid. All I have to do is call 911 on my cell, and the cops will be here in a few minutes. Or maybe I'll go chase your friend, who's almost certainly hiding around the corner, let the two of you decide who wants to take responsibility."

The mention of his accomplice seemed to increase Lloyd's rage and panic. "FUCK YOU, YOU MOTHER-FUCKIN' WHITE-ASS BITCH! I will cut you if I get out of here, I will fuck you up, I will—"

"Nice talk. Look, we've got you on auto theft, hit-and-run—enough charges to put you back in Hickey for several months, if not central booking at city jail, where people are staying up to forty-eight hours these days before they even see a judge. But we're reasonable people. You can make a deal."

"I DON'T TALK TO COPS!"

"You don't have to talk to anyone but me. For now."

"Where?" Whitney asked, ever practical. "Your house?"

"Yours. I'll drive your mother's car back to her while you take mine." She thought she should be behind the wheel of the Mercedes if Lloyd did anything unpredictable. "Plus, your house is so remote that he can't run away that easily. Even if he gets away from us, he won't get far."

Once at Whitney's house, Lloyd came out of the luggage compartment feetfirst, aiming straight for Tess's midsection. Again, she had expected nothing less and needed nothing more than a simple sidestep to avoid the blow. Still, without Whitney to help her, she would never have been able to subdue the young man. Thin as he was, he had a feral strength, twisting and turning in their grasp, cursing them all the while. The two women ended up straddling him, so his face was scraping the gravel in the driveway.

"Fuck you, bitches," he said. "The minute you get up, I'm going to kill you both."

Tess pulled out her gun, just to remind him that she had one—and he didn't have any weapon at all. Not even a knife, based on her inexpert pat-down, for all his talk of cutting people.

"You ain't gonna use that on me. That's not your way."

"What do you know of my ways?"

"All I did was try to steal your car. White folks like you don't shoot you for shit like that."

"You're right." Tess put the gun away and pulled out her

cell phone. "Calling the police is more my style. *County* police. I'll tell them that Whitney and I caught you trying to break into her carriage house out here and that you attacked her. You want to get picked up by county police on attempted rape and burglary?"

"That won't hold."

"It will hold long enough for someone to beat the crap out of you in an interrogation room in Towson."

Tess didn't actually believe that county cops would automatically brutalize any black teenager in their custody, not even one accused of an attack on a Valley resident. But she thought the threat would be credible to Lloyd—and it was. He allowed the two women to escort him inside, where Whitney produced a length of rope.

"What's that for?" Tess asked.

"To tie him up. He doesn't have the best record for staying put."

"Fuck you." Lloyd spit on the floor and started to writhe in Tess's grasp. Whitney dropped the rope and grabbed his other arm.

"Look," Tess said, forcing Lloyd to make eye contact. "We'll give you a chance to sit and talk to us. If you run, we call the police. It's that simple. The driveway is a mile long, Lloyd. By the time you get to the end, a squad car will be waiting for you. And if you try to cut across the property, you'll find that picturesque fence is electrified."

He considered her offer.

"I'm hungry," he said at last. "You got any food or soda?" Then, as a hasty afterthought, as if remembering the chipotle muffins that had so distressed him: "I mean *normal* food."

"Well, there are several bags of those cookies, although they're now broken into pieces," Whitney said. "Other than that, I think I have some olives. And maybe some gin."

Lloyd settled for a glass of tap water and a bag of the shattered lemon cookies.

"When you were at my house, you saw a photograph of Gregory Youssef," Tess began.

"Who?" He wasn't very good at faking ignorance—or masking the nervousness that the name always seemed to inspire in him.

"Don't be coy, Lloyd. Youssef is the federal prosecutor who was killed the night before Thanksgiving. You knew that a federal prosecutor had been killed, because the dealers in your neighborhood were pulled in for questioning. You knew Gregory Youssef's name. But the two weren't linked in your mind. Who was Gregory Youssef to you?"

"Never met the man."

He seemed sincere, but Tess had already observed that Lloyd had a knack for technical truths that sidestepped larger ones.

"How do you know his name, then? And why do you try to avoid the subject when it comes up? Are you scared?"

"I ain't likely to be scared of *you*."

"Not of me. But definitely of someone, something. Someone who can link you to Gregory Youssef. And perhaps indirectly to his murder."

Lloyd finished a bag of lemon cookies and started in on the chocolate chip ones. Tess couldn't help envying his metabolism. She had once been able to eat that way, but that had been on the other side of thirty.

"I didn't know anything about no murder," he said. "Not a bit of it. All I was told is there was a guy and he'd crossed some folks, and they were going to scare him a little, take his money to show that they could, that he was a fool to think he was a player. Guy gave me the card and the code, told me when to use it and where."

"A guy?"

"I ain't naming names. I don't know a name to give. He was just some guy, an associate of a man I know."

Tess didn't believe Lloyd, but she let it go. "What about the security camera? Didn't you realize you'd show up on it?"

"I wore a hoodie pulled up tight so hardly any of my face showed." He demonstrated with his hands, cupping them around his face so only his eyes and the bridge of his nose were visible. "My North Face jacket was over it, but it got stole that very night. Which is why . . . well, that and the fact that I didn't get no money . . ."

"You're losing me, Lloyd. Take it step by step, minute by minute. When did you get the card?"

"Around eleven that night. Near Patterson Park."

"And who gave it to you?"

He shook his head. "There were no names. I don't know his, he don't know mine."

"Really?"

"Uh-uh. Just a friend of a friend of a friend."

"Okay, but he gives you the card and the code, tells you an ATM and a time. Right?"

"Yeah, I was to hit this machine on Eastern Avenue at exactly twelve-thirty A.M. So I did. And I get rolled like fifteen minutes later, guys take my jacket and the cash. And I'm thinking—" He stopped himself. "I'm thinking the guy who hired me done fucked me over, told his boys what he had me do, so he could get the money that was s'pose to be mine. They got my jacket and the cash, but I still had the card in my back pocket. And I was hungry. So I go to an all-night deli, use the card to buy a sub and a bag of chips."

"The deli had an ATM machine?"

"Just for purchase, but it takes Independence Cards and shit."

Tess had to fight the urge to tell Lloyd that "and shit" was not equivalent to "et cetera." Listening to Lloyd was like some hip-hop version of *The King and I*.

"Does the deli have video surveillance?"

"Don't think so. Korean's too cheap. He got a baseball bat instead."

"Even if he did," Whitney put in, "he would have reused the tape by now. Most of those places recycle the tapes every twenty-four hours if nothing happens."

Tess knew this to be true. "What time was this?"

"Like going on two."

Tess made a note. Youssef's killer had been tracked by E-ZPass along the I-95 corridor about the same time. Investigators must have noticed that discrepancy—Youssef's car in the northern reaches of Maryland, perhaps already in Delaware, his ATM card still in Baltimore. By using the card when he did, Lloyd had raised the possibility that there was an accomplice, a key fact the police had managed to hold close.

Tess wondered if Lloyd understood he would be seen as just that—an accomplice. His ignorance of the larger plan would be of no protection to him. He could be turned into a scapegoat, an easy arrest to assure the public that some progress had been made.

"Was that the last time you used the card?"

"Yeah, that was it. For food."

"Was it the last time you used the card for *anything*?"

Lloyd extended his feet sheepishly, showing off his whiter-than-white Nikes. "I figured I deserved a pair of new shoes and a jacket, to make up for the one that got stole. I went to the Downtown Locker Room at Towson Town Mall on Friday. Then I cut the card up and threw it in the sewer, like I was s'pose to do in the first place. I didn't see how anyone could mind. I was just trying to stay even."

"The person who gave you the card, Lloyd—did he kill Youssef? Would he have known that was the plan?"

"I dunno. He didn't look it."

"How did he look?"

"Just like, I dunno. Like a guy."

"Still, this stranger asked you to use an ATM card at a certain time and place. To use it just once, then throw it away. You noticed the name and you memorized the code—you still know the code, by the way?"

"Two-four-one-one," he shot back. Another detail that would matter, another detail that only a very small circle of people could know.

"Here's the thing I don't get, Lloyd. How did it escape your notice that the name on the card was the same as the name of the man who was killed that night?"

He shrugged. "Don't follow that news shit unless it's, like, a good chase or something. Everybody kept talking about the lawyer that got killed, but no one was saying his *name*, you know? And this guy, he had said what we were doing was no big thing. He said they were just going to teach a guy a lesson, fuck with him a little."

"You ever see him again?"

"Naw."

Tess glanced over at Whitney, who had been taking notes on a cocktail napkin, which must have been the closest thing at hand. She held up the monogrammed scrap so Tess could see what she had written:

> *Hoodie pulled tight*
> *Deli at 2 a.m.*
> *Downtown Locker Room two days later.*
> *Nikes and a new North Face.*
> *2 4 1 1*

"It's pretty damn specific," Whitney said. "If it's all true, everyone's going to want to talk to him."

"NO COPS," Lloyd said. "No cops, no names. Not mine, not nobody's. You know they'll lock me up, and I ain't done shit. They'll hang a charge on me to get me to talk, but I got nothin' to say. I done told you what I know. You promised you ain't gonna make me."

"I did promise," Tess said. "And I'll do my best to keep my word. But will you talk to a reporter if I can guarantee your confidentiality?"

"Will they make my voice sound all funny?"

"Will they— Oh, no. A newspaper reporter. Not television."

This seemed to disappoint Lloyd, but he nodded.

"I don't get it," Whitney said. "So he had the card. So some stranger who claimed he had a grudge against Youssef gave it to Lloyd and asked him to use it at a certain time and throw it away. What does that really establish?"

Lloyd also looked puzzled, as if he couldn't see how he fit into this larger story.

"I'm not sure," Tess said. "Someone went to a lot of trouble to make it appear that Gregory Youssef was the victim of a certain kind of crime, something personal and a little tawdry. Something that would make everyone squeamish. But if this can be traced back to a local drug dealer, then Youssef's death actually could have been a consequence of his job after all."

"I didn't say anything 'bout a drug dealer," Lloyd said, but the denial rang hollow to Tess.

"So what do we do?" Whitney asked. "Call the cops?"

"NO COPS!" Lloyd roared.

"No, no cops," Tess said. "But if Lloyd tells the *Beacon-Light* everything he knows, the cops will get the information just the same."

It also would smooth over her own relationship to the newspaper and make amends to Feeney. As his friend, she had tainted him a little with that outburst the other day. This would put them back to even, or closer to it. And she had a hunch that Feeney would agree with her that Marcy Appleton deserved this juicy plum of a story. She *was* the federal courts reporter.

"We won't even risk going down to the newspaper. We'll make the newspaper come to us. Tonight, in fact. And then we'll be out of your hair for good, Lloyd."

"Better be some dinner involved," he said. "Real food, too. Not that weird shit."

"Whatever you want. Chicken box? Sub? Pizza? Burgers?"

"Yes," Lloyd said.

Good Friday
into Bad
Sunday

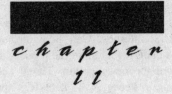

chapter
11

EVEN IF MARCY APPLETON HAD BEEN ABLE TO MEET all her editors' various directives and second guesses in one day of reporting, Tess had always assumed that the *Beacon-Light* would hold Lloyd's story for the Sunday edition, when it would make the biggest splash. Besides, it had taken most of Thursday and then Friday morning for Marcy to play the time-honored reporting game of "Would I Be Wrong If?" *So would I be wrong if I wrote that the ATM card was used at these locations? Am I right about the code? I won't print it, but would I be wrong if I said the* Beacon-Light *has a source who knows the code? Would I be wrong if I said the videotape showed someone in a hoodie and a North Face jacket?*

The multilingual, smoothly confident Marcy had started with the Howard County detectives. While the suburban county had its pockets of bad neighborhoods, it was overall a blandly peaceful place. Great for kids, as its residents said defensively, but not so great for homicide detectives, whose skills didn't get much of a workout. Even over the telephone, Marcy picked their bones clean. She then took on the interim U.S. attorney, Gail Schulian, who lost her much-admired cool, revealing in the process just how little she knew about the investigation. Marcy never got flustered, according to Feeney, who kept Tess apprised of the story's movements—and reiterated his pledge, in each conversation, that Lloyd's name would never, ever be mentioned, not even inside the newsroom. Reporters at the *Blight* were now required to reveal anonymous sources to at least one superior. But Feeney counted as a superior, hilarious as Tess found that fact.

"It's gone," he told her wearily Friday evening. "We lawyered it this afternoon, and it cleared the copy desk about five minutes ago."

"Are you their bright and shining star now?"

"More Marcy than me, although she's been good about sharing credit. She told the bosses that an old source of mine was the go-between. Guess that's true enough. Only downside is we both have to work Easter Sunday, doing the jerk-off react."

"Better than covering an Easter-egg hunt or the perennial gang fights that break out in the harbor when everyone goes promenading."

The bulldog, the early Sunday edition, goes on sale Saturday morning. Tess Monaghan remembered the jargon, if not the reason for it. Something about the bulldog chasing the other editions off the street. But that was simply by virtue of its heft. There was precious little news in the bulldog most weekends. People bought it for the real-estate ads and the coupons, not the stories. However, a big investigative piece, such as Marcy's article on the new facts in the Youssef case, would be anchored on the front and stay there throughout the run. Only an event of great significance—another 9/11, the death of a world leader—could knock off an exclusive this strong. The Associated Press and the out-of-town papers would start working it immediately, but the *Beacon-Light* had a head start, while the other news outlets would be trying to find officials willing to pick up their phones over the Easter weekend. The television stations would settle for rip-and-reads, all but reciting Marcy's story into the camera while standing in front of a suitable backdrop—the federal courthouse, the riverbank where Youssef's body had been found.

Running errands Saturday morning, Tess stopped at her neighborhood coffeehouse, Evergreen, to skim the article. Feeney and Marcy had kept all their promises. Lloyd's identity was cloaked, and not a single one of his assertions had been shot down. Marcy also had been careful, as Tess had insisted, not to assign Lloyd's gender. It had made for some awkward writing, with endless repetitions of "the source" and "a person with firsthand knowledge." Marcy hadn't even used the name of the store where Lloyd had purchased his jacket and shoes, not that Tess believed that a store clerk could remember who bought a North Face jacket on the day after Thanksgiving. In fact, neither Tess nor Lloyd would have cared if the newspaper had named the Downtown Locker Room, but the *Blight*'s advertising department had pleaded with the editors to omit that detail.

Satisfied, Tess went about her day, convinced she had done a good deed.

But just as she no longer remembered the rationale behind the name of the bulldog, she had forgotten how much a story could change from bulldog to Sunday final.

*   *   *

In the gym, sweat pouring onto the paper as he pedaled a stationary bike, Gabe Dalesio read the story with a mix of despair and pride. *He had been right, he had been onto something, he had been so close.* But who would believe him now? He *knew* that Youssef wasn't at the wheel of his car when it left the city, and now this story all but proved it. It was an elaborate ruse, an electronic trail meant to conceal Youssef's real movements. But his brainstorm was moot now. There was no point in being right unless others knew about it. Fuck Collins, for being so dismissive. He probably wouldn't even remember that Gabe had said anything. The only thing that Collins carried away from that conversation was that Gabe spent a lot of time thinking about getting blow jobs from other guys. Damn it. Damn his own self. He should have told the boss lady what he had figured out.

He wondered how Marcy Appleton had found this anonymous source anyhow. She was a decent reporter, well liked around the courthouse, but better known for her exotic looks than her smarts. A house cat, not a shit disturber. Maybe a defense attorney had acted as matchmaker, offered up his client in hopes of spinning the story. No matter how ignorant the source was of the larger crime, he could still be squeezed as an accomplice. But if it were a matter of trying to protect a client from other charges by giving up valuable information, no seasoned attorney would do that through the media. He would come straight to the prosecutors, put his cards on the table. And if the source didn't have a potential charge hanging over him, then why talk at all? If the source had been picked up for something else, perhaps by city cops, Gabe could see him making this deal, but there didn't seem to be anyone official involved. Just the reporter and the source.

Absentmindedly Gabe rose from the bike and grabbed a cup of water.

"You're supposed to wipe the equipment down," a middle-aged woman berated him, one of those frightening, pared-to-the-bone types who thought having no body fat was the same as being attractive.

"Sorry," he said, running his towel over the seat.

"It's just hygiene," the dried-up skank said, clearly on a mission to humiliate someone to make herself feel better. "A lot of people 'round here think the rules don't apply to them, but your sweat's not nectar, you know? I don't want to sit on your sweaty seat."

"Trust me, ma'am, I don't want that either." She didn't get it, just hopped on and began pedaling away, as if she had somebody's little dog in her basket.

Hell, Gabe's problem was that he had been too circumspect, too mindful of rules and protocol, wasting opportunity after opportunity. He had planned to make his bones on the Youssef case, but this damn reporter had pulled the rug right out from under him.

Still, might as well drop by the office, see what was buzzing. He could at least get brownie points for showing his face in the middle of what was shaping up to be a real clusterfuck.

Jenkins spent weekends out in West Virginia, in an unassuming built-to-spec A-frame near Berkeley Springs. Inside, it had some nice touches—a plasma television, vast leather chairs, high-end bathrooms, a kitchen with all the extras. The latter had been done with an eye to his ex-wife's taste, although Betty was long gone before he started building the place. In the back of his mind, he thought she might come back. If not for him, then at least for granite countertops. But

Betty found West Virginia even less appealing than Balti-more.

He was settling in for a day of NCAA basketball, brack-ets and a Sam Adams at his side, when his cell phone rang. It was the fake-o switchboard number that showed up on of-fice calls, and he almost said fuck it—his days of worrying about work 24/7 were long gone. He had done that, and look what it had gotten him. Demoted, humiliated. Still, few work emergencies could be so severe that they would order him back from the mountains, a two-hour trip, so he decided to risk it.

"There's something in the paper today," Collins said with-out preamble. "Someone who used Youssef's ATM card talked to a reporter. And the Howard County detectives all but verified it. Remember how cagey they were with us? Well, one of the things they were sitting on was some info about the card. Turns out it was used two more times after the initial withdrawal, even as Youssef's car was heading up the interstate. We knew about the first withdrawal, which matched up with the E-ZPass—northbound car came through the lane at ten forty-five, it was used on Eastern Av-enue at eleven-oh-five. So now they know the killer wasn't the one who used the card, assuming the killer is the one who drove Youssef's vehicle up 95 to the turnpike."

"Interesting," Jenkins said. He liked to be taciturn on the phone, holding his cards as close as any target would. Not because they had any reason to worry about what they said on the phone, just because Jenkins liked discipline for disci-pline's sake, and he had taught Collins to do the same. It helped, thinking like the people you were targeting, aping their habits. "Should I come back today, face the music? They let me act as liaison on this because they thought the Howard County cops would be open with me, so I guess I'm in the shitter now."

"Actually, they're saying Gail is spitting nails about Howard County, but your name hasn't come up."

So Jenkins was so far down on the shit list he wasn't even worth getting mad at. There were worse things than being invisible, although he couldn't think of any just now. "Thanks. Who you like in Syracuse-GW?"

"Orangemen versus Colonials? Orangemen. Pussy names, I have to say."

"Spoken like a true Poet." Collins had played for the Dunbar Poets, a Baltimore powerhouse that had sent some big players to college and even the NBA.

Jenkins hung up, mourning the loss of what should have been a sweet, relaxed day. He could understand the cops fucking over Gail, but why had they withheld the ATM stuff from *him*, when all he'd ever done was smile and charm and do his aw-shucks-we're-all-in-this-together routine? He hadn't leaked anything. Howard County had let the E-ZPass stuff out, but maybe they had realigned the facts in their mind, decided Jenkins was to blame. It wouldn't be the first time he'd been scapegoated that way. Bastards. They were going to do him again. He just couldn't win.

Not even in the brackets, as it turned out. By the end of the afternoon, Jenkins was already statistically eliminated from the NCAA pool, which he once ruled. He was losing his touch across the board.

Lloyd spent Saturday the way he normally did, roaming the neighborhood with Dub, looking for financial opportunities, as they liked to call them. He had been taken aback to learn that there was no money to be had from the newspaper. Maybe he should have gone to the cops after all. Cops *paid* for information. But no, he couldn't risk that. Once the cops got him, they wouldn't let him go until he gave them what they wanted, and he had nothing to give. Besides, he had gotten some good food out of it. He had told his story to the man and the lady from the newspaper over a huge meal in that crazy lady's house, the scary blonde. They had let him have anything he wanted to eat, from anywhere, so he had ordered up a feast—subs and chicken boxes and pizzas, eating from it all as if it were just a big motherfucking buffet, not worrying about what would go wasted, then taking the leftovers away, along with the last two bags of cookies.

He had eaten and talked, talked and eaten, and almost come to enjoy it, the way those people hung on his every word. He was going to help solve a big-ass *murder*. He was almost inclined to brag on himself to Dub, but then he remembered: If the ATM card was linked to some murder, the murder was almost certainly linked to Bennie Tep, and Lloyd did not want to be crossways with any drug dealers. He'd have to keep it quiet. Still, he had a private thrill when he and Dub stopped in the Korean's and he saw the front of the newspaper framed in the box on the corner. He leaned closer, reading a few lines, until Dub punched him and asked what he was doing, looking at the newspaper like some old-timer.

They walked across Patterson Park, the fields still muddy. The day was cold and bright, but it held the promise of spring. Lloyd liked spring. People seemed nicer in the days after the cold weather snapped, and it was easier to bum money from the tourists who flocked to downtown. If you got too close to the harbor proper, the cops or the purple people ran you off, but a block or two away, near the parking garages, was just as good. Yes, spring would be great this year, he promised himself. He'd get something going this spring.

*   *   *

Crow worked at the Point all day Saturday and into early Sunday, arriving home at 3:00 A.M. Restless, he prowled the house. Since going to work at her father's bar, he had tried to keep to Tess's more normal hours as much as possible, but he just couldn't throw himself into bed upon coming home, especially when a band like the Wild Magnolias had played. His head still buzzed with the music, and he hummed a few bars of "Smoke My Peace Pipe." He wished he could get out his own guitar and play, but that would be unfair to the slumbering household. Instead he went into the den, thinking to smoke himself into serenity, but the unicorn box was gone. *Oh, Lloyd.* Tess wouldn't miss the dope. A little more law-and-order every year, she seldom smoked anymore and was nervous about Crow's occasional indulgence. But the box was a recent gift from a little boy named Isaac Rubin, who had purchased it at the Metropolitan Museum of Art while on a pilgrimage to visit the location of his favorite book of all times, *The Mixed-up Files of Mrs. Basil E. Frankweiler.* Isaac had given the box to Tess for agreeing to speak to his class on Career Day. The loss of the box would kill Tess, who could be surprisingly sentimental about objects. Maybe Crow could go online, order her another one.

At 5:00 A.M., still wide awake, he heard the thud of the newspaper on the front steps, decided the *Beacon-Light* would be as good a soporific as dope. He settled in at the dining room table, reading Marcy's story. He read the same words that everyone else had read in the bulldog edition, except for one key change. Now, in the home edition's second paragraph, it said, "In a meeting arranged by private investigator Tess Monaghan, the source told *Beacon-Light* reporters . . ."

Shit. Crow skimmed the rest of the story. Lloyd was safe, as promised. Marcy and Feeney, covered by state shield laws, couldn't be compelled to reveal his identity. Even if the feds decided to get involved, it would take months to play out. So they, too, were protected, if only in the short run.

But Tess wasn't. Neither were Crow and Whitney, if it came to that. Citizens had no shield protection. But Tess was the only one whose name had been served up to the authorities, a fat, juicy target for what were probably some very angry people.

He let her sleep until seven-thirty, then woke her with breakfast. "What's wrong?" she demanded the moment she saw the tray with fresh pastry and coffee purchased from Evergreen.

She was gone by eight, about an hour ahead of the Howard County detectives, as it turned out.

"Where is she?" asked a freckled, redheaded detective, who brandished his badge as if it could make her reappear magically. "When is she coming back?"

"I have no idea," Crow said, and it was the absolute truth.

PART TWO

Mobtown

Monday

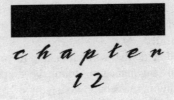

chapter
12

"TESS, I DON'T KNOW WHAT TO TELL YOU. I EDITED THE story myself and baby-sat it every step of the way through that first edition. I checked midday Saturday to see if anything had cropped up, if the top guys were second-guessing so much as a comma. Sunday editor told me everything was okay. Even so, I had my cell phone on every moment, and no one called me."

Tess almost felt sorry for Feeney, who was so upset that he couldn't be bothered to sip the martini in front of him. But Feeney wasn't the one who had to move out of his own house Sunday morning and go into semi-hiding. Feeney was going home to his own bed tonight.

"So how does my name end up above the fold and before the jump? It might as well have been in neon."

"Hector called Marcy at home at six P.M., began badgering her. Said one anonymous source was pretty thin, and couldn't we source it at all? She only told him about your role to buttress the case that the source was trustworthy. He didn't tell her that he was going to put it in the story, just turned around and called the desk himself. That's why it reads a little stilted."

"How could he do that without talking to you first?"

"As an assistant managing editor, he outranks me. He doesn't need my permission to do anything."

Neither one of them mentioned the obvious fact—that the AME might not have been so quick to insert Tess's name in the story if she hadn't pissed him off earlier in the week. Her mother had frequently told Tess that there was a cost to speaking one's mind, but Tess had never imagined that it could be jail time. But that would be the outcome if she was brought before a grand jury and refused to testify.

She chewed her lip, found that unsatisfactory, and decided to try the olives the restaurant had provided. Baltimore had discovered tapas, or vice versa, and the city was now thick with variations—Greek, Spanish, Middle Eastern. Tess and Feeney had agreed to meet at Tapas Teatro because it was reliably chaotic, the kind of place where no one attracted attention and even the most determined eavesdroppers were thwarted. Plus, it had windows on the street and several exits through which Tess could flee if any official types showed up.

"I promised Lloyd. I gave my word that I wouldn't tell the police his name. You did, too, but you're covered by shield laws."

"Only on the state level, although I'd never reveal an anonymous source. But what's Lloyd got to lose by coming forward?"

"He thinks that the police won't believe he's told all he knows, that they'll hold him as an accomplice to the homicide until he's revealed the name of his contact—and he doesn't have it. He's given us everything he's got."

"Can you argue that your position in this is privileged, that Lloyd falls under the attorney-client exemption?"

"Lloyd's not a client, and he didn't sign the usual paperwork. Tyner's never heard of him, and I can't ask an attorney to lie about that."

Tess drained her sangria as if it were fruit punch and looked around the restaurant. So many happy, normal people with such uncomplicated lives, chatting about the films they had just seen at the Charles Theater next door, eating with gusto and joy. Not a single one of them under the threat of federal investigation.

Actually, neither was she. Yet. For the past thirty-six hours, only the Howard County detectives had been trying to find her for questioning, sending increasingly urgent messages via Crow, then her lawyer Tyner, who was able to say truthfully—and, because he was Tyner, loudly and brusquely—that he didn't have any idea where she was. No one did. She had packed a bag, turned off her incoming cell phone, and checked into a nightly rental at a North Side high-rise. Even some of the residents didn't know about these by-the-day rooms, so Tess was confident that she had bought herself a little time. Very little.

"They're saying you did it for the reward money."

"*What?* What they?"

"The feds. It will be in the paper tomorrow. The U.S. attorney says if you're a good citizen, you'll cooperate with the investigation. But then she floats the possibility that you arranged for the interview to get part of the reward."

"I didn't even know there was one."

"There is, and it's hefty as these things go, a hundred thousand. Hey, maybe that would be enough to get Lloyd to come forward voluntarily."

"Maybe. But it's not a sure thing, right? You usually only get the money upon the conviction of a suspect. Lloyd's not going to have the patience to play those odds. And Crow won't forgive me for betraying Lloyd."

"Even if it comes down to you being jailed for contempt?"

"Crow idolizes the Catonsville Nine and some group called the Baltimore Four. He expects me to live up to their lofty example."

"The Baltimore Four? Crow expects you to have twenty winning games as a pitcher?" It made Tess feel better that Feeney's brain also jumped to the Orioles, not some long-forgotten incident at the Customs House.

"Have you been paying attention to spring training? *I'd* have a shot at the number-five spot in the Orioles rotation."

Tess chewed an olive pit. She had no appetite, and there was no better barometer to her mood. She was in very deep shit. She never got herself in more trouble than when she was being clever.

The thing that killed her was that Lloyd was wandering clueless through the city, with no inkling of what he had set in motion. Ignorance *was* bliss.

At the relatively advanced age of fifty-seven, Bennie Tep was still in the game, but he had been trying to grow the legal side of things, rely less on the game itself, which was so volatile. He planned to enjoy his old age, retire like any citizen, although he wasn't going to play fuckin' golf. Last thing he wanted at this point was another homicide on his calendar, but once it was explained to him, he understood. The boy had talked, the boy had to go. Okay, so he'd been clever enough not to throw Bennie's name around, or so they assumed, because the cops hadn't dropped by to talk to him yet. It was only a matter of time. They would get to the boy, and the boy would give them all up. The newspaper might not know or care who'd given the order, but the investigators most certainly did. The boy had been given a job, and he not only screwed it up, he had talked. The consequences for the second were more dire than for the first. And it wasn't like it was the first time this kid had fucked up. Bennie understood why it had to be done. But his heart wasn't in it. Heart wasn't in it, and his hand couldn't be anywhere near it.

Toad wasn't crazy about being the triggerman, but disloyalty pissed him off, so he took on the job. Toad could be trusted. Tell him to do a thing and he did it. No muss, no fuss. Thing was, they could have done it this way in the first place, just popped the guy on a downtown street. Bennie didn't believe in making things more complicated than they had to be. If the lawyer needed to die, he needed to die. But why all the to-and-fro? The whole plan had made Bennie's head hurt. Bennie already knew how to commit the perfect murder. He had done it many times over, coming up. Shoot the guy. Make sure there are no witnesses. Get rid of the gun. Doubt his system? Well, he was here, in his own house—titled to his aunt, but his house nonetheless—fifty-seven years old and forty years in the business, and they'd never even gotten so much as a felony indictment against him. There were men in so-called legitimate businesses who couldn't make that claim.

Bennie puttered around his kitchen looking for something he was allowed to eat or drink. This was usually the time of night that he liked to have a little cognac, but his doctor was down on that. Said his liver was fatty, although Bennie himself was lean, just a little paunch. Apparently he was like that guy on the commercial, the cut one who belly-flopped because his cholesterol was so high. Wine with dinner was okay, he had been told, but wine was something you wanted with a steak, and he wasn't allowed to have that either. He looked at the doctor's diet suggestions, taped to the side of the refrigerator. Fish, but not fried. Chicken, no skin. Nasty.

The usual rabbit food. He could have some low-cal microwave popcorn, but his dentist looked down on that. Bennie's heart was simply on notice, but his gums had crossed the line to rotten. He could have popcorn or nuts only on the night before a trip to the periodontist, but he was so sick with dread about the pain the night before that he didn't have the appetite for much.

He settled for a York Peppermint Patty, a mini, only fifty calories, low-fat, and no trouble for his teeth. With a cup of hot tea, it was almost as good as a real dessert. Almost.

Waiting for his water to come to a boil, he turned on the late news. Slot machines—shit, he hoped they didn't come to town, the legal numbers were bad enough—something else about the governor. Had Toad missed his chance? But when the news came back from commercial, the anchorgirl had on her serious face, signaling a sad story. That meant a homicide, a fatal car accident, or something about an injured pet.

"We've just gotten word that police have been summoned to the 2300 block of East Lombard Street for what appears to be a drive-by shooting. A young man was shot multiple times while standing on the corner there. Police say there were no witnesses. Those with information are asked to call . . ."

Bennie winced, poured a little extra sugar in his tea. The boy was so young. Bennie hadn't even started at sixteen, and here was a young man already dead. But it had been a different business in Bennie's day—more time to learn on the job, get some savvy. The young ones today were too impatient, hotheaded, wild to use their weapons. Plus, no one diversified anymore. Bennie, for example, still carried some gambling action, a daily street number and some sports book from time to time. Now he had the real estate and the sub shops, although those were wearing him out. Damn health department. They were more formidable competition than the New York boys, citing a man for every little thing. It was the *ghetto*. Of course there were roaches and rats.

Damn. He felt bad for the kid. If they had done things Bennie's way to start, none of this bullshit would have come to pass. He hated fancy shit. All that hoodoo with ATM cards and bank machines and surveillance cameras, and they weren't any more in the clear than if they had just shot the guy in the head and left him in Patterson Park. Everybody had to be so got-damn smart all the got-damn time.

But it was over. Now only two of them knew what was what, and they would never tell. They both had too much to lose.

Tuesday

chapter
13

IN HIS DREAMS CROW HELD FAST TO TESS WHILE SHE TRIED to wriggle out of his grasp. She wasn't attempting to escape out of malice or rejection, only because her curiosity had fastened on something bright and shiny and just out of reach. It was like trying to hold on to a squirming child, and eventually he had to concede her strength and let go.

Plus, she smelled awful.

He awakened to find his arms around the greyhound, who was not trying to evade his touch at all but had instead burrowed into him, exhaling bursts of fishy breath. A mere two nights since Tess had decamped, Esskay had usurped Tess's place in the bed, even using her pillow. Miata, less conflicted about the idea that she was a dog, was draped across the foot of the bed.

It was odd, being in Tess's house—and he always thought of it as *her* house, despite the work he had done on the rehab—without Tess. He felt off balance and tentative. But perhaps what he really felt was superfluous. The rational part of his mind understood that Tess was protecting him by concealing her whereabouts, but another part wondered if she had expected him to wilt when confronted by various authorities. "I don't want to put you into the position of lying," she had said Sunday when she packed her bag and left the house. They had been in regular phone contact since then, and she had let slip that she was less than a mile away, somewhere in North Baltimore. "I can almost see Stony Run Park from where I am," she said, then stopped abruptly. But Crow knew that meant one of the high-rises near Johns Hopkins.

What if the newspaper had reported that Edgar "Crow" Ransome was the actual go-between in this tale? Would he now be on the run, while Tess was kept in the dark? True, he had not ferreted out the connection between Lloyd and Youssef, much less gone out and plucked the kid off the streets of Baltimore and forced him to tell what he knew. Crow had found that part of the story a little appalling, in fact, an echo of nineteenth-century bounty hunters rounding up slaves. Whitney and Tess didn't have good sense sometimes. But none of this would have happened if he had not brought Lloyd home that first night.

Right now Tess probably wished this were so, although Crow thought the Howard County investigators had been given a promising lead, if they could just focus on it. Even if Lloyd couldn't or wouldn't say who had asked him to use Youssef's ATM card, the detectives now knew this wasn't a case of a man being murdered by a piece of would-be trade.

He glanced at the clock: 11:00 A.M. With Tess gone, he had honored his own night-owl nature instead of trying to fit his schedule onto Tess's days, playing weft to her warp. It had felt good, sleeping in, obeying his own body's needs for once.

The dogs, poor things, hadn't adjusted to the new routine. They needed to be walked immediately. He threw on his clothes, Esskay leaping around him in giddy circles while Miata just panted in excitement. They preferred Crow, for he was focused on them during the walk, while Tess's thoughts tended to drift and her pace to slacken. Eager and anxious, they burst through the door—and almost tripped over the huddled form of Lloyd Jupiter, who seemed to be trying to fold himself behind a yew-berry bush.

"You gotta help me, man. They killed Le'andro. They killed *Le'andro*."

"Le'andro was the one who was supposed to use the card, but he had a chance to get with this girl. So he gave me the card, told me I could have the money. But that was a secret, see? Between us. Because he had a direct order to do it his own self. So they think he done it. And if they think he done it—"

"Then they think he's the source in the newspaper article."

"Yeah." Lloyd picked up a rock and threw it as far as he could—which turned out to be pretty far. The kid could probably be a decent baseball player. But inner-city kids seldom played baseball. It took too much equipment, too many people, whereas basketball could be played with two guys on a cement playground covered with broken glass.

They were walking along Stony Run Creek, a narrow stream in a park known mainly to those whose houses bordered it. Esskay and Miata were compassionate dogs, but it was hard to explain to two walk-bound creatures that anything was more important than their twice-daily routine. They scampered ahead, towing Crow behind them as if he were a water-skier. Lloyd had refused to hold either leash on the grounds that he hated dogs. Crow had a hunch it was more fear than hate but didn't press the issue.

Along the way Lloyd's story had tumbled out quickly, as if trying to keep pace with the dogs. Le'andro was a low-level player in an East Side drug gang, one run by a man that Lloyd knew as Bennie Tep, although he admitted that probably wasn't his full and proper name. Still, he whispered it, as if it were a powerful thing in its own right, almost like an Orthodox Jew saying Yahweh or spelling G-d. And before he told Crow the name, he made him promise it was a *secret*-secret, one just between the two of them. "Not for your girlfriend or those damn reporters," he said. "They got Le'andro killed."

Crow didn't have the heart to point out that Lloyd had helped. In trying to protect his contact, he had only made him more vulnerable.

"But Le'andro was involved in dealing drugs, right?"

"Yeah."

"And you said he was shot to death on a corner where there have been disputes over territory. It could be unrelated."

"There ain't been no quarrels over that corner for at least three weeks. That thing was settled when Buck Jackson was locked up."

Three weeks didn't seem like a true truce in a drug war, but perhaps Crow didn't understand how time was calculated in Lloyd's world. Perhaps three weeks in East Baltimore was three years in Iraq.

"So if they killed Le'andro, you're off the hook. They think the informant is dead."

"Yeah, but your people"—Crow was charmed despite himself by the concept that he had people—"have to make it official, tell police that Le'andro was the one they talked to. That's the only way I can be safe."

"They can't, Lloyd. Not if they get hauled in front of a grand jury. Perjury is a big deal."

"Yeah," Lloyd said. "They got Lil' Kim on that, but Baretta and his parrot go free on murder. World is *fucked* up."

Crow couldn't disagree on that last point, although he remained as mystified as ever by Lloyd's cultural markers. A hip-hop star like Lil' Kim, sure, but how did he know about Baretta? Then again, even the poorest homes in Baltimore were usually wired with premium cable, and why not? Crow couldn't find it in him to begrudge the poor any luxury, no matter how shortsighted it seemed.

"Tess told me that the reporters who know your identity can invoke state shield laws," he said. "If brought before the grand jury, they'll testify that everything in the story is true, but they can't be compelled to say anything else. Not under state law. And Tess is trying to figure out a way to avoid being interviewed at all, because she has no privileged status. Maybe if police *assume* it was Le'andro . . ."

But even ever-optimistic Crow couldn't see how this would happen. They would demand that Tess verify that Le'andro was the source, and Tess couldn't risk lying to local investigators when the stakes were so large.

"Lloyd, here's the thing: If you stay with me at the house, someone's going to put it together really fast that you're the source."

"Why?"

"Well, because, it's just that . . ."

Lloyd laughed at his discomfiture. "I was just messin' with you, man. I know you got no black friends."

"That's not true. That's absolutely not true."

"Yeah? So who you hang with who's black?"

"Well, Tess's friend Jackie and her daughter. And I sometimes have lunch with Milton Kent, the talk-show host."

"On 1010 AM?" Lloyd looked impressed. The station was the only talk channel in Baltimore programmed for a black urban audience. Crow sometimes toggled between it and the all-conservative WBAL, marveling at the wide world of conspiratorial thinking.

"No, the NPR affiliate." Lloyd was no longer impressed. Meanwhile Crow was reeling inside his own head. Of course he had black friends, he must have black friends. There was, well, Seth, back at college. They had been tight. And some musicians, from his days as the lead singer of Poe White Trash. Certainly he had never made a conscious choice *not* to have black friends.

But this was Baltimore. Sixty-six percent black, and most of its white citizens lived inside an all-white bubble. Just walking through the park, Crow and Lloyd had drawn more than their share of odd looks from the stay-at-home mothers who speed-walked at midday. That's why he knew he had to get Lloyd out of Roland Park as soon as possible.

"Lloyd, you have to go to the police. Tell them the part about Le'andro, and they'll understand you've got nothing more to tell. Tess will do everything she can to keep her promise to you, but you can't expect her to go to jail to protect your identity."

"I never asked for this trouble. She *made* me do it. She was just looking out for her own self. Now I'm looking out for me."

This was all too true. Not particularly noble on Lloyd's part, but true. Tess, driven by insatiable curiosity as sure as Kipling's elephant was, had dragged Lloyd into this, not the other way around.

"But it's the only way you'll be safe. Once you talk to the police, they'll do everything they can to protect you. You can't get in trouble for giving a dead man's name."

"Yeah, right. You know how many witnesses been killed in my neighborhood? Even locked up, you're not safe. They want you, they *get* you. Besides, if I say Le'andro, they gonna go to Bennie Tep and he'll have me killed. Snitchin' don't *play* where I'm from."

They had come full circle, in the conversation and in the walk. Lloyd was right. Well, not right exactly, but logical in his own way. Outing himself would achieve nothing. Lloyd had already told everything he knew. True, he had omitted a key detail, Le'andro as middleman, but now that Le'andro was dead, Lloyd truly had nothing more to offer. Police would charge him and hold him. Worse, they might release him to streets where he, too, would be hit. Meanwhile Lloyd couldn't stay with Crow, because even Barney Fife would quickly ascertain the identity of the black teenager who had suddenly taken up residence in Tess Monaghan's North Side home. He needed to get away, somewhere safe.

Why not take a page out of Tess's playbook? If Crow and Lloyd disappeared, she could then say in all innocence that she didn't know where her source was. He'd have to work it out with Pat—no, let Tess explain to her father why Crow was on the lam and couldn't come to work. *On the lam.* He couldn't help finding the idea somewhat romantic. He and Lloyd would take off today, disappearing into the city. He'd need cash to avoid leaving any trail, but cash was never a problem. They would use disposable cell phones, the kind available from every convenience store now, to stay in touch with Tess; he had learned about that scam from watching HBO. No, no, he wouldn't call at all. If Tess's phones weren't already tapped, they would be soon. He'd have to buy pairs of cell phones, send one to Tess in the mail.

"Lloyd, are you sure no one knows that Le'andro handed the card over to you?"

"Absolutely." His answer was swift, emphatic. Perhaps too much so.

"Lloyd?"

He sighed, put-upon by his own unreliability. "I got a friend."

"The kid you run the tire scam with?"

"Uh-huh. But he's good people. You don't need to be bothering with him."

"What if he tells someone?"

"He won't." The swift conviction was sincere this time.

"How much does he know?"

"He knows Le'andro gave me a chance to make some money last Thanksgiving. And he was with me when I used the card, out at the mall. I bought him something, too. But he don't know I talked, and I don't want him to."

"Lloyd—you were supposed to tell the reporters *every-thing*. That was the deal."

"I told 'em about what I bought myself. The DVD player was for him. He likes movies, and it got a battery pack, so he can charge it up at the library, watch it in the night."

Crow remembered the pile of DVDs he had found on the floor of the spare bedroom the day after Lloyd's memorable first visit, the copy of *Throne of Blood* in the Volvo.

"You steal the Kurosawa movie for him?"

"What? Oh, no, I just thought it looked cool."

"It is cool. If we had time, I'd let you watch it."

"Where we going?"

"To hide in plain sight."

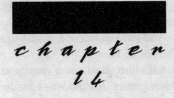

chapter 14

IN PRINCIPLE TESS DISLIKED PEOPLE WHO USED CELL PHONES in restaurants. But she was getting ready to make an exception for herself, rationalizing that she hadn't spoken to Crow all day, when Tyner arrived for their meeting. His face was stormy with general disapproval—of her cell phone, of the restaurant, of Tess, who had chosen it—and she meekly slid the phone back into her knapsack.

"You can't keep playing this silly game of hide-and-seek," he said as soon as he had barked his drink order at the waitress. Tyner wasn't big on social preliminaries. "You need to decide what you're going to do when you finally surface."

"I could take the Fifth."

"You haven't broken any laws."

"Maybe I *think* I have," Tess said.

"Your lawyer," Tyner said, pointing to his chest in case she had forgotten he was here in a professional capacity, not a family one, "is informing you that you haven't. You can't invoke self-incrimination if you haven't in fact done anything incriminating. That's a kind of perjury, too."

"I could marry Lloyd and refuse to testify against my husband."

"Don't be droll, Tess. Besides, if you married the boy, you'd create a legal trail that would lead police right to him. That's the one thing you've managed to do right so far, through no real fault of your own. The boy's name isn't recorded anywhere. If Crow had given Lloyd's real name to the police the night of the accident, the detectives would eventually have pieced it together. As it is now, they're probably searching Baltimore for Bob 'One O' Smith."

"I know," Tess said. "That's Crow's karma. He's also refused to help the insurance companies, who are just as keen to find our little friend."

"He won't be able to stonewall them forever, you know. And you won't be able to evade the cops much longer. They'll put you in front of the grand jury when it meets next month. You'll be asked to name the source you brought to Marcy and Feeney. If you refuse to name a person of interest in a homicide case, you could be jailed. In fact, they'll take great delight in locking up a middle-class white woman."

"A lot could happen before the grand jury convenes. Lloyd could decide to come forward on his own—"

Tyner, a champion snorter, gave a short, elegant whiff of air. It was the equivalent of a teenage girl's "as if."

"Or they could develop leads in the case that make Lloyd irrelevant."

That earned a shake of the head and an even more contemptuous snort. Tess didn't take it personally. Tyner was grouchy with everyone but Kitty, his wife of almost six months. (He insisted on calling her his "bride" with a kind of starry-eyed, gooey devotion that Tess found far more alarming that his usual cantankerousness.) But his mood was particularly dark today, a fact that Tess chalked up to her choice of lunchtime rendezvous, the Club 4100. She had picked the old bar in the Brooklyn section of Baltimore for its twin advantages of cheeseburgers and an off-the-beaten-track location. No one ever ended up in the Club 4100 by accident. She also loved the décor, which had been built around Baltimore sports in general and Johnny Unitas in particular. Alas, the restaurant did have a habit of serving red wine chilled, and she hadn't warned Tyner off the cabernet in time. The icy grape wasn't improving his mood.

"Outside a grand jury setting, I can't be compelled to tell the cops anything, right?"

"No."

"And it's not illegal to lie to cops in an interview?"

"It depends, but no, it's not like with the feds—only why would you even think of trying to lie at this point?"

"I could give them a fake name or say I honestly don't know the kid's name, that I met him through someone."

"They'd want to know who made the introduction, then."

Tess shrugged. It would be ironic if the cops used the same trick on her that Marcy had played on them, asking her if they would be wrong to assume the source was the kid who had stolen her car. Of course, cops didn't need to play such games. They could jack her up now, apologize later. After all, that's what Lloyd said had happened in the wake of Youssef's death. The drug dealers had been arrested and held on whatever pretense the investigators could manufacture, then let go when a different scenario emerged.

Seemed to emerge. That's what intrigued Tess. Youssef's murder had been a mise-en-scène, an elaborate play. Yet the multiple stab wounds still struck Tess as awfully personal.

Thirty-nine stab wounds wasn't an act. The scenario had been faked, but the rage had been real.

She reached for the scar on her knee, remembering the night she had used far more bullets than strictly necessary to defend her own life. She had fired until the gun was empty, and she would have done that if the weapon had held ten, twenty, a hundred bullets. If she could dig the man up and shoot him again, she would.

"I wish I could talk to the widow."

"I hardly recommend that course of action." Tyner was cupping his hands around the frigid glass of red wine, but not the way a wine lover might. He was rubbing them back and forth like a Boy Scout making a fire from twigs, trying to bring his drink to room temperature.

"No, no, of course not," Tess agreed automatically. "Why not?"

"Because to Mrs. Youssef you're the woman who's shielding someone who could help police solve her husband's murder. Besides, what would that accomplish?"

"Lloyd told us everything he knew. He's done as a source of information. Whatever happened to Youssef, Lloyd was at arm's length from the origin of the plan, an errand boy, assigned to use the card and create an alternate reality."

"So he claimed. Did it ever occur to you that Lloyd might have been directly involved in the murder and that he's spinning the story to deflect suspicion?"

The question caught Tess off guard. She was so sure she had considered every angle of Lloyd's story, processing it through what she thought of as her cynic meter.

"No," she said. "He didn't recognize Youssef's face. Lloyd's not sophisticated enough to lie on that many levels. How can you be an accessory to murder if you don't know what the guy looks like?"

"By helping to cover up the crime," Tyner said, his voice

uncharacteristically gentle, which always troubled Tess more than his usual rages. "Which is what Lloyd did, Tess. Don't lose sight of that. He helped someone conceal a murder and create a chain of evidence designed to confuse investigators."

"But until he met me, he didn't even know that the two things were related."

"So you say. So you believe. But you can see why homicide detectives might be a little more dubious. It's not unreasonable to think that Lloyd is now trying to cover his ass, distance himself from a crime."

"Sure, if they had him on another charge and he offered up this story to save his own neck. But no one had any leverage over Lloyd."

"*You* did. You could have turned him in to the police for stealing Crow's car. Which, with Lloyd's record, meant more time inside."

"Only, what he told us checked out. The police have confirmed now that they always knew about the ATM charges but had been sitting on them because they thought it was something that only Youssef's killer could know."

Youssef's killer—Tess heard the echo and made the same argument in her head that she had been making to Tyner. Lloyd didn't know what Youssef looked like, so he couldn't be directly connected to his murder. Youssef was dead in a state park when Lloyd bought his sandwich, while Youssef's car was crossing into Delaware. He couldn't have been there. Right?

Tyner took a sip of his wine, frowned at the taste and the temperature but pressed on. "Even if you're not going to cooperate with Howard County police, I think you should go down there—with me of course—and pretend to be a good citizen. Okay? Maybe we can argue that Lloyd was a client who made an oral contract with you to keep his identity secret and that you expose yourself to a civil lawsuit by breaching that promise."

"But no contract entitles me to shield criminals, right?"

"True."

"And Lloyd has broken the law. In fact, on just the first ATM withdrawal, I think he might be in felony territory. Or some kind of fraud?"

"Yes, it's a serious charge. Why don't you introduce me to Lloyd, let me take him on as a client? I can't make your deal with him privileged after the fact, but I can help him."

"I made a promise—" she began.

"Yes, but you didn't know you could face jail time for it. Crow will understand, Tess. Lloyd has to speak to the police. I'll get him immunity, if possible, protect him every way I can. But this can't go on."

"I guess not." Tess pulled out her cell phone again. "Crow and the dogs will be glad to have me home. You know, it's not that I gave my word to Lloyd so much. It's the promise to Crow that I would keep my promise to Lloyd. That's the one I can't break."

"I'm sure the Howard County detectives will be very moved by that sentiment," Tyner said, but Tess hardly heeded his sarcasm. The phone was ringing unanswered at home, kicking into voice mail after the usual five rings. She tried Crow's cell. It went straight to voice mail, which indicated it was off. Should she try the Point? No, he didn't work Tuesdays. She felt a little clutch of panic, silly, she knew. But he was usually so accessible. If not at her beck and call, at least at her call. She was the one who forgot to check in, neglected to say where she was going to be. They had spoken—when had they spoken? Last night. A sweet, easy call. He said he missed her but he understood why she couldn't say where she was. She assured him that she didn't think he would ever tell anyone where she was. She just

wanted him to be able to claim ignorance of her whereabouts with a clear and sunny conscience.

Privately, she thought Crow a rotten liar. But she hadn't
told him that. No, their last encounter had been nothing but
pleasant.

"Tyner, you have my permission to set up the meeting
with Howard County for tomorrow. But if you don't mind,
I'm going to throw some money down and run home."

Jenkins knew he should just leave the Howard County cops
alone, let them do their jobs. But they were such incompetent mopes. Nice but ineffectual. When were they going to
find the broad and drag her in? He couldn't keep from calling just one more time, checking to see if they had made any
progress.

"So," he said, knowing that small talk was neither expected nor welcome. "You got the name yet? You got the
broad?"

"No," admitted the detective, a feeb named Howard Johnson, poor guy. Worse yet, he had hair as orange as the old
restaurants and eyes the same blue color as the trim. It was
like his parents had peeped into the bassinet and said, *Let's
make his life hell!* "The PI has dropped out of sight. Not at
home, not in her office, not answering her phones."

"You sitting on her house?"

"Not yet."

Rubes.

"But her lawyer just called. She's willing to meet."

Really. But then he had expected as much. Still, he gave
an impressed whistle, as if he chalked all this up to Johnson's formidable skills. "Huh. Look, Howard, I know I
promised to keep the fed's collective nose out of this, but
can I come to the interview? Not participate," he added

hastily, sensing even over the phone line that he had pushed a little too hard. "Just watch, through the glass."

"Sure, but . . . why do you want to watch some stupid woman PI stonewall her way to the grand jury?"

"Just got a feeling about this one."

"Me, too. But my feeling is that it's the kind of red ball that's going to sink me. I almost wish you guys had taken over this one."

Jenkins hung up. He did have a feeling, a literal one in his gut, which was cramping from nerves. He poured himself a tumbler of Jameson and forced it down, reasoning that his stomach and his throat would just have to get over it and live with the burning reflux, because the rest of his body needed it bad. *Take one for the team, esophagus. Take one for the team.*

It was dusk when Tess came home to two strangely exhausted dogs. Still, they were never so tired that they couldn't greet her properly—Esskay doing the little vertical jumps that Crow called leaping and posturing, Miata circling Tess's shins.

"Where's Crow?" she asked, but the dogs just kept up their welcome-home dance.

The house had a too-neat look, as if it had been picked up in anticipation of something. Newspapers were in the recycling bin. Crow's breakfast dishes had been rinsed and placed on the drain board. Her heart clutched a little, for the scene reminded her of the other times Crow had left. But no, when he *left* her left her, he did it with more obvious ceremony. Crow had a weakness for the grand gesture. Besides, his cell was on the kitchen counter, plugged into its charger.

She checked the cell phone she used for incoming calls. The technology was still quirky; calls were received and dropped into her voice mail without the phone ringing. Wait, she had placed it on vibrate while working from a coffeehouse in South Baltimore that afternoon. Still, there were no familiar numbers on the log and only one message, which had came from the home number.

"Lloyd's in danger," Crow said, his tone as light and uninflected as if he were telling her to pick up milk at the store. "The guy who gave him the ATM card was killed, and Lloyd is sure it's because of the story. Yeah, he lied about being the only one involved. So I've taken him somewhere he'll feel safe—and I'm not telling you where we are, so you'll be able to claim ignorance without lying. We'll keep in touch via disposable cell phones, changing every few days so we can't be tracked. You should get your first one tomorrow or Thursday."

Lord, he sounded cheerful, as if this were some Hardy Boy adventure. Crow and Lloyd, a Frank and Joe for the new millennium, a postmodern variation on all those black-white buddy movies of the 1980s: *48 Hours, Lethal Weapon.*

Weapon—*shit.* Tess went to check the gun safe in her bedroom. She had her Beretta with her, as always, but she still owned the Smith & Wesson that she'd used before trading up last summer. The safe was empty, which almost made her weep in frustration and anger.

But it was the handwritten note on her pillow—*I love you! Trust me on this!*—that did the trick. She sat on the neatly made bed and cried. In frustration, in anger, but more in loneliness and fear.

If Lloyd was in danger, then it followed that anyone with him was, too. Crow had thrown himself on a very live grenade. Didn't he realize that? Now she was in an impossible position. If she gave up Lloyd's name without knowing where he and Crow were, how could she protect either of them?

If she didn't, then how could she protect herself?

Wednesday

chapter 15

CROW HAD THOUGHT HE WOULD FIND IT EASY TO SPEND A night in a homeless shelter—after all, he'd been working with various soup kitchens and shelters for the past three months—but he was wholly unprepared for the difference between life as a come-and-go-as-you-please volunteer and the lot of a client. Or guest, as this Southeast Baltimore shelter called the twenty-odd men it took in every night. It wasn't so much the smells or the sounds that threw him, although those were plentiful and strange. It was the lack of autonomy, from when the lights were turned out to when the men themselves were turned out onto the streets the next morning. As a benefactor Crow had power. As someone in need of the shelter's services, he felt at once meek and surly.

It was a safe haven, however, and he had planned to return there for a second night until the director pulled him aside after breakfast.

"Look, I'd do anything for you," said Father Rob, short

for Roberto. A Lutheran minister, he had convinced his church to let him use the parish hall as a shelter as the congregation's neighborhood members dwindled over the years, replaced by yuppies who thought churches were only good for condo rehabs. "But if you're trying to hide, this isn't going to work for you."

"Why not?"

"You stick out, Crow. I mean, Lloyd—sure, we could keep Lloyd forever and no one would give him a second look, although he's a little young. But Lloyd's not going to put up with that. He's going to go back to his own neighborhood the minute he gets bored or frustrated."

"His life's in danger. He's the one who came to me, the one who sought my help."

"I know Lloyd, Crow. I've known him a lot longer than you have. You think this is the first time he's slept here?"

"I thought you didn't take teenagers."

"We don't—officially. What would you do if a kid showed up on a snowy night?"

Buy him a meal, Crow thought. *Take him into my own house. Wreck my girlfriend's life.*

"Anyway, Lloyd's ideas don't have a lot of what I'll call staying power. Yes, he's scared now. But the fear will pass. It has to pass. His part of East Baltimore might as well be the Middle East. There's so much violence he's numb to it. This isn't his first friend to be killed. It won't be the last. He'll persuade himself that Le'andro's death doesn't have anything to do with him after all. Or that he's cool as long as he doesn't talk to the police. Once out of your sight—and he'll try to lose you, sooner rather than later, no matter how many good meals you buy him—he might go to the very drug dealer he fears, beg for some kind of clemency."

"So I should take him to the police."

Rob hesitated. "The good-citizen part of me says yes. The part of me that knows this city— Crow, a man was beaten to death in jail this winter. By the guards. So if I'm honest, I can't tell you there's a way to guarantee Lloyd's safety. Yet you definitely can't control him as long as he's in Baltimore. Two days from now, he'll be chasing a sandwich or a girl, forgetting all about how scared he was. You need to get him out of town for a little while, figure this out from a safe distance."

Crow studied Lloyd, slumped in an old plastic chair in the shelter's foyer, his posture and attitude radiating the typical adolescent sullenness. What would Crow do with him all day in Baltimore? He'd thought they could go to the library, a prospect that had filled Crow with joy. A day to read and think, hidden away in the gracious main library's nooks and crannies. Then down to the harbor for lunch, maybe a long walk for exercise, back to the library until closing time, dinner somewhere in Canton, and here to sleep. Given the circumstances, Father Rob had even agreed to hold two beds for them, waiving the usual first-come, first-served rule out of gratitude for the favors that Crow had done the shelter.

But Crow saw now how delusional he was. Lloyd would never spend a day in a library, much less see the point in taking a long walk on a cool spring afternoon. He would fight Crow every step of the way.

"Where should we go?"

"I don't know, Crow." Father Rob gave him a rueful smile. "I really shouldn't know, should I?"

"If anyone comes here asking after us, even someone who knows me—"

"Crow who? Lloyd who? *Vaya con Dios.*"

Before Tess's father had taken over the Point, it had belonged to Tess's uncle, Spike. At least she called the old man

Uncle Spike. The nature of his relationship to the family remained vague. No one even seemed sure if he was a Monaghan or a Weinstein. There was also the hint of some scandal about Spike, a criminal past that the usually voluble Tess skirted in conversation. Whatever Spike had been, whatever he had done, he was now a proper retiree, living in a condo in South Florida and going to the greyhound tracks. Not to bet but to monitor the treatment of the dogs. It was Spike, in fact, who had rescued Esskay, although he always insisted that Esskay had rescued him.

From a sub shop in South Baltimore, a place with a video game that would keep Lloyd occupied as long as there was a supply of quarters, Crow called Spike on the cell phone he had just purchased, a twin to the one he'd overnighted to Tess.

A man of few words, Spike listened to Crow without comment or interruption, reason enough to be fond of him.

"There's a man," Spike said. "Friend of the family, will look after you for a while. Edward Keyes."

"Isn't he the former cop who signed off on Tess's paperwork so she could get licensed?"

"Yeah. Good people. He lives down the ocean." Spike may have retired to South Florida, but his Baltimore accent had not diminished at all and he pronounced this phrase with the classic Baltimore *o* sounds: *Downy eaushin.* "I'll call him. I'll also call a guy in Denton, who will swap out cars for you. Give you something nice and legitimate, put yours on a lift for the duration. But look, Fast Eddie—"

Spike, despite being Spike, did not approve of Crow's nickname and had settled on "Fast Eddie" as a suitable substitution.

"What, Spike?"

"You got enough cash? 'Cuz I'll front you, wire some to Keyes."

"I have all the cash I need, Spike," Crow said, knowing

that Spike would not ask how that could be, bless him. Spike was a great respecter of secrets, having had a few himself. "Enough to last for weeks, if necessary, especially with the accommodations you're arranging."

"But what you're doing, it's short-term, right?"

"Probably no more than a week or so. Just until we figure some things out."

Even over the telephone, Spike was capable of eloquent silences. This one was skeptical.

"I need Lloyd to trust me," Crow rushed to explain. "Once he trusts me, he'll understand that I have his best interests at heart, and he'll come in voluntarily, do what he has to do."

"You don't think he's told you everything." Said flatly, a question and a statement. Spike had his opinion, but he still wanted to know what Crow thought.

Crow glanced over at Lloyd, whose every cell seemed focused on the game in front of him. He held on to the controls, swaying side to side, his right hand darting out to pound the button that unleashed his artillery. His grace, his dexterity, his rapt concentration—what could Lloyd accomplish if those gifts could be directed elsewhere? But how could anyone persuade him to redefine the future as something more than the next four to six hours?

"No," Crow admitted. "I don't think he's told me the whole story. But I also think he's right that his only choices just now are being killed or being locked up."

"Don't lose sight of that," Spike said.

"That he's in danger?"

"That he's a liar."

"That's harsh, Spike."

"Also true. I bet you've already caught him in one lie." Crow's silence answered that question for Spike. "Just because he's 'fessed up to one doesn't mean he's done yet. Lying's a way of life with some people."

                        *   *   *

It was 2:00 P.M. when Crow called Tess on the disposable
cell phone that was not yet in her possession. She could retrieve the message tomorrow.

"Lloyd and I are on the road," he said. "Details to follow
via these lines of communication."

Lloyd meanwhile was looking around the increasingly
flat countryside, sniffing the air suspiciously. "What's that?"
he asked.

"Salt. The ocean's maybe thirteen miles from here."

"Which ocean?"

Honestly, Baltimore schools. Even a sixteen-year-old
dropout should know which ocean bordered Maryland and
Delaware. "There's only one we could have reached in three
hours, the Atlantic."

"Ain't *nothing* here, if you ask me."

"Not in March, no. Not down the ocean." Crow took a moment, for he always needed to prepare himself before he
launched into an imitation of Spike's Bawlmer accent. "We've
gone downy eaushin, hon."

"Hate that 'hon' shit," Lloyd said, going back to the X-Men
comic book that Crow had bought him at the same convenience store that provided the phones. But a few miles later,
when they pulled up on the street that dead-ended into a small
boardwalk and the Atlantic came into full view, Lloyd found
it hard to maintain his studied nonchalance. There was a pal-
pable awe in his silence, although he tried to hide it.

"There sharks in there?" he asked.

"No. Dolphins sometimes."

"Is it always so loud?"

"Loud?" Crow hadn't thought of surf as noisy, more of a
soothing music, one that took him back to his childhood, the

summer nights on Nantucket. "I guess so. It's a beautiful sound, isn't it?"

Lloyd shrugged. Crow wished that it were warmer, that they could take off their shoes and socks, roll up their pant legs, and wade into the surf. It seemed almost criminal to him that Lloyd had reached the age of sixteen without knowing what it felt like to wiggle one's toes in wet sand, to feel the sensation of the tide rushing out, so it seemed as if one were moving while standing perfectly still.

"So what we going to do now?"

"This is our new home for the next few days. Until we figure out what's best for you."

"The ocean?" Lloyd's voice squeaked a bit.

"No, this place here." Crow waved toward a faded white square of a building, the red lettering on its side weathered by the winter. FRANK'S FUNWORLD.

"What's there to *do*?" Lloyd looked at the tiny strip of boardwalk, the largely empty houses, with a sense of desperation. "No fun that I can see."

"Don't worry," said a short, squat man who came waddling out of a side door. Because the door was centered in the face of a grinning clown, it appeared as if the man had crawled out of the clown's belly. "I got plenty to keep you busy."

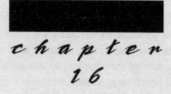

chapter
16

GABE DALESIO STILL COULDN'T BELIEVE HIS LUCK. HE HAD
all but given up on ever getting a piece of the Youssef
investigation—too big now, too radioactive. Plus, all the
agencies had to present a united front, pretend they were on
top of things, not start pointing fingers across jurisdictional
lines and glory hogging. Gabe had tried to drop some hints
in front of the boss woman that the case interested him, that
he had some experience with shield laws if she wanted to
pursue that angle. (A lie, but what of it? He'd get the expertise if he needed it.) But nobody cared about what he had
to offer.

And then boom, out of the blue, this FBI agent Barry
Jenkins calls up and asks if he'd like to watch the interrogation of the private investigator, the grandstander who was refusing to name the source.

"Why me?" he asked, then wanted to kick himself. That
wasn't the comeback of a natural-born winner, all grateful

and pathetic. *Why me?* He should have asked for the time and place, said he'd be there.

Jenkins, to his credit, didn't bust balls. "I'm sort of the un-official liaison on the Youssef matter. Collins at DEA told me you'd been challenging the, um, received wisdom on the murder before any of this broke. I asked your boss, and she said she could spare you on this."

"Sure." Trying now for the cool, hard-as-nails stoicism that he should have shown from the start. So Collins didn't think he was a faggot after all. "I could fit it in."

"We're just going to watch, mind you. The state people don't want us breathing down their necks. They want our help, but they want to run the show."

"I've been thinking about this," Gabe had said. "If Youssef is a kidnapping victim—"

"Who said that?"

"That's my theory. It all goes to the E-ZPass, what I told Collins. I don't think Youssef was at the wheel of his vehi-cle when it passed through the toll on its way south, but he wasn't dead yet either, so it's a kidnapping charge, which makes it a federal case even if you don't know he's a U.S. attorney—"

"Let's not get ahead of ourselves here, young'un." The guy actually said "young'un," as if he were John Wayne and Gabe was some kid, Ron Howard in *The Shootist* or one of those boys from the movie about the cattle drive.

But that was okay. Those boys came through for the Duke in the end, proved they were men. And now Gabe was here in the Howard County public safety building, arms folded, eyes squinted, staring through the one-way glass at what appeared to be a remarkably average woman. She had wavy, almost shoulder-length hair that begged to be shaped and styled in some way, light hazel eyes, and a nice shape if you liked that buxom type, which Gabe usually did. Her

voice was low, her words clipped, although Gabe sensed
that this was not her natural way of speaking. With each
question she glanced sideways at her lawyer, an old geezer
in a wheelchair. Ironside and Perry Mason, all rolled into
one. It was unclear why they made eye contact each time,
as the lawyer didn't seem to signal her in any way, didn't so
much as shake his head yes or no. She looked at him, then
said, over and over again, "I'm sorry, but I consider that information confidential." Gabe didn't get that. She had volunteered to come in, presumably to cooperate. What was
this shit?

"You have no standing to assert privilege," the Howard
County assistant state attorney reminded Tess.

"I'm not saying it's privileged. I'm saying I made a promise, a binding oral contract. Breaking it would make me liable to civil action, which would be ruinous to my business.
I literally can't afford to tell you what you want to know."

"And this promise is more important to you than solving
the murder of an officer of the court?"

"Let me remind you," Tyner put in, "that my client has already shown her willingness to do her civic duty by getting
her source to share his—or her—information with reporters.
It's up to investigators to use this information as they wish."

"A newspaper article is no substitute for a true criminal
investigation. There are unanswered questions."

"Such as?"

"The source didn't name who provided the ATM card."

"Maybe, maybe not," Tyner said. "Given that I was not
present for the interview, I can't speak to that."

"*She* was present."

"That hasn't been established for the record," Tyner said.

"Were you present?"

"Not for the entirety of the interview." Tess had made the food run.

Detective Howard Johnson could not hide his exasperation. Tess didn't blame him. Semantic games pissed her off, too. "Did the source tell the reporters who gave him the ATM card?"

"Or her."

"Excuse me?"

"Him or her," Tess said. "I've never put a gender to the source, nor did the reporters. I'd like to establish that for the record."

Detective Johnson picked up a piece of paper. "The purchases—the Nikes, the North Face—they were men's, according to the receipts."

"I buy men's shirts at the Gap," Tess said. "I'm wearing one right now. At any rate, I'm not going to answer questions that imply the gender of the source is known."

"Okay. Did *he* or *she* identify the person who gave *him* or *her* the ATM card?"

"Not to me."

Tess was walking a very fine line here. Lloyd had not identified the source of the card at the time of the interview. But he had told Crow yesterday, prompting their flight. She didn't know the name, but she knew it was gettable. All one had to do was look at who had been killed late Monday or early Tuesday—something that Tess had steadfastly avoided. With so many secrets to protect, a little genuine ignorance *was* bliss.

Poor redheaded Howard Johnson was beginning to sweat. "Your source is protecting a killer, which makes him—"

"Him or her," Tess said.

"*Him* or *her* an accessory. Which means *you* are obstructing justice."

"Charge her with that and we'll proceed from there," Tyner said. "Until then it's an empty threat."

"The source knew nothing about the murder of Gregory Youssef. The source believed the whole incident to be some kind of low-level scam. But—" Tess looked at Tyner. They had spent much of the morning trying to decide if they should share the new information that Crow had provided, brainstorming every ramification and possibility. It was hard to know sometimes how a piece of information would land. To Tess it was obvious that the murder buttressed her position. But it might not appear that way to the detectives and attorneys. "I do have some new information. New to me."

She was aware of the anticipation in the room, the hope that she would tell them something significant, the worry that she was setting them up for the anticlimax.

"I still don't know the name of my source's contact. But I do know that the contact is dead."

"Dead?"

"Homicide."

"Who? When? How could you know this?"

"As I said, I don't know his name. But I can give you some information about my source's contact."

Detective Howard Johnson leaned forward.

"The victim was one of the city's sixty-some homicide victims since the beginning of the year. So you have a finite universe of cases to examine."

"We will put you in front of the grand jury," the detective said, his temper beyond lost. "We will hold you in contempt. We will let you sit in the detention center until you get over yourself and stop this stupid shit."

"I don't doubt that," Tess said. "But the person I'm protecting honestly believes this to be a matter of life or death. Someone has already been killed. We don't know for certain that it's connected to the Youssef case, but it's a possibility we have to consider."

"Only, the person who was killed wasn't in protective

custody," Johnson pointed out. "Your source would be a lot safer, coming to us."

"You think? There's a tradition of dead witnesses in Baltimore that belies your confidence. Besides, even though I could tell you who my client is, if I were so inclined, I can't tell you *where* the client is. The source has created his—or her—own brand of protective custody. Has left the area and has no plans to return for the time being."

"Are you being truthful?"

"I've been truthful at every point in this interview." Tess couldn't keep a little heat out of her voice. When the circumstances suited her, she was perfectly capable of lying, but she had been extremely precise today. True, she hadn't been particularly helpful, but that wasn't the same as lying. She had walked the line, as the old song had it.

And was hovering right above a ring of fire, to keep it in the Johnny Cash canon.

On the other side of the glass, Jenkins popped a Pepcid, although he kept his face impassive, unreadable. Sanctimonious bitch. Where did she get off?

No matter. He had been smart to heed his stomach's queasy instincts and invite the AUSA last-minute. This eager beaver next to him was the key to finding out what he wanted to know. All he had to do was unleash Fido here and he would cheerfully, happily, and quite legally proceed to press this bitch until she was begging for mercy. Jenkins hoped she was smart, or at least pragmatic, the kind of person who would abandon a principle when things got rough. Let her play this half-assed game with him and he would own her. Sure, she could be all noble here, when the only thing she was risking was some penny-ante shit from county cops. But when it was her life versus someone else's, those lofty principles would fall away. They always did.

The thing is, he sort of got where she was coming from. In a different context, he might have respected her. He knew what it was to believe in something and how hard it could be to give it up, even in the face of overwhelming evidence that those to whom you were loyal had no loyalty to you. She had been taken in by this kid, whoever he was, bought into the idea that he needed her protection. Couldn't see the forest for the trees, a figure of speech that had long puzzled Jenkins, who had always been able to see everything all at once. She had placed herself at the center of the Youssef matter, losing sight of the fact that it wasn't about her, that she was an insignificant player. This wasn't her story, but he could see why she might think it was. To her credit, she was trying to do what she thought was right.

But she believed in the wrong thing, she had chosen the wrong side, and that was reason enough to dismantle her life.

Thursday

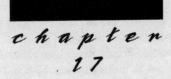

chapter 17

"Ocean's hell on paint and wood," Edward Keyes said, handing out scrapers and brushes to Crow and Lloyd. "Ocean's hell on everything, corrosive as a sonuvabitch. I usually paint in the fall, but my Mexican crew up and quit on me."

"Do you have to stereotype them by race?" Crow said automatically, then regretted it. They were dependent on this man's generosity, after all.

"What I'd say? Just said they quit, and they did. Left me high and dry last fall, and now I'm way behind if I'm gonna open for Mother's Day weekend. I should give up on shingles, go with something more mod-ren I know, but I like the old-timey look. It's not as much work as it looks to be, not once you get a rhythm."

Lloyd, who had glared at Edward Keyes throughout his overview of the seasonal preparation required by Frank's FunWorld, spoke for the first time. "Why Frank?"

"What?"

"Your name ain't Frank. So why this place called that?"

"Sounds better, don't you think? Allitter-something."

"Alliteration," Crow put in, and the other two regarded him as if he were the nerdiest kid in the class.

"Had a cat named Frank once. Mean old tom. By the way, you'll want to get as much painting done as you can in the morning. Wind kicks up in the afternoon something fierce. That's why I usually do it in the fall." And with that, Edward Keyes left them, whistling a happy tune.

Crow supposed that he would be cheerful, too, if he were dispensing the supplies for this backbreaking work, then retiring to the sheltered interior of the park to tinker with the rides and reassemble the Whac-A-Mole games, with a radio to provide some mental distraction. Crow and Lloyd remained outside on this bright, windswept day, with nothing but their own companionship. Which could have been pleasant, but the only conversation Lloyd seemed capable of was a litany of complaints.

"Why we got to paint? We're paying our way, aren't we? You givin' him cash for our food and our rooms, which ain't much. So why we got to *work*?"

"What else are we going to do with our time?"

"I don't know. Watch TV and shit. Anything but this."

"What would you be doing back home, a day like today?"

"Find some action. Hang." Lloyd made a few desultory passes with the paintbrush. "Why can't we use a roller at least? Go a lot faster."

"Roller won't cover shingles. We'll be able to use it on the concrete, though, on the other side. And when we get to that part, it will seem so easy it won't be like work at all."

"Were you a teacher?"

Crow was flattered. "No, but it interests me. I think sometimes of going back to school, getting a certificate." *Only
how would I explain to Tess that I could afford it?*

"Yeah, that sounds like teacher shit." Lloyd pitched his
voice high and took on a bright, prissy tone. " 'Really, it's
not that hard, boys and girls, if you just *try*.' That kind of
thing. They was always saying shit like that."

"Was there anything you liked about school?"

"It was warm," Lloyd said pointedly. "They didn't make
us stand outside in the cold, painting shit."

"Look, if we talk, pass the time, this will go a lot faster."

"I got nothing to talk about with you. Seems to me talking is what got me here."

"Here" was actually beautiful in its way, a short, old-
fashioned stretch of boardwalk in the town of Fenwick, just
above the state line and Maryland's far-busier resort, Ocean
City. The early-spring light, the empty beach, the careworn
buildings—they made Crow's fingers itch with the desire to
paint again, although not in this way, applying coats of latex
to the battered surfaces of Frank's FunWorld.

"World" was a little grandiose for this bunkerlike rectan-
gle that contained one bank of Skee-Ball machines, several
video machines, a single Whac-A-Mole, and a couple of
booths for the hand-eye coordination games that spit out
tickets good for schlocky items at the so-called Redemption
Center. The rides were geared toward small fry for the most
part—little motorcycles that went 'round and 'round, little
boats that went 'round and 'round (although their basin was
dry), and a ringless, currently horseless merry-go-round.
The only concession to anyone above age ten was a bumper-
car ride, with the obligatory You Must Be This Tall sign.
They would have to paint that, too, Mr. Keyes had said. That
and the clown's face. Well, Crow had just complained to
Kitty that he never got to paint anymore.

"No, I mean we could just talk *talk*. About life. Or movies and books. What do you like?"

"I like them dinosaur books and movies," Lloyd said. "*Jurassic Park.*"

"Michael Crichton. So you like futuristic plots, science fiction."

Lloyd made a face, but Crow decided it was the word "science" that was putting him off.

"You liked *Minority Report*, right?"

"The one with the *Top Gun* dude?"

"Yeah, sure. Anyway, the guy who wrote that also wrote this one called *Do Androids Dream of Electric Sheep?*, which they made into a Harrison Ford movie. *Bladerunner.*"

"*Bladerunner*'s a better title."

"Maybe." Crow began with bounty hunter Rick Deckard and his mood organ, his argument with his wife, Iran, whose name confused Lloyd no end. Crow's memory was shaky at first, and he sometimes conflated film and book, but slowly the beloved story came back to him in detail, almost every sentence intact.

Once the mix-up over Iran's name was cleared up, it wasn't apparent if Lloyd was listening. Then he asked a question about midway through, a clarification of some plot point. Other than that, he was quiet and thoughtful. The wind seemed to settle down and the sun grew stronger, so the work wasn't quite as hard on their exposed hands. Before they knew it, they had finished scraping and painting most of the shingles.

"That guy write any other stories?"

"A few," Crow said.

When the wind kicked up as predicted and they had to suspend painting for the day, Crow prevailed on Edward to come to the library with them. He was paranoid enough to want to avoid using his own card to check out materials, even if it turned out that Delaware and Maryland had some sort of reciprocity agreement between their library systems. A silver-haired volunteer with an accent that reminded Crow of his Virginia roots showed them the library's books-on-tape, which included several unabridged editions. With the tapes running up to twelve hours, they couldn't get through more than two in a week of work, and it was hard for Crow to imagine they would be in this limbo much longer than that. He encouraged Lloyd to make one of the selections. Lloyd picked Stephen King's *The Stand*, despite Crow's subtle lobbying for *The Girl Who Loved Tom Gordon*. "No girls," Lloyd had said. Crow chose Robert Parker's *Early Autumn*, then picked up several books as well—Chester Himes, Walter Mosley, Elmore Leonard's *Rum Punch*, which Lloyd seemed to find mildly intriguing after being assured it was the basis for Quentin Tarantino's *Jackie Brown*.

"That was kind of conspicuous," Edward Keyes said when they were back in Fenwick, sitting down to a lunch of warm soup and grilled cheese sandwiches, made on the hot plate in Frank's office. Crow had considered his own appetite remarkable until he watched Lloyd consume four sandwiches, three glasses of sweet tea, and most of the Utz chips in under ten minutes.

"What? Choosing Stephen King and Robert Parker? Or buying a boom box with a tape deck to play them?"

"The three of us going up to the South Coastal Library. Me getting a library card after living here almost twenty years without needing one, then helping some white kid and some black kid check out books on tape. They'll be talking about that for months, up to the library."

In Baltimore fashion he pronounced it "lie-berry." The

very sound of Edward's vowels made Crow a little home-sick.

"It's not as if anyone is looking for us," Crow said. "Not in this, um, configuration. True, the authorities are keen to find Lloyd. Maybe," he added hurriedly, noting Lloyd's pan-icky look. "But as far as everyone else is concerned, I'm down south, looking for bands to book at the Point."

"I told Spike I'd take you in, no questions asked, and I'm not asking any. I'm just making a few commonsense obser-vations. You're supposed to be laying low. What you did today—that was about as laying low as a mallard tap-dancing at the edge of a duck blind."

"Okay, so we won't go to the library again. We probably won't need to. I'm sure we'll have this sorted out in less than a week."

"No hurry," Edward said. "It's not like I'm going to run out of work for you two to do. You might not be able to paint in this breeze, but there's plenty of other stuff to do around here."

Crow had been afraid of that.

Jenkins decided to take Gabe to a restaurant where he still had some residual drag, dating back to his first tour of duty in Baltimore. McCafferty's was a Mount Washington steak house, sort of the Palm Lite, with caricatures of Baltimore celebrities hanging on its walls. "Baltimore celebrities"—now, there was a phrase that could never be used without in-voking in-the-air quotation marks. But the steaks were excellent and the location obscure, so the likelihood of being overseen or overheard was practically nil.

"What do you think?" Jenkins asked Gabe, who was studying the caricatures with what appeared to be a mix of yearning and contempt. He was a New Yorker. Well, a New

Jersey kid, but the biggest snobs often came from across the river. He probably wanted to be up on that wall, but felt sheepish about it, as if he were aiming too low.

"It's a good New York strip, although a little pinker than I normally like. Restaurants just don't believe you when you ask for medium, but it's what I prefer."

Dumb-shit. "No, I mean about the case. Is there a way we could sort of slide our way in, without actually breaking faith with the county police?"

"Oh, the case." At least the Youssef investigation excited the kid more than the food in front of him. "If you really want to take it from them, we need to press my kidnapping theory. Although we could argue that the mere fact it appears to be job-related—a federal prosecutor, probably killed on orders of a drug dealer—gives us an entrée as well."

"Yeah." Jenkins swirled the red wine in his glass, watched the legs run down the side. He had gotten very enthusiastic about wine for a while there, started learning the basics and the vocabulary, then lost interest. Dinner was going to cost him about $140, and he would have to put it on his personal card, given that none of this was authorized, although he would tell the kid it was on the government. Not that he couldn't afford it, but it seemed unfair somehow. Why shouldn't an agent be allowed to take an AUSA to a meal, no questions asked? They were talking about a case, damn it, the murder of a federal prosecutor. But it was that kind of loose thinking about his expense account that had caused Jenkins so much grief when they started gunning for him.

"Yeah," Jenkins repeated. "Thing is, I'm not so sure we want the case, officially. Not the way it is now."

"What do you mean?" Oh, the kid was a glory hound, wild for the scent.

"They're gonna drag her to the county grand jury, right? And she'll probably give in, tell them what she knows. But that's too public, too drawn out. It builds expectations—and it gives her too much power. I'd like to get to him—and I'm sure it's a him, fuck that 'he-or-she' shit—before this whole thing gets out of hand. Plus, the trail gets colder every day. She says he's out of town. With our luck he'll be in Mexico by the time she gives up the name. She could be stalling us for just that reason."

Gabe chewed thoughtfully, although not thoroughly. When he opened his mouth to speak, he still had a little steak moving around.

"But what else can we do except wait, if we're not willing to take the case away from the county cops?"

"You're a federal prosecutor."

"Yeah." Realization was dawning, but it was a slow, ponderous dawn. Jenkins preferred young men who thought a little faster on their feet, but he was stuck with this one.

"Example: Collins did a little door-to-door in her neighborhood yesterday, while we were at the interview. One guy said she had a houseguest recently, a black kid who caused all sorts of problems. I say it's the source. We figure out who his contact is, this allegedly dead guy, and I'll bet anything it's a drug dealer. That links her guest to drug dealing, and that means she had a drug dealer staying under her roof."

Jenkins turned over the palm of his right hand, gesturing Gabe to follow him. But he was still chewing his undercooked-by-his-standards steak.

"RICO statutes," Jenkins prompted. "You accuse someone of allowing drugs to be dealt from her house, you can file to seize the house, the car. Once her own assets are threatened, she won't be all Joan of Arc, will she?"

"Bit of a reach. It presumes that we can figure out who the dead contact is and that he's a drug dealer."

"Collins said he could have that name in twenty-four hours," Jenkins said. "Besides, no harm in bluffing, right?

We don't have to actually do any of this. We just have to make her think that we can. But okay, put RICO aside. We also could have her bank records in a day or two, depending on what bank she uses. So many of our old guys are in security gigs around town, they'd let you eyeball her records, probably, if we tell them the paperwork is coming."

"I'd have to go to Gail. . . ." The kid looked at once nervous and eager, wanting this opportunity, yet fearful of breaking chain of command. Jenkins would never have gotten anywhere if he thought this small. Then again, he might not have gone too far either. It had been such a shock when they came for him, especially when he realized how his colleagues gloated at his fall. Yes, he had been a little pushy and he had courted the media more than he should have. But he'd also been genuinely collegial, a good guy, friendly and helpful. He hadn't realized that small-minded types could hold even innocuous stuff against you. Pygmies. Fucking pygmies. He wondered if that was a word you were allowed to say anymore, if it was now officially insensitive. But "fuckin' little people of tribal origin" didn't have the same ring, did it?

"We don't need to involve the boss lady just yet. No authorization memo, nothing in writing. You and me, we could just go visit the chick dick at home, unofficial-like. Talk to her. Let me tell you, once you start poking around people's affairs, you always find something. If all else fails, just say IRS. Everybody cheats on his taxes."

"I don't."

"Well, yeah, of course. *We* don't." Jenkins winked at the boy over his wineglass. *He* was drinking iced tea and had seemed judgmental when Jenkins ordered alcohol with lunch.

"No, I don't. For real. I don't even itemize deductions. Without a house it's not worth it. And when my dad rigged up an illegal cable box, I told him to take it down or I'd turn him in."

"You didn't." Jenkins tried to make his tone sound admiring, but he was actually thinking, *What a stiff-necked little prick.*

Ah, well. That just made him even more perfect for the task at hand.

chapter
18

M ISS MONAGHAN?"

Tess was used to being accosted anywhere, anytime in Baltimore, her personal and professional identities
forever overlapping. Relatives crashed meetings with
clients when she was foolhardy enough to conduct her affairs in public places, while those who knew her through
her work had no qualms about confronting her during obvious downtime. Once, a disgruntled city official, unhappy
with the effect that Tess's research had on his divorce settlement, kept up a running commentary on her ethics during a screening of *Lawrence of Arabia.* He had finally been
led out of the Senator Theater by two young ushers, still
hissing invectives all the way—"Bitch! Whore! CUNT!"—
while Tess stared straight ahead, trying to lose herself in the
restored glory of Peter O'Toole's gaze.

Still, it was disconcerting to have someone address her
formally while she was naked except for Jockey underwear.

"Yes, that's me," she said, pulling on her bra and T-shirt as quickly as possible.

"I'm sorry to bother you, but you looked too, um, focused to interrupt on the gym floor. I'm Wilma Youssef."

The first irrelevant thought that crossed Tess's mind was, *But you're so blond.* Silly, she had imagined Youssef's wife more as a sister—dark-haired, dark-eyed, olive skin. The woman standing at the end of this row of lockers was a petite, blue-eyed blonde. Tess's second, still-not-on-point reaction was, *You've kept your face out of the news.* Gregory Youssef's image may have been as ubiquitous as the girl on the Utz potato chip bag, but his wife had managed to stay off camera, no small feat for a grieving widow.

Then, finally, an almost appropriate observation: What did one say to a notorious widow? What did one say to a widow who almost certainly believed that you were an obstacle in her husband's murder investigation?

"Hi," Tess said, offering her hand, once her T-shirt was in place. Mrs. Youssef declined to shake.

"I really need to talk to you, but I don't have much time. My mother-in-law spells the nanny at day's end, but I hate to impose on her longer than necessary. Can we speak in the café upstairs?"

Tess made a face. There was nothing wrong with the bar-restaurant in the Downtown Athletic Club, but gym was like church to her—a sacred place, yet not one where she wanted to linger once her ablutions were done.

"The Brass Elephant is just a few blocks away. Could we have a drink there?"

"Oh, yes. That bar you like so much."

"How do—"

The widow Youssef's smile was at once sad and superior. "We've been making quite a study of you. Do you think it's a coincidence that I'm at this particular gym at this particular hour? I don't exactly have time to work out."

Tess wasn't sure what was more unnerving—the idea that someone could so easily discern her patterns or the woman's use of the first-person plural. Who was this "we," exactly?

"I can be there in five minutes," she said. "It's not a bar that stands on formality, but it does prefer that the patrons wear something below the waist."

It wasn't clear if Wilma Youssef understood that this was a joke or if she simply didn't see the humor in anything. She gave Tess a chilly smile and nodded her assent.

"Club soda," Wilma Youssef told the bartender.

"Nursing?" asked Tess.

"Yes, but I never drank. Neither did Greg. We met through a Christian fellowship group at Cornell."

The information seemed at once pointed and defensive to Tess, but all she said was "Oh." And then to the bartender, "I'll try that weird gin drink you make, the one with peach schnapps. Maybe it will make me feel as if spring is on the way."

"We're not what people mean when they speak of the religious right," Wilma said, picking up on Tess's unvoiced skepticism. "But we were conservative by most people's standards. Didn't drink or use drugs. We also happen to believe that homosexuality is a sin. So I always knew that Greg's death was not as it appeared. Nothing could make me believe *that*."

Funny, the Christian fellowship stuff was the one piece of information to date that made the scenario *more* plausible to Tess. She wondered if Youssef's killer had known this and factored it in.

"When the story with the new information ran in the

Beacon-Light, I was so hopeful. At first. I thought it meant that Greg's killer had been found and the truth would finally come out. But now police tell me that you're determined to shield the killer."

"Not the killer. Just a—" Ever vigilant, Tess stopped herself short of using Lloyd's gender. "Just an individual who was holding a piece of the puzzle, unawares."

"Some lowlife."

"Is that part of your doctrine, too? Assigning people their value on earth?"

Nothing seemed to shake Wilma Youssef's eerie poise.

"I'm a widow with a three-month-old child. A boy who will never know his father. It's important to me that Greg's name be cleared."

"It seems to me that it has been. We still may not know who killed him, but it seems more likely now that it had something to do with his work, right?"

She chewed a piece of ice. Tess wouldn't be surprised to learn that the Widow Youssef subsisted solely on ice.

"I received something . . . unexpected," she said, once the ice cube had been crunched into oblivion beneath her small, perfect teeth.

"What?"

"I prefer not to say."

"I won't tell anyone." The woman clearly wanted to confide in someone. Perhaps she had been drawn to Tess in part because she thought Tess owed her that much. "If you know anything about me, it's that I keep my promises, that I'm willing to go to extraordinary lengths to do just that."

"I *can't* say."

"Which is it? Don't want to or can't?"

"Both. I don't know what this *thing* means. I don't want to know, because then I can say I didn't know, if someone else finds out. Greg had . . ." In Wilma's pause, Tess supplied a thousand possibilities, an array of wonderful and intriguing nouns. It was a bit of an anticlimax when Wilma Youssef finally said, "A safe-deposit box."

"So? Lots of people do."

"This one was secret, kept in a bank down in Laurel, quite a distance from where we live. I wouldn't even have known it existed if the renewal paper hadn't arrived in the mail last month. Apparently the bank doesn't even know he's dead."

"That's awful," Tess said, meaning it.

Wilma sighed. "You get used to it. Almost. The telemarketers that call and ask for Mr. Youssef—they don't even lose their place in the script when I say, 'He's dead.' They just plunge ahead, telling me about the new 'products' available on my charge cards."

Wilma Youssef was making it awfully hard to out-and-out loathe her. Her values may not have been Tess's, but her situation engendered sympathy. All the more so because she didn't seem to expect it.

"Well, if you need help getting access to it, that can be accomplished pretty quickly through probate. I know some lawyers— Well, you know some lawyers, obviously. I'm sure there are ways to expedite."

"I don't have a key."

"Still, there has to be a way—"

"I didn't come to you for legal counsel. I'm not worried about straightening out Greg's estate."

"What are you worried about?"

She gave a tiny, embarrassed shrug.

"Have you told the police about the safe-deposit box?"

"No. It's not required, not by law."

"But it could be relevant to his murder."

"I don't see how."

"Neither do I. But that's because we don't know what's in

it. And maybe it will be something silly or inconsequential. But the fact of its existence is not going to go away."

"You promised not to tell." Said swiftly, almost accusingly.

"That I did."

"We told each other everything, Greg and I. Everything. We didn't have secrets from each other."

"With all due respect, you clearly had at least one."

To Tess's horror the woman burst into tears—gusty, loud sobs that seemed all the more enormous coming from this doll-like woman. Tess and Wilma were the only customers in this part of the bar, but it was still mortifying. Luckily, her sobs ended as quickly as they came, like a summer cloudburst.

"Sorry," she said with a sniffle. "Hormones."

"Ms. Youssef—"

"You may call me Wilma."

"Wilma. That's a hell of a name to settle on a kid."

"Yes, a life of Flintstones jokes. When I found out I was having a boy, I immediately insisted that he would be called Gregory Jr."

"Anyway, Wilma"—it was hard not to give it the Fred Flintstone inflection, now that the fact had been acknowledged, but Tess resisted. "What exactly is it you want from me? To break the promise I made to someone else while keeping yours? To assure you that what I know can't have anything to do with a safe-deposit box in Laurel? Or do you want my permission to keep your secrets as I'm keeping mine?"

The woman sat quietly, her hands folded in her lap. "I want the truth, but I'm frightened."

What could Tess say? It was in the end what everyone wanted—painless truth. Problem was, she wasn't sure such a thing existed.

Wilma Youssef, however, had the damnedest ability to

squander whatever sympathy she managed to arouse. She continued, "My husband and I were good people. We worked hard. We didn't deserve this."

"The implication being that some people do deserve what happens to them."

"Well . . . yes. Yes. I'm sorry, but people who take drugs, who sell them, who live without benefit of marriage, who have children as if they're throwing litters of puppies—they bring their problems on themselves. Greg was trying to do good in the world."

"That's one way of looking at it."

"The only way of looking at it."

"No. No, not even close. Imagine being born into that world. Remember how it was said that Bush, the first one, was a guy who was born on third base and thought he'd hit a triple? Well, these kids aren't even in the ballpark and they don't have any equipment—no bats, no balls, no field. It's like they're in some weird reality show where they have to play the same game with rotted tree limbs, spoiled grape-fruits, and hundred-fifty-pound sacks of rocks tied to their backs."

Wilma's cool blue eyes were thoughtful. Shrewd, actu-ally. Tess remembered, perhaps a beat too late, that Wilma Youssef was a lawyer, too, already back in the office less than three months after her baby's birth—and less than four months after her husband's death. A tough cookie and an an-alytical one, accustomed to parsing every word.

"So the source is someone young," Wilma said. "Rela-tively. A juvenile?"

Tess waved a hand as if impatient, although her only frus-tration was with her own big mouth. She had been so strong, so taciturn in the police interview, only to natter away with Youssef's widow.

"I'm speaking in generalities."

"Sure. Of course." Wilma sipped from her water glass, her gaze downcast. Tess had a sickening feeling that she was being played.

"Is there really a safe-deposit box?"

"What? Oh. Yes, of course."

"And is that the reason you came to see me? Because you think what I know can somehow render that fact inconsequential? That whatever your husband may have hidden becomes irrelevant as long as his murder is solved before you gain access to it?"

"What could my husband possibly have to hide?"

"You tell me."

Wilma Youssef took some bills from her purse. "I really shouldn't impose on my mother-in-law. She adores Gregory Jr.—I sometimes think his birth is the only thing that kept her grief from tearing her apart—but I don't like to leave her alone too long. And it's such a trek down to Sherwood."

"What about your father-in-law?" Tess meant only to be kind. "How's he holding up?"

Wilma allowed herself another tight, mirthless smile. "Hasan has been dead for almost a decade. He was shot to death in Detroit. A robbery in the neighborhood deli that he owned, where he had done nothing but perform a thousand kindnesses to the very people who ended up killing him. So you see, my husband knew something about being born outside the ballpark, too. Perhaps you'd like to come home with me, explain to my mother-in-law your theories about the underclass and why they deserve your sympathy and protection more than her son."

It wasn't often that Tess allowed someone the last word, but Wilma Youssef had earned it. She bent over her drink, her face hot in a way that no cocktail could ever cure, no matter how light and springlike the recipe.

When she looked up again, Wilma Youssef was gone.

chapter
19

TESS NEVER PRETENDED TO GREATER STREET SMARTS THAN she had. There was strength to be gained by admitting one's weaknesses, if only because one could then compensate for them.

But even her most naïve neighbor—that would be Mrs. Gilligan, a blithe eighty-five-year-old who still slathered pinecones with peanut butter in order to bring chickadees to the evergreens outside her kitchen window—would have made the car parked outside Tess's house as a government vehicle. Boxy and nondescript, it could serve no other purpose than the transport of Very Official People on Very Official Business.

I could just keep going, Tess thought. Head to Mr. Parrish's drinking spot of choice, the Swallow at the Hollow, down a few beers, eat some fried mozzarella sticks. Wilma Youssef had put Tess over her daily limit for unplanned encounters.

Problem was, she was going so slowly that she had already been made by her men-in-waiting. There was nothing to do but suck it up and find out what they wanted.

The three men who emerged from the car struck Tess as a mismatched set, although she couldn't have said why. *One of these guys is not like the other,* as they might have sung on *Sesame Street.* It wasn't that two were white and one was black, or that two were young and one was on the far side of middle age. If anything, she would have picked the young white guy as the odd guy out. He was so filled with nervous energy that his dark, bristly hair practically danced with static. The other two seemed calm and stoic, more self-contained.

"Miss Monaghan," the manic one began, giving it a hard *g*.

"Let me guess, you're here from the government and you want to help me."

At least the older one smiled at the old joke, or pretended to.

"We want you to help us, actually," he said, stepping neatly into the role of good guy. So what was the third one's function? "If we could go inside . . ."

"IDs," she demanded. "Not business cards, but whatever official-issue stuff you've got."

She studied the two badges and plastic ID that were handed to her as if she could spot fake ones: Barry Jenkins, FBI; Mike Collins, DEA; Gabriel Dalesio, U.S. attorney.

"Quite the task force," she said. "No ATF? Customs? Postal inspectors?"

"All in good time," the old one, Jenkins, said, and although he was just playing along, Tess felt the goose-prickly chill that her mother described as someone walking over her grave.

"I don't talk without my lawyer present."

"Oh, it's not that official," Jenkins said, the epitome of avuncular. "In fact, Gabe and I watched your interview with Howard County, so in a sense we've already done the lawyer thing. This is more of a friendly conversation. A social call."

"Then I can ask you to come back when I feel more like having visitors?"

"Well, no." He smiled, ever so apologetic.

"Would you please wait here while I go inside and call my lawyer?" She unlocked the door, peeling a "We missed you" sticker from FedEx off the glass. Must be something Crow had ordered. She scrawled her name on the back, reattached it, and closed the door pointedly behind her.

They ignored her, of course, filing in behind her as if she hadn't asked them to stay outside. Tess would have done the same thing if she had their authority. The dogs inspected the men with interest. Esskay, the attention slut, showed her usual lack of discrimination. Miata, however, reared back when Collins reached out to scratch her behind the ears. Great, her dog was acting like a racist.

"Back up, guys—I mean the dogs. Although, well . . ." She hustled the dogs into the kitchen, where she dialed Tyner from behind the closed door. No answer at home or office, and he didn't pick up his cell. Damn his unending honeymoon bliss with Kitty. He was probably feeding her raw oysters at Charleston, or sharing the gingerbread with lemon chiffon sauce at Bicycle. She left messages at all the numbers—his office, his cell, Kitty's business, Kitty's cell, their home above the bookstore—but if Tyner and Kitty were having a romantic evening out, voice mail wouldn't be his first priority upon arriving home.

Desperate, she dialed one last number. "Get here *now*," she hissed, allowing no greeting, offering no explanation. She then returned to the living room, where the three men were inspecting her home décor in such a way that the most innocuous items now seemed sinister, redolent of meaning—the Mission-style furniture, the small legal bookcase filled with Crow's most precious books, not rare titles per se, but ones he prized highly nonetheless: *The Hitchhiker's Guide to the Galaxy, Confessions of a Mask, Don Quixote, Tally's Corner.* Determined not to betray her own persona, she turned on a neon sign that Crow had given her for Christmas a few years back, the one that proclaimed HUMAN HAIR in bright red letters.

"Can I get you anything?" she asked, as if she were vapid enough to confuse this with a social call. "Water, beer, wine, crackers, cheese, raisins, nuts—"

Jenkins raised his hand, uninterested in the contents of Tess's pantry. "That won't be necessary. We just need to talk to you, unofficial-like."

"I really don't want to talk without a lawyer here."

"We could take you downtown, wait for your lawyer to meet us there. If it's going to be like that, we might as well go all the way, right?"

His tone was friendly as ever, his manner casual, but Tess didn't miss the implicit threat in his words. She took a seat at the head of her dining room table, and the men followed her lead. Perhaps she could bluff her way through this, speaking without saying anything.

"We just want to impress upon you how important it is that you tell us *now*, without further delay, who your source is."

"And where he is," put in Collins, the DEA agent. Why DEA? That was still troubling her.

"I can't answer those questions."

"You mean you won't."

"Okay, to be precise, I won't answer the first, but I can't answer the second."

"You told Howard County police that he left town."

"He or she. That's my understanding, yes. I haven't spoken to the source directly, however. In fact, I haven't had any contact with the source since I arranged the meeting with the *Beacon-Light* reporters a week ago."

"Tell us this," said the prosecutor, Dalesio, the one who struck Tess as the odd man out. "Was your source a number-one male?"

Tess actually understood the police jargon, although it seemed strange for a federal prosecutor to speak as if he were on police radio.

"A black man," Jenkins supplied when she didn't answer right away. "African-American."

"I'm not going to answer that question."

"Why not?"

"I'm not going to provide any identifying information. And I want to point out that I still haven't assigned a gender to the source. You may use 'he' and 'him' if you like, but I'm not going to do that."

Jenkins rested his hands on his belly in the manner of a beloved uncle settling in after a particularly satisfying Thanksgiving meal. "African-American, that's not exactly a big clue in a city that's sixty-six percent black—and where ninety percent of the homicide victims are black men."

Tess raised an eyebrow. She was conscious of what she was doing—by refusing to give the expected answer, she was making them consider the possibility that the source was white, throwing them off the trail. The main thing was not to say anything untrue, no matter how trivial. That required a lot of self-control for Tess, who was used to lying in work situations.

"So if the source *isn't* a black man," Jenkins continued, his voice a calm and easygoing drone, "then we can rule out that he's the young man who was staying at your home last week."

Any sense of control she had vanished.

"Collins here canvassed your neighborhood yesterday, asked some questions about you. Your neighbors find you a, uh, colorful personality. Your comings and goings attract more attention than you might realize."

This was news to Tess, who thought she had successfully disappeared into this leafy, quiet neighborhood, taking on the camouflage of seminormalcy, just another working gal. Oh, sure, there were her dogs, especially Esskay, who was notorious for trying to eat the smaller dogs in Stony Run Park, mistaking them for squirrels and rabbits. And Crow, with his handsome face and exuberant personality, was much beloved by the not-so-desperate housewives who swapped recipes with him at the local coffeehouse. There was the time she had come home to find an intruder in the house and had ended up crawling across the yard on her belly, skirt up to her hips, gun in hand. But even this had seemed all so Anne Tyler idiosyncratic, the kind of gentle lunacy on which North Baltimoreans prided themselves. Certainly she was no more notable than Mr. Parrish, with his nightly drunken coasts.

Mr. Parrish. Fuck. And the police report on the incident. What was that fake name that Crow had given?

"Bob Smith," the prosecutor read from a photocopy. "Believed to be age sixteen, of 400 Battery Avenue, an address that would put him in the middle of the harbor. Is Bob Smith the correct name for the young man who was staying with you?"

"If it's the name in the report, then it's the name my boyfriend gave the police. He's the one who brought the kid home."

"Yes, and given that the police decided that fault couldn't

be ascertained in the accident and left it to the insurance companies to untangle, they probably don't care if the name is correct or not. But we do. Is this the name of the young man who stayed with you, Miss Monaghan? And is this young man the source you're protecting?"

There's no time limit, she reminded herself, no penalty for not speaking immediately. *Think this through, anticipate where they're going.*

"I should probably have my lawyer with me," she ventured.

"As I said, we can go downtown to wait for him."

She should do that. But she was tired and hungry, two factors on which they were clearly banking, and she didn't want to sit in some uncomfortable chair all evening, waiting for Tyner to return home. The opera, she remembered. He and Kitty had season tickets. Box seats—hardly an indulgence for a man in a wheelchair. She imagined them holding hands, lost in some nineteenth-century melodrama while she was caught up in this twenty-first-century one.

"I can't lie to you," she said, her voice sorrowful.

Jenkins nodded in kind empathy, while the younger men just stared at her, sharp and impatient.

"I can't lie to you—because it's a federal crime to lie to you. If there was anything for the average American to glean from the exhaustive coverage of the Martha Stewart case, it's that it's against the law to lie to federal investigators. So I can't lie to you. I just *won't* answer that question, if that's okay."

Jenkins's smile vanished. "This is your source," he said, pointing to the photocopy of the police report. "This is your source, and your boyfriend made a false statement to a police officer, and *he* can be prosecuted for that."

Tess said nothing, focusing all her energy on remaining

impassive. It took an amazing amount of effort, but she imagined herself as the Sphinx. Of course, Oedipus had defeated the Sphinx, but these three men didn't appear to be anointed by destiny.

"We can't find Bob Smith at his nonexistent address on Battery Avenue. But we did find a Bob Smith in the database of people who have been convicted of drug crimes. Can we assume that's your Bob Smith?"

Sphinx. Sphinx, sphinx, sphinx. The word repeated in her head like a key on a tinny piano, pressed over and over again, or a drip from a faucet. *Sphinx, sphinx, sphinx. Plink, plink, plink.*

"Okay, we're going to assume that it is. And given that Mr. Smith has served time for distribution-related charges, we're going to assume that you're working with him. And given that Mr. Smith had permission to use your vehicles, we can seize those, along with your personal and professional accounts. To keep that from happening, all you have to do is set the record straight and tell us who stayed at your house last week. Once we establish that your Bob Smith is not the convicted drug dealer, we won't have to pursue these charges against you."

Tess did not doubt that they could do everything they said they could. But she was reasonably certain they could not do it this very minute and that they were not prepared to charge her with anything. If they were, they would have taken her downtown at the outset. They were bullies and bluffers—for now. They were trying to do an end run around the grand jury proceedings, bigfoot the case on the sly, and grab all the glory for themselves.

"What's the DOB on your Bob Smith?" she asked on a hunch.

"January thirtieth, 1969," the prosecutor said swiftly, one

of those bright boys who can't resist giving an answer he knows, even as the older man frowned at him.

"Well, as you said, you're looking for a teenager."

"Enough," said Jenkins. "Tell us the name of the boy who stayed here. You'll regret it if you don't, Miss Monaghan. I'm sure you think you're being noble, but your loyalties are misplaced."

"I can't continue this conversation without my lawyer," she said, much the way a polite child might say, *The brussels sprouts look delicious, but I happen to be full.*

It was the kind of moment that actually deserves to be called pregnant, a full and bursting moment in which it was clear that something was about to happen, but not what or how.

Then Whitney Talbot arrived.

"I was at Video Americain, so I grabbed a movie from the recommended shelf—*Funny Bones*, have you seen it? I thought we could order in from the Ambassador. Oh, and I picked up red wine and beer at Alonso's, because Indian food is so hit-and-miss in terms of beverages, and I don't trust your taste in wine." She turned to the agents and rolled her eyes. "She *still* likes merlot."

It was always interesting watching someone meet Whitney for the first time, trying to take in what would have been a sedate, preppy prettiness if she were ever quiet for more than twenty seconds. She made an especially striking impression tonight, dressed in ratty sweats that appeared to date from their college days. Tess must have caught her as she headed home from doing erg pieces at the boathouse.

It was also interesting to see how quickly Whitney could size up a situation. Her own breathless monologue finished, she regarded the three suited men in Tess's dining room, dropped the alcohol and videos on the table, then disappeared into the kitchen and began noisily gathering plates and glasses as if nothing unusual had happened. After pointedly setting two places at the table, she headed into Tess's office, where she could be heard noisily punching the buttons on the phone and demanding Indian food. All for show, Tess assumed. The Ambassador didn't deliver.

"Where is your boyfriend, Miss Monaghan?" Jenkins asked.

"I don't know exactly."

"Is that the truth?"

"He told me he was scouting bands for the club where he works."

"He *told* you—interesting choice of words. It almost sounds as if you don't quite believe him."

"They've had a lot of off-and-on moments, those two," Whitney said, coming back into the living room with Tess's digital camera. "Tess, did you forget your ritual?"

"Ritual?"

"Taking everyone's photograph when they cross your threshold. You know, like John Waters does." The local film director did in fact take Polaroids of everyone who entered his home, an obsession he had detailed for several magazines. Whitney quickly shot three photographs of the visitors, not giving them time to protest, then handed the camera to Tess. "Me, too. Remember, you shoot me every time."

Tess followed her instructions, not sure what Whitney was up to, but confident there was, as always, a plan.

"There's only going to be enough food for two," Whitney said, her voice den-mother brisk, her hands on her barely existent hips. She looked as if she were about to start a rousing game of I'm a Little Teapot. "So unless you want to watch us eat—"

"I didn't get your name."

"Whitney Talbot."

"As in the county?"

"As in the *congressman*," she said. "The one they named the bridge after, on the upper shore? A Republican, but a moderate one in the Maryland tradition. Well, the old tradition. Life is so partisan now. We love Uncle Deucie dearly."

"Uncle Deucie?"

"Trevor Sims Talbot Jr. The second. Therefore, Deuce. Therefore, Deucie."

The three men exchanged a look, and the older one jerked his chin upward, indicating they should leave. It wasn't Whitney's name-dropping that had done the trick, Tess was sure of that much. Whitney's uncle was the kind of gentlemanly pol who had gone out of style in these more strident times, and it was doubtful he had any clout in Washington. No, it was the sheer fact of Whitney's presence, which was what Tess had counted on when she summoned her. They didn't want a witness to this interview, however unofficial, especially someone like Whitney, whose remarkable confidence made her difficult to scare or cow. She was simply too much of a variable to control for.

"Enjoy your dinner," Jenkins said. "We'll get back to you."

Whitney and Tess did not speak again until they heard the car's engine turn over, the crunch of gravel, the disappearing whine of the motor. They sat at the table in silence, poured themselves red wine and sipped—contemplatively in Whitney's case, numbly in Tess's. Minutes later another car pulled up, and Tess tensed, but it turned out to be the Ambassador. Whitney had somehow cajoled them into making this one-time-only delivery. Lamb saag, savory meat samosas—it should have been great comfort food, but Tess was beyond being comforted.

"Project Zeus?" Whitney asked when they were alone again, using the code they had agreed on when Tess realized that Whitney also could be pressured to provide Lloyd's name if anyone guessed her part in this whole affair. Other friends might have used an astronomical reference, but this Roman-to-Greek transposition of Lloyd's surname was a natural for two former English majors.

"Yeah. Feds."

"Shit."

"What was that thing with the photos?"

"I couldn't be sure who they were. If they weren't official, they would have balked, right? Besides, it freaks people out when you pull a camera on them. When you call me like that, I know it's because you're trying to fuck with someone. I was just doing my part."

Tess raised her glass to her friend. "You did beautifully."

"So what do they want? I mean, I know what they want, but why are the feds stepping in? They were content to let Howard County have this investigation when it was a gay pickup gone wrong."

"I guess there's glory in it now, avenging a fallen colleague whose death may have something to do with the drug cases he prosecuted. I don't want to think about it, much less talk about it. Let's hope this movie you brought over is good for a few laughs."

Funny Bones was good for quite a few laughs, although not quite in the straightforward way the title had seemed to promise. Things went unexplained—Oliver Reed and those strange eggs—and there was a moment in which everything literally hung in the balance. It was, in fact, one of the few films that Tess had ever seen in which she could not predict the tenor of the ending, could not figure out if she was watching a comedy or a tragedy.

It made for an admirable quality in a movie, she decided, but an unnerving situation in one's own life.

Friday

chapter
20

GABE DIDN'T HAVE A PHOTOGRAPHIC MEMORY, ALTHOUGH he had a good one. Gabe's talent was that he *knew* paper, as if it were a language unto itself, an unmapped country. Gabe was good at paper even when it wasn't paper, when it was just a facsimile of a document captured in a computer screen. If files and forms were women, Gabe would have been the Casanova of his time. In fact, if Gabe had been content to play to his greatest strength, he would be a forensic accountant, being summoned to testify as an expert witness in corporate scandals.

But Gabe had disliked the idea of life on the sidelines, waiting for things to happen. That wasn't how he saw himself. So he had chosen the prosecutorial track, hoping that his knack for paper, for details, would pay off.

Finally it had.

"Barry told me that you expect to get a subpoena soon," said the point guy at the bank, a former fed, just as Jenkins had predicted. "Until then we can't give you copies. And, technically, you shouldn't even take notes, so I'll pat you down for pad and paper."

He waved his hands in front of Gabe, maintaining three feet of space between them. "Nope, I don't feel anything. Anyway, enjoy yourself."

The files were so straightforward that Gabe didn't really need to take notes. Tess Monaghan maintained only two accounts at the bank, one personal, one corporate, both small. There were bumps of incoming cash here and there, but in amounts that jibed with the nature of her business.

But not for a while, he noticed. She was living pretty close to the margins these past few months. Interesting, but not necessarily of use. In fact, kind of the opposite. He wanted to find some big, mysterious sum, something that he could say looked like it had come from a drug dealer or an individual otherwise involved in a criminal enterprise. But this was just, well, pathetic. He wondered how she could afford that house up in Roland Park. According to the property-tax records he had checked this morning, she had bought it at a bargain price, $175,000. Even accounting for Baltimore's overheated real-estate market and the fact that it was probably a falling-down wreck when she acquired it, that was a suspiciously good deal. City rolls had it assessed at $275,000 for tax purposes, and that was low, based on his quick eyeballing of the place. She had probably made some of the improvements on the sly. Great, he could get the city to fine her for not pulling the proper permits. Yeah, that would scare her. Given her father's juice as a former liquor-board inspector, she probably had the city types eating out of her hand.

The father—that was another lead. Gabe called up Patrick Monaghan's records, but the old man didn't keep the corporate account at this bank, just the personal ones. Wait, here was some overlap—a check from daughter to father, for $7,000, made out last fall after she had a fairly respectable deposit in her business account, which she then transferred to her personal account. Like a lot of self-employed types, she didn't appear to pay herself a salary per se, just transferred a regular amount to her personal checking every month. Anyway, the father was still worth pursuing. All relatives were good. Even the toughest targets got upset when you started dragging family members into things.

Which brought him to the boyfriend. Gabe pulled out his pad to remind him of the full name—Edward "Crow" Ransome IV. Sounded like some inbred preppie to Gabe, the kind of guy that he had loathed in law school. The type who didn't study, didn't sweat making law review because he had a soft place to land at Daddy or Granddaddy's firm. Barry's preliminary inquiry had established that Ransome kept a brokerage account, but he had his checking at this bank, too. God bless consolidation. Five years ago they might all have been at different places, but there were fewer and fewer banks these days.

Fuck. He did a double take, counted the zeros again. Oh, this was rich, pun intended. This was fascinating. He should check into this further. No—back up, rethink. He didn't need to know any more about this, not yet. He just had to be there to see the girlfriend's face when she was asked how much she knew about her boyfriend's finances. Gabe had seen how they lived, what they drove, what they owned, and it didn't correlate with this kind of dough-re-mi.

It was going to be sweet, lobbing this little grenade at that self-satisfied bitch.

The last thing Tess felt like doing on Friday was starting a new job, but there it was on her calendar, indifferent to her red-wine hangover and generally jittery state. It wasn't even supposed to be her gig; Crow had agreed to do the under-cover work on this one, which would have come much more naturally to him. In fact, it was one of Crow's do-gooding buddies who had hired her. A board member of a local non-profit had asked Tess to investigate its "public face"—an up-from-welfare success story who had effectively branded the charity with her name and image. Ellen Mars was the char-ity, the charity was Ellen Mars. She was a beloved figure, an inspirational role model—and the world's shoddiest book-keeper, putting the organization at risk for an IRS audit. In-competent or crook, that was the question bedeviling the board member, who didn't dare pursue the inquiry openly. He had asked Tess to volunteer for the organization on a part-time basis. It had been her plan to send Crow in her stead—he was the philanthropist, after all, and would arouse far less suspicion. He also had some context for how a char-ity should be run, given his work recycling leftovers. But Crow was gone and the client was anxious, so Tess got up Friday morning and reported for her afternoon shift at the Ellen Mars West Side Helping Hand.

As soon as she turned off her block, she saw a familiar car idling at the small traffic island on Oakdale, not far from where Mr. Parrish had collided with Lloyd—and Tess's life. The beige sedan followed her, not even bothering to lag back or disguise its intentions. Mike Collins was at the wheel, Barry Jenkins in the seat beside him. Tess gave them a little wave in the rearview mirror, but they didn't acknowledge her in any way. That made it creepier somehow. They were following her yet refusing to concede the fact that she ex-isted, that she was another person on the planet. Tess wanted it to be like the cartoon with the sheepdog and the wolf punching in and out at the time clock. Just a job, nothing personal. But these guys seemed to feel it was extremely personal. She wondered if they had known Youssef, worked with him. How would she feel if she believed that someone was obstructing the investigation into a colleague's death?

Then again, how would she feel if she turned Lloyd over to them and he was charged with a murder he clearly didn't commit or was killed by those keen to obscure their own involvement? If only they could make an arrest without Lloyd. They knew everything that Lloyd knew. Why wasn't that enough? After her second missed stop sign, she reminded herself that she needed to look at the road in front of her, not the car behind her.

A half-dozen volunteers had gathered at the West Side rowhouse that served as Ellen Mars's headquarters, all first-timers, an excellent setup for Tess's intentions, although it gave her a pang to realize how easily she blended with these middle-aged North Side types in their embroidered sweaters and pressed jeans. Ellen Mars was nowhere to be seen, but a younger woman who bore a strong resemblance to the eponymous founder came in and began assigning jobs—someone to sort the donated clothing for the women's shelter, someone to inventory the foodstuffs that had come in the day before, someone to open the mail, helping record the checks and cash—

"I could do that," Tess said. "I was an accounting major in college."

The woman—she had yet to introduce herself—led Tess to a beyond-cluttered desk behind the kitchen. Tess couldn't help notice how ratty the little rowhouse was. Upkeep was difficult on those old places, which hadn't been built with the expectation of lasting for centuries. But this place was simply unclean. She watched a roach meandering along the baseboard. It was headed, no doubt, for the food-encrusted dishes in the sink.

"Bills here," the woman said, placing her hand on one stack. "Other correspondence here." She indicated a stack of similar size. "You write down our obligations in one column and the day's incoming receipts on the other."

"Write them . . . ?" Tess opened her empty hands, bereft of pen, bereft of paper.

The woman dug around in the desk's drawers, unearthing a legal pad and pencil.

"I didn't get your name," Tess said.

"Phoebe. I'm Ellen's sister."

"Is Ellen here?"

"She's in Annapolis for Ellen Mars Appreciation Day."

"I'd think you'd want to be there."

"Chil', if I went to every ceremony honoring Ellen, I'd never get anything done. If it ain't the White House or the queen of England, I can't see taking the time. Okay, Verizon— we owe nine hundred and fifty dollars."

"How can the phone bill be that large?" Tess, almost forgetting her role, was on the verge of advising Phoebe that Verizon had packages with limitless long distance for as little as seventy-five dollars a month, and there were probably better deals still.

"It's three months past due. Plus, Dwayne—that's my cousin—met some woman on the Internet, ran up a bill. Turns out she lives in Poland. Or maybe it was Prague. One of those *P* places."

"So it's a personal expense."

"No, he used the phone right here."

Tess started to object, then remembered this was the kind of information she was here to gather. Apparently Ellen Mars didn't recognize any division between Ellen Mars the nonprofit and Ellen Mars and family. Within thirty minutes Tess had a neat column of numbers, showing almost three thousand in obligations for the organization, with most of the bills marked as second or third notices, and an incoming haul of eighteen hundred dollars. It had been almost touching to see the small checks and creased bills that made up that amount. Some people sent in as little as five dollars, often with handwritten notes.

"Is this a typical day?" Tess asked Phoebe, who hovered close, snatching and examining each check as it emerged, recoiling from the bills.

"Oh, it gets slow toward spring and summer. 'Round Thanksgiving we start bringing in real money."

Tess began doing the math in her head. Assuming, conservatively, that Ellen Mars West Side Helping Hand brought in seventy-five hundred a week on average, times fifty-two—that was almost four hundred thousand a year. Yet the board member who hired her said there were no salaried employees. And there didn't seem to be much money spent on the headquarters, so— Phoebe's sharp scream interrupted her thoughts.

"Police!" she said, and Tess thought she was calling for them, but she was simply identifying them, after a fashion. Mike Collins stood on the other side of the barred window above the desk, looking in at them. When Phoebe jumped and started, he gave her a wave and then pointed to Tess, effectively miming, *Don't worry, it's her that we're interested in.*

"You got troubles?" Phoebe demanded.

"N-n-not exactly," Tess said.

"But he's police, right? Black man in a suit, gun on his hip—in this neighborhood he better be police."

"Well, DEA. But he's just . . . keeping an eye on me. It's not what you think."

"Honey, we can't have that."

"But—"

"No *thank* you. I don't know what's going on in your life, but we don't need that around here. Thank you for coming in. You're a good worker, and we'd welcome you back any day. But not your friend."

Furious and embarrassed, Tess left. Her client's suspicions were clearly justified, but what should have been a nice leisurely gig, with steady hours mounting up every week, had just been ruined. She'd have to wait for Crow to come back, and when would that be? For a moment she tried to persuade herself that she was no longer obligated to keep her promise to Lloyd. She hadn't bargained for the disruption it was causing to her life.

Then again, Lloyd hadn't bargained on his friend's being killed. Neither one of them had known what they were getting into, and now they were both stuck. Tess remembered a Yiddish folktale that she had heard when she was in court-ordered therapy. Her therapist was big on Yiddish folktales. He told her of a woman who set out on a journey that she had long intended. On a bridge a man handed her a rope, told her not to let go, and then jumped over. If she left him, he would die. The woman had to see that the man's choices were not hers and that she was not obliged to stand there and hold the rope.

Tess had always assumed she was the woman in that scenario, but now she was beginning to think she was the man. She had handed the rope to Lloyd, and he had walked away without a qualm. Or would it be the other way around, if she gave him up?

She started up her car and began to head home, then thought better of it. The sky was overcast, but the promise of spring was in the air. Why not take a little drive? Drawing on a knowledge of Baltimore's streets that is unique to firefighters, patrol cops, and former reporters, she made her peripatetic way through the city, stopping as the mood struck her. She went to Louise's Bakery for chocolate drop cookies and a loaf of stale bread, which she then distributed to the geese and ducks along the banks of the Gwynn's Falls. And everywhere that Tess went, her little lambs were sure to follow. She headed back downtown, ducked into the parking garage beneath the Gallery shops—then shot right back out on the other side. The maneuver gained her only a minute, but a minute was enough to lose them in downtown traffic, a victory in principle. They would be there tomorrow and the next day and the day after. But, for today, she was triumphant.

Her victory proved to be even shorter-lived than she had thought. She and the dogs were coming back from a longer-than-usual evening walk when she saw Collins on her front porch. She tried, for one valiantly optimistic moment, to imagine a piece of good news that had brought him here. He was working for Publishers Clearing House in his off-hours. She had been recognized as a point of light. No, that was a previous administration. Perhaps it was all a mistake and the federal government wanted to apologize for its treatment of her.

But she didn't think the federal government did apologies. Waco, Ruby Ridge, WMDs. No, not their forte.

"Mike Collins, DEA," he said, as if they had never met.

"I remember," she began as Esskay lunged forward, her nose jabbing into Collins's crotch. Miata, however, held her ground and semigrowled. It was more throat clearing then menace, a sound indicating that Miata could be trouble if she deemed it necessary. Jesus, what had the Doberman's previous owner done to create this knee-jerk racism in a dog?

"We'd like to talk to you downtown."

"Didn't we just go through this yesterday?"

"New info."

"What?"

"Downtown," he said.

"I'll need my—"

"Lawyer. That's fine."

"May I tell him what this is about?"

"They'll tell you both together."

"Are you going back to the idea that I sheltered a drug dealer and you can use that to begin forfeiture on my house and car? Because—"

"Downtown." If his voice had any inflection to it, he could have been Petula Clark.

"May I change?" She indicated her sweats, streaked with mud. The dogs had decided it was a good idea to ford the creek, in search of quarry that turned out to be a falling leaf.

"No."

"*No?*"

"No."

"I need to call someone about the dogs—"

"Your *boyfriend*?"

Something about the question—an underlying keenness, a just-perceptible sharpening in Collins's tone—made Tess uneasy.

"No, the kid who takes care of my dogs when I'm not around. Am I coming home tonight?"

He shrugged. "Remains to be seen."

"Then you should let me change."

"Look—" He took a step toward her, and Miata produced a full-throated snarl. Tess was touched by the Doberman's devotion but doubtful that it would help her, in the long run, for Miata to bite a DEA agent.

"Let me put the dogs away, call my sitter, and change into jeans, okay? It's not like I'm going to pull a Goldilocks, jump out a window. I'm not under arrest, right?"

"Not yet."

Tess studied his face, hoping for a wisp of a smile, the tiniest crack in the stony façade. The FBI agent, Jenkins, had seemed human at least, and there had been a blustery quality to the young prosecutor that allowed Tess to believe she could outwit him. Collins, however, made her feel like growling, too, if only because she sensed he was enjoying himself a little too much.

"I'm going inside. Don't follow, okay? Stay on the porch. My dog doesn't like you, for whatever reason, and with Crow gone, she's super protective of me. I can't guarantee your safety if you follow me inside."

"I guess she hasn't seen a lot of brothers in this neighborhood."

"Brothers?" The word sounded strange in Collins's mouth, which was funny. Usually it was only white people who sounded ridiculous aping street slang. "Oh, well, I mean, she's seen—"

She caught the name, just, before it teetered off her tongue. She had been about to say, *She's seen Lloyd, and come to think of it, she didn't like him much either.*

"She's seen . . . ?"

"A lot," Tess said flatly. "Her former owner was very badly beaten when Miata wasn't there to protect him. That's why she's so territorial."

"I'm not worried. If the dog comes at me, I can always shoot her."

"Is that your idea of a joke?" His noncommittal shrug didn't fill her with confidence. "Just stay here, okay?"

She opened the storm door, stumbling in her haste over a FedEx package that had been left there. She scooped it up and ran inside, shutting and locking the door behind her. Moving quickly, she did all she said she would do, then tried to think if there was anything else to be accomplished before surrendering. Her eyes fell on the package, which she had thrown aside. It had been shipped from Denton, Maryland, and the sender was listed as E. A. Poe of Greene and Russell streets. Crow had been named for the poet and storyteller, and he knew that Tess was familiar with Poe's final resting place at that downtown intersection. Inside was a cell phone, and when she powered it up, there was already a message.

"Use this phone for seventy-two hours," Crow's voice said in her ear, and she almost wept at the familiar sound. "Then a new one will arrive. That way, even if they put a trace on your known numbers, they can't track these calls to a cellular tower and figure out where I am. We're okay. We're safe. I've been trying to persuade Lloyd to come back on his own and cooperate, but he's just not ready yet. If I bring him back now, I think all he'll do is run."

Collins began rapping on the front door. It was a hard yet matter-of-fact knock, dull, steady, and utterly unnerving. Miata barked and snarled, while the usually silent Esskay gave a high yodel, almost as if in pain. Tess shoved the "safe" phone in the laundry hamper, below some truly disgusting workout clothes that should keep anyone but the most determined searcher at bay. It wouldn't matter if they came back with a warrant, but it was all she could do for now.

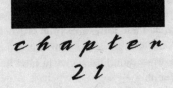

chapter
21

"WHEN I WAS GROWING UP, IF WE WANTED A JACUZZI, WE had to fart in the bathtub."

"*Trading Places*," Crow said. "That movie was made before you were born, Lloyd. I'm surprised you know it."

Lloyd shrugged, leaned back in the small hot tub. "It was on all the time when I was little. It's still on all the time. There's, like, a million movies in the world, but on television it's always *Trading Places, Die Hard,* and *Pretty Woman.*"

The two were soothing their sore muscles at the Clarion, a beachfront hotel south of the Delaware-Maryland line. Ed had long ago arranged a swap of sorts with the hotel's manager, giving him free passes to FunWorld in exchange for offseason privileges at this small exercise room, with its indoor pool, its hot tub, and a few ancient exercise machines. A gym snob such as Tess would have been appalled by the antiqueness of it all, but it was a fine place to soak at day's

end. Ed told the manager that Crow and Lloyd were his
workers, and that was the simple truth, after all. They had
put in two days of scraping and painting now. When they
weren't painting, they were applying oil to the dried-out
hinges on the ten garage doors that ringed the amusement
park. The merry-go-round horses were next in line, waiting
to be reunited with their poles.

On the first day of April, the pool area was empty, with
not even a lifeguard on duty. But then this whole part of the
world felt empty this time of the year. It was pleasant, Crow
thought. He wouldn't mind living here, September through
May, where the loudest noise was the ocean and there
seemed to be more room in the sky for the light, pale and
diffuse. But Tess could never leave Baltimore for more than
an extended vacation.

Lloyd looked over at the pool, which had a slide at the
shallow end. "I knew they had big water slides, but I didn't
know they had little ones."

"You like to go to water parks?"

He shook his head. "Been to Great America and seen the
wave pool, but I got no use for that."

"Do you know how to swim, Lloyd?"

He gave an elaborate shrug, as if to suggest that swimming was esoteric or exotic. Crow might as well have asked
him if he took ballet lessons or made sushi at home.

"You want to learn?"

"Naw."

"Why not?"

Lloyd shook his head again, as if Crow were being will-
fully igorant.

"I could teach you."

"Uh-huh."

"You know, that's a stereotype."

"What?"

"African-Americans and swimming."

"Ain't my fault." Said quickly, defensively, as if Lloyd were used to being blamed for all sorts of things that weren't his fault.

"But you could challenge it. Upend it."

Lloyd continued to shake his head, uninterested.

"What if knowing how to swim could save your life?"

"How that gonna happen? Flood gonna come down Monument Street one day?"

Even here, more than a hundred miles from East Baltimore, Lloyd still couldn't imagine a life beyond a small nexus of streets.

"You're not on Monument Street now. You're sitting a couple hundred yards from an ocean. And it was only a few months ago that an entire ocean rose up and killed almost two hundred thousand people."

"I don't remember nothin' about how the people died because they didn't know how to swim."

Crow laughed. "You've got me there. There are some situations you can't prepare for."

Lloyd nodded wearily, as if Crow had just realized something that Lloyd had been born knowing.

"When we get to go back?"

"You tell me. We can go back anytime you agree to talk to the police."

"Uh-huh. That's gonna get me killed."

"And going back without talking to the police might get you killed, too. So what's it going to be?"

"I'm so bored." He tilted his head back against the lip of the Jacuzzi, stared at the ceiling.

"So you want to go back?"

"I don't know. Maybe. If I could just go to a club or something, get out for a night."

"No clubs around here, Lloyd. And we can't go back to

Baltimore just to go clubbing. We could go to the movies, though."

"Seen all that shit at the Sun 'n' Surf."

"Maybe we could find some decent paperbacks at the bookstore up in Bethany Beach."

Lloyd rolled his eyes. "Man, we *listen* to books all day. Do we have to read 'em at night, too?"

"Ed said he might finish blowing out the bumper-car machines with the air hose today."

"He saves all the good jobs for himself," Lloyd grumbled. "He gets to stay inside, out of the wind, tinker with shit, while we just paint and scrape, scrape and paint."

"You're missing the bigger picture, Lloyd. Once the bumper cars are up and running, Ed will need to do some test drives."

"Now, that," Lloyd said, "is something I could do."

Given Lloyd's experience behind the wheel of the Volvo, Crow somehow doubted that. Then again—no stick shifts on bumper cars. Maybe Lloyd would do better.

"Your finances look pretty shaky," Gabe Dalesio informed Tess an hour later. She was in an office in the federal courthouse, not an official interrogation room, but that didn't comfort her.

"It's been a thin few months, but things are turning around. I started an excellent job today—although you guys pretty much ruined it for me. And the *Beacon-Light* owes me quite a bit of money."

"They paid for you to turn over that source? I didn't think legitimate newspapers played that way."

"I did a seminar on investigative techniques. The two things aren't related." *Not directly.*

"You were asked to teach their reporters how to report? You think they would have picked someone more successful."

Tess supposed that Gabe thought this would hurt her feelings. She simply looked away, not even bothering to shrug.

"It's been established," Tyner said, "that my client doesn't have a lot of cash in her accounts. Is that a federal crime now? Is federal enforcement going to be part of the overhaul of Social Security, with citizens being rounded up if they're not putting away enough for retirement?"

"It's just I don't get why she's carrying her boyfriend and all. Why doesn't he pitch in?"

"He does what he can. The house is in my name, so I pay the mortgage, and that's how I want it. But we split everything else."

"That's big of him, going dutch when he's sitting on almost a hundred fifty thousand in his checking account."

Tess didn't have to fake her laugh at the bluff. "Don't be ridiculous. Crow doesn't have that kind of money."

Jenkins didn't literally elbow the young prosecutor aside, but he did square his shoulders back, signaling that the interview was now his. "According to bank records, he deposited that amount in his account on Tuesday, right before his . . . um, road trip. That was what you told us, wasn't it? That he went out of town for business?"

Again she had to tell the truth without telling too much. "He's out of town, and I don't know where he is."

"Have you spoken to him?"

"No." *Listened to his voice mail less than an hour ago, but not spoken to him.*

"Heard from him?"

"He left a message, said he was safe."

"Safe?" Shit. "Unusual choice of words, don't you think? Why wouldn't he be safe?"

"It's what he said. I didn't think about it."

"Safe," Jenkins repeated. "Safe. Is it dangerous, what he does?"

"I don't really know."

"Of course, he's got five thousand in cash on him, so maybe that's why he's worried. See, the deposit was for a hundred and fifty K, less five thousand."

Five thousand? Five thousand dollars? Crow didn't have enough money to fix the muffler on his Volvo.

"You and your boyfriend ever use illegal drugs?"

Tess glanced at Tyner. "She doesn't have to answer that question. Self-incrimination."

"Okay, your boyfriend ever use illegal drugs?"

Tess sat, stony-faced.

"Your boyfriend *dealing* in illegal drugs? Because I have to tell you, that's the only thing that makes sense. The cash, the road trip. I bet he deals out of your daddy's bar. Lord knows that business needs all the help it can get, too."

"He would never do that."

"How can you be so sure?"

"I know him."

"Yet you didn't know he had all this money."

"I never said that."

"Did you? Did you know?"

Again there was the not-lying problem. The federal rules seemed so unsporting. "His parents are very well-to-do."

"I guess we'll have to put them on our list."

"List?" She hated the way her voice squeaked, making the word two syllables.

"Yeah. We've already started checking into your finances, your father's. I mean, when there's a drug dealer in the family, who knows how far it goes?"

"You keep saying that as if you've established the fact." Tyner spoke, as Tess was having trouble with complete sentences. "I know the young man. He is *not* a drug dealer."

"We think he is."

"Based on?"

"Information that we've gathered."

Tess's mind felt as if it might split in two. One part was stuck on this stupid accusation, trying to shoo it away, but wondering maybe, what if, did he . . . ? The other part was trying to be heard over these shrill fears, signaling to her urgently. *You can't lie to them, but / You can't lie to them, but / You can't lie to them, but . . .*

They can lie to you.

"It's illegal for me to tell you anything that I know to be untrue, right?"

"Yes," Jenkins said, leaning forward on the table, hands clasped as if in prayer. So friendly, so kind, so inviting.

"Then why is it legal for you to lie?"

Jenkins's mask of collegiality slipped then. Just for a moment, but Tess saw the angry man behind the warm and fuzzy façade. "We haven't said anything that's demonstrably untrue," he said.

"But you can, right? You can say anything you want to get me to talk, but if I say the least little thing wrong, you'll pounce on me. It hardly seems fair. If you've got proof my boyfriend is a drug dealer, then show me. Get a warrant to search my house." She remembered belatedly the phone buried beneath her dirty underwear, as well as the minuscule amount of marijuana concealed in her unicorn box, and regretted the offer, but there was no turning back. She was on a roll. "Show one iota of evidence that he's done anything but turn up with a lot of money in his checking account. If he deposited it in one lump sum, the bank has to report it, right? Hardly seems like the work of a criminal mastermind trying to launder money. And where did the funds come from anyway?"

"That's for us to know," said the young prosecutor, sounding for all the world like a peevish eight-year-old. He might as well have added, "and for you to find out."

"You don't have anything," Tess said. "You're just bullies."

Collins stiffened, the first time Tess had seen him show any unwilled reaction. Gabe Dalesio looked as if he wanted to fling himself on the ground and drum his heels until Tess did or said whatever he wanted.

Jenkins, however, was back to playing nice.

"Look, I have a daughter about your age. I know how things happen. You meet a fellow, you're in love, you don't look too closely or ask too many questions. You know what I mean? Or there are those girls, the ones who get, like, life sentences in federal prison because they took a bag on the train to New York, no questions asked, and it turned out to be heroin. I'd hate to see that happen to you."

Tess widened her eyes, so ingenuous as to be disingenuous. "What's her name?"

"What?"

"Your daughter."

He paused just a beat. "Marie."

"You got a photograph of her?"

"What?"

"Your daughter. I figure you must have one, you being so loving and all. So concerned."

Jenkins leaned back, no longer making a pretense of affection and concern. "Okay, so I got two sons. But we're not talking about me. Where the hell is your boyfriend?"

"I don't know," Tess said, never happier to be ignorant. "I just don't know."

They kept her for another hour, then released her, reminding her that she was making a grave mistake, that she should demand Crow's whereabouts the next time he checked in, that they were far from finished prying into her life. In front of them, she was at once blithe and resolute, but she began sagging as soon as she got into the elevator and felt strangely dizzy by the time she and Tyner reached the street level.

"Are they lying?" she asked Tyner as they made their way into the parking garage, where homeless men slept on the steaming grates. "Could Crow really have this kind of money?"

"I don't know, but it would shed some light on his happy-go-lucky nature. Easy to be a blithe spirit when you don't have to worry about making a living."

"He was stone-cold broke when I found him in Texas. He's always refused his parents' attempts to help him out. Where does he suddenly come up with a hundred fifty grand? And why would he keep it secret from me?"

"You can ask him when he calls," Tyner said. "But just remember—anything you know, these guys will make you tell eventually. I wouldn't ask any question just now if I wasn't sure of the answer."

Ed made Crow and Lloyd wait until after dinner to test the bumper cars, delivering a rather ponderous lecture about how they worked. And while Lloyd took great pleasure in ramming Crow's car from every angle, Ed delighted in gliding around and away from them, demonstrating a level of control that would do a NASCAR driver proud. "Try to catch me," he yelled over his shoulder, and the younger men happily gave chase, futile as it proved to be. At one point Lloyd even demonstrated with an unmanned car exactly how the accident with Mr. Parrish had happened, and Crow could see that it had indeed been Mr. Parrish's fault.

He knew he would sleep particularly well that night, and

Lloyd didn't even complain about the cool, salt-laden breeze that came in through the open window. Sleeping with the windows open had been an ongoing contest between them since they first arrived.

"Crow?" Lloyd said, his voice drowsy.

"Yes?"

"What we gonna do *tomorrow* night?"

It was almost eleven when Tess, just on the edge of sleep, heard her laundry hamper ringing. She could have reached the phone before it switched into voice mail, but she didn't even try. She lay in bed, listening to the burst of music, one of the few classical airs she recognized, the beginning of *Madama Butterfly.* Had Crow programmed that into the phone for her before he slipped it into the FedEx pouch? Puccini gave way to the double beep indicating that a message had been left. She got up then, but not to retrieve the phone. Suddenly wide awake, she decided she would need a hit of pot to recapture the unconsciousness that had been so close just a few minutes earlier.

Do you or your boyfriend use illegal drugs? You betcha, Mr. FBI man. Especially now that you showed up in my life.

The unicorn box was gone. Had Crow taken it in anticipation that the house might be searched? Where did Crow buy the little bits of pot he brought into the house anyway? Where was Crow? Who was Crow? She had met his parents, seen the house where he had grown up. He was no drug dealer. If he were one, he'd be the world's worst, extending credit to junkies, declining to maximize profits by cutting the purity of what he sold. Where had the money come from? Why had it popped up in his account on the very day he ran away? Was Crow with Lloyd, truly?

The only thing worse than having so many questions

about the man she loved was being afraid of the answers. Not so much because she feared that Crow had done something nefarious, but because Tyner was right: Knowledge was dangerous in this case. The three caballeros were going to come back to her, again and again. Right now the only thing Tess had going for her was ignorance. For Crow's own good, she should avoid speaking to him directly. She wasn't even sure she should listen to the voice mail he had left.

But in the end she could not maintain her resolve that strictly. She pulled the cell from her laundry hamper and, after a few fumbling missteps, retrieved the new message.

"I miss you," a familiar voice said. "I love you. Call me on this number when you get a chance."

She meant to press 2 to save it, but she hit 3 instead, erasing it forever.

Check yes or no. Wasn't there a country song by that title a few years back? Not that Gabe listened to that shit, but that lyric had somehow wormed its way into his consciousness, one of those songs you want to forget but can't. Check yes or no. *That's my story and I'm sticking to it,* another country song. *My wife ran away with my best friend, and I sure miss him.* Okay, he watched CMT sometimes late at night when he couldn't sleep. So sue him. He liked the female singers, that kind of big-hair denim-and-lace femininity— like Jersey girls but softer, more pliant. Better than counting sheep and quicker, too, because it just took one. Robert Bork laws be damned, Gabe wasn't going to have a pay-per-view porn bill come back to haunt him. Besides, who needed porn when regular cable went as far as it did? *Proud to be an American, yes siree, because at least I can say that I'm free*—free to have my mortgage application pulled, along with tax returns for the past five years, and never be the wiser for it.

Gabe was back in his office, his real one, not the fake-o one they had used to interview the Monaghan woman. He had thought that was pretty sly on Jenkins's part, taking her to the offices that the U.S. attorney had so recently vacated for this plusher joint across the street. The courthouse had an ominous vibe after hours, a real ghost-town feel. Plus, it meant no snooping colleagues would see what they were up to. But he could do the paperwork at his own desk late into the night, and no one would ever notice. It was going on 1:00 A.M., and here was the bull's-eye, all he needed.

Gabe found it ironic, the ultimate proof that what you didn't know *could* hurt you. People were running around, all steamed because the Patriot Act let authorities examine one's fuckin' library records, and they had no clue what the government already had the power to do. Of course Gabe was for the Patriot Act. It was an essential tool. It didn't go far enough, to his liking. That civil-liberties crap killed him. He wouldn't blink an eye if someone wanted to open up his life. He had nothing to hide. But he didn't need the Patriot Act for most of the penny-ante idiocy he pursued, not even in this chick's case.

The boyfriend's cash had been interesting, but it hadn't done the job, had it? He had tried to tell Jenkins and Collins that was the risk of jumping on it so fast. They should have let him find something else before they threw that one at her, but they were so impatient. They had stretched and come up empty. If they had waited just a few more hours, he could have delivered this whammy to them. They called it the head shot. Once you had this on a person, they had no wiggle room. He was still going to go through the dad's files, because bars were such sleaze magnets, but it was all gravy now. He had her. Pops was going to be the bonus.

Gabe had wanted to go after the reporters, too, but Jenkins had shot him down. At first, Gabe didn't see why. The state shield laws didn't apply in federal cases. And the press had no public support these days anyway. The reporters would probably fold in a second. But Jenkins had been adamant, said going after the newspaper would tip their hand. He was probably right. The too-many-cooks approach had spoiled this broth in the beginning. They needed to keep things close, keep the team lean and mean.

Gabe looked at his notations again. So simple, so lethal. A photocopy of a form that thousands of people filled out every day. Three checks—one from her father, two from her. Put it all together and it added up to thirty years in the federal system.

Saturday

chapter
22

"S ALISBURY?" LLOYD SAID, MAKING A FACE. "YOU TAKING
me to a club in Salisbury?"

"Where did you think we were going to go?"

"I dunno. Philly. Wilmington, even. A *city*."

"Salisbury's a city."

"Sh-it."

They were driving along U.S. 50, the route they had taken
east three days earlier, which now felt like a lifetime ago. It
was the weekend of daylight savings time, so what was
today's nine o'clock would be tomorrow's ten o'clock. The
sky was inky black, with just a few stars poking through,
like rips in a scrim. Crow enjoyed the quiet and the dark-
ness, which reminded him of the countryside close to his
hometown of Charlottesville. But Lloyd was too busy pout-
ing about their destination to notice the world around him.

"A club?" Ed Keyes had echoed when Crow consulted
him, scratching his red-stubbled chin. "I might could get

you in my VFW lodge, although I don't think they allow minors."

"You belong to the Veterans of Foreign Wars?"

"Vietnam," he said. "I only joined to get access to the lodge parking lot. It's near a good clamming spot, but you can't park there unless you're a member. They tow."

"Lloyd wants to go hear music, be around people his own age."

"Shit, I don't know. Ask the cashier over to the Shore Farms. I think she's got family down there."

The bright-eyed young woman did know of a club, which she described in rushed, excited tones, clearly hopeful of an invitation. Crow felt almost guilty not taking her elaborate hints, but it would have complicated things, getting too close to anyone over here.

The club, such as it was, was in an abandoned bank in downtown Salisbury. From the outside there was little sign of the activity that marked the hot Baltimore clubs—a valet parker for the high-end SUVs, dolled-up women teetering on their high heels, the occasional gunshot—but the Shore Farms cashier had sworn by the place.

"Doesn't look like much," said Lloyd, every inch the world-weary connoisseur. But how much experience could he really have in clubland? He wasn't of legal age, and he wasn't someone who could pass for older than he was, even with the best fake ID. They wouldn't have been able to come here if it weren't for the fact that it was "Teen Night," an alcohol-free evening for the high school set.

Lloyd pimp-walked toward the door, determined to be unimpressed. But when the second set of doors opened, revealing a packed room of girls in filmy tops and tight jeans dancing to a hooky hip-hop song that Crow recognized from listening to WERQ, Lloyd couldn't help smiling just a little. *'Twill do,* his expression seemed to indicate, *'twill do.*

"Sorry." A bouncer's thick arm came down, a swift and certain barrier, blocking Crow from the club.

"But I'm with him."

"Teen Night," the man said. "No one over nineteen admitted."

"But—"

"You can come back and pick up your . . . *son* at midnight."

"Today's midnight or tomorrow's midnight?" Crow asked.

"What?"

"Never mind. Look, I need to keep a watch on my friend. I promised his, um, people that I wouldn't let him out of my sight."

"He somebody?" Asked with 90 percent skepticism, 10 percent hope. Lloyd could be some on-the-rise rapper, up from Atlanta, passing through.

"You could say that." Crow tried to load his voice with subtle insinuation, as if anyone who was anyone would recognize the young man who had just entered the club.

"And you're, what? Like his bodyguard?"

Crow gave the slightest of nods. It was true, in a fashion.

"Tough shit," the bouncer decreed, folding his arms across his chest. "See you at midnight. Tonight's midnight."

Crow waved frantically at Lloyd, who was disappearing into a group of teenage girls, but he paid no attention. Crow would simply have to sit outside the club for the next three hours. Ah, well, it was an opportunity to find a convenience store, pick up new phones. He wondered why Tess hadn't called as instructed or at least left a message. Maybe he had chosen a provider that didn't work too well in her area. He'd try a new one this time. It was strange, not speaking to Tess directly for almost a week. She must be up to her eyeballs in work. Shit—the Ellen Mars case. He had forgotten that he was supposed to help Tess with that. But she had to understand that nothing was as urgent as keeping Lloyd safe.

While part of Lloyd felt superior to the teenagers dancing to what was an outmoded song back in Baltimore, a tired old thing that had been at the height of its popularity last fall, the girls were as pretty as any he'd seen back home. A stranger in their midst, he wasn't getting much play, but when he started cutting up, doing his trademark comic moves, they began to notice him. He set his sights on a dark-skinned shorty with processed hair and a juicy body. She didn't seem to be with anyone in particular, and she let him dance closer and closer to her. Now he had her eye, and she was smiling at him, matching her moves to his. He was smoothing it out now, toning it down so he looked serious about what he was doing but keeping his face clownish because she seemed to respond to that.

Thing was, he didn't have anything to tempt her with. Crow had paid his admission fee but neglected to give him any spending money, and he didn't want to go in search of him now to ask. That would be weak. He didn't have a car he could take her to, although he could always get one. That's why he had started learning to steal cars in the first place, to impress girls. But that would probably be a bad idea here. Country police didn't have enough work to fill their days. And the cracker types around here would probably come down hard on his black ass. No, he couldn't invite her outside for a ride.

He felt the bump in his inside breast pocket, the unicorn box. *Weed,* now that was something he could offer.

He leaned in, his mouth close to her ear. She had a nice fruity smell. Might be gum or something she put on her hair.

"You smoke?" he asked.

Wide-eyed, she shook her head. What was this, like, Teen *and* Church Night?

"Wanna try?"

To his delight she nodded and took his hand, leading him to the bathrooms at the rear of the club. With a quick glance around for lurking authority figures, she ducked into the men's room, and he followed. The stall's lock was broken, but the old metal frame was warped enough to hold the door.

"You're pretty," he said, not thinking clearly, allowing what was in his head to pop out. That was a punk thing to say. Le'andro always said you shouldn't compliment a girl too early in the game. "What's your name?"

"Glory."

"Gloria?"

"Uh-uh. *Glory.* You're not from here, are you?"

"Naw," he said pridefully. "I'm from Baltimore. East Side."

There was an awkward silence, and he tried to think of something to ask her, but to his amazement and delight she started kissing him. She might not have smoked before, but she seemed familiar enough with this. Maybe he wouldn't have to break out the weed after all.

But she stopped as abruptly as she had started. "Show me."

"Show—"

"What you promised."

He pulled out the box, showed her the cache within. Shit, he didn't have papers. How was he going to make use of it?

"That sure is pretty," she said, running her fingers over its surface. "When it's empty, can I have it?"

"Ain't gonna be empty for a while. There's more than an evening of fun here." Trying to hook her, set up the long-term play.

"Maybe you could put it in a Baggie, let me have the box tonight."

"I don't know. . . ." He was reluctant to give up the box, for reasons he wasn't sure he could explain even to himself. Glory began kissing him again and this time added the extra touch of placing one shy but game hand down the waistband of his pants. Okay, maybe she could have the box. He put the top back on it and returned it to his pocket so his hands could tend to her. Dancing, she had looked young, a babyish fourteen who just happened to have a grown girl's body. He hadn't counted on getting a lot from her. But now she seemed ready to do just about anything. He was trying to figure out if he should let it go now, give himself up to that warm hand or get her somewhere he could get inside her. Maybe if he sat down on the toilet seat and pulled her on him—

"What the *fuck* you doing?"

The stuck door was dislodged with such force that it caught Lloyd in the back, catapulting him forward into Glory, who all but fell into the toilet, which made her sputter and squawk in indignation. It would have been funny if he hadn't been scared to death. Lloyd grabbed her and swung around, so she was between him and the invader, a tall guy with dark, angry eyes. And a gun. Fuck, even in the country, the niggas had guns.

"You her boyfriend?" he asked, trying to think how he would plead his case.

"I'm her *brother.*"

A boyfriend, Lloyd might could deal with. It would still be bad, he'd probably get the crap beat out of him, but a boyfriend might get that it was an honest mistake, the kind anyone can make when a girl leads you to a bathroom and begins kissing you. After all, if this was Glory's boyfriend, that was probably how *they* had started. A brother—no chance. A brother would kill you if he could, just like that scene in *Scarface*. Lloyd did the only thing that seemed likely to save his ass, dropping to his knees and crawling out from under the stall, then running full-tilt into the club, trying to lose himself in the crowd.

He thought he heard a shot but told himself it had to be something else, a balloon popping, a car backfiring. At any rate, he didn't look back, just kept running for the door. Out on the street—fuck, no Crow. *No Crow!* And Lloyd didn't have time to look for his worthless ass. He just had to run as fast and far as he could and hope he was running away from trouble, not into it.

An hour before Teen Night was to end, Crow returned to the street with two new cell phones and a couple of magazines he had been delighted to find at the local Shore Farms—the *Atlantic* and *Harper's*. He ran the heater as necessary, dispelling the chill from the car. The solitude was a nice break. He hadn't really been alone since Lloyd had shown up on the doorstep Tuesday morning. He liked the kid, who could be good company when he wasn't brooding or complaining, but it was nice to be alone, too.

As midnight approached, other cars began pulling up, parents fetching their kids. Crow hung back, aware that he was all too visible, a white guy picking up someone who obviously was not his son or younger brother. Ed was right. They had to be careful about drawing attention to themselves.

It was only when the bouncer, the one who earlier had denied him entrance to the club, padlocked the door that Crow realized that Lloyd was never coming out.

PART THREE

Tiny Towns

Sunday

chapter
23

"Tess? It's Whitney. Just FYI—an IRS agent called out of the blue, wants to go over the foundation's books. Not a problem, but I thought it was awfully coincidental."

"Hey, hon, it's Kitty. This man—I didn't get his name—came by the bookstore late, just before closing. He wanted to talk to me about my arrest outside Supermax, when I was protesting the Thanos execution. He had a photo. Of me, that is. He's tall, African-American, close-cropped hair, maybe thirty. He would be handsome if he smiled."

"Tess, it's your mother—" But that one she answered.

"Hey, Mom. What's up?" As if Tess didn't know. She had been getting these calls and messages all weekend.

"Not much. A strange man just rang our doorbell, said we should talk to you about what you were 'into.' An FBI agent, very nice, but I let him know in no uncertain terms that I work for NSA and I am *not* intimidated by such tactics, that he had another think coming if he thought—"

"Great, Mom. Is Dad there? Did they talk to him?"

Her father picked up another extension, but Tess could still hear her mother breathing on the line.

"Hey, Dad."

"Hey."

"So who talked to you?"

"IRS."

"You worried?"

"Not really."

Patrick was the world's most laconic Irishman, but Tess was expert at listening to what he *didn't* say, and the anxiety in his silences was chilling. It was one thing to destroy her own life by keeping her promises to Crow and Lloyd. And even Whitney had sort of signed up for this. But her parents hadn't. She wondered how long it would be until Crow's parents were called, what insinuating questions would be poured into their ears. That would be unfortunate on many levels. For one thing it would alert them to the fact that their son was missing.

She assured her parents that everything would be fine and hoped it wasn't a lie. She then called Tyner, told him to be on standby, certain that the three caballeros, as she now thought of them, would come for her again. And, sure enough, Jenkins and Collins arrived just after eleven.

"Back to the courthouse?" she asked, trying for chipper but coming closer to chirpy, her voice high and crackly as a teenage boy's.

"For now," Jenkins said. "But don't be surprised if you end the day in federal lockup."

"What, you're going to charge me with a crime?"

"Probably," Jenkins said, expressionless. Collins simply smiled a terrible smile.

*   *   *

Crow had driven around Salisbury until dawn, but he couldn't imagine where Lloyd had gone, not in the short term. The kid had probably headed back to Baltimore, catching a ride with someone who lived west of Salisbury, planning to hitchhike the rest of the way. Scared for his life just five days ago, he was now bored out of his mind and wanted to go home. With someone like Lloyd, boredom trumped mortality. Father Rob had warned Crow about that. It had probably been a plan, using the club as a ruse to get away.

Of course he couldn't have known, going in, that he and Crow would be separated. But he had seen the opportunity once it presented itself, concocted a plan on the spot. Lloyd was smart that way.

Stupid, too.

At least Crow could go home now. Or would, once he called Tess and told her Lloyd was missing. He hoped that information wouldn't make her waver in her resolve to protect Lloyd. Then again, if Lloyd was stupid enough to go back to Baltimore, maybe he didn't deserve their protection anymore.

Thing was, the police couldn't take care of Lloyd even if the kid would allow it. Wasn't that why he had come to Crow in the first place? Stupid, self-destructive kid. If he didn't care about his life, why should Crow?

He took out the new cell phone and dialed Tess's home phone again. The phone rang twice, then kicked into voice mail, a sign that she was on the other line and ignoring the call-waiting signal. He started to text-message her cell but didn't think it was a good idea to relay the news about Lloyd in such a fashion. He called the house one more time, just in case. No answer now. Where could Tess be on a Sunday morning? A creature of routine, she should have walked the dogs and grabbed her usual coffee by now. Even with the return of mild weather and the reopening of the boathouse, she never went out on the water on Sunday mornings. She preferred to go at day's end, in the last hour before sunset, when the light was kind to the eyes and the weekend boat traffic had thinned.

Where could she be? Where could Lloyd be? He thought of mice and men, he thought of *Of Mice and Men*, he thought of Lennie and the rabbits, and the source for the book's title. The best-laid plans of mice and men often aft a-gley.

Well, here he was, living large at the goddamn intersection of Aft and A-gley.

Lloyd had slept outside many times, in weather more biting than this, yet he never knew a berth as cold and hard as the field he'd found near what appeared to be a highway. Once the sun came up, it was a little better, and he burrowed down into the narrow groove. A furrow. The word came back to him, unbidden, a lesson from long ago. Furrows and Pilgrims and planting fish heads to make better corn. Satchmo? Sasquatch? Something like that. But as the sounds of traffic grew louder on the road, he decided to get up and get going.

Where, was the only question. Where should he go? Where could he go? The question was complicated by the fact that he had missed the sunrise, so he wasn't exactly sure which way was east and which way was west. And even once he figured it out, which way would he choose? He was a lot closer to the amusement park than to Baltimore, had to be, but it was hard to imagine he could walk all that way. It had taken Crow almost an hour to drive it.

Baltimore was farther still. But once he got there, at least he would have his life back. No more working for nothing. No more of Crow's conversation, which just drove him nuts sometimes. He was the *talkingest* guy, although he did know some interesting stuff. The older guy, Ed, at least he knew how to chill, just sit back and be quiet. He was almost cool, although Crow said he was an ex-cop, which meant he wasn't cool. It had made Lloyd nervous, being so dependent on a cop, ex or no.

He walked along the road, determined to let someone else decide where he would end up. He'd stick out his thumb and catch a ride, and wherever he went, that's where he would be. That was as good a way to plan as any. Just let life take you where it goes. Hadn't that been the way he always lived?

Come to think of it, wasn't that why his life was so fucked up?

He stumbled along the soft, crumbling shoulder, whipping around when he heard cars approaching, but no one slowed. That didn't really surprise him, black man with leaves and shit in his hair. What did shock him was the minivan that rolled to a stop next to him, big black woman at the wheel, six kids packed into the two rows of seats, all in churchgoing clothes.

"Where you trying to get to, son?" she asked, her voice all sweetness. The kind tone surprised him more than anything. Somehow he had figured she would yell at him, make a lesson of him for all those kids. *Look at this stupid nigger walking down the highway. This is what happens if you don't go to church regular.*

"I . . . I don't know."

"Where your people?"

Where indeed. *Who* were his people? His mama and Murray? Dub? Not Bennie Tep and his folks, not since they killed Le'andro. Lloyd felt something strange in his throat and his eyes, a stinging sensation. Why did this woman's gentle voice and manner make him want to cry when he had held his ground through ass whippings? He'd be more comfortable if she were bitching him out. He was used to that tone, at least.

"I been staying over to, like, the boardwalk," he said.

"In Ocean City?"

"Northa there." It took him a second, but he pulled the name out. "Fenwick."

"So why you going the other direction?"

He shrugged, not wanting to admit that he didn't know where he was going.

"We're from Dagsboro, but we're on our way to lunch, up to the Denny's in Salisbury. You want to come with us?"

"I thought Denny's was the place that didn't like black people to eat there," he said.

"That's why we go there, every Sunday." The woman had a single dimple in her left cheek, sharp as a diamond winking in a ring. "We go and we say grace, and I have to say they're always *real* nice to us. You're welcome to come, too, although no soda. And no dessert unless you clean your plate. You gotta play by the same rules as my owns."

Two little girls on the bench seat in the far back scooted apart, pulling in their full skirts and making room for Lloyd.

"You smell funny," said one, but not with any real meanness to it.

"Shavonda Grace," the lady scolded, but her tone was mild. "What are you thinking, talking to our guest that way?"

Guest. He was a *guest.* Lloyd didn't remember anyone ever calling him that before.

Wait—Crow had, the first night he'd brought Lloyd to his house. Thing was, Lloyd had been so busy being a thief in his own head, he hadn't even noticed, or cared, what Crow considered him. If only he hadn't tried to steal the car, if he had just accepted the kindness for what it was. If he hadn't stolen the car, then that woman wouldn't have been so hell-bent on coming after him and he wouldn't have told them what he knew to get her off his ass and Le'andro wouldn't have been killed.

He thought he'd been so clever, telling the story the way he did. He had thought he was smart, leaving out those details that complicated things. But it was his own cleverness that had gotten Le'andro killed. Maybe he should have told the whole story from the beginning. But it was his nature to hold back what he could, to squirrel away a little extra.

Besides, if he had told the story in full, the only difference would be that he and Le'andro both would be dead.

"You smell," Shavonda Grace repeated, but she was giggling.

"You'd smell, too, you spent the night in some got-damn cornfield."

The children gasped in horror at the mild profanity, but the woman behind the wheel kept her company manners.

"Son—I'm sorry, I didn't get your name."

"Lloyd."

"Well, Lloyd, we don't permit bad language, especially if it involves taking the Lord's name in vain. I'd appreciate it if you'd keep that in mind."

Her manner couldn't have been sweeter, the same easy tone she had taken with the little girl, but for one moment Lloyd was reminded of every woman, every teacher, every person who had told him what to do, where to go, what to say, and how to say it. He wanted to unleash a string of curses, things that would sear the ears of these little church-going prisses, show them just how tough he was. *Fuck you. Fuck them. Fuck everybody. Fuck the whole got-damn world, and all the people who think they know what you should be doing and saying and thinking and breathing.*

Then his stomach sent up a sad, sour rumble, and Lloyd recognized it for the plea it was. *Go to Denny's. Get a meal.*

Maybe borrow some bus fare, you lucky. Then you can be as got-damn tough as you want to be. Just take this little kindness, for once.

"Yes'm," he said, meek as a girl.

"You smell," Shavonda Grace repeated, giggling behind her hand.

"Yeah, well, at least I don't—" He was going to say something mean about her dress, her hair, her nose, her ears, whatever he could find, and although she was a pretty thing, there was no shortage of material to work with. There was always something you could find to use against a person, tear her down. But she was just a little girl, and her mother—or aunt or whoever—was doing him a kindness. Besides, he remembered the insults flung at him when he was her age, the way they stuck. He wouldn't do that to her.

"Don't what?" Shavonda Grace demanded to know.

"Don't take up too much room, so you can scoot as far from me as you like and hold your nose. I won't take no offense."

Shavonda Grace made a great show of pinching her nose shut and fluttering her eyes, but she didn't slide one inch away. If anything, she seemed to move a little closer.

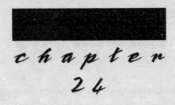

chapter
24

"EBRUARY TWO YEARS AGO, YOU TOOK A LOAN OUT FOR your house," Gabe said, pushing a photocopy of the mortgage application toward Tess. She didn't have to see the paper to remember the transaction. She had been almost nauseous after the hour at the title company, stunned by the dollar amounts, the commitment she was making. Thanks to Baltimore's real-estate market, she looked brilliant now, but at the time all she could fixate on was the actual cost of a $140,000 loan over thirty years.

"You got me there," Tess said. "I bought a house."

"And you made a down payment of twenty percent."

"Sure. That's mandatory to avoid private mortgage insurance."

"Where did you get thirty-five thousand?" Gabe asked.

"I had just closed a case that included a generous reward for information about a long-missing girl."

"So you made the down payment on your own?"

Were they trying to bring this back to Crow and his mystery money? Tyner looked as mystified as she was. Tess nodded tentatively.

"You didn't borrow any of the money for the down payment?"

"No."

"Didn't take money from your father?"

"My father's contribution was a gift."

"Right." Gabe produced another piece of paper from the file. "And here's his notarized statement that the money was a gift. Nine thousand nine hundred fifty dollars—just under the limit for taxable gifts under the codes then."

"Uh-huh."

"And here's where you swore on the application that no borrowed money was used for the down payment. You remember checking that?"

"I checked a lot of things in the process of buying the house, but sure. As my father's letter said, it was a gift."

"But you've since made two payments to your father— five thousand dollars year before last, seven thousand last fall."

Last fall. Tess remembered wistfully how flush she had been.

"I was grateful to my father. He had helped me buy my house. When times were good for me, I wanted to repay the favor."

"In other words, it was a loan, and you repaid it with interest."

Tyner ran his fingers through his hair, a sign that he was nervous, but only Tess would know that.

"No," Tess said. "He gave me a gift. I gave him a gift. It's like—if my dad gave me a turkey for Christmas and I gave him a ham for Easter."

"I'm afraid the federal government doesn't see it that way.

Call it turkey, call it ham, but it was a loan, and you lied about it."

Tess flounced in the hard plastic chair, impatient and out of sorts. They had been trying to scare her with their talk about federal charges, but this was so chickenshit. She thought of the blatantly illegal things she had done as part of her job. Taking confidential documents out of the governor's trash, for one. And this was the best they could do? Nitpicking over payments from a father to a daughter and back again.

"Fine—" she began, ready to concede the point, but Tyner put a cautionary hand on her arm and interrupted.

"They were gifts," he said. "It's our position they were gifts."

"Well, it's our position that your client lied on a federal form," Gabe said. "And we plan to charge her with that."

Tess rolled her eyes. Jenkins, who had been letting Gabe run the interview, caught her exasperated expression, but it didn't seem to bother him. The three men were like proud hens sitting on some monstrous egg.

"The penalty for what you've done," Gabe said, "is thirty years in federal prison."

"Oh, get *out*," Tess said. But even as she spoke, she saw Tyner nodding unhappily.

"And your dad has done the same thing. Lie in this notarized statement." Jenkins held up the letter for Tess's edification. "So we can go after him, too. And we will, unless you tell us the name of your source. Give it to us and all this will be forgotten. We'll cut an immunity deal for you and your dad, and this will never come up again."

Tess felt dizzy, weak—and almost bizarrely grateful. It was going to end now. This had gone too far. Her dad was already unnerved by their inquiries into his business. This would drive him over the edge. But even as she readied herself to break her promise to Lloyd, her brain clicked along, hearing the false note, the sour chirp of illogic, but not being able to pounce on it.

Tyner could, however.

"You're saying this is an official plea bargain, something Gail Schulian has approved?"

"Well . . ." Gabe glanced at Jenkins, lost for just a second. It was a fatal mistake. Tyner's instinct for weakness and ineptness was as sharp and astute as that of anyone Tess had known. She sometimes felt that Tyner had learned to compensate for his physical limitation, the paralysis caused in a car accident almost fifty years ago, by developing a sixth sense that allowed him to discern the tiniest frailty on a cellular level. If you were going to go up against Tyner, not a single mitochondrion could be having an off day.

"Does Gail know about this?" Tyner pressed.

"Gail?"

"Your boss. Gail Schulian. Has she signed off on making an official plea agreement, in which the government agrees never to prosecute Tess for what we've yet to affirm is a violation of this federal statute, in return for naming the confidential source in the Youssef case?"

"We don't take everything to the boss," Gabe countered, but his optic muscles seemed to have snapped, so his gaze went everywhere around the room, avoiding Tyner's. "I have the authority to offer this plea."

"I don't doubt that," Tyner said, in a tone that indicated he had no faith in the young man whatsoever. "But given that your boss is an interim U.S. attorney, I think it's important we involve her in these discussions from the beginning. It would make me feel more comfortable, especially since her replacement could be named at any time. Also—should Tess tell you what you want to know, are you going to share the information with the Howard County detectives? It is their

case, after all. Seems odd, the feds expending so many resources on a case they didn't even want to investigate. Let's
get everyone in the room—this suspiciously bare-bones,
underdecorated room—and do this just once."

Why was Tyner talking about interior decorating now?

"Gregory Youssef was my colleague," Gabe said. "Of
course I care what happened to him."

"Yes, now that you believe he wasn't killed by a male
prostitute. But when that was the going scenario, this office
couldn't get far away enough from Youssef."

Gabe gathered up the papers he had spread so lovingly
across the desk, straightening and bouncing them ostenta-
tiously in an obvious delaying tactic.

"Your client is guilty of a felony," he said. "We're offering *you* a deal. Take it or leave it."

"Are you prepared to charge my client?"

"Absolutely."

"Then do it. Enter the charge and let me get her in front
of a federal magistrate, so bond can be set and she can be released. We don't have to work out a plea today. You think
she broke the law? You think you can prove it? Go ahead."

"There's no need to be all official—" Jenkins put in.

"Really? I guess that would explain why we keep meeting
in an office that the U.S. attorney vacated back in January of
this year. Are you that paranoid about your colleagues looking over your shoulder, Mr. Dalesio—or that nervous about
the boss finding out about this little freelance investigation?"

"Look, this is just beginning." Gabe Dalesio's olive-
skinned complexion was now more of an eggplant shade, his
forehead perspiring. "I've got the paperwork to seize her car
today. And to start the process on seizing her house."

"On what grounds?"

"She told the Howard County police that her source feared
for his life because his contact has been killed. Our office has

been able to establish that the dead man was Le'andro Watkins, killed last Monday night in a drive-by shooting."

"I don't know the contact's name," Tess put in. She had gone to great lengths not to know it. "It was never revealed to me, so I can't verify it one way or another."

But she did know when he had died, and the timing was right. How had they pinpointed this? How could they be so sure? They must have assumed the murder was subsequent to the newspaper story and examined only those homicides that occurred in that five-day window, from when the story first appeared to her interview with the Howard County cops.

"Le'andro Watkins is a drug dealer," Jenkins said. "He was part of Bennie Tep's organization over on the East Side. Low-level, but he was rising up. So if he trusted your friend to do something for him, your friend was probably involved with drug dealing, too."

"Not my 'friend,'" Tess said sharply. "And your logic sucks. If Androcles took the thorn from the lion's paw and the lion turned out to be a drug dealer, would he be vulnerable to these seizure laws?"

"It's up to a federal grand jury to evaluate our logic," Jenkins said, long past pretending to play second chair behind the young prosecutor. "We're going to link you to a dead drug dealer. We're going to figure out if anyone ever connected with drugs worked out of your house or used your car. We're going to look into your father and your aunt, see if their businesses are used as fronts for drug money. And all because you insist on protecting someone who's almost certainly a criminal."

Tess was speechless, her mouth shut tight in order to combat the instinct that was dying to scream "Lloyd Jupiter" over and over again. She had every right to break the promise. They were probably on the verge of figuring it out themselves. They had identified the dead kid, Le'andro Watkins, with no help from her. With that lead they could definitely flush out the secret to Lloyd's identity. So why didn't they do it? Why was it so important for them to get *her* to tell what she knew? It was childish to think of this as a battle of wills, but this had gotten personal in a way that Tess couldn't fathom.

"Bring Gail in," Tyner said, "and we'll do this properly. Tess is not telling you anything until we have her promise that all of this goes away. Forever. And we're going to want some assurances about the rest of her family as well."

"Your *wife*," Mike Collins said, making the commonplace word sound uncommonly rude, and Tess knew that Tyner longed to strike him for insulting Kitty.

Instead he said, "Everyone. Tess, her father, her aunt, her boyfriend, her friend Whitney."

"We don't offer blanket immunity for life—" Gabe began, but Jenkins's voice rose over his. "We'll get back to you."

"Is she free to go?"

"Sure." Jenkins paused in the doorway. "We never have any problem finding her, do we?"

The trio left them alone in the room. It was only then that Tess noticed how odd she felt. Her face was flushed, feverish, as if she were a kid with a guilty conscience called to the principal's office. Her hands and feet were ice cold, as if no blood were getting to them, yet her palms were sweating, too.

But it was Tyner's hand, placed gently on her shoulder, that worried her the most. She must be in a lot of trouble if Tyner was being so kind to her.

"The thing about the office—how did you figure that out?" A trivial question, but she couldn't quite bring herself to form the more central one.

"I had thought the surroundings pretty bloodless, even by

government standards. On a hunch I called a friend who does a lot of federal bankruptcy work, and he confirmed that they relocated across the street."

"Am I . . . could they . . . I mean, shit, thirty years. How can that be?"

"The prosecutor's not particularly bright," Tyner said. "And he clearly jumped on this hobby horse without getting Gail's say-so. But I think she'll take his side and they'll charge you. That max really is thirty years. They use it all the time to squeeze people they can't get on anything else."

"We could go to the press. . . ." She must be desperate if she was considering trying to manipulate the local media.

"Thing is, I don't think we can win this public-relations war. The average citizen sees it their way—you're protecting a person of interest in the murder of a federal prosecutor. And if it drags on even a little while, the cost of defending yourself would be exorbitant. You'd have to hire someone else, for one thing, someone with more expertise in the federal system—a system in which more than ninety percent of all cases plead out, because more than ninety-five percent of the people who go to trial are found guilty."

"Maybe I could borrow some money from Crow," she said. "Crow, with his secret money-market account. I still don't know what to make of that. I don't know what to make of any of this. And I've been terrified to speak to him on the phone, for fear he'll tell me something that these guys will ask about and then I'll be at risk for lying and incurring more federal charges."

Tyner gave her shoulder another squeeze. She turned away from him, and using the wheeled chair to motor across the floor, like a toddler astride a Big Wheel, she rolled to the trash can in the corner and threw up.

THE AFTERNOON WAS GRAY AND OVERCAST, A PERFECT complement to Crow's mood. Yet he kept postponing his departure, finding another chore to do for Ed, another errand to run. He dropped the Books on Tape in the library's off-hour boxes. He and Lloyd would never listen to *Early Autumn* now. On the way back to FunWorld, he stopped at Ed's trailer park and found the older man sitting on the screened-porch annex to his motor home, wearing shorts and clutching a beer.

"It's Opening Day," Ed said. "And on Opening Day I sit on my porch in shorts and drink beer."

"I thought there was only one game and it's tonight on ESPN, the Red Sox at the Yankees. Everyone else plays Tuesday."

"Tradition," Ed said. "You find the boy?"

Crow winced a little at the "boy" part, conscious of how it would land on Lloyd if he were here. Then again, Lloyd was a very young sixteen. Maybe not a boy, but boyish, as evidenced by his disappearing act.

"No," he said. "And he doesn't know how to call me, because I switched burners last night, dumping the other phone. I suppose he could try to call FunWorld if he knew the number, or get your listing from directory assistance. But why would he call? He clearly wanted to get away."

"You know I was a cop, right?"

"Yeah. A cop, but also a friend of Spike's. You held his liquor license, in fact. What was that about?"

"Spike has a past. The kind of past that keeps you from having a liquor license. Not even his family knows about it. He was . . . a little out of control as a young man. I locked him up."

"You locked him up, but then you helped him get a liquor license when he got out?"

"What he did— Look, it's not my story to tell. One day you'll have a past and you'll want people to keep it to themselves. Trust me."

"I already have a few mysteries in my life," Crow said.

Ed snorted, as if Crow didn't know from secrets, and he had a point. Most people would think that Crow's secret was a cause for joy and celebration, but Crow felt marked by it, shamed and unsure. "Anyway, let's just say I could see the bigger picture, see that maybe Spike didn't have any choices in what he did. So when he did his time and wanted a fresh start, I helped him out."

"What's your point?"

"I don't know. I kind of lost it." He scratched a pale, freckled calf. "Oh, yeah. Like I said, I was a cop. The boy?"

"Lloyd."

"Yeah, him. He's hiding something, too."

"He was *in* hiding because he had stopped hiding something."

"I get the distinction, but that's what I'm telling you. He ain't told you everything he knows. That's why he's so jumpy-like. There's another shoe going to drop with him. Maybe you're better off, not being around him. Someone wants to kill the kid, you're trying to protect him, and he's not straight with you. That means he's risking your life along with his."

Crow wanted to indulge the older man, but he didn't think a retired cop's instincts were worth much.

"Well, I guess we'll never know. I don't think I'll ever see Lloyd Jupiter again."

"You want a beer?"

Ed was drinking Pabst Blue Ribbon, which had enjoyed a brief, strange vogue among the wannabe hipsters that came to the Point. Crow was pretty sure, however, that Ed had been drinking PBR since before those kids were born and would still be drinking it after some of them died.

"Sure."

They sat in companionable silence, pretending the day was suitably warm and sunny, and listened to the callers on WBAL, whose signal was faint but clear here on the shore. It was the happiest, most optimistic day of the baseball season, with the Orioles fans convinced that they were going to go 162–0. Hey, it could happen. Anything could happen.

Tess dug the cell phone out of her laundry hamper and called the only number on the message list. No answer. How else could she get in touch with Crow? She examined the phone, which had more bells and whistles than hers—pictures, video, Internet access. She could e-mail him, then. She went to her computer and sent Crow a message headed SIX INCHES FOR YOU, a long-standing joke with them.

Call me. Urgent.

All she could do was hope he would check the e-mail via phone—he was clearly too canny to use a computer that could be traced. Oh, she had raised her little spy boy well. Spy boy made her think of flag boys, and she put on a CD of the New Orleans music that Crow loved so much—and kept booking into the club, despite mixed results. "Jockamo fee-NO-MONEY," her father had complained privately to her.

My flag boy told your flag boy. . . .

She should forward those photos that Whitney had taken of the three caballeros, she decided, although if that trio got close enough for Crow to identify, it would be too late. But at least he would recognize his hunters should they come for him, understand how serious things were. Not that it mattered. Tyner figured she had perhaps seventy-two hours before she would be charged officially and faced with the choice of giving up Lloyd Jupiter or rolling the dice on the federal charge. Of course, once she identified Lloyd, they would still have to find him, and she couldn't help them with that. Would they believe her? Or would they deny her the promised immunity, thinking she had reneged?

As for Crow's disappointment when she caved—well, who was Crow to be disappointed with her? Crow, who had listened to her fret about money while he sat on his secret nest egg. She didn't believe that Crow would be involved in anything illegal, but then—she had never thought he would be cruel or selfish either. He had been playing poor. She really was.

Tess downloaded the three photos, then sent them as e-mail attachments. The nausea came back, and she couldn't think of anything to do except to lie on the floor, although what she really needed to do was put something, anything, in her stomach. The dogs came over and comforted her, pressing their damp, cold noses to her neck and ears. She was touched—until she realized they were simply petitioning her to take them for their afternoon walks. Man's best friend, sure, as long as your interests were congruent with theirs.

Her restless, association-prone mind leapfrogged back to the motto she had invoked the first time the happy trio had come for her. It was one beloved by her father, a longtime public servant. *What's the most frightening sentence in the English language?* he would ask her when his friends came over. Other kids did the itsy-bitsy spider, but this was Tess's shtick.

She'd lisp back, *We're from the government, and we're here to help.*

Her father's friends, most of them employed by the city and state and feds, would laugh until they were bent double.

Jenkins was so frustrated that he didn't trust himself to speak. Dalesio was an inept asshole. If Jenkins had controlled the interview from the start . . . But he hadn't wanted to do that. He needed that stubborn bitch to focus on Gabe, wanted her to see *him* as the enemy. Thing is, good cop–bad cop worked only when the bad cop was good at being the bad cop. He should have left Gabe out of it, worked this exclusively with Bully. But the DEA agent was a little *too* good at playing bad cop. Plus, verbal wasn't Bully's strength. Poor guy. He'd never really found his niche after they had taken him out of the undercover unit.

No, the kid had folded, weak and ineffectual. Jenkins had told him repeatedly that they needed to extract the information *now*, that it was imperative to get her to give it up without going for the actual charge. They didn't want to do this in public. Her lawyer would certainly leak details of an official deal, if only to embarrass them. Sure, Schulian would go for charging Monaghan; she was furious about the way the Youssef case had played out in the press. She'd be happy to throw the full weight of her office toward obtaining the lead. Hell, she might even be proud of Gabe Dalesio, which was all he really cared about, his own career and standing. But then there would be too many players, too many people in the loop. This asshole kept ignoring Jenkins's admonition to keep this close, among the three of them.

"There are some other leads in the paperwork," Gabe was burbling now, not getting how badly he had screwed up—or else covering for his embarrassment. They had gone for a late lunch at a steak house in the harbor, where the misty weather had held down the usual weekend crowds, and while the place wasn't bad, it made Jenkins wistful for the joints he'd known in New York. Keane's, Peter Luger's. The New York office was considered a bum assignment by most of the agents, but it was the only place Jenkins had wanted to be, and it had outstripped his fantasies. The best way to live in New York was to be rich, of course, but there was a second way to do it—having a job that encouraged people to shower you with perks. Access to restaurants and clubs, forgiving owners who let you slide on checks because you were FBI, you were keeping the city safe.

Even with those hidden bonuses, it had been a stretch, living—and dressing—to the heights he desired on his government salary. And Betty had been expensive, surprisingly so. She'd been a waitress when they met, making jewelry on the side, seemingly down-to-earth and low-maintenance. But once he was disentangled from his wife and family, Betty's needs grew and grew.

Then it had all gone to shit in a way he could never imagine. A tip had come into the Bureau about a possible terrorism suspect, a dark-skinned man photographing bridges around New York on a curiously regular schedule, almost like clockwork. Who wouldn't have jumped on the guy, brought him in, hammered away at him? He was a young Egyptian, a college student allegedly, and he claimed he was taking the digital photos for a school project, but Columbia University had never heard of him.

Turned out the kid went to Columbia *College*, in Chicago. He was in New York on spring break. Oh, and he was a Christian, too, not a Muslim. Jenkins might have ridden out the private embarrassment of it all, but then the media had gotten it. Once it was public, someone had to take the fall. The Bureau couldn't blame Barry for the investigation itself, which had been totally by the book, but they found a way to discredit him. They started going over his expense reports, questioning every line item. In the end they never found enough to fire him, but they found enough irregularities and missing documentation to send him back to a make-work job in Baltimore. To add insult to injury, his new colleagues treated him like a short-timer, a man of no worth. He was given bullshit duties, things that didn't use 30 percent of his brain. At his lowest he had thought of putting a gun in his mouth a couple of times, but then he met Bully, who'd been even more thoroughly screwed by his bosses—but wasn't so defeated by it. Bully's fury had stoked his own, gotten him to take his tail out from between his legs and reclaim himself.

"There's the articles of incorporation for her business—"

The dumb shit was still babbling. Figured. Guy had wilted in front of the old cripple, but now he couldn't shut up. Collins hadn't said a word since he placed his order. Jenkins loved that about Collins, the way he didn't talk unless he had something to say.

"Look, we have what we need," Jenkins said, cutting the kid off. "Don't get carried away."

"I'm just saying that there's still more ways to get at her."

"We *had* her," Jenkins said. "The point was trying to get her to tell us today, to keep this from turning into some huge public deal. That's why I told you not to go after the reporters, because that would have been all over the newspapers the minute you even questioned them."

"Well, what about the information that Bully developed?" Collins frowned at Gabe's use of his nickname, but the kid was too insensitive to notice. "What do we know about the dead kid, Le'andro, his known associates? Why not jack up Bennie Tep, lean on him?"

"Brilliant," Collins said, and Gabe beamed, not hearing the sarcasm.

"We go to Bennie, we alert him that we know he's involved," Jenkins said. He was no longer trying to disguise his exasperation. In fact, he was amping it up, hoping that the kid would finally understand how badly he had screwed up. "He'll kill half of East Baltimore rather than risk being linked to the murder of a federal prosecutor."

"But he's such a small-timer in the scheme of things, and you said he's always tried to avoid violence—"

"He's small by design. Like a boutique, you know? He keeps his business close in order to reduce risk. He doesn't like to kill, but he will if he has to."

"Oh," Gabe said, getting it at last, or seeming to. "Well, there's nothing hard and fast about the timeline. We can wait to bring her back in. If anything, it will probably make her even jumpier. Sword of Damocles and all that."

"Sword of damn what?" Jenkins asked. He was a college boy, too, but that one got by him.

"He was a man who sat under a sword, hanging by a thread," Collins said. Gabe, the poor sap, couldn't hide how impressed he was. Bad form. Bully wouldn't forgive him that.

"You learn that in college?" Gabe asked.

"High school. Dunbar."

"Right—you were a *Poet*." Fuck, the kid was teasing Bully now, making "poet" sound like "faggot." But Collins wouldn't even waste a look on the guy.

Crow's body was completely disoriented. He had stayed up until 3:00 A.M., which was the new 4:00 A.M., then gotten up at the new 10:00 A.M., which was the old 9:00 A.M. Drinking three PBRs on a practically empty stomach hadn't helped matters much. He should probably grab a meal before heading back. Or maybe stay here, get a good night's sleep, rather than risk nodding off at the wheel. Was he honoring his body's needs or postponing the re-union with Tess, who would be full of questions he couldn't answer? He felt foolish, running away to protect Lloyd only to lose him in a Salisbury nightclub. Some protector he'd turned out to be.

A dusty gray minivan was idling in one of the spaces on the side street along FunWorld. For one stupid, panicky moment, Crow worried that the authorities had caught up with him. But he was pretty sure no law-enforcement agency used minivans.

"Mr. Crow?" a woman called from the car.

"Just Crow," a familiar voice corrected. "He's not a mister."

"I found Lloyd hitchhiking this morning, and he said he lived here. But I didn't want to leave him until I saw a grown-up." The driver, a full-faced black woman with a se-rious Sunday hat—a tall, golden straw concoction that de-served to be called a crown—looked him up and down. "I guess you count."

The side door slid open, and Lloyd climbed out of the minivan, at once sheepish and defiant. "Where were you last night, man? You left me."

"I left—" But Crow saw that insisting on this technical point might cost him something larger. "I'm sorry. I went to buy new cell phones. It didn't occur to me that you would be looking for me before closing."

"We fed him a good lunch," the woman said. "My, he does have an appetite."

"And he smells!" a little girl's voice called from within the depths of the minivan, provoking peals of childish laughter. Crow thought the insult would throw Lloyd into his worst defensive posture, that he might ball up his fists or say something inexcusably obscene. But he just mock-scowled and said, "Not as bad as you, Shavonda Grace," which earned another round of delighted giggles.

"Looks like you made some friends," Crow said after the woman at the wheel—Mrs. Anderson, he had learned, of Dagsboro—made a three-point turn and headed back to the highway.

"Naw. More like acquaintances."

"Acquaintances can become friends."

"If you say so."

Did Lloyd mean to imply that Crow was more acquaintance than friend? It didn't matter. His actions undercut his cruel adolescent words. He had come back here. On his own, free to choose, he had directed Mrs. Anderson to bring him here. Perhaps he trusted Crow after all.

Monday

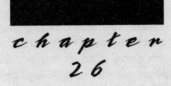

c h a p t e r
26

TESS WOKE UP ABOUT 7:00 A.M., HER HEAD FOGGED FROM restless dreams. They hadn't been real dreams, more a state between consciousness and unconsciousness in which her mind was stuck in a single groove, like a car spinning its tires in the sand. *Crow's secret account, Crow's secret account, Crow's secret account.* The fact nagged at her not only in its own right but because it was pointing her somewhere else. She did the only thing she knew to clear her head, the thing she would have done anyway on any weekday morning from mid-March to Thanksgiving. She went to the boathouse.

Unlike the college crews and the local rowing club, a self-employed and solitary sculler such as Tess had the luxury of going out a little later, which allowed her to avoid the traffic jams during the peak times on the rickety docks. And while the middle branch of the Patapsco was far from pastoral, it provided the serenity and isolation she needed to think. Or not think, as the case might be. Here her brain could empty itself, sit still while her body did all the thinking. Tess had tried many things to reach that in-the-moment state that some call Zen—yoga, wine, bad television. But it was only on the water that her busy mind surrendered.

Tess's body was pretty smart, as it turned out. Today her leg and arm and back muscles went through their paces with great gusto. By the time she was heading to the dock in a nonstop power piece, she had the detail that had been nagging at her.

Tess wasn't the only woman who shared her life with a man who had a secret account. Gregory Youssef had left behind a safe-deposit box. Was there something to that? Should she try to persuade Wilma to open it before Tess gave up Lloyd?

Her mind moved in time with the oars, thinking of other things she could do before she had to knuckle under to the feds. They had identified the young man, Le'andro Watkins, killed in Lloyd's stead but didn't seem interested in pursuing that lead. Tess could follow and even endorse that logic. Such an inquiry might end up alerting the killer that he had missed the real target, which could make Lloyd all the more vulnerable. The only thing Lloyd had going for him right now was that Youssef's killer assumed he was dead. That and the fact that only five people—Tess, Crow, Whitney, Feeney, and Marcy—knew who Lloyd was.

Or was that *six*? This thought came to her as she was running the hose over her shell. There was at least one other person Lloyd trusted to the extent that they shared a scam and split the cash. Tess might not know the boy's name or whereabouts, but she did know what he looked like and how he might be found. She would locate him first, then surprise Wilma in her lair, much as Wilma had caught Tess off guard in a place where she had expected to be free from questioning.

*   *   *

After another morning of painting, Crow and Lloyd used their lunch break to go to the library, check out the Books on Tape that Crow had returned just yesterday, already back in circulation at this small and efficient branch. Crow seized the opportunity to check the Internet as well, curious in spite of himself to read the accounts of Opening Day. Given his mother's Boston roots, he had been raised a Red Sox fan. It was, he reflected now, excellent preparation for being in a relationship with Tess—frustrating, infuriating, heartbreaking, exhilarating. But the Sox had persevered.

After a mere eighty-seven years, a voice in his head reminded him as he closed the computer's browser.

He and Lloyd continued to the FedEx box, dropping Tess's new phone in the mail to her. It would arrive tomorrow morning, and Crow could call her then.

And tell her what? The long-term flaws in his plan became more apparent every day. Lloyd still didn't want to go back to Baltimore if it meant talking to authorities. When Crow had fled with him, he'd hoped there might be another break in the case, making Lloyd a moot topic. He saw now that an arrest in Youssef's murder wouldn't make Lloyd any less interesting to the various law-enforcement types. If someone was charged, Lloyd would still be expected to testify—and still face the street justice meted out to those who cooperated with the police. Crow had been naïve to think that time would buy Lloyd anything but more grief.

He found himself wishing that Tess were here to argue with him, boss him, tell him to do things differently. But for once he was on his own, without Tess second-guessing him.

Funny, it was what he had always thought he wanted.

*   *   *

When it came to his house, his car, and himself, Gabe Dalesio was neither neat nor messy. He sometimes went too long without a haircut or didn't notice his shoes needed a shine. The remains of his latest Starbucks Americano often sloshed around for days in his Acura's cup holder. But where his actual work was concerned, he had systems upon systems upon systems. One of his trademarks, as he thought of it, was his use of a sketchbook, the largest one he could find, and a set of color-coded pens and Post-its. He had first started using this method when he was tracking money in drug and RICO cases. But now he deployed his colored pens in an attempt to figure out how everyone in Tess Monaghan's life interacted—and to gain back Jenkins's faith and trust. Look for the person or place with the most overlaps, Gabe decided, and he could figure out where they had stashed the source.

The boyfriend should be the key. He worked for Patrick Monaghan, and his sudden absence was simply too convenient. Plus, he had a pocketful of cash, based on the deposit slip for the hundred and fifty thou, which meant he could go for days without using an ATM or a credit card. Gabe wished he could get a wiretap for the Monaghan telephone, but he knew he couldn't meet the standard, not yet. Down the road, maybe, but Jenkins didn't have the patience for such maneuvers. Gabe riffled his papers, looking for the yellow Post-its. Yellow—the color for cowards—was the boyfriend.

The boyfriend's family was dull, which is to say that they were everything they appeared to be, a university professor and a sculptor, living the proper academia-social life in Charlottesville. Where had their son gotten his money, then? Tax filings should provide leads, but those weren't due for another two weeks. What would Gabe do if he had a pile of cash like that? Just what he was doing, he realized. He loved his job.

The Monaghans and the Weinsteins, now, they were more promising. Steeped in local politics, and local politics always had a nut of corruption. Clearly, the more he leaned on her father, the more they got to her. That was when she had wavered in the interview, when they threatened her father. The Monaghans were green, the Weinsteins were purple. There had to be something to play with in those two worlds.

He hadn't missed Jenkins's exasperation and disappointment yesterday. Gabe was just self-aware enough to realize how clueless Jenkins and Collins thought he was. He knew that they blamed him for screwing up this latest round. But what could he do, once the old guy sussed out that they were taking an unauthorized flier on this?

The yellow path wasn't leading him anywhere. But he had put a pink Post-it on the liquor license, the Monaghan bitch's color. Why had he flagged this anyway? She wasn't listed anywhere on the license, and she didn't appear to have anything to do with her father's business. The liquor license had been passed from Ed Keyes to Patrick Monaghan, so green was the only flag that should be flying here.

Keyes. That was the name of her detective agency. Keyes Investigations, Inc. He had thought it was some stupid local reference, as in Francis Scott Key, "The Star-Spangled Banner." It was the name of the owner. Yes, there it was on the corporation papers. Keyes. Keyes. *Key!*

He crumpled a paper cup, the only nonessential piece of paper in his office, and sent it sailing into his wastebasket. It bounced off the rim, teetered, then fell in. Gabe Dalesio. He shoots, he scores.

*   *   *

Tess called Health Care for the Homeless, figuring the agency would have a ready list of the soup kitchens open on Mondays. There were fewer than ten, led by Our Daily Bread. The huge soup kitchen in the heart of downtown served every day, with almost a thousand people passing through its line. But she had a hunch that the young man she was searching for would stick closer to home. There was a small church-run program over on the East Side, which started serving at three to accommodate schoolkids. Lloyd hadn't gone to school, but his friend might. And it was over in that part of town, on a Monday, that Crow had met Lloyd.

Holy Redeemer's director didn't bother masking her hostility to Tess and her mission. "Our kitchen is a haven," said Charlotte Curtis, a short, compact black woman with graying braids. "I don't want any of our guests to feel as if we've betrayed them. It's part of the reason I don't take federal or state money. I don't want anyone thinking they have a right to my records."

"I'm not trying to get anyone in trouble," Tess said. "Sort of the opposite. I've been trying to help a kid named Lloyd Jupiter."

It felt strange to say his name, given how fiercely she had concentrated on *not* saying it for the past week. But this woman was so protective of her clients that Tess couldn't imagine her cooperating with the authorities.

"I know Lloyd," Charlotte Curtis said, her voice ever so cautious. "He's a sweet kid, underneath it all."

"And is there another kid he hangs with, round, a little heavyset, but very quick and light on his feet?" Tess still remembered how speedily and casually the boy had moved after piercing Whitney's tire.

"Dub."

"Dub?" Tess was thrown by the name's redneck vibe.

"Short for Dubnium, an element. His mother liked chemistry when she was in high school." Charlotte Curtis sighed. "Unfortunately, his mother likes chemicals, too. She's in the wind. But Dub is some kind of genius. Seriously. He's not only doing well in school, he's managing to evade the Department of Social Services, which is determined to put him and his siblings in foster care and collect his mother's public assistance before she can get to it. No one can find Dub if he doesn't want to be found."

The warning registered only as a challenge to Tess. "No one *official*," she countered. "But you can, can't you? I bet you know where he is."

"If I knew where he lived, I'd be obligated to do something about it, wouldn't I?"

"Would you? Do you believe that Dub would be better off in DSS custody?"

Tess felt Charlotte Curtis taking her measure, putting her on some metaphysical scale that weighed and evaluated every bit of her—brain, heart, soul. The woman said at last, "I can't swear to where he is. He moves a lot. Last I heard, they had a place over on Collington. Look for a red tag on the lower portion of the plywood that covers the door."

"Tag?"

"Graffiti mark. Dub has an open-door policy for other kids who need a place to stay, Lloyd among them. But he doesn't give out the address, just the block, because he and his mother are always tussling over the benefits. Dub gets the card, she reports it stolen, he changes the PIN code somehow, has the replacement card sent to him care of . . . Well, let's just say he has a regular address he can use. High school is easy for Dub after five years of trying to outthink his mother."

*   *   *

Tess got to the rowhouse on Collington before school was out, giving her time to explore it. The house was boarded up, with No Trespassing signs stapled to the wooden surfaces, but there was a red squiggle in the lower-right-hand corner, and the plywood over the door swung open easily.

Her stomach lurched a little at the conditions inside— pallets on the floor, no running water, dim even in the afternoon because of the boarded-over windows. Even as a flophouse, it was far from adequate. Charlotte had confided in Tess that the church allowed Dub and his siblings to use their bathroom in the mornings, and the children then relied on the facilities in the branch library the rest of the time. In fact, that was where they spent each afternoon throughout the cold-weather months. Would they stay outside, now that dusk came later and the air was almost warm? Tess waited in her car, certain she would recognize him by his walk.

Not long after five, Tess saw a trio coming down the block, a heavyset teenager and two younger children. Yes, that was the silhouette she remembered, the same light-footed Jackie Gleason grace. She waited until they slipped into the house, then followed about five minutes later.

"Shit," Dub said.

"I'm not DSS," Tess assured him. "Just a friend of Lloyd Jupiter's. He's in trouble."

"Don't know any Lloyd."

"So it's just a coincidence that you puncture tires and Lloyd comes along five minutes later, ready to change them?"

Dub didn't make the mistake of speaking when surprised.

"I *saw* you, Dub. Week before last. You and Lloyd pulled the scam over on Mount Street. Old Mercedes station wagon. Only Lloyd didn't show up for a while, did he? And when he did, I bet he had a story about how he didn't make any money, but he had bags of cookies, maybe some leftover carryout. Am I right?"

"Them cookies were good," the little girl said wistfully. She looked about eight, and she wore her hair in a timeless style—three poufy plaits, sectioned off as precisely as city blocks, fastened with plastic barrettes at the ends. Tess marveled at the care that had been taken with the little girl's hair. The boy, slightly taller, was spick-and-span as well, although his trousers were a tad too short. She hoped kids no longer got teased for wearing high-waters.

"I haven't seen Lloyd for a while," Dub said. "I don't know where he is."

"That makes two of us. But did he come to you after Le'andro Watkins was killed? Did he tell you he feared for his life?"

Dub felt in the pocket of his jacket and took out three limp bills, dollars that looked as if they had been dug out of a trash can or a gutter, and perhaps they had. "Go down to the corner store, buy yourselves a treat," he instructed the younger ones. His voice was gentle, yet the tone defied them to argue back. "Whatever you want."

The boy grabbed the bills and bolted, the girl at his heels. "You've got to share," she said. "Dub, tell him he's got to go halves."

"Be nice, Terrell," he said. "You know you have to look after Tourmaline when I'm not around." He waited until the plywood door swung back into place before he spoke to Tess again. "They don't need to know everything I do. Besides, I stay away from that side of things. Lloyd and me, we run a few low-risk games, when there's time and opportunity."

"Like a snow day," Tess said, remembering that school had been canceled the day that Crow and Lloyd first met. "But on Wednesday—"

"That day with the Mercedes? Staff-development day at the school, so they let us out two hours early. But I always told Lloyd that I would draw the line at anything to do with Bennie Tep."

"Bennie Tep?"

"He's the drug dealer that Le'andro worked for. Lloyd, too, for a while, but Bennie got no use for Lloyd. Says he lacks focus, can't be trusted to do even small things right. But Le'andro liked Lloyd, if only because Lloyd was fool enough to think that Le'andro was someone worth looking up to. He let him hang around, threw him some little things he didn't want to do."

"Things like using an ATM card in a very precise way, at a very precise time?"

Dub didn't answer, so Tess continued. "That's practically public record at this point. Lloyd's admitted as much to me. It was in the newspaper a week ago Sunday, only without Lloyd's name attached. Which is probably the reason that Le'andro was killed—because Lloyd pretended he was the only one in on the scam."

"Yeah, okay. Back last fall, Lloyd bragged on how they put one over on this guy big-time—that he tried to double-cross Lloyd, but Lloyd triple-crossed him."

"They? You mean Le'andro and Lloyd fooled this guy Bennie?"

"No, not Bennie. Lloyd wouldn't never have fucked with Bennie. This guy, you know, he wasn't gonna to be around ongoing. I think he was from out of town. So Lloyd thought he could put a few extra things on the card. What was the guy gonna do? And, sure enough, we—he—didn't catch no flak over it. No one ever came around, asked what was up, told him he had done wrong. If anything, Lloyd wished he'd held that card a little longer, charged a little more."

Of course, that would have created a longer, more detailed trail for investigators in the Youssef murder. Which meant, Tess realized, that Lloyd really didn't have any idea at the time how radioactive that ATM card was, how much trouble it could cause.

"So Lloyd told you about this?"

"Yeah."

"Did he have any details about the guy who hired Le'andro?"

"Naw. He didn't know him."

"But did Le'andro mention a name, say where he was from? Any new scrap of information would help, maybe keep the police from trying to charge Lloyd with being an accomplice."

Dub thought. "Lloyd said the man drove a punk-ass car. Some shitty Chevy, like a Malibu or something. Said thieving wasn't what it used to be if a player like this had to drive something that raggedy."

"But I thought he never met the guy."

"He didn't."

"So how could he know what he drove?"

"Maybe Le'andro told him."

Tess tried to work this through. Lloyd hadn't met the man who hired Le'andro, but he knew the make of his car. Had Lloyd been lying all along? Was Dub lying now, intent on shielding his friend? But then if the man who gave the ATM card to Le'andro had met Lloyd, knew who he was or at least what he looked like, why hadn't he killed them both once the story got out?

"Lloyd ever mention Gregory Youssef to you?"

"Who?"

"It's been on the front page of the papers just this past week—"

Dub's blank look persuaded her to abandon the story before she began it. She was talking to a homeless seventeen-year-old, a kid who was trying to go to school, keep his family together, and stay one step ahead of whatever forces—his mother, the Department of Social Services—would break them up. Dub had heard Lloyd's side of things, nothing more.

"Look, is there anything I can do for you?"

He looked wary. "Naw. We fine."

"I mean money, groceries. I know you don't want DSS in your life, but there's got to be a better way to keep your family together."

"We'll be okay. I got one more year of high school, then I'll get a scholarship, go to community college part-time, work the rest. When I'm eighteen, I can petition for custody of Terrell and Tourmaline, official like, and I won't have to fight my mom for theirses checks anymore. Then I'll get those two through. Long as we show up for school and don't cause trouble, no one needs to know anything about us."

"What do you use for a mailing address?"

Dub smiled as if he found Tess naïve. By his standards, she was.

"How much do you and Lloyd get for the tire trick?"

Dub shrugged as if he had no idea what she was referencing, although he had already admitted his role. He might not have been born this cagey, but life had schooled him as well as the Baltimore city school system, probably better.

"Twenty? Forty?" Tess took three twenties from her wallet. "The way I see it, my household has thwarted you twice." When he didn't reach for the money, she added, "I pay for information all the time. You earned this, same as anyone. No special treatment, no handout."

"I didn't tell you much," he said, his fingers closing over the bills.

"You know, I can find odd jobs for you," she said. "My office isn't two miles from here, and my aunt has a bookstore nearby. Between us, there are lots of little jobs, things that would work around your school schedule. And my aunt's store stays open late. She'd let you hang there until closing—"

"We fine," he repeated.

chapter
27

Back in her car, Tess checked her watch. Almost six, but that was early in high-powered-lawyer land. The secretaries and receptionists might have gone home, but she was betting that a young comer such as Wilma Youssef was still at her desk—depending on her day-care situation.

Wilma worked at one of Baltimore's better-known firms, a string of Italian and Jewish surnames where politicians came to roost when they tired of public life or, in some cases, the public had tired of them prematurely. In fact, the most recent U.S. attorney, the one who had seen Youssef's death largely as a publicity bonanza, had dropped hints about how much he would like to work here, to no avail. It wasn't his Republican affiliation; the firm was apolitical, throwing its weight behind power and money and those who already had them. But the firm also valued discretion, and the former U.S. attorney had failed to impress on that score. High in the glossy white IBM tower near the harbor, this was a genteel, old-fashioned law practice, one that eschewed criminal cases in favor of civil ones. Again, it was all about money.

Wilma Youssef, squirreled away in a small office far from the pristine reception area, did not appear to be getting her share, not yet. This was not where partners sat, Tess decided after sweet-talking a custodian into unlocking the main doors for her and pointing her toward Wilma's office. She had claimed to be a client with an appointment, which barely seemed a lie.

Wilma jumped a little when Tess appeared in her doorway.

"Have you decided to cooperate with the police?" Wilma asked, skipping past any pretend niceties.

"I'm prepared to make a deal with you. You get your husband's safe-deposit box open, find out what's in it—and then I'll name my informant."

Okay, she would name Lloyd in a few days in order to avoid prosecution on the mortgage charge. It was still the truth. Why shouldn't she leverage it any way she could?

"What do the two things have to do with each other?"

"Nothing, probably. But I want to be sure of that. See, I've been thinking. Someone made your husband's death look like what it wasn't. So then we all jumped to the conclusion that it must be the other, a virtuous prosecutor cut down for his work. Maybe that's not it either."

Wilma was one of those fair, thin-skinned blondes who blushed readily and deeply from emotion.

"I've lived through the past five months with all this crap innuendo about my husband, delivered our child even as the nurses were gossiping about Greg. Was he gay? Did he have a lover? You, better than anyone, should know that my husband was murdered because of something he had worked on. Why do you persist in protecting these people?"

"These people?"

Once in full blush, a person can hardly moderate the meaning of the blood that has rushed to the face. But Tess thought she saw a flicker of shame in Wilma's expression.

"Drug dealers, I mean. Criminals."

Tess plopped herself into the chair opposite Wilma's desk, tired of waiting for an invitation. "My source isn't pure, I'll grant you that. In fact, if the informant in this case didn't have a record, I doubt I would have ever extracted any information to begin with. But the source *isn't* a drug dealer, I can guarantee you that."

"Still—"

Tess had read of people tossing their heads but seldom seen it done with any true flair. Wilma, however, managed to execute the gesture with style, lifting her chin with the force of a skittish racehorse being led into post position at Pimlico. Too bad that her blond hair was too short and too lacquered with spray to make a satisfactory mane.

"*Still,*" Tess echoed. "You mean there's your husband's death, which matters, and the life of my informant, which matters to you not at all."

"My husband is dead. Your informant is a lowlife who needs to be coerced into doing his civic duty."

"Less than forty-eight hours after the newspaper article appeared—the one that detailed how your husband's ATM card was handed over, along with the code and explicit instructions on how and when to use it—a teenager was killed in Baltimore. Shot to death while standing on a corner."

"So?"

"So the kid, Le'andro Watkins, was the one who was supposed to handle the ATM card, but he passed it on to someone else—my source. My source talks, Le'andro is killed."

"These things happen."

"Exactly. Young black kids get shot and killed in East Baltimore. And, by the way, men who live secret lives sometimes end up on the wrong side of a trick, too. 'These things happen.' But what if they're happening this time because someone knows what it looks like, how the crimes will be perceived? We have two homicides that are meant to look like something they're not. *That's* the connection."

Wilma was settling down, listening to Tess's words, allowing intellect to trump emotion. Met under the best of circumstances, Wilma Youssef was never going to be a kindred spirit. She struck Tess as incurious and self-centered, a woman who lived her entire life as if she inhabited some abstract gated community where all evil could be kept at bay. Her religious beliefs and early good fortune in life had made her smug, dogmatic.

But for Tess to dismiss her because they agreed on so little would be no different from Wilma's disdain for "those people." She was a widow, a single mother trying to perform in a job that was demanding and exhausting under any conditions. She yearned for the truth, but she was terrified of it, too.

And that, more than anything, seemed to Tess the universal human condition.

"If I open the box and what's inside doesn't have any relevance to Greg's death, will you agree to keep it confidential?"

Tess wondered just where Wilma's imagination had taken her over the past few months. Some very dark places, no doubt, places far scarier than any gossiping nurse could imagine.

"Absolutely. But we need to expedite this, okay? I don't know how it's done—you're the lawyer—but there's got to be a way for you, as your husband's heir, to get into that safe-deposit box quickly. Maybe a judge in Orphans' Court, maybe—"

"A judge already has ruled," Wilma said, sheepish for

once. "It's actually pretty automatic when a spouse dies. In fact, the bank has told me they'll open it for me whenever I can make it in."

"So why haven't you examined its contents if you had the right all along?"

Wilma shook her head, clearly not trusting herself to speak for a few seconds, then said, "Pandora's box, you know? I'm scared what might be unleashed."

"Hope was in Pandora's box, too. Don't forget that. The last thing that came out was hope."

chapter
28

GABE COULD TELL THAT COLLINS WAS SURPRISED BY THE invite—a drink? just the two of us?—prompting another bout of anxiety for Gabe. *What if he really does think I'm a fag?* The rejoinder in his head—*but he's black, and I'm not into black chicks, so why would I be into black guys?*—made him feel only more squirmy and strange. Even on the telephone with Collins, he felt awkward and tongue-tied, like he was a teenager calling a girl.

But all Collins said, after an interminable pause, was "Okay, where?"

Even that simple question provoked another round of second-guessing. It had to be a *guy*-guy place, but not so obvious a guy place that it would look like Gabe was insecure about that stuff. Besides, a sports bar would be too rowdy for conversation.

"Um, that martini bar? The new one on Canton Square?"

"Sure," Collins said. "What time?"

"Eight?"

Shit, he had to figure out a way to stop speaking in questions around the guy. He decided to get to the bar early, so he'd have a drink in progress, be in control of the situation. But the lack of street parking undermined him, and he arrived fifteen minutes late, which clearly irritated Collins. Gabe's rushed apology, his explanation that he had parked far away, didn't seem to help much.

But once Gabe got going, laid out the connections he had uncovered, he could tell that Collins was impressed.

"Do you know for a fact that this Keyes guy helped to hide the source and her boyfriend?"

"No, but we always figured they went by car, right? It's the beach, off season. The locals probably notice every out-of-towner, especially some salt-and-pepper combo."

Shit, what he wouldn't have given to take that back.

Collins took a long swallow of his Heineken. He was drinking from a glass, which made Gabe feel as if there were something unmanly about settling for a bottle, Sam Adams at that, although he was drinking shots of Jameson on the side.

"What makes you so sure," Collins said, "that the informant is black? The fact that he bought Nikes at the Downtown Locker Room? Could be some punk-ass whigger, you know."

"Um, I didn't— I mean . . ."

Collins smiled, gave him a playful punch in the shoulder, one hard enough to leave a bruise. "I'm just busting balls. Of course the source is a black kid. Just like . . ."

"Just like?"

"Just like the ATM photo. Can't see his face, but we can see his hands."

"Right," Gabe said. "Of course." He wasn't a bigot. He had simply forgotten how he knew what he knew.

"You keeping this close, this insight to where they might be? Or have you gone to Schulian, opened up an official file?"

"Hell, no. It's our secret so far. I haven't even told Jenkins." Gabe was feeling the rush of camaraderie now, burbling in spite of himself. "I gotta say, I don't have utter confidence in him. Those FBI guys are so full of themselves. I mean, what's he ever done? You, you've been out there, did undercover. You risked your life." He sensed he was entering dangerous territory, but he decided to chance it. "That was bullshit, what they put you through."

"Before your time. How do you know of it?"

"People talk." Collins clearly didn't like the idea of being gossiped about, so Gabe quickly added, "Everyone thinks you got a raw deal."

"It turned out okay. The lawsuits were dismissed. You can't sue a federal agent doing his job—even when he botches it and shoots a citizen."

"But it ended your time undercover after the newspaper ran your photo, and I heard you were one of the best. That sucks. It was an honest mistake, under the circumstances."

Collins, back in his usual taciturn mode, said nothing, but Gabe thought he caught a wisp of a smile on his face, a moment of understanding. Finally, with Jenkins out of the way, they were bonding.

"Another round?" he asked. "My treat."

"Sure," Collins said. "Night's young. Night's so young that R. Kelly would date it."

It was almost midnight when Gabe and Collins finally left the bar. Gabe was a little lit—not so much that he couldn't drive, given that it was basically a series of straight shots and left turns until he coasted into his parking pad off Hanover. He just felt fuzzy around the edges. The air was soft, the first true spring evening so far. The season got here a little faster here than it did in Jersey, not even two hundred miles to the north. Just twenty-four hours ago, the Yankees had almost been sleeted out on Opening Day in the Bronx, but here you could see buds on the trees.

"Where you parked?" Collins asked.

He had to think about it. "I'm on Fait, like four blocks from here."

"I'm around the corner from there," Collins said. "I remember when this neighborhood was nothing but toothless old Polacks, the kind who would call the police if a black kid so much as rode his bike down the sidewalk."

It was the longest sentence Collins had ever uttered in Gabe's presence. It was so cool, them becoming friends. He could ask Collins about being a star on the Poets, or whatever that local basketball team was called. Hadn't Juan Dixon played for them? Steve Francis? Somebody good in the NBA.

"This your ride?" Collins asked when Gabe stopped by his Acura. "Nice."

He laughed, getting that Collins was still busting his balls, but in a friendly way. "Not particularly."

"Nicer than a Malibu. Nice enough to get carjacked for."

"Yeah, right. Not in this neighborhood."

"I'm dead serious."

Gabe hiccuped, but only because he had been laughing too much, sucking in air much of the evening. Collins could be pretty funny when he made an effort. He did an imitation of Jenkins that was to die for—the super concerned manner, the fatherly sighs.

Collins's fist shot out, hitting Gabe so quickly and violently in the midsection that he just crumpled into the street as if his spine had been removed. *What the*— The last sensations he knew in this life were all metal—the scrape of the keys being dragged from his fingers, the barrel of a gun at

the back of his head. He didn't piss himself, but only because Collins was moving even faster than Gabe's instincts
could. He was going to die, and the only thing he managed
to figure out before it happened was that it had absolutely
nothing to do with his car. *Did I—*
   Gone.

Tuesday

c h a p t e r
29

T ESS AND WILMA HAD AGREED TO MEET AT THE BANK
 when it opened, which meant Tess had to leave Baltimore at 8:00 A.M. and fight rush-hour traffic every inch of
the trip. Even without all the frazzled commuters, it would
have been a charmless journey. The bank, a branch of a
multinational that was relatively new in the state, was on a
strip clogged with chain restaurants and stores catering to
every part of one's automobile—fast-lube places, tire joints,
brake jobs, windshield glass.

"Why here?" Tess asked Wilma. "It's quite a haul from
where you live and where he worked. It's not like he could
get here on his lunch hour."

"Probably because it's one place I'd never come. I don't
think I've ever been here before in my life." Wilma's face
was grayish, as if the suburb of Laurel were a disease she
was worried about catching.

The bank manager studied the court order in a way that

made Tess fear complications. A chubby Latina packed into a bright yellow suit, the manager had the air of someone who would make things difficult just because it would make *her* day more interesting. But perhaps she was simply a slow reader, for she handed the paper back to Wilma and led them into the small area the bank kept for safe-deposit boxes.

"*She* can't come in," the woman said, pointing at Tess. "And I gotta watch."

"I'm an officer of the court," said Tess, who had prepared the lie ahead of time, along with a reasonably official-looking ID, created on her computer and then laminated at a twenty-four-hour hardware store last night. She had also talked to Tyner, who'd assured her that there was no law requiring a bank employee to observe, but some insisted on it, if only out of sheer nosiness. "The order specifies that this has to be done under supervision because the estate is still in probate. She's allowed to inventory the contents but not to remove them."

The woman looked skeptical—as well she should, because nothing Tess had said was remotely true—but fate decided to throw Tess a bone. Another bank employee arrived at that moment with a pink, orange, and white Dunkin' Donuts box. Saved by the cruller. Anxious to make her selection, the woman waved them in.

Wilma's hands shook as she fitted her key into the lock. She then took the box, a medium-size one, to the semiprivate area set aside. She lifted the lid and revealed a black-and-white photocopy of a bearded man in a straw hat, a man who looked strangely familiar to Tess. There was a layer of pink tissue paper beneath it. When Tess pushed it aside, the overwhelming impression was a landscape of green, a veritable Emerald City in a box.

"I thought you were the earner and Greg was the one who was bound for glory," she said.

Wilma was silent for a moment. "That—that—*asshole*," she said at last. Tess regularly heard—and said—far worse words, but it was a shock to see the prim and self-righteous Wilma let loose this way. "If you knew how tight things were for us at times—college loans, the baby, the mortgage on the new house. Although now I understand where he got some of the cash to buy the new house. He *said* that he had borrowed money from his mother."

"I hope you reported it as a loan on your mortgage application," Tess said.

"What?"

"Nothing. Should we count it?"

"Not really. If I know how much it is, I think I might get angrier. Whatever Greg was doing, there wasn't . . . It couldn't be . . . It had to be . . ." *Illegal*, Tess wanted to say, but Wilma still wasn't ready to concede that. "He got himself killed, and for what? We would have been okay, in the long run. I would have made partner. He could have gone into private practice if it came to that. What was the rush?"

Tess had extracted one bundle of cash, counted it, and done some quick multiplication in her head. Sixteen packs, $10,000 per pack—$160,000, give or take. "He was shaking someone down. Who?"

"I don't know," Wilma said. "Honestly."

Tess pulled up each pack of bills, to make sure there was nothing left in the box.

"What are you looking for?" Wilma asked, her voice at once bitter and teary. It was clear that this secret cache, if not exactly what she had feared all along, was also anything but an innocuous discovery. "Waiting for hope to fly out? I don't think she's here."

"A note. But I guess that would be too easy, right? A nice and neat confession about what he was into."

"To write something like that, he would have to believe he

was in imminent danger. And the one thing I'm sure about the last time I saw Greg alive is that he was buoyant, happy. In fact, he was happier in the weeks before his death than he'd been in a long time. He went into a horrible mope around the time I got pregnant. At the time I thought it was money woes—"

"Could be. Maybe this was a sudden windfall, and that's why he cheered up. He was in antiterrorism, right? This would be chump change to some of those Saudis." Tess was studying the log—Greg had last visited the bank in September. The account had been opened in August year before last, and he had been here monthly, through July. Then—nothing.

"Maybe." Wilma's eyes were on the money, but she wasn't seeing it. She was trapped in her own thoughts. "Only, we bought the house last winter. I found out I was pregnant in March, and he was irritable from then on. I worried that he felt trapped in a way he hadn't before. But come fall his bad mood vanished. On Halloween, when the kids came to the door, he was just so into it. He said to me, 'I can't wait until our little boy does that.' Something changed over the summer."

The employees' doughnut buzz was fading fast, and Tess thought it would be best to put the drawer back in place, continue their conversation elsewhere. At the last minute, she grabbed the Xeroxed photograph, stashing it in her pocket.

She steered Wilma to the Silver Diner, not even fifty yards up the highway. It was an ersatz diner, the kind of faux-fifties place that Tess didn't normally condone, but it was the best bet for breakfast in these parts.

"Think back to Greg's work," Tess said. "Was there anyone he might have blackmailed?"

"No. The terrorism unit was having virtually no luck. Truth is, Greg was kind of floundering since the transfer.

He was brought on for PR, a suitable face to put before the cameras. The dirty little secret about the FBI's antiterrorism work is that there *is* no work. Until, well, there is again. Get me?"

Tess did, but she didn't want to think about it.

"What about his earlier cases, the drug stuff he did?"

"He was known for being a hard-liner and getting convictions. In fact, he was contemptuous of his colleagues who couldn't nail suspects no matter how close they got. So who would pay him off? He got the federal death penalty for that one group of gang members."

Wilma said the last with great pride, reminding Tess that the two of them did not see eye to eye on many things. Tess opposed the death penalty in theory, and it pained her that she had taken another man's life so readily. But she was learning to hold her tongue and her opinions. She and Wilma weren't here to become BFFs.

"In the terrorism unit—was there anything he said about his work that centered on a single individual? They might not have been making arrests, but they still could have been up on wiretaps, monitoring someone. A wealthy Saudi Arabian might have paid money to know what his unit was doing, skimpy as it was."

Wilma shook her head. "I'm telling you, all he did was speak of their incompetence and the futility of the whole operation."

"So why did he volunteer for it in the first place?"

"I'm not sure. He'd been working a few things with a guy named Mike Collins, but he said Collins couldn't bring him anything good since he stopped working undercover. You have to understand—the way the office is set up, the AUSA's are often dependent on agents to bring them good cases."

"But he must have known other agents."

"He liked Mike best and thought he'd gotten a raw deal. Do you know him?"

"Yeah, I know him." Tess decided not to share that she wasn't his biggest fan.

"Greg really admired him. An authentic Horatio Alger story, up from the streets, basketball star at Langston Hughes."

"Dunbar," Tess corrected absently. She dug the photocopy out of her pocket, stared at the old man in the hat.

"Whatever."

"He talked about Mike a lot?"

"I don't know if I'd say 'a lot.' Enough that I knew he resented the agency's treatment of him."

"Wilma—"

"What?"

"Did you ever have a crush on a guy?"

"Sometimes." Wilma's tone was smug, as if to suggest she was far more familiar with being an object of crushes, not a holder of them.

"So when you were obsessed with some guy, didn't you say his name over and over, whenever you could, bring him up in the most irrelevant conversations, just to have the thrill of saying his name?"

Wilma blushed her furious blush. "Greg was *not* queer for Mike Collins."

"No, but they might have shared a secret that they would be even more desperate to conceal." Tess showed her the photocopy. "This is taken from one of those literary postcards you can buy at Nouveau or Barnes & Noble. It's Walt Whitman."

"So?"

"Poet. *Poet.* If Mike Collins played for Dunbar, then he was a star on the Poets. I guess he couldn't find a Dunbar postcard, so he settled for Whitman. 'I sing the body electric'? 'I dote on myself, for there is that lot of me, and all so luscious'?"

Wilma, despite her Ivy League education, still looked mystified. But Tess had no doubt that her husband had hedged his bets, leaving this subtle clue for someone who would eventually make the connection but treat Youssef's old friend with dignity and respect. Who else had to know that Collins played for the Poets?

Jenkins had been surprised to find Mike Collins at his door first thing that morning. As much as he liked the young man, he'd never had him to his apartment. In fact, he didn't even realize that Mike knew where he lived.

He wondered what else Bully knew about him.

"You want coffee?" he asked, although the kid seemed so wired that a shot of Jameson might have been more appropriate.

"No, I'm fine."

"Well, I need some."

He motioned Collins to follow him into the apartment's kitchen, not that it was a trip that required a tour guide. Since returning to Baltimore, Jenkins had lived in one of those sterile, rent-by-the-month gigs, already furnished. The kitchen was separated from the so-called great room by a Formica-topped bar. Collins sat there, perched on one of the wicker stools that had come with the place, rocking a little from side to side. Kid was het-up. Jenkins hoped he wasn't doing drugs, a curious but not unheard-of liability for DEA agents. But Collins's disdain for drugs had always been persuasively virulent. He saw them as a plague that had swept through his once-middle-class neighborhood, destroying almost every young black man in their path. No, it was impossible to imagine Collins using drugs.

Jenkins pulled out his filters and the can of grounds he kept in the freezer, although he was always hearing conflicting opinions on that method of storage. It seemed to him that they kept changing the rules about everything. *Plastic cutting boards, wooden cutting boards, back to plastic. Coffee with tap water, coffee with purified water, coffee with eggshells and old socks, back to tap water.* Whatever Jenkins did, he made crap coffee, but at least it was cheap. Jenkins didn't like giving someone two dollars for something he could make at home for a fraction of the cost. Made him feel like a sucker. He thought about Gabe Dalesio, who never seemed to be without a large cup of pricey coffee. The guy must have spent at least four, five dollars a day on coffee drinks. Four dollars a day, almost thirty dollars a week, over fifteen hundred dollars a year on coffee. Jenkins's first wife, Martha, had criticized Jenkins for the way he tipped, the ones and fives and even tens that had slipped through his fingers so readily. But a tip went to a person at least, not some corporation. You hand a girl a five-dollar tip for checking your coat and you make her day. Give Mr. Starbucks or Ms. Seattle's Best Coffee three dollars for some fancy hot drink and you were just one of the multitudes of suckers.

The coffee machine puffed and huffed, quite a production for the task of pouring hot water over a paper filter of coffee grounds. It tasted better if you waited until the whole pot brewed, but Jenkins could never resist pulling the carafe out and letting his mug catch the first syrupy cupful.

"You sure you don't want any?"

"I'm fine."

It was only when Jenkins turned back to the counter, FBI mug in his hand, that he saw the gun on the counter. *Not a service revolver,* his mind registered. A street weapon, a piece of shit. Then: *Why does Mike have it? Why is he showing it to me?*

"Mike," he said, his voice soft and pleading. "Bully. What's this about? What's wrong?"

Even in this agitated state, he was so very handsome. Extremely dark-skinned, with features that had always seemed vaguely Native American to Jenkins—strong straight nose, high cheekbones, a bow-shaped mouth. That mouth was trembling, just a little now. Yet any show of emotion in Collins's face was noteworthy.

"Mike . . . ?"

The young man picked up the gun, studying it as if he wasn't quite sure what it was or where it had come from, then put it back down.

"I . . . I may have overstepped, Barry."

"Overstepped?"

"Gabe Dalesio learned something, and it struck me as key, but I knew if we acted on it, he might begin to put things together. So, um, I killed him."

This was a new situation to him. As a father to his own sons, Jenkins had been the one who disappointed, who stood before his children's sorrowful and disapproving faces again and again. Here at last was his chance to assure someone that it was okay to screw up, to give comfort and succor.

Succor. Funny word. Say it out loud and it sounded just like "sucker."

"You used this gun?"

"Yeah. Out on the street, like it was a carjacking or a robbery gone wrong. I took it off a drug dealer years ago. There's no paper on it."

"You take the car?"

"No, but I grabbed his wallet and his keys. Then I went to see a woman I know out Hunt Valley way, one who's not too fussy about advance notice."

"What you kids call a booty call?" Collins managed a feeble smile at Jenkins's deliberate squareness. "That was smart, Bully." This earned a genuine smile, one of relief and pride. "And you didn't use your service weapon, smarter still. Now we just have to throw this one down the sewer."

"And go to Delaware?"

"Delaware?"

"That's what Dalesio found. There's an ex-cop, held the liquor license on the dad's bar, and he's also listed as the founding partner in the girl's business. He figured that a guy like that was probably in the habit of doing the family favors."

"Well, that sure is interesting." *But not worth killing another federal prosecutor for.* "I mean, it's worth checking out. Still sounds like a bit of a long shot to me. Why would an ex-cop shield someone wanted in a murder investigation?"

"Dalesio did some preliminary checking. He pulled a reverse directory, started calling some of the guy's neighbors. There was some strange guy drinking beer with him just yesterday."

"Strange?"

"Unknown, not a familiar face. White, youngish. Could be the boyfriend. We should go over there."

"Throw the gun down the sewer. Then go to work."

"Work?"

"A federal prosecutor was killed last night. You don't know that now, but it will be all over your office soon after you get there. And while you may have his wallet—throw that down the sewer, too, okay?—police will have already traced the car registration back to him. Go into work and be glad, for once, that they treat you like shit. I'll do the same thing, and we'll do what we've been doing all along: keep our eyes and ears open, figure out who knows what, then proceed according to an orderly plan of *my* devising."

Collins winced a little, picking up the implicit criticism in that one stressed word, and Jenkins realized that he had to modulate his tone. "It's okay, Bully. You did okay. Just let me do the thinking. It worked with Youssef, didn't it? We took our sweet time, and it was just about perfect."

"Except for the kid using the ATM card again. And then that private eye came along."

"Yeah, well, she's got other fish to fry now." Jenkins wondered fleetingly how they would continue to press her without Gabe. Maybe it didn't matter. Maybe they really did have the information they'd sought all along. "The thing is, we've got to do this without involving civilians. Mike? You feel me?"

Another wisp of a smile from Collins for the way Jenkins sounded when he aped that ghetto talk.

"If this little fucker is at the beach, we've got to take him into custody and isolate him. Set him up to run from us, then do the old throw-down. Nothing fancy, nothing complicated."

"I get it."

"You sure? Because we're up to two more bodies than we ever planned to have. I don't blame you for Youssef—he tricked you into telling him what we had going, demanded in, then wanted out. He was a liability, and we had to get rid of him. But this . . ."

Collins's shoulders sagged. The kid meant well. But his central flaw could not be fixed. When in doubt, he went for his gun. It was a weird defect, one usually found in female officers, but it had been okay as long as Collins kept shooting criminals. It was only when he shot that civilian that he'd gotten in such deep shit. Irony was, he'd been absolutely justified for once. The guy had refused to stop, just kept coming at Collins, one of those old-timers who thought he could beat a drug dealer with a rake, fucking up a big buy that Collins had spent eight months getting to that moment. The geezer was lucky to have survived, in Jenkins's opinion.

"Go to work, Bully," he said. "The minute someone tells you about Gabe, say, 'Holy shit! I was having a drink with him last night. He was telling me his theories about the Youssef case.' Don't say anything that can be contradicted by an eyewitness. You walked out with him. Walked most of the way to his car with him because you were parked in the same direction. Admit that you were a little lit—"

"I wasn't, actually."

"Admit that you were a little lit, that you went out to visit your lady friend and barely had time to change your clothes before coming in to work. Get me? We're in assessment mode today."

Collins left, and Jenkins sat at his kitchen table, head in hands. How had it all gone so wrong? It had been so perfect on paper, so bloodless and simple, money coming in and no one going out. He added up the death toll in his head. Youssef, Dalesio. Oh, and the kid, Le'andro Watkins, not that the world could really mourn a lowlife who was going to kill or be killed before his twenty-first birthday.

And now they had to find this other kid, set him up. But then they would be done. It had to end there. Please, let it fucking end.

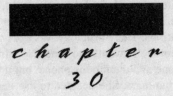

chapter
30

TESS HAD PLANNED TO GO STRAIGHT TO HER OFFICE FROM
Laurel, but she headed home instead. WBAL was reporting on a street murder in Canton, the kind of crime sure
to spook the area's yuppies and tourists. When the newscast
yielded to the morning call-in show, she could hear people
trying to extract the detail that would establish that the crime
was somehow the victim's fault. *Was it a domestic?* No, it
appeared to be a robbery and attempted carjacking. *Was it
someone driving a flashy car?* Not clear. *A man cruising
for . . . um, female companionship?* The callers were desperate for proof that no crime or misfortune was ever truly
random. Tess thought it more remarkable that such murders
were so infrequent. It was less than a mile from the swank
condos on the Canton waterfront to the desperate neighborhood where Dub, Terrell, and Tourmaline squatted in an
abandoned rowhouse.

At home she found another FedEx with another cell

phone—Crow had thought to waive the signature this time—but after several futile minutes with the instructions, she realized she had hit the wall of her own technological limitations. There probably was a way to download the digital photos she wanted to send Crow from her camera to the phone and then to his phone, but it would take a better mind than hers. She decided to use her laptop, setting up a neutral Hotmail account, then forwarding the photos there. She would call Crow on the new phone and give him the password, then hope he could get to a computer to view them.

The problem was, she had no proof that Mike Collins was anything other than the concerned federal agent he purported to be. She called her one good friend in the Baltimore City homicide squad, Detective Martin Tull.

"Not a good time," the detective said with his customary curtness. "Got a red ball so far up my ass that it might end up coming out of my nose the next time I blow it."

"Canton, yeah, I heard it on 'BAL. I'll be quick. You got an open case on a kid named Le'andro Watkins? He was killed last week. Shot, typical drug-murder stuff." *Or so it would appear.*

A moment of silence. Tull must be glancing at the board that carried the cases, listed by number and victims' last names. The board was color-coded—black for closed ones, red for those still open. Tess would bet anything there was a sea of red on the board this year.

Tull came back on the line. "Yeah, that's Rainier's."

Shit. If Tess had only one friend in homicide, she also had only one enemy. Still, she didn't carry a grudge, and maybe Rainier didn't either. In the end she had done right by him, handed him a bouquet of clearances. Tess had probably helped Rainier earn his highest clearance rate since he joined the department.

"He around?"

"That worthless fucker called in from the field this morning, said he was doing some interviews. He's hiding, worried that he'll be pulled to help on this case."

"Got a cell for him?"

"Yeah. And maybe he'll answer if he doesn't see the 396 prefix." All city numbers, including those from police headquarters, began with those three numbers.

"Good luck," Tess said. "I owe you one."

"You've lost count if you think all you owe me is one."

"Final question: If you were the kind of homicide detective who ever pretended to be out in the field to avoid a difficult assignment—we all know you'd never do that, just being theoretical here—but if you *were* that kind of detective and you weren't working and you didn't want to be found, where would you be?"

Tull began laughing.

"What's so funny?"

"Truth be told, I'd go to your father's bar, because no one's ever going to find anyone in that little bend of Franklintown Road. But if I were Jay Rainier—and I thank God every day that I'm not—I'd be on Fort Avenue. He came up through Southern District patrol, has a soft spot for Locust Point."

"Tull, there's a bar in almost every block of Fort."

"Yeah, but it's only, what, two, three miles long? And it's a nice day for a pub crawl. Cool, but sunny."

Tess called Crow's new number but got no answer. She left careful instructions about how to access the Hotmail account, then made a quick costume change before heading to South Baltimore, trading her suede jacket for a nylon windbreaker of a startling bright blue, lined with synthetic plush of the same color. It had belonged to her father and still had his name, Patrick, embroidered on the front.

But it was the back, proclaiming Tess a member of the
Colts Corral, No. 34, that should make the Fort Avenue bartenders warm to her.

Crow and Lloyd were loading supplies at the 84 Lumber off
Route 26 when the cell rang, and Crow couldn't get his
hands free to answer it without dropping a two-by-four on
Lloyd's toe. It was wonderful just to hear it ring, to know
Tess was trying to get in touch with him. He checked the
message on the drive back, listened to her breathless instructions to get to a computer and review the photos she
had sent.

But the South Coastal Library, so helpful in all other re-
spects, thwarted him. Its computer network was loaded with
virus protections that refused to allow him to download the
images Tess had forwarded. One of the librarians could
probably help him bypass the program, but Crow didn't
want to risk drawing that much attention to himself. Maybe
Ed had a computer.

"We take technology too much for granted," he said to
Lloyd as they drove back to Fenwick.

"What you mean?"

"We assume everyone has a cell phone, computers, Internet access—or that cell phones will always work or we'll
be able to find a wireless hot spot when we need it. Can you
imagine the chaos if terrorists or hackers brought down all
the landlines and cell access and wireless connections for
even an hour? If you couldn't call anyone, use an ATM, send
an e-mail?"

"I'd be okay," Lloyd said.

Crow started to explain that Lloyd was missing the larger
point of what he was trying to describe, the global nature of
technological dependence. But Lloyd had spoken a simple

truth. Lloyd would be okay, probably better than most. On the day that the shit *really* came down—when buildings fell again or if a similar nightmare scenario played out—Crow wouldn't mind having Lloyd Jupiter at his side.

Fort Avenue dead-ended into Fort McHenry, the star-shaped fort where a pivotal battle in the War of 1812 had inspired Francis Scott Key to write "The Star-Spangled Banner." In honor of that deed, the fort had commissioned a statue of Orpheus—or, as locals called him, that naked guy with the harp. Tess parked in the public lot and began heading west along a street where there was a bar, on average, every two blocks.

She had not been in the Locust Point section of Baltimore for two years, and the area had changed considerably, like most of the city's waterfront. She could see the shells of expensive town houses—at this width and price, they would never allow themselves to be called rowhouses—rising by the harbor, and there was a fancy-schmancy bakery, the kind of place where a cupcake cost almost as much as a Lady Baltimore in the old-fashioned stalls in Cross Street Market. But most of the old bars were hanging on, with only a few chichi interlopers. Given that her father was once an inspector for the liquor board, Tess couldn't help speculating why so many licenses had been granted in the area. It had to be tied to political patronage; the question was whether it implied a surplus of clout or a complete lack thereof. She also wondered how many of the places made illegal payouts on the video poker games where, even at midday, stonefaced zombies sat pressing buttons forlornly.

The bartenders at such places were expert at protecting their regulars, especially from women inquiring after them. But with reasonable deployments of charm and cash, she managed to ascertain whether Jay Rainier was known in these parts. "Captain Larry's?" the bartender at Truman's volunteered, but the skipper there sent her to Hogan's Alley, which recommended the End Zone, a cruel joke, as that bar had been replaced by a yuppie joint, the Idle Hour. She had worked her way almost two miles down Fort Avenue when she found the man himself in Dorothy's, a pale lager and a large cheeseburger in front of him.

"Don't you worry about mad cow disease?" Tess asked, taking the stool next to him.

"Hmmmph," Rainier said, his mouth full.

"Me neither. I'll have what the gentleman's having, medium rare, Swiss cheese if you've got it."

"And a Coors Light, too?" the waitress asked.

Tess didn't believe in the light version of anything. She studied the handles on the draft taps. "Yuengling."

"You want fries with that?" The waitress's tone suggested she had a vested interest in Tess's weight.

"I want fries with *everything*."

"Hey, Monaghan," Rainer said after a hard swallow. He seemed wary but not unfriendly. "Is this a chance encounter?"

"Not exactly."

"Fuck me." There was no edge to his words, however. He studied the silent television above them, tuned to ESPN. "Second real day of the baseball season and probably the last one that the Mets will be in first place."

Tess nodded in pretend empathy. She had been brought up to hate the Mets more than any other team in major-league baseball. The very mention of 1969—the year that Baltimore teams had lost to New York ones in the World Series, the Super Bowl, and the NBA championships—could ruin her father's day.

"I hear you caught a case—"

"Of the clap? You doing STD investigation now for Public Health? That would be a step up for you, prestigewise." Rainier's tone remained listless, as if he really couldn't summon the energy to taunt Tess.

"Le'andro Watkins. Teenager, killed last week."

"Yeah, that's a winner, ain't it?"

"You've developed any leads?"

"None at all. Usual drill. No one saw anything. No one knows anything. He was a low-level solider in a small-time drug gang."

"Worked for Bennie Tepperson—Bennie Tep. Am I right?"

"Yeah," he said, now more alert. "You got something for me, Monaghan? Because this one's a total loser."

"I might. Eventually. Was there anything to suggest that it wasn't what it appeared to be, a straight-up retribution shooting?"

"Naw. Although I will say the East Side has been quiet lately, and Bennie's far from a player. He's an old-timer who's stayed in the game by not taking a lot of risks. Hell, he'll barely defend what territory he does have, and he's getting a rep for putting out really weak packages. He's never been a significant player, except in his own head."

"You hear that from DEA?"

"Naw, our own guys are more up on it. The feds got no use for the drug stuff now, unless it's big federal-death-penalty stuff with lots of gang violence, like those M-13s down in southern Maryland."

"Still, the DEA was interested, right? Came around, asked a few questions?"

Rainier gave her an odd look. "Nope. No DEA involvement at all. What makes you think that?"

"You sure? I know you're the primary, but could they have spoken to someone else?"

"Anything is possible, but I sure as hell didn't talk to anyone. It's not exactly one of our high-priority cases. And if a DEA agent came sniffing around, there would have been talk, you can be sure of that."

It was what Tess had expected to hear, even feared. If Mike Collins hadn't talked to the primary on the case, then how could he know that Le'andro Watkins was the dead kid that had scared Lloyd into running? Chances were he was the man who had killed him.

"You know a DEA agent name of Mike Collins?" she asked Rainier.

"Know of him. He's the poor bastard who shot that geezer who tried to interrupt his drug buy. Honest mistake, and they hung him out to dry."

"But you've never spoken to him, haven't had any contact with him in the last week?"

"Nope. Never met the man."

Tess's lunch arrived, and she decided to abandon herself, however briefly, to the reliable pleasure of grilled meat, melted cheese, and deep-fried potatoes. "So what sent you into hiding today?"

"I'm working," Rainier said, in on the joke for once. "Hey, it's bad enough I'm saddled with this piece-of-shit Watkins case. I don't see why I have to be collateral damage in a red ball as well."

"Tourist?"

"Worse."

"A relative of the mayor?"

"Some federal prosecutor. Probably a random thing, a straight-up carjacking, but they're sending guys out to grab every lowlife in a five-mile radius, just in case it's related to his work. Two AUSA's in six months. It's making people a little jumpy."

The cheeseburger, which would have been a contender in

any best-of-Baltimore survey, turned to ash on Tess's tongue.

"You happen to hear the name?" she asked after a hard swallow.

"Something Italian."

"Dalesio?"

"Yeah, like the restaurant. Dalesio. You know the guy?"

chapter
3 1

*L*IVE AND LEARN, JENKINS THOUGHT. GAIL SCHULIAN WASN'T
going to make the same mistake that her predecessor
had, calling press conferences and vowing to avenge the
death of Gabe Dalesio. She was playing this as close to
the vest as possible. Here it was almost four o'clock, and the
name hadn't been released to the public yet. As far as the general population knew, the Canton carjacking was just some
unlucky civilian.

Collins had done as he'd been told, gone to the bosses and
spoken about his drink with a dead man. He said Dalesio
had been working on some leads in the Youssef case, but it
was all about trying to get the female PI to give up her
source, nothing inherently dangerous.

Collins had reported the details back via cell phone, although even that made Jenkins nervous. Just their luck,
some hobbyist with a scanner would pick up their conversation. But whatever Collins was, he was disciplined, and

while an eavesdropper might wonder why he felt the need to relate all this to Jenkins, there was nothing in the content of their conversation to cause trouble. Yes, Collins had been a most satisfactory protégé all around.

Until he murdered Gabe Dalesio.

Killing Youssef had been bad enough, but necessary. The whole beauty of Jenkins's scheme was that it was low-risk, a fed's version of playing stickup man. They were stealing money from a drug dealer, and a mediocre drug dealer at that, one who was unlikely to be a target but had the old-school arrogance to think he might be. It was a scheme Jenkins had dreamed up and polished while in exile in Woodlawn, waiting for retirement and contemplating suicide. The thing was, such a scheme required a collaborator. A defense attorney had seemed the likely go-between, and Jenkins couldn't stomach the thought of that. Then he had met Mike Collins, another former wonder boy covered in shame. As an East Sider with contacts on the ground, Bully could do what few other feds could: go straight to the source. Collins hashed out the deal, told Bennie Tep that he was coming up on wiretaps but that Collins could hold him harmless for a monthly fee. It was like selling real estate on the moon; the only way that Bennie Tep could prove they weren't protecting him was if he got arrested by the feds, and that was never going to happen.

How had Youssef figured it out? That bugged Jenkins to this day, because if Youssef could figure it out, someone else could as well. He was such a smarmy bastard, cutting himself in when he hadn't done any of the work. But okay, Jenkins was fine with giving him a cut, letting him collect a little Bennie Tep money, too. It didn't even cost him and Bully anything; Mike just told Bennie that they had to bring an AUSA in to guarantee his protection, so the monthly fee went up. No, it was okay when Youssef wanted in.

It was when he wanted *out* that things came to a head, and the fact that he wanted to do it because he had a kid on the way just made Jenkins more nervous. Once Youssef opted out, it would be all too easy for him to turn on them if the shit ever came down. But Jenkins had smiled and shook the young man's hand, told him there were no hard feelings, congratulated him on his soon-to-be-born son, and let him go his own way, thinking everything was peachy.

Bennie hadn't wanted any part in killing Youssef; that would be a death-penalty crime, and he was too cautious for that. But he let Mike have one of his low-level kids set it up. Le'andro wasn't the brightest bulb on the tree, but he had faked his way through his part. He got in touch with Youssef, claimed to know something about a Pakistani who was funneling money into local drug gangs, asking questions about weapons and dirty bombs. The night before Thanksgiving was supposed to be Youssef's big score, a meeting with someone close to the Paki, arranged by Le'andro. He had headed downtown, thinking he was on his way to being a hero.

He hadn't died heroically. He had given up the ATM number readily enough, thinking it might save his life, but the punishment had just begun. Make it look personal, Jenkins had impressed on his protégé. Make it look angry. Truth be told, Collins had succeeded a little too well at that part. In the end, when they were parked along the Patapsco in the state park, Jenkins had turned away, not wanting to see what Collins was capable of.

But it had gone according to plan, except for the moment that Youssef tried to get away by wading across the river. Collins had caught him on the other side, and he didn't have to make it look angry then, because he was. Funny, that unplanned contingency had worked for them, too, sending the case into Howard County, where the detectives had even less experience handling homicide than Baltimore County did.

Looking back, Jenkins regretted all the thinking and conniving. The overreaching, really. He knew better. The shrewder you tried to be, the greater the likelihood that something would trip you up. The E-ZPass, for example. That little discrepancy had brought Dalesio into the investigation, and they would have been better off without him in the long run. Better off without his death for sure. And he should have known not to rely on some street kid like Le'andro. Why had he handed the ATM card off to someone else, who then screwed it all up? What had he told the other kid, if anything? Maybe they could stop now, play the odds that this other kid didn't know anything that could implicate Bully, much less Jenkins. But if the kid dragged Bennie Tep into this, he'd sell them out in a minute. Well, sell Collins out. Bennie Tep didn't know Jenkins existed. No, it couldn't be risked. They had to plug this last leak.

But they had a plausible reason now. Collins was going to go to Delaware and find this kid, assuming Dalesio was right about where they were. Collins was going to finish the job that his new best friend wouldn't be able to do, being shot down and all in the prime of his young life. They were going to find the source—no, the *accomplice*, which would explain why he was so desperate to evade them—and whose fault would it be if the kid pulled a gun on them, refused to be taken alive?

The only question was whether they should leave tonight or tomorrow morning. Tomorrow, he was thinking. Sick days all around. As the afternoon wore on, he started blowing his nose, talking a little raspier than usual, complaining about the pollen. He even sneezed a couple of times, not that a single one of his so-called colleagues said so much as gesundheit or bless you. Well, fuck you guys, too.

*   *   *

Tess hadn't realized how lucky she'd been, getting Tull on her first try that morning. Despite her multiple urgent voice mails and pages, even with the "911" code appended, it was almost seven before he got back to her. It was hard, competing with the murder of an assistant U.S. attorney—even when you had what might be relevant information. Tull sounded weary and stressed, the end of his day still distant.

"There's this DEA agent, Mike Collins—"

"We've talked to Mike Collins," he said: "He had a drink with Dalesio in Canton, said good-bye to him in front of the bar, and headed out. He told his boss, and his boss told him to come talk to us. And yes, we know that Gabe Dalesio was pressing you on the Youssef murder."

"Tull, Collins is the killer. There was no carjacking. This is what this guy does. He makes murders look like, well, *other* murders. A carjacking in this case. I think he also did Youssef and that street kid I was asking you about, Le'andro Watkins. See? He plays with the stereotypes of homicide, makes us see what we expect to see."

"Tess, I know they've been leaning on you, but this is beyond paranoid."

"But he could have done it, right? He was with him right before."

"Sure, if we're talking about the mere physics of the situation. As a problem of time and space, it's possible. But why in hell would a DEA agent kill this guy, much less the other two?"

It was an excellent question. Tess pondered the stray bits of information she had gathered—the money in Youssef's account, the death of a teenager who worked for a drug dealer, a teenager whose name that Collins knew, a teenager who was connected to Youssef's ATM card. She felt like she was working a monochromatic jigsaw puzzle. The pieces fit theoretically, but trying to piece them together could make you go blind. Or mad.

"Would you pull him in for questioning tomorrow, hold him on that pretext until I make some . . . um, arrangements?"

"Not without a lot more information."

"I'm sure that Collins killed Dalesio, Martin." The use of his first name, which Tull loathed, was almost a code between them, a sign that Tess was as serious as she ever got. "Maybe because Dalesio figured something out that he wasn't supposed to know."

"Is this insight coming from your elusive source?" There was an unmistakable edge to Tull's voice. He was a loyal friend, but he couldn't possibly approve of Tess's refusal to cooperate with a homicide investigation.

"Mike Collins is one of three feds who's spent a lot of time in the past ten days trying to get that information out of me. Dalesio was one of the others, and the third is an FBI agent, Barry Jenkins."

"I knew Barry Jenkins on his first pass through Baltimore. He's a good guy."

"Okay, sure." Tess had no desire to argue this point. It was Collins she feared, not Jenkins, who was probably in the dark as well. She assumed that photo of Whitman had been meant for him, or someone else familiar with Collins's life story. "But keep all this in mind, Tull. If anything happens— to me, to Crow, to our . . . um, friend—remember this conversation, okay? Remember that I tried to tell you."

"Don't be so melodramatic, Tess. You're talking about a DEA agent and a longtime FBI guy. They don't go around killing civilians, much less assistant U.S. attorneys. Hell, the DEA and the FBI don't even work together under normal circumstances. They got no use for each other."

"If you say so. But if I bring . . . my source to you, can you offer true protection? Can you guarantee anyone's safety?"

Tull paused, all the answer Tess needed. "It's hard, Tess. Put aside your whole conspiracy theory. This kid is afraid because he's double-crossed a drug dealer, right? Unless he's got family someplace well outside Baltimore, unless he's willing to stay off the streets, I'd be a liar if I promised anything."

"That's what I thought. What if I can bring you proof that Collins is connected to all of this?"

"Whatta you got?"

"I'll tell you in an hour."

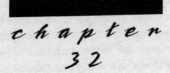

chapter
32

THE POLICE HAD COME AND GONE AT GABE DALESIO'S
rental house, which was what Tess was counting on. If
time hadn't been at a premium, she would have hunted down
the landlord and talked her way in, used one of her official-
looking ID cards. "Death inspector" for the state medical ex-
aminer's office was good. So was any kind of public-utility
business card, which allowed her to claim reports of a gas or
carbon monoxide leak. But it was past 7:30 P.M., and she
didn't want to waste time trying to track down the registered
owner of this property on Hanover Street. Even if she did
find the landlord, he could turn out to be an out-of-town in-
vestor who used a local property-management firm. More
time wasted.

And with the sky still light, thanks to daylight savings
time, breaking and entering wasn't the best option. So Tess
decided to go straight at it, knocking on a neighbor's door
and asking if he had a spare key.

"I'm a friend of Gabe's family. . . ."

"From Jersey?"

"Yes." It was amazing, the information that people would plant in a well-timed pause, then give one credit for knowing. "They want me to go into the apartment, make sure certain things are there. The police"—she wiggled her fingers—"don't always leave things as they found them."

"I saw the cops. They wouldn't tell me anything, but . . . it's him, right? The guy killed in Canton?"

The neighbor was in his late twenties or early thirties, an aging frat-boy type with a paunch. His shock at his neighbor's death had been dulled by a beer-bred complacency. Again, perfect for Tess's needs. An older, more vigilant neighbor would have been inclined toward hard-nosed skepticism, while a young woman would have been outside her charm range. This was her optimum demographic for manipulation. Tess nodded, eyes downcast.

"The thing is, Gabe had my keys, but he never gave me his. He was kinda paranoid."

Shit. "Darn."

"But you know what? I bet you could get into his place via the roof."

"The roof?"

"We both got decks. You go up through mine and cross over. It's no big deal. We do it all the time. You hear about those barge parties people have on lakes? We have, like, roof parties running most of the block."

Rooftop decks were a divisive feature in South Baltimore, beloved by the newcomers, decried by the preservationists. Suddenly Tess was all for them. Her new best friend led her through a house notable only for the smell of mildewing laundry and the large-screen televisions in at least three of the rooms she glimpsed. Once on his deck, he seemed prepared to follow her over the railing and into Gabe's house, but she persuaded him that it would be better if she were alone, in case any official authority questioned her presence there. "I'm a friend of the family, but if I take someone else in with me, I become just another burglar."

He sent her off with a cheerful, vigorous wave, as if she was going on an ocean voyage, and Tess clambered from his deck to Gabe's. The door was locked, but flimsy. Not so flimsy, however, that she could force it with her weight. She was about to summon help from her new best friend when she saw the window overlooking the deck. There was the tiniest gap at the bottom, which meant it wasn't locked. She knocked out the screen, lifted the sash, and climbed into what proved to be Gabe's home office.

His desk was covered with stacks and stacks of paper, but orderly. Her eyes fell first on a notebook, its lined pages covered with the same sentence over and over again: *I will be a Supreme Court justice. I will be a Supreme Court justice.* He had been writing this up to twenty times a day for months, apparently, the poor dumb mook. Her gaze then fell upon her own name, on a chart: T. Monaghan. There was also P. Monaghan, J. Monaghan, K. Monaghan (Kitty had not taken Tyner's last name upon marriage, bless her). E. Ransome—that was Crow, of course. Each name had been inked in a different color. If she hadn't been the target, she would have studied and admired this impeccable organization. Tess had thought she was pretty good at charting and delineating her projects, but Gabe Dalesio made her look like a rank amateur.

The color scheme was mirrored, she realized, in the Post-its fluttering like banners from various stacks of paper. She glanced back to the chart—Crow was yellow. There were at least a dozen yellow flags, and the first one she grabbed was a statement from a brokerage firm up in Towson. A million dollars. More than a million dollars, invested in a mutual fund whose acronym meant nothing to Tess. For a moment she was swamped with doubt and fear. Where could this money have come from? But it was a legal account, not a secret safe-deposit box. And the feds hadn't bothered to taunt her with this information. Crow's money wasn't the issue, not as far as they were concerned.

She needed to be systematic, logical. She pulled every piece of paper with a yellow Post-it, even those with other colors attached. Here was her father's liquor license, which had been triple-flagged in yellow, pink, and green, and scored with exclamation marks. A name had been circled in those three colors as well, Ed Keyes. Tess had never known that Keyes held the Point's license before it was transferred to her father, but she wasn't surprised. Spike had not been much of one for legalities, much less the kind of sucking up that helped a man get a liquor license. Other yellows held brief dossiers on Crow's parents, but no excited punctuation.

She searched for another triple flag and found the articles of incorporation for her business. How could this be of interest? Were they so desperate for leverage on her that they had hoped to find she was operating without a proper license?

Another multicolored circle, another series of *!!!*—next to Ed Keyes's name.

An interesting overlap, but why would it matter to Gabe Dalesio unless Ed was a crook, and Tess, although she had never met her nominal partner, doubted that. Her Uncle Spike had sworn by the former cop's loyalty, his reliability.

Uncle Spike. Crow, working in Spike's old bar, might have called the old man for help in getting out of town. And Spike could have sent him to Ed, his old reliable. Did that mean Crow was with Ed, or simply that Ed had helped him hide somewhere else? That would explain the exclamation marks, which appeared nowhere else in Gabe Dalesio's notes.

Tess took out her cell and a business card she had saved despite being sure that she would never use it.

"I'm ready to meet," she told Barry Jenkins. "I'm ready to talk, to tell you everything. But it has to be tonight."

"Really?" he said. "I guess that can be arranged."

"And it has to be in public. A restaurant or a bar."

"Just name the place and the time."

"My dad's bar on Franklintown Road. Ten-thirty."

"That's kind of late for an old man. Can we do this to-morrow?"

"No." She modulated her voice. "Tonight. Tonight or I'll let the *Beacon-Light* have it first."

"I thought they were more intent on protecting the source than you are."

"I have his permission to go public if I think it's necessary to protect his safety."

"His, huh? You *must* be ready to identify him, throwing the big secret of his gender around."

"Ten-thirty," she said. "All of you—Collins and Dalesio." She was just a citizen. There was no reason she would know that Dalesio was dead.

"I can't guarantee anyone but myself."

"All of you or it's no deal."

"Ten-thirty, your father's bar."

She hung up, satisfied she had the only thing that mattered— a head start. She began trying to call Crow as soon as she was on the highway, then continued at ten-minute intervals, only to be bounced into voice mail every time.

Crow was falling asleep on the sofa while Lloyd was trying to coax something watchable out of the black-and-white tel-

evision that Ed had bequeathed to them. After clicking back
and forth between the Delmarva Peninsula's two channels,
he gave up in disgust, popping in one of the videos they had
checked out from the library, *The Hot Rock*. Tired as he was,
Crow found himself drawn into the film, an old favorite. He
loved the shambling, low-key quality of seventies films, the
small stakes, the human scale. True, Redford was all wrong
for Dortmunder, but his miscasting didn't hurt the film.
Thinking of Westlake made Crow think of *The Grifters*.
Would Lloyd like that? *Should* Lloyd like that? Wasn't John
Cusack's character named Lloyd? No, it was Roy. Would
Lloyd appreciate *Grosse Point Blank*? Crow's brain was
soup tonight.

"A hundred thousand dollars for five guys," Lloyd said in
disbelief as the caper took shape. "That's crazy."

"Lloyd, you made yourself an accessory to murder for
two hundred, a sandwich, a pair of shoes, and a jacket. Oh,
and a DVD player for your buddy."

"I was gonna get my mama some earrings, too," Lloyd
said. "But it was crowded at the Hecht's counter."

It was the first time that Lloyd had ever spoken of his
mother voluntarily. Perhaps the experience with the Anderson family yesterday was making him wistful for home.
Crow decided to mine that vein of feeling, play on those
emotions to see if Lloyd could be persuaded to go back.

"You miss your mom?"

"She okay."

"Yeah, but do you *miss* her?"

An adolescent shrug.

"You want to call her?"

"Thought we couldn't tell people where we are."

"I'm getting rid of the cell phones every forty-eight
hours, remember? Besides, no one's going to be coming

around to talk to your mother, much less get up on her phone, unless they figure out who you are. And there are only four people who know that. Me, Tess, and the two reporters."

"And that crazy blond bitch with the cookies."

Normally Crow would have reproved Lloyd's careless misogyny, but the description of Whitney wasn't that far off base. She *was* a bit of a bitch. In a good way. Whitney's WASP bitchery was a kind of superpower, one that had extricated Tess out of many a jam—and gotten her into almost as many.

"Here, call." He handed Lloyd the cell phone and paused the film on the wonderfully anguished face of Paul Sand as he swallowed the diamond.

Lloyd punched, listened, punched the number in again. "Phone's dead. Lost the charge already. You gotta stop buying this cheap shit."

"Dead?" Crow took the phone and examined it. "No problem, it'll work while plugged in to the charger."

Lloyd punched in the number, listened poker-faced.

"Number disconnected."

"Try information. Maybe she changed it."

"Phones get disconnected," Lloyd said.

"I thought your father—"

"Stepfather."

"Yeah, I thought he was pretty, um, together. Steady."

"Even people with jobs get their phones cut off. It's the easy one to let go, this time of year."

"This time of year?"

"Still too cool to let the gas and 'lectric get turned off, especially with all those kids. Plus, Murray's got a cell, so they can get by without the home phone."

"Call on Murray's phone."

"I don't wanna waste my time trying to get past him. He's big on questions. My mama will get the phone turned back on next month, probably."

There was no recrimination in Lloyd's tone, no self-pity. He spoke of the world he knew as casually as Crow might speak of playing Little League in Charlottesville or going to Luray Caverns on field trips.

"Hey, you get Internet access on this phone," Lloyd said. "You know that?"

"Probably costs an arm and a leg to access it."

"Everything cost, man."

"True. Hey—see if you can get that e-mail from Tess. The one with the photos attached."

It was as if technology were Lloyd's second language, Crow marveled. A week ago he hadn't known what instant messaging was. Now he quickly opened three e-mails from Tess, each with a photo attachment. "White dude," he said, showing Crow a photo of a youngish man. "Old white dude." A middle-aged man. "Brother— *Shit.*"

"What?"

"Nothin'." Lloyd's face was closing down, his eyes slanting sideways.

"*Lloyd.* No more secrets. You agreed."

"I know this guy. Well, I don't know him, but I seen him. He's the guy who gave Le'andro the card."

"You always said Le'andro gave you the card, that you didn't know where he got it from."

Lloyd shifted uncomfortably. "I thought we'd all be safer if I left that part out."

"You were supposed to tell us everything, Lloyd. That was the deal—no lies, no omissions."

"I *know*," Lloyd said. "But I didn't know the guy, and he doesn't know I was there. I was hiding. Le'andro didn't want him to know that he was going to contract it out, you know? So I stayed in the car when he went for the meeting, but I could see them in the rearview mirror. Didn't seem no harm to it."

"You're saying this guy is connected to Gregory Youssef's murder?"

"I'm saying he had the card and the code, and he told Le'andro what to do with it. I didn't know him. Bennie Tep told Le'andro to do him a favor, no big deal. We thought this guy was from New York or Philly. He didn't dress like anyone special, and his car was really shitty. He looked trifling."

"Lloyd, this is a DEA agent. This is one of the guys who's been trying to get your name out of Tess ever since the article appeared. Tess thought it was because the feds want you as a witness, but he may just want *you*."

"Shit."

Lloyd's face was as frozen in desperation as Paul Sand's, although Crow didn't find it the least bit comic.

"I'm going to call Ed," he said. "He's a former cop. Maybe he knows someone over here who can take us in, protect us."

Ed's phone rang and rang, and Crow had a moment of wondering where he could be at ten o'clock. No answering machine either. How typically Ed. But he picked up on the eighth ring, and his voice sounded sharp, not as if he had been asleep or outside.

"Ed, it's Crow. I think Lloyd and I need to turn ourselves in to someone, but someone we can absolutely trust. Definitely not anyone in the DEA or the FBI. Do you have any contacts in the department back in Baltimore, anyone you can vouch for—"

"Wrong number," Ed said.

"Ed, it's *Crow*—"

"I'm telling you, you've got the wrong number. You call

here again, I'm gonna Star 69 your ass, turn you over to the local cops. You hear me? The *local cops*, the Delaware state troopers up to Rehoboth. You think they're small-time, but they'll know what to do with your punk ass. I'm sick of this shit."

He's giving me instructions, Crow realized—*and maybe risking his own life in the process.*

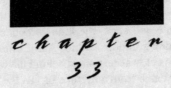

chapter
33

WAS THAT HIM?" BARRY JENKINS ASKED WHEN ED
Keyes hung up the phone.

"Was that who?"

"Edgar Ransome—the young white man who's traveling with a young black man who happens to be a person of interest in the murder of a federal prosecutor. You've practically been harboring a fugitive, Mr. Keyes. How did a former cop get mixed up in something like this?"

Jenkins and Collins had arrived at Keyes's trailer-park address just after ten. It had been Collins who pointed out that it would look weird, calling in sick and then going to arrest the suspect in the Youssef case. This way they could say honestly that they'd followed up on a lead that Dalesio had shared with Collins before he died. But Jenkins always forgot how long it took to cover the 130 miles between Baltimore and the Delaware beaches, even in the off-season. The first hour flew by, making you cocky, but then came

Delaware and the long, dark stretch of 404, a two-lane road where one stubborn farmer could bring the average speed down to forty-five miles per hour. At night the landscape seemed desolate and eerie, the kind of countryside where people broke down in horror films. And Collins, so bold in every other respect, was restrained behind the wheel of a car. That probably came from a lifetime of DWB.

They could have left earlier, but Jenkins wanted to go through the motions, walk through the steps that they would later claim to have taken. One less lie to keep track of. They had even gone by Gabe's house, although they didn't need to go in. After all, Gabe had already told Collins what they needed to know—the name of the likely contact, his address over in Delaware. They were almost to the Bay Bridge when that cunt called, suddenly ready to play, and Jenkins had agreed to meet her rather than let her know that he was nowhere nearby. She wouldn't be the first woman he'd stood up.

Once they arrived in Fenwick, they had decided not to go straight to the ex-cop's trailer. They chatted up some neighbors in the trailer park. They were skeptical types, but again official ID and badges worked wonders, and they eventually loosened the jaw of one old biddy, who had noticed a strange young man hanging around.

"White or black?" Jenkins had asked.

The woman had cast a nervous look toward Collins, as if unsure of the propriety of referencing race in his presence.

"Why, white," she said, lowering her voice to a whisper. "He sat outside and drank a beer with Ed on Sunday, bold as you please."

Bold because it was Sunday, because it was beer? Jenkins wasn't sure of her logic.

"You get a name, or any information about him?"

"I think Ed said he's a seasonal worker, helping him out at the park."

"The park?"

"You know, the place he runs down to the boardwalk."

Of course Jenkins didn't know. But she volunteered the info eventually, in her own scattered way. So while Jenkins was sitting with Ed Keyes, sharing a beer with him and trying to get him to open up about his "seasonal worker," Mike Collins was already en route to FunWorld to make his acquaintance.

Then the phone rang. Jenkins wasn't fooled. He knew what the old guy was trying to do—but he also knew he was too late. Collins probably would have shot the old guy, but Jenkins was trying to do this right for once.

Mike Collins sat parked outside the shuttered amusement park, trying to figure out where all the entrances were. Fearlessness had always been his greatest strength—and his largest liability. He never doubted that he could outrun, outshoot, outfight anyone. Outthink? No. But in any physical contest, he would win.

But that was in Baltimore, on occasion Prince George's County, places where it was never truly dark. Off-season, the town of Fenwick sat in inky blackness, clouds blotting out whatever light the stars might have provided tonight. The ocean, which Collins could hear but not see, should have been a comfort. Wherever they went, they couldn't go east. That was one direction he didn't have to worry about. Still, it bothered him, this unknown territory. He saw only one door, in the center of a clown's leering mouth, but what about all those garage-type entrances? He had to get the kid now or risk losing him, losing everything.

Just the kid, Jenkins had said over and over, as if Collins were stupid. *Just the kid. Take him into custody, and we'll stage our final act out on the road.* Jenkins's idea was that they would stop for a bathroom break somewhere, or so they would tell folks later on. That lonely stretch of 404, the bypass around Bridgeville. The kid would demand a chance to whiz on the side of the road, and Jenkins would join him, then the kid would go for Jenkins's gun, and Mike would have to shoot him. Would they throw down the knife, too, or was that overkill? Collins was fuzzy on that part.

Just the kid.

Well, he'd do his best.

He eased out of the car and positioned himself in a doorway opposite the side entrance to the amusement park. Could they raise those big shutters? Not quickly, he guessed, and not without a lot of noise, chains rattling and shit. Damn, he wished he knew the layout of the place inside. Maybe he should wait for Jenkins so they could control for someone trying to go out the windows. Maybe—

But here they were. Two men, about the same height and build, moving silently and quickly toward an old Jeep. He was on them before the driver was in the car, his gun in the guy's back. Normally he would have roared, too, used the adrenaline-fueled bluster he'd been trained to employ in such situations. But it was almost as if the guy expected him. His hands went up in automatic surrender. A civilian, as Jenkins had predicted. A candy-ass.

"Mike Collins?" the man asked.

"Yes," he said automatically even as he thought, *How? How do you know my name? The girlfriend, shit, the girlfriend—*

"Run, Lloyd!" the man screamed. *"Run!"*

And the boy took off toward the ocean of all places, ran toward the sound of that angry surf. Surprised, then furious, Collins caught the man across the face with his weapon, then hit him again, and he would have kept going if he hadn't remembered that the man, infuriating as he was, wasn't the quarry. *Just the kid,* Jenkins had said. Should he finish the man off, was he still off-limits? No, he had to chase and catch the kid. He'd have to do the throw-down on his own. Jenkins would understand.

The kid had a good head start, and it took Mike a moment to realize he'd have to shuck his shoes if he wanted to be competitive on this wet sand and surf. Still, the kid was just a runt and a slacker, underfed and underexercised. He had no chance. The distance between them was closing, and the stretch of beach ahead was increasingly desolate. Mike wouldn't even try to catch him until they got past that last line of houses, where he could be sure that they were alone, unseen.

Lloyd thought briefly about Crow's advice that he should learn to swim. If he could get out in the ocean, would he be safer? Guy was a brother, maybe he couldn't swim either. Too late now, and he'd freeze to death in that water anyway. His lungs were on fire, his legs felt like lead, churning in the sand, but he had to keep going, not daring to look back. He was pretty sure that cops, even dirty cops, couldn't shoot you in the back. Someone had told him that. Who?

Le'andro. Fuck.

He wished he could take it back, every bit of it. Rewind his life as if it were a video, go to that night before Thanksgiving. *No, Le'andro, I can't help you out. No, Le'andro, I'm not going to hide here and listen to what this guy tells you to do, then do it for you.*

Two hundred dollars and a North Face jacket. Crow was right. It was a piss-poor payment for one's life.

The houses seem to be giving way, disappearing. He was now on an open stretch of beach, and he could hear that guy grunting behind him, steady as the Terminator. Crow was wrong. He shouldn't have run. Guy might not have killed him in front of a witness, but he'd sure as hell do it out here in the middle of nowhere. Crow was just protecting his own ass, maybe, like in *Robocop*, where all those guys keep running from the guy that the machine had targeted for assassination. Fuck Crow. Fuck everybody. Lloyd could sense the other man gaining on him, and he was beginning to think he couldn't go another step when light flooded the open beach and that pathetic ugly Jeep crested the dunes just ahead of him.

Crow hadn't abandoned him after all. But what could Crow do anyway?

Crow's nose was broken, he was pretty sure of that, and something felt off in his cheek. Whatever had happened, it was the worst pain he had ever known, worse even than being stabbed, because at least then he had gone into shock, been beyond pain.

Still, he knew he had to get to Lloyd. He didn't even take time to deflate the Jeep's tires, not caring if it got stuck in the sand. The thing was to get there, to be present, to bank on the fact that a witness would take the air out of this scheme. He raced up the stretch of Highway 1, wishing that the summer speed traps were there so he could lead them into the chase, pulled into the parking lot of the public beach, and then rammed up the path used by the surf fishers. His headlamps picked up two running figures. The one in front looked ragged, on the verge of collapse, while the other moved with a brisk, confident stride.

"Stop!" he screamed. "We'll come with you together! We'll both—"

To his amazement, the man on the beach turned and fired straight at him, hitting the Jeep. The lights probably made it hard for him to aim with any accuracy, but now he was approaching, coming toward the Jeep's side, his weapon drawn. And for the first time in his life, Crow understood that he was in danger, that he could be killed. Lloyd, yes. Lloyd, sure. Lloyd, of course. He had been protecting Lloyd all along. Lloyd was vulnerable because he was the kind of disposable kid whose death no one would notice, as long as it was under the right circumstances. But not *him*. People like Crow didn't get killed, not by cops, no matter how crooked and desperate.

Yet here was a man approaching him with a gun, a man who was going to shoot him and then Lloyd. How would he explain it? Crow backed away, moving behind the car, but it seemed unlikely that they could maintain this game of ring-around-the-rosy, like in some old retro movie where the boss chased the comely secretary around the desk.

"You *can't*," he shouted to Mike Collins. "It's over. You can't—"

Yet the man's very posture made clear that he could, that he would. Crow bent down and grabbed a handful of sand, flung it in Collins's face. It wasn't clear if he hit his eyes as he had hoped, but Collins flinched instinctively, and it was all Crow needed. He dove into the Jeep and grabbed the gun he'd taken from Tess, the .38 Smith & Wesson that she retired when she bought her Beretta. Lloyd, as if sensing his plan, threw himself on Collins from behind, knocking him down in the sand. Like a child, at once single-minded and unfocused, Collins turned his attention on Lloyd, pushing him off, positioning himself in the sand, taking a two-handed grip on his gun and aiming straight at Lloyd's forehead.

"Don't!" It was unclear if the man could hear, if he ever heard, if he understood anything other than his own need to survive. Lloyd closed his eyes, surrendering, ready to die.

Lloyd opened them again at the sound of the gunshot, watched in seeming amazement as Collins crumpled. Crow, who hadn't handled a weapon since he earned a merit badge in riflery, had made the first shot count, because he knew this was not a night for second chances.

Jenkins wasn't surprised when he heard the knock at Ed's trailer door. He had been expecting Mike to come back and tell him the boy was safely in tow, that they needed to head back. In fact, he wasn't sure why it had taken this long.

He *was* surprised to see the two men he'd been searching for. They had become abstract to him, somehow, objects, one with a name and one without. He knew the one face, from driver's-license databases, although it had been far more handsome in that official photo, without the nose bloodied and crooked.

"Call the police," Crow said to Ed. "And then I need to call a lawyer."

"Did you . . . ?"

"I can't talk to you. You're FBI, right? Barry Jenkins. Tess sent us pictures of you. Are you crooked, too? Were you part of this?"

Jenkins took out his service weapon.

"Shit," Ed said. "Give it up, man. It's over."

Jenkins could blame it all on Collins, of course. Pretend ignorance. Say he'd been duped as everyone else had, that it was Youssef's plan and Collins had killed him. That had been built into the equation from the beginning. No one could link Barry Jenkins to anything directly—not Bennie Tep, not Youssef, no one. True, he'd been there the night Youssef died, driven behind Collins up the highway to the turnpike exit where they dumped the car, and the very setup suggested an accomplice. But no one could prove it was *him*. Except Collins.

"Is he dead?"

The boyfriend, what's-his-name, considered the question and nodded.

"How?"

"I'd prefer to wait for the local police and an attorney before I say anything else." Even now the old man was moving toward the phone. Like Jenkins gave a shit.

Jenkins pointed his gun at the boy. "Tell me your name."

"I'm calling 911," the old cop roared, grabbing the phone. "Don't think that I won't."

"Just your name. That's all I want. Tell me who you are."

"Lloyd Jupiter," the boy whispered. He was trembling, the little shit.

Jenkins thought fleetingly of going outside. But Jenkins was afraid he would lose his nerve if he took another step, and he was determined to do the right thing, the honorable thing, as awful as it was.

"Lloyd Jupiter," he echoed.

With that, Barry Jenkins nodded, put his weapon in his mouth, and pulled the trigger.

May

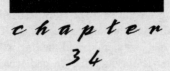

chapter
34

I *ALMOST* MADE IT," TESS SAYS TO ME, PERHAPS FOR THE twentieth time. It's something of a sore point.

"Almost," I agree, crushing the Metro section of the *Beacon-Light* into a ball and tossing it into a trash can. Two men were killed in Baltimore yesterday, their deaths dutifully reported on page B-3. Meanwhile City Man is on the cover of the Maryland section again, arrested by federal agents for alleged ties to terrorists.

In other words, in the immortal words of the Talking Heads—same as it ever was. But Tess can't let go of that night in particular, or the past in general. That's what makes her a true Baltimorean.

"The thing is, there's this sign, at the intersection of 26 and 20, tells you to go right to Fenwick? But 20 takes you around to the south end. I would have been better off going through Bethany and then heading down the coastal highway. And I *still* got there before the Delaware police, although not before . . ."

"Uh-huh."

We're sitting on the steps of Holy Redeemer, as we've done every Monday, hoping to get lucky. The afternoon lunch service has just started, and the line is long, because Holy Redeemer is serving chicken and word travels fast. People come from as far as West Baltimore on Chicken Day.

"I mean, I thought it out. I had a plan. They were going to be in Baltimore, waiting for *me*, while I went and got you. I kept trying to call you, too, just in case anyone beat me there—but your goddamn cell phone was off."

"It lost the charge."

"Whatever. All that folderol with the phones, and do you realize we never once spoke on them? That they were off, or out of range, or out of juice—"

"I know, Tess. I overthought it."

It isn't—for once—that she has to prove she's right. Tess needs absolution. She feels bad about my nose, which is healing just fine with no damage to the sinuses, and that's all I care about. It isn't quite as straight as it once was, but I like the bump. Makes me look like more of a tough guy. It was just that night, seeing me all bloody and fucked up in Ed's trailer, that threw Tess. She came galloping in, gun drawn, not even two minutes after Jenkins killed himself, frantic because she recognized the boxy sedan parked outside. *Now you know how it feels,* I wanted to say.

And I know how she felt, so it all evens out.

My nose is just a portion of Tess's guilt. She thinks this is all her fault. If she hadn't decided to track down Lloyd and force him to tell what he knew about Greg Youssef, none of this—the deaths of Gabe Dalesio and Le'andro Watkins— would have happened. But if I hadn't brought Lloyd home in the first place . . . if Lloyd hadn't slashed my tire . . . if I hadn't borrowed the Lexus that day because the brakes on my Volvo were squishy . . . if I hadn't concealed my inheritance from Tess, making it difficult to explain to her how I could afford to fix my squishy brakes. The bottom line is, if it doesn't snow on that particular Monday in March, none of this happens. But it did, and it has, and that's that. We'll keep circling back to the subject again and again, each making the case for our central role. *My fault. No,* my *fault.* But I also know that there is as much ego as guilt in this argument, and time will wear it down. Eventually. If you think about it, Tess and I actually came in at the end of this story. The people who should feel guilty aren't alive. And I don't think Mike Collins ever felt much of anything, although there was something akin to remorse and sorrow in Barry Jenkins's face that night.

The question is whether he felt it for himself and the failure of his grand scheme or for the people who had died because of it. I suppose it could have been both.

Strange to say, the worst part of the whole ordeal wasn't that night on the beach, when I at least had adrenaline on my side. The scary part was the three days when I was held for the death of Mike Collins. Killing a DEA agent is serious stuff, even if you can persuasively make the case that he was going to execute an innocent kid in front of your eyes, even if you had good reason to think he was going to kill you as well. No one believes in law and order more than those charged with keeping it, and things were rough for Lloyd and me those first seventy-two hours in Delaware. But Tess's call to Martin Tull proved helpful, along with the information about how hard Jenkins and Collins had pressed her for Lloyd's name. Turns out Jenkins had wormed his way into the Youssef investigation, but Collins had no official role, and it was beyond bizarre that an FBI agent and a DEA agent were working together. Nothing to get a bureaucracy's attention like the flouting of its own precious rules.

And when investigators started discovering the assets in the two agents' names, it began to come together. Wilma was the one who delineated it for us, who saw how easy it would be for federal agents to blackmail a drug dealer who was at no risk of indictment. They were stickup men with badges instead of guns. Wilma made a semiclean breast of things, telling investigators she had found fifty thousand dollars in a safe-deposit box in her husband's name. "Triple that," Tess told me, but she kept still. Me, I think that Wilma's motive wasn't greed so much as spin. The smaller the amount, the more likely it was that her dead husband was a blackmailer instead of a full-fledged coconspirator. It may seem like a silly distinction, but I'm not going to begrudge her that. We all need certain myths to get by.

"Are you going to tell Lloyd about the money?" Tess asks me. "*Your* money, I mean."

"First I just want to find him."

Secrets are corrosive. Remember that. Oh, I suppose it's okay to conceal birthday gifts and Christmas and other pleasant surprises, but every other deception leads to rot. If I had told Tess about my inheritance when I came into the trust at the beginning of this year, then it wouldn't have mushroomed into such a big deal. But I hated the money, loathed the very thought of it. It was blood money twice over, and I couldn't bring myself to speak of it.

The first part of the story, Tess knew. Years ago my grandfather had disinherited my mother for running off with my father. Grandfather—and it was always "Grandfather," nothing shorter or sweeter—saw money as a cudgel, a whip, a means of control. He thought he could bend my mother to his will with it. Much to his surprise, my mother was perfectly happy with her life as a professor's wife. But after I was born, she sent me to her father in the summers, an olive branch of sorts, an indication that she was willing to make amends if he would meet her halfway. Unfortunately, my grandfather saw me as another weapon, another way to punish my mother. He made me heir to a trust that she had to administer, thinking that would shame and hurt her. My mother didn't mind, but I did. I hated being a pawn in the old man's game.

And that was before my mother told me last fall, just before I came into the trust, that it was time I knew the origins of the family's fortunes.

"Whaling," I said. "Grandfather never shut up about it." My Nantucket summers had included a lot of briefings on my ancestors.

"Whaling in the nineteenth century," she said. "But earlier, in the eighteenth . . . well, they had started with a very different kind of cargo."

"Oh."

Growing up in Charlottesville, I had gone to schools with various Lees and Jacksons and Stuarts, marveled at classmates who actually looked forward to joining the Sons of the Confederacy. I always wondered how they lived with their family's legacies. And now it turned out my own history was just as complex. A million dollars. Did time wash money clean of its sins? Was I culpable for my ancestors' moral relativism, in which the men enabled the slave trade and the women then protested it, achieving some kind of karmic equipoise? And wasn't I guilty of the same kind of hypocrisy, giving it away a dollar a time but not ready to relinquish it whole? My very approach to philanthropy was cavalier, ill-conceived. My Monday-morning food drive, which recycles food from area bars and restaurants? Pure bullshit. I drive down to the wholesale market in Jessup and buy what I think the soup kitchens can use. Without me there is no Chicken Day at Holy Redeemer. I was straddling, too.

Charlotte Curtis, the director at Holy R, says Lloyd is in

the wind again. He tried to go home, but it was the old
Thomas Wolfe story. Within days he and Murray had
clashed and he was back to his old life—scamming, loafing,
scrounging. Lloyd turns seventeen this summer, and he
missed most of tenth grade. How can anyone reasonably expect to help Lloyd if he won't help himself?

The thing is, I'm not particularly reasonable. So I'm sitting
on the steps of Holy Redeemer hoping against hope that
Lloyd shows up. It's Chicken Day, after all. Chicken and
mashed potatoes and bags of Otterbein cookies to go. How
could anyone stay away? In fact, Charlotte thinks I overdid it
a little. But I keep thinking Lloyd will come, especially after
Tess sees Dub, Terrell, and Tourmaline leaving with the red-
and-white bags of gingersnaps clutched in their hands. They
stop, exchanging cautious greetings, but when Tess begins,
"If there's anything I can do—" Dub waves her off.

"We fine," he says. And he will be. Like the genetic mar-
vels that emerge from inner-city neighborhoods to play pro
sports, Dub was born with something extra. He'll make it
out through sheer will and intelligence. Lloyd, on the other
hand . . .

Go figure, he comes in just under the wire, getting in line
at one minute before four. He sees us, but he's clearly anxious for his food, so we hang back, letting him go inside and
eat. He must inhale it, because he's back out in under ten
minutes, Miss Charlotte locking the door behind him. Last
man standing.

"Hey, Lloyd."

"Hey." A beat. "Crow." I can't tell if he's forgotten my
name or isn't sure he wants to grant me that much intimacy.
He blames me for Delaware. Nothing really bad happened to
him while we were detained, but he was terrified every
minute of it, and he begrudges my knowing this. But that
was a month ago, and with no evidence to lead the federal

authorities back to Bennie Tep or any other local drug dealer, Lloyd's in the clear. The only person he could identify, in the end, was Mike Collins. In Howard County the death of Greg Youssef is a closed case.

In Baltimore City the death of Le'andro Watkins remains open, probably forever, and the only person who cares is Rainier, stuck with another stone-cold whodunit.

"How you doing, Lloyd?"

"Things're cool," he says, taking a few steps backward. Maybe he thinks we're going to grab him and throw him in a car again.

"You know, there was a reward. . . ."

"Ummmm." He's still moving backward.

"It was supposed to be for information leading to the arrest of Youssef's killers, but they decided we're entitled to it. Tess, me. You."

This gets his attention. "Yeah? How much?"

"Here's the thing: Because you're a minor, I'm going to hold your share in trust. To get it you have to go through me."

"Shit." He makes it two syllables. "That's just a way of saying you're never going to give it to me."

"No, I'm going to safeguard your share. It's not a lot of money, Lloyd, but it's enough. Enough to go to college, even set you up in your own apartment. Buy a car, assuming you ever get a license. But I am allowed to set conditions."

"Yeah?"

"Yeah. Condition number one: you're going to work this summer. At FunWorld. Room and board, plus two hundred sixty-five dollars a week."

"Fuck, I already done that."

"Did you hear me? There's a wage this time."

"*Slave* wages."

That makes my skin jump. But there will be time enough, as Prufrock learned, to tell Lloyd my secrets. After all,

Lloyd hasn't always been forthcoming with me. "During the summer the dormitories will be filled with kids your age. And Mrs. Anderson, that nice lady who helped you out? She said she'll make sure you get to church every Sunday. And you get a bonus if you stay the whole summer. You'll come home with over two thousand dollars, if you don't blow it on fried dough and saltwater taffy."

"Then what?"

Good question.

"Your choice—back to school or you start tutoring for your GED. Then college or a job. The trust will be used for essential costs. But if you keep up your end of the bargain, you'll come out of school with no debt and a nice lump sum to start your life."

Lloyd stops moving backward, but everything in his posture suggests that he still wants to cut and run, get away from me. He likes his life just the way it is, or thinks he does. He can't imagine what else it would be, so he has to pretend he's happy.

"When I got to start?"

"Most of the kids begin after school lets out. But since you're not enrolled—*this* semester—Ed could use you starting Mother's Day weekend. In fact, he says your whole family could come down, spend the weekend."

"Even Murray?"

"Even Murray," I say, knowing it's not what he's hoping to hear.

"And where do I live when I come back? Not with you?" The idea clearly horrifies him. Give Tess credit: It horrifies her more, but she doesn't let it show.

"We'll work something out, maybe rent a place that you can share with Dub and his people. But it would be my name on the lease, so you'd have to live according to my rules."

"Rules," Lloyd said, his voice crackling with contempt.

"School. Books and shit. Like all the answers are written down someplace and all I have to do is learn them."

"Yep."

"I'll think on it." He takes a few steps forward, shakes my hand. Then he ambles away before I can find out how to get in touch with him, where to find him. As Miss Charlotte said, Lloyd Jupiter's in the wind these days, aiming to please no one but himself.

"Go ahead," I say to Tess, who's clearly bursting to say something. "Tell me I'm crazy. Tell me I'm a fool for trying, for caring."

"It was easier to save his life one night than it will be over the long haul," Tess said. "But you already know that. You've always known that."

Miss Charlotte comes out, locking the door behind her. "Did you see Lloyd?"

"Yeah."

"I wasn't sure, because he gave me something to give to you."

She pulls out Tess's unicorn box and hands it to her. Tess starts to open it, then thinks better of it. She passes it to me instead, and I shake it gently. Hollow, not even a seed swishing inside. Nobody's perfect.

"Do you think," I ask Tess, "that it's a good sign? Or does this mean he's through with us entirely and doesn't want any unfinished business between us?"

She traces the crooked line of my nose with her index finger. At some point the face of one's beloved becomes so familiar as to be abstract. What does she see? What do I see? Is Tess pretty? Are her features even? I don't know. All I can absorb are the expressions that play across the surface, the amazing nuance. In this instance there is mockery, yes, the impression that she's always amused by me. But there is sympathy, too, a shared weakness for lost causes. Sadness and respect for the bond we now share. I finally understand that when Tess fingers her scar, it's not because she's scared but because she wants to remind herself that she has what it takes to survive.

She touches my scar and concedes the melancholy bond between us. My grandfather arbitrarily established that my life as an adult would start on my twenty-sixth birthday, December 15. But I know it began on April 5, on a deserted stretch of beach north of Fenwick, Delaware. Not because I killed a man but because I realized that a man could kill me, that immortality was not my birthright.

"Go for it," she says at last. "God forbid another native should come of age not knowing who the Baltimore Four were."

"The Oriole pitching staff of 1971, right?"

"Berrigan, Lewis, Mengel, and Eberhardt. The Customs House, 1967."

This surprises me more than anything. "I didn't think you were listening that day."

"Well, I was."

AUTHOR'S NOTE

READERS OFTEN ASK WHERE WRITERS GET THEIR IDEAS, and in the case of *No Good Deeds* it seems more important than usual to anticipate and address that question. In December 2003, I heard a radio report that a federal prosecutor in Baltimore had been killed on the eve of closing arguments in a big case. Jonathan Luna's death remains unsolved, and my knowledge of it goes only as far as what was reported in the media. It was someone else's casual observation about the *coverage* of the case that sparked my imagination and led to this story, which has been built on what-if upon what-if upon what-if.

Yet Baltimore really is Smalltimore, and when I turned to a neighbor to help me research a day-in-the-life of an assistant U.S. attorney, I found out I was talking to one of the two coworkers who delivered eulogies at Luna's funeral. I am extremely grateful to AUSA Bonnie Greenberg and keen that this be understood: Nothing in this book is meant to reflect on the life of Luna, a man about whom I know almost nothing. The same is true of Luna's family, friends, and coworkers.

To continue the Smalltimore theme, I am indebted to Julian "Jack" Lapides, a longtime family friend, for some crucial background on probate and safe-deposit boxes.

Randy Curry, part of the multigenerational family that has run Rehoboth's Playland since 1962, gave me some insight into how a seaside amusement park readies itself for summer. There is no Frank's FunWorld, alas, but if you're looking for a good time on the Delaware seashore, Skeeball at Playland is still twenty-five cents for nine balls. Curry also confirmed my long-held belief that you must bank your shots to get the highest possible score.

Books, articles, the *Frontline* documentary *The Man Who Knew*, and other sources provided insight into the day-to-day life of an FBI agent. John O'Neill was killed on September 11, 2001, in his new capacity as director of security for the World Trade Towers—a job that he took, in part, because he felt he had been unfairly scapegoated by the FBI. A source that must remain anonymous was extremely helpful in detailing the ins and outs of the federal justice system.

I learned about the Baltimore Four, a precursor to the better-known Catonsville Nine, from Brendan Walsh of Viva House. Brendan and his wife, Willa Bickham, hate it when they're singled out for credit—and here I am, doing it twice in one book. Dave White provided another esoteric bit of knowledge for Crow, while Mike Ollove deserves credit for the best headline that the *Sun* never used. Thanks to David Simon, whose chance remark inspired this novel. Like Tess, I'm listening even when you think I'm not.

Finally, it's worth pointing out that there were 269 homicides in Baltimore last year—a slight decrease from 2004, but far from the large-scale reduction promised by Mayor

Martin O'Malley when he ran for office in 1999. As I write this, the city has just paid five hundred thousand dollars to a consultant to help remake its image in the eyes of tourists and convention planners. But visitors to our city enjoy remarkable safety in an increasingly vibrant downtown. It's our own citizens, in neighborhoods where executives would never want to tamper, to paraphrase a favorite poet, who are most at risk. I'm just saying.

LAURA LIPPMAN
Baltimore, Maryland
December 2005

Don't miss the next exhilarating novel from
award-winning author

LAURA LIPPMAN

*What the
Dead Know*

Turn the page for a first look at
Laura Lippman's new stand-alone novel
about an unsolved crime that rocked
Baltimore and an unknown woman
who may or may not be the only
clue to solving the mystery.

HER STOMACH CLUTCHED AT THE SIGHT OF THE WATER tower hovering above the still bare trees, a spaceship come to earth. The water tower had been a key landmark in the old family game, although not *the* landmark. Once you spotted the white disc on its spindly legs, you knew it was time to get ready, like a runner crouched in the blocks. *On your mark, get set, I see—*

It hadn't started as a game. Spotting the department store nestled in this bend of the Beltway had been a private contest with herself, a way to relieve the tedium of the two-day drive back from Florida. As far back as she could remember, they had made the trip every winter break, although no one in the family enjoyed the visit. Her apartment was cramped and smelly, her dogs mean, her meals inedible. Everyone was miserable, even their father, especially their father, although he pretended not to be and took great offense if anyone suggested that his mother was any of the things that she undeniably was—stingy, strange, unkind. Still, even he couldn't hide his relief as home drew nearer and he sang out each state line as they crossed. *Georgia,* he growled in a Ray Charles moan. They spent the night there, in a no-name motor court, and left before sunrise, quickly reaching South Carolina—"Nothing could be finah!"—followed by the long, slow teases of North Carolina and Virginia, where the only points of interest were, respectively, the lunch stop in Durham and the dancing cigarette packs on the billboards outside Richmond. Then finally Maryland, wonderful Maryland, home sweet home Maryland, which asked for only fifty miles or so, barely an hour back then. Today, she had needed almost twice that much time to crawl up the parkway, but traffic was thinning now, back to normal speeds.

I see—

Hutzler's had been the city's grandest department store and it marked the Christmas season by setting up an enormous fake chimney with a Santa poised on its ledge, caught in a perpetual straddle. Was he coming or going? She could never decide. She had taught herself to watch for that flash of red, the promise that home was near, the way that certain birds told a sea captain that the shore was within reach. It had been a clandestine ritual, not unlike counting the broken stripes as they disappeared under the front wheels of the car, a practice that quelled the motion sickness she never quite outgrew. Even then, she was tight-lipped when it came to certain information about herself, clear about the distinction between eccentricities that might be interesting and compulsive habits that would mark her as odd as, say, her grandmother. Or, to be absolutely truthful, her father. But, one day, the phrase had popped out, joyful and unbidden, another secret dialogue with herself escaping into the world.

"I see Hutzler's."

Her father had gotten the significance instantly, unlike her mother and sister. Her father always seemed to understand the layers beneath what she said, which was comforting when she was really little, intimidating as she got older. The problem was that he insisted on turning her private homecoming salute into a game, a contest, and what had once been hers alone then had to be shared with the entire family. Her father was big on sharing, on taking what was private and making it communal. He believed in long, rambling family discussions, which he called rap sessions in the language of the day, and unlocked doors and casual seminudity, although their mother had broken him of that habit. It you tried to keep something for yourself—whether it was a bag of candy purchased with your own money or a feeling you didn't want to express—he accused you of hoarding. He sat you down, looked straight into your eyes, and told you that families didn't work that way. A family was a team, a unit, a country unto itself, the one part of her identity that would remain constant the rest of her life. "We lock our front door against strangers," he said, "but never against each other."

So he seized "I see Hutzler's" for the family good and encouraged everyone to vie for the right to say it first. Once the rest of the family decided to play, that last mile of Beltway had been unbearable in its suspense. The sisters craned their necks, leaning forward in the old lap seat belts, the ones worn only on long trips. That's how things were back then— seatbelts for long trips only, no bicycle helmets ever, skateboards made from splintery planks of wood and old roller skates. Pinned by her seat belt, she felt her stomach flip and her pulse race, and for what? For the hollow honor of being the first to say out loud what she had always been the first to think. As with all her father's contests, there was no prize, no point. Since she could no longer be guaranteed victory, she did what she always did: She pretended not to care.

Yet here she was again, alone, guaranteed the win if she wanted it, and her stomach *still* flipped, unaware that the store was long gone, that everything around the once-familiar clover-leaf had changed. Changed and, yes, cheapened. The refined dowager that had been Hutzler's was now a tacky Value City. Opposite, on the south side of the highway, the Quality Inn had morphed into one of those storage places. It wasn't possible from this vantage point to see if Howard Johnson's, home of the family's weekly fish-fry suppers, remained at the intersection, but she somehow doubted it. Did Howard Johnson's exist anywhere, anymore? Did she? Yes and no.

What happened next transpired in seconds. Everything does, if you think about it. She would say that later, under questioning. *The Ice Age happened in a matter of seconds; there were just a lot of them.* Oh, she could make people love her if absolutely necessary and although the tactic was less essential to her survival now, the habit was hard to break. Her interrogators pretended exasperation, but she could tell she was having the desired effect on most of them. By then, her description of the accident was breathlessly vivid, a polished routine. She had glanced to the right, eastward, trying to recall all her childhood landmarks, forgetting the old admonition, *Bridges may freeze first,* and felt a strange sensation, almost as if the steering wheel was slipping from her grasp, but the car was actually separating from the road, losing traction, although the sleet had not started and the pavement looked bone-dry. It was oil, not ice, she would learn later, left over from an earlier accident. How could one control for a coating of oil, invisible in the March twilight, for the inactions or incomplete actions of a crew of men she had never met, would never know? Somewhere in Baltimore a man sat down to supper that night, unaware that he had destroyed someone else's life, spared the unbearable knowledge she herself had long carried.

She clutched the steering wheel and pounded on the pedals, but the car ignored her. The boxy sedan slid to the left, moving like the needle on a haywire tachometer. She bounced off the Jersey wall, spun around, slid to the other side of the highway. For a moment, it seemed as if she were the only one driving, as if all the other cars and their drivers had frozen in deference and awe. The old Valiant—the name had seemed a good omen, a reminder of Prince Valiant and all that he stood for, back in the Sunday comics—moved swiftly and gracefully, a dancer among the stolid, earthbound commuters at the tail-end of rush hour.

And then, just when she seemed to have the Valiant under control, when the tires once again connected to the pavement, she felt a soft thump to her right. She had sideswiped a white SUV and although her car was so much smaller, the SUV seemed to reel from the touch, an elephant felled by a peashooter. Later, she would come to believe that she saw a girl's face, not so much frightened as surprised by the realization that anything could collide with one's neat, well-ordered life at any time. The girl wore a ski jacket and large, cruelly unflattering glasses, made worse somehow by white fur earmuffs. Her mouth was round, a red gate of wonder. She was 11, maybe 12, the same age—and then the white SUV began its lazy flip-flops down the embankment.

I'm sorry, I'm sorry, I'm sorry, she thought. She knew she should slow down, stop, check on them, but a chorus of honks and squealing brakes rose up behind her, a phalanx of sound that pushed her forward in spite of herself. *It wasn't my fault!* Everyone should know by now that SUVs were prone to tip. Her mild little nudge could never have caused that dramatic-looking accident. Besides, it had been such a long day and she was so close. Her exit was the next one, not even a mile ahead She could still merge into the I-70 traffic and continue west to her destination.

But once on the long straightaway toward I-70, she found herself veering right instead of left, toward the sign that read "Local Traffic Only," to that strange, unfinished road that her family had always called the highway to nowhere. How they had gloried in giving directions to their house. "Take the interstate east, to where it ends." "How can an interstate end?" And her father would triumphantly tell the tale of the protests, the citizens who had united across Baltimore to preserve the park and the wildlife and the then-modest row-houses that ringed the harbor. It was one of her father's few successes in life, although he had been a minor player—just another signer of petitions, a marcher in marches. He was never tapped to speak at the public demonstrations, much as he longed for that role.

The Valiant was making a terrible sound, the right rear wheel scraping against what must be a crushed fender. In her agitated state, it made perfect sense to park it on the shoulder and continue on foot, although the sleet had now started and she became aware with each step that something was wrong. Her ribs hurt so that each breath was like a jab with a tiny knife, and it was hard to carry her purse as she had always been instructed—close to the body, not dangling from her wrist, a temptation for muggers and thieves. She hadn't been wearing her seatbelt and she had bounced around inside the Valiant, hitting the steering wheel and door. There was blood on her face, but she wasn't sure where it was coming from. Mouth? Forehead? She was warm, she was cold, she saw black stars. No, not stars. More like triangles twisting and turning, hung from the wires of an invisible mobile.

She had been walking no more than ten minutes when a patrol car stopped alongside her, lights flashing.

"That your Valiant back there?" he called out to her, lowering the window on the passenger side, but not venturing from the car.

Was it? The question was more complicated than the young officer could know. Still, she nodded.

"You got any ID?"

"Sure," she said, digging into her purse, but not finding her wallet. *Why, that*—she started to laugh, realizing how perfect that was. Of course she had no ID. She had no identity. "Sorry. No. I—" she couldn't stop laughing—"It's gone."

He came out of the patrol car and attempted to take the purse, look for himself. Her scream shocked her even more than it did him. There was a fiery pain in her left forearm when he tried to slide the purse past her elbow. The patrolman spoke into his shoulder, calling for assistance. He pocketed his keys, walked back to her car and poked around inside, then returned and stood with her in the sleeting rain that had started. He mumbled some familiar words to her, but was otherwise silent.

"Is it bad?" she asked him.

"That's for a doctor to say when we get you into the ER."

"No, not me. Back there."

The distant whirr of a helicopter answered her question. *I'm sorry, I'm sorry, I'm sorry.* But it wasn't her fault.

"It wasn't my fault. I couldn't control it—but, still, I really didn't do anything—"

"I've read you your rights," he said. "The things you're saying—they count. Not that there's much doubt that you left the scene of an accident."

"I was going to get help."

"This road dead-ends into a park-and-ride. If you wanted to help them, you'd have pulled over back there, or taken the Security Boulevard exit."

"There's a pharmacy at Forest Park and Windsor Mill. I thought I could call from there."

She could tell that caught him off-guard, her use of precise names, her familiarity with the area.

"I don't know of any pharmacy, although there's a gas station there, but—don't you have a cell phone?"

"Not for my personal use, although I carry one at work. I don't buy things until they work properly, until they're perfected. Cell phones lose their connections and people have to yell into them half the time, so you can't safeguard your privacy. When cells work as well as landlines, I'll buy one."

She heard her father's echo. All these years later, he was in her head, his pronouncements as definitive as ever. *Don't be the first to purchase any kind of technology. Keep your knives sharp. Eat tomatoes only when they're in season. Be kind to your sister. One day, your mother and I will be gone, and you'll be all that each other have.*

The young patrol officer regarded her gravely, the kind of awed inspection that good children reserve for those who misbehaved. It was ludicrous that he could be so skeptical of her. In this light, in these clothes, the rain flattening her spiky short hair, she probably looked younger than she was. People were always placing her at a full decade below her real age, even on those rare occasions that she dressed up. Cutting her long hair last year had made her look younger still. It was funny about her hair, how stubbornly blond it remained at an age when most women needed chemicals to achieve this light, variable hue. It was as if her hair resented its years of forced imprisonment under those home applications of Nice 'n' Easy Sassy Chestnut. Her hair could hold a grudge as well as she could, which was saying a lot.

"Bethany," she said. "I'm one of the Bethany girls."

"What?"

"You don't know?" she asked him. "You don't remember?

But then, I guess you're all of, what—twenty-four? Twenty-five?"

"I'll be twenty-six next week," he said.

She tried not to smile, but he was so much like a toddler claiming two-and-a-half instead of two. At what age do we stop wishing to be older than we are, stop nudging the number up? Around thirty for most, she assumed, although it had happened to her far earlier. By eighteen, she would have done anything to renounce adulthood and be given another chance at childhood.

"So you weren't even born when—and you're probably not from here, either, so, no, the name wouldn't mean anything to you."

"Registration in the car says it belongs to Penelope Jackson, from Asheville, North Carolina. That you? Car didn't come up stolen when I called the tag in."

She shook her head. Her story would be wasted on him. She'd wait for someone who could appreciate it, who would understand the full import of what she was trying to tell him. Already, she was making the calculations that had long been second nature to her. Who was on her side, who would take care of her? Who was against her, who would betray her?

At St. Agnes Hospital, she continued mum, answering only direct questions about what hurt where. Her injuries were relatively minor—a gash to the forehead that required only four stitches, something torn and broken in her left forearm. It would be stabilized and bandaged for now, but would require surgery eventually, she was told. The young patrolman must have passed along the Bethany name, for the billing person pressed her on it, but she refused to speak of it again no matter how they poked and prodded. Under ordinary circumstances, she would have been treated and released. But this was not ordinary. The police asked the hospital to keep her and told her that she was not free to leave even if the hospital determined it was appropriate. "The law is very clear on this, you have to tell us who you are," another cop told her, an older one. "If it weren't for your injuries, you'd be in jail tonight." Still, she said nothing. The doctors entered the name "Jane Doe" on her chart, adding "Bethany?" in parentheses. Her fourth name, by her count, but maybe it was her fifth. It was easy to lose track.

She knew St. Agnes. Or, more correctly, had known it once. So many accidents, so many trips. A calf sliced open when a jar of fireflies was dropped, the shards ricocheting up from the sidewalk and nicking the roundest part. A fly-swatter applied to a chicken pox wound with sisterly good intent. A knee opening like a flower after a fall in the underbrush, revealing the terrifying interior of bone and blood. A shin scraped on the rusty valve of an old tire, a huge inner tube from some tractor or truck, their father's makeshift version of a bouncy castle, obtained and erected in deference to their mother's Anglophilia. The trips to the emergency room had been family affairs, more father-enforced togetherness— terrifying for the injured party, tedious for the sister who had to tag along, but everyone got Mr. G's soft ice cream afterward, so it was worth it in the end.

This is not the homecoming I imagined, she thought, lying in the dark, allowing self-pity, her old friend, to come for her, envelop her.

And she *had* imagined returning, she realized now, although not today. Sometime, eventually, but on her own terms, not because of someone else's agenda. Three days ago, the hard-won order of her life had jumped the track without warning, as out of her control as that pea-green Valiant. That car—it was as if there were a ghost in the machine all along, nudging her north, past the old landmarks, toward a destiny not of her choosing. At the I-70 exit, when it would have been so easy to go west, toward her original destination, and possibly escape detection, the car had turned to the right and stopped on its own. Prince Valiant had brought her most of the way home, trying to trick her into doing what was right. That's why the name had popped out. That, or the head injury, or her anxiety about the little girl in the SUV.

Floating on painkillers, she fantasized about the next day, what it would be like to say her name, her true name, for the first time in thirty years. To answer a question that few people had to think about twice: *Who are you?*

Then she realized what the second question would be.

Edgar®, Agatha and Anthony Award winner
LAURA LIPPMAN

BALTIMORE BLUES
978-0-380-78875-0/$7.99 US/$10.99 Can

Suspected killer Darryl "Rock" Paxton hires ex-reporter
Tess Monaghan to do some unorthodox snooping to
clear his name.

CHARM CITY
978-0-380-78876-7/$6.99 US/$9.99 Can

In a city where baseball reigns, a business tycoon wants to change
all that by bringing pro basketball back to town—until he's
found asphyxiated in his garage with his car's engine running.

BUTCHERS HILL
978-0-380-79846-9/$6.99 US/$9.99 Can

A notorious vigilante who shot a boy for vandalizing his car
has just gotten out of prison and wants to make amends.
When Tess agrees to start snooping, the witnesses to
the crime start dying.

IN BIG TROUBLE
978-0-380-79847-6/$6.99 US/$9.99 Can

A new case takes Tess out of her element to a faraway place
where the sun is merciless and rich people's games can have
lethal consequences.